CW00690197

CAROLINE the CRUEL

JENNIFER M. WALDROP

Caroline the Cruel: A Joined Kingdoms Novel

Cover Design: Vivien Reis

Editing: Roxana Coumans, Roth Notions

Proofreading: Belle Manuel

www.jennifermwaldrop.com

July House Publishing | Your story, your way

www.julyhousepublishing.com

The Maidenwall

The Green Sea

Ripenik

The Faraway Lands

Narcissa

Mantia

The Ice Sea

Kierengaard
Attica

Veetula

The Great Frozen Plain

Avondale

Warrik
Bowring

Gulf of Aar

Everstal

Vineyard

Galloway

Roskíde

Bridgewater

Breaker Bay

The Sommer Ocean

Caroline the Cruel

PART ONE –

THE MAKING OF A QUEEN

CHAPTER I

"HOLD STILL, CARA." EMMY giggled, raising the stolen tailor's shears awkwardly hooked around her adolescent fingers at Caroline's temple making her tremble. "If I give you a jagged crop because you're wiggling, it's your own fault."

Emmy's bright blue eyes met Caroline's silver in the large, gilded mirror they sat in front of. Mischief lit Emmy's features, and a self-indulgent smile crept across her sun-speckled face. The all-too-familiar expression sent a flood of dread charging through Caroline's limbs, which crashed into the walls of her stomach before settling there in a gurgling pool.

"Please, Emmy. I don't want to cut my hair." Fat tears dripped down Caroline's pale face as chunks of her onyx locks floated down to the floor.

"Stop crying." Emmy poked her in the shoulder with the point of her scissors, eliciting a cry. "This is your punishment. You chose. I'll give you a cut, or I'll tell father what you did to Cook."

Hot shame burned on Caroline's damp cheeks and her mind drifted.

❧

Her and Emmy had made a game of forcing their cooks to eat the meals which dissatisfied them, heaping on seconds and thirds until the cooks were rubbing their protruding bellies and dripping with perspiration. The punishment, which had been Caroline's idea, was an effective tactic to improve the quality of their food.

It wasn't her fault the entire kitchen was preoccupied with feeding the envoy from Veetula here for the Peace Ball. Feeding her and Emmy should be a priority. The portly older man they called Cook, who had the unlucky task of feeding them on more days than not, served Caroline a rabbit stew with chewy bits and a flavor that made her insides roll.

Caroline suspected the soup was from the day before—and it hadn't *smelled* spoiled. Before Cook served them, an attendant came and fetched Emmy. *Too convenient.* Emmy's mother, the Queen of Everstal, requested her only daughter's presence, probably to gloat over the blonde-haired princess in front of their foreign guests.

The intuition in Caroline's heart told her that Cook would have never served Princess Emmy day-old soup. She hadn't meant to be vindictive, but when he'd set the bowl down in front of her, pin pricks crawled up her neck to her cheeks and her teeth ached like they might crack, she was clenching them so hard. Cook should have seen Caroline's ire, and replaced the bowl immediately with something more palatable, but he had been too busy to notice.

After one bite, Caroline spit a slimy piece of rabbit on the cold stone tiles and pushed the dish across the table in protest. A passing castle cat called Red jumped down from his perch on a windowsill to inspect the food which had splatted into its domain. The castle cats were blue and orange, speckled and striped, but they were all called Red after Roskide, the red castle which was the crown of Everstal. Red took a sniff of the discarded meat and turned its nose to the ceiling, flicking its tail disappointedly as it sauntered from the room, which set Caroline seething.

"Cook, come over here right now and take your punishment." Caroline stomped her foot twice and crossed her delicate arms across her still flat chest. She motioned with her chin to the steaming bowl and even Cook wrinkled his nose.

With a shaky hand, he picked up the spoon and brought it to his lips, blowing across the contents. Cook shot her a wary glance and slurped the rotten stew.

"All of it," she insisted in the most terrifying monotone a fourteen-year-old girl could muster.

Emmy clicked her scissors open and closed, snapping Caroline out of her memory and back to the present. "Cook had to be taken to the infirmary," Emmy said, prancing around the room, circling Caroline like a shark. "You know what that means, don't you? You need to be punished."

"The infirmary?" Caroline swallowed the knot in her throat. She didn't mean to make him that sick, but he *had* planned to feed her the foul dish.

Cook had been retching whenever she gushed out of the little dining area where he served them their meals. The man hadn't made it two steps past the table before he heaved the contents of his stomach onto the floor. The smell had been too much for her. A guilty little tingle crawled across the back of her shoulders.

Emmy brought the shears in front of Caroline's face with a final clack, closing them a little too close to her nose. "I will give you a choice, Caroline," the older girl said haughtily, pursing her lips into a prim pout. "You can either let me finish your haircut, or I will tell father."

That's how Caroline found herself sitting in front of her half-sister, and all her beautiful onyx locks littering the floor around her feet.

She wiped her clammy palms down her skirts. The motion soothed her rowdy gut, which was still churning from the stew or the debasement, possibly both.

Emmy picked up one of the longer strands and twirled it between her fingers. Then she let a crazed cackle escape. "What is Father going to think? You're no longer his raven-haired love child."

Caroline had favored her mother, the beauty who King Thom Dallimore had taken as a lover on his final campaign against Manula fifteen years ago. He took one look at the raven-haired woman and fell in love. Caroline resulted from their union and when Queen Cerise discovered the king's lover, she sent her own spies to locate the woman, and then she sent an assassin.

King Thom never confirmed it was his own queen who was responsible for the death of his love, but he knew in the way a king knows those things. That unspoken suspicion was why Caroline, his illegitimate daughter, was allowed to live in the keep alongside his other child, Princess Emmaline, his heir. He was the king after all.

His two daughters were opposites in all things: coloring, beauty and in temperament. One girl had the love of her father, the other her mother. One was soft, the other all angles.

Caroline's lovely sister, who was two years older, despised her for having the king's heart. It was a rift she appeared to ignore on most days. And because Emmy was the heir, when it was not *most days*, she was untouchable. She used that advantage against Caroline every chance she got.

Caroline ran her fingers through her shorn hair. It stuck up in little tufts, making her cheekbones poke out even more dramatically and her large silver eyes bug out of her face like an insect. She could only blink at her reflection as numbness eclipsed the searing of the fresh wound given to her by her half-sister.

"I don't know, Emmy. Let's go find out if Father still loves me." Caroline shrugged and pulled her sagging body from the stool. She kicked the hair with the toe of a satin slipper, and put it out of her mind, stomping off in search of the king. Emmaline skipped eagerly behind her.

King Thom was in the training yard when Caroline and her sister found him. Sweat glistened off the brow of the brawny man as he removed a layer of steel plate which he always wore during his sparring sessions.

The patter of footsteps drew the man's attention. Her father lifted his head in the girls' direction as they approached, the start of a grin was replaced by a deep frown. He ran his sturdy hand through the spiky mop that sat atop Caroline's head.

"Oh, sweetheart, what have you done with your beautiful hair?" He sighed, resigned to the antics of children.

Both Caroline and the king had loved her hair. He had told her one night after they had read stories that her hair was exactly like her mother's. A shiny, almost iridescent black, long and stick straight. Heavy, beautiful hair that seemed to absorb all the light and attention it received. It was the one thing that had made her feel pretty, special even. And now it was gone.

Caroline's lip trembled as new tears sprang to her eyes. She tried to tell on Emmaline in the past, but the other girl's mother always came to the rescue. It was no use.

"Oh, don't cry, my darling. It will grow back," the king soothed, petting his daughter.

"But what about the ball tonight?" Caroline brought quaking fingers up to her forehead.

"I suppose we'll have to get you a lovely bonnet," the king teased, testing the resilience of his youngest daughter.

A small grin cracked across Caroline's face before she fell into a giggling fit with her father.

Emmy, who had been quietly observing them, huffed, and stormed out of the training yard.

CHAPTER 2

C AROLINE'S PRIDE SWELLED, MAKING her chest full. Another year had passed with no conflict between Everstal, her father's kingdom, and Veetula, the frozen kingdom to the north. The peace ball represented everything good her father was, the event marking the fifteenth year since King Thom Dallimore had ended the centuries long conflict between the two enemies. No one had believed it possible and now each spring, either Everstal or Veetula would host the other for a full week of gaming, drinking, feasting, and dancing.

It was their turn to host, and while it was typical for the red castle to be covered in roses, for this event Queen Cerise brought in crates of different flowers, fruits and vegetables and commissioned sculptures to be made with the bounty. She was even invited to help, but Caroline decided decorating wasn't her thing. Not that she was going to rebuff the rare kind gesture from the queen.

Caroline almost bumped into a topiary that wasn't usually there. Roskide was in full bloom. She circled the statue plucking a strawberry from a live vine and sunk her teeth into the ripe end. Bright sweetness burst into her mouth mirroring the rush of giddy flutters that lifted her spirits, almost making her forget about her hideous hair.

Caroline tried to catalogue who would be in attendance and which royals would be missing. She would make her father proud and represent Everstal well, even though she was the bastard princess.

Agna, their queen, had four children. Twin girls, Lissa and Leeza, and Natalia, who were married off to princes from far away kingdoms Caroline couldn't pronounce. A fifteen-year-old son, the heir, Jaden, who was rumored to be just as dashing as the other men in the Ivanslohe line, never attended for 'security reasons', which she supposed made sense. And the fertile queen expected another child within months. Carrying a child to full term at her age was a delicate thing, so she was excused.

That left King Hollis in attendance, along with his younger brother, Prince Breicher, and several royal cousins and other important men and women and their families whose names weren't important. Caroline had only gotten brief glances at them, but the rumors had been true. With their blazing sapphire eyes, an Ivanslohe trait which could be seen from across the room, their rugged features, and tall, broad stature, they seemed like warrior princes from a storybook. Butterflies danced in her stomach. One day, she might meet Jaden Ivanslohe, the handsome prince, who was only a year older than her. And since her father had united their Kingdoms, who knew? Maybe one day one of those blue-eyed royals would sweep her off her feet.

Caroline tapped her toes anxiously, unable to stand still as she and Emmy waited on their parents. It was the first time they were allowed to attend the festivities, which culminated in the glamorous dance in Roskide's Great Hall set to open in less than an hour.

Emmy was on the dancefloor, preening before an invisible gentleman, who'd apparently asked her to dance as she was now twirling in his invisible arms. The queen had gone all out for Emmy's attire, having Everstal's finest dressmaker customize a multi-layered, red, chiffon gown befitting a sixteen-year-old princess. Twisted flourishes and sashes adorned the monstrosity. It was supposed to bear a resemblance to one of the thousands of crimson roses that were scattered about Roskide and the surrounding villages, but Caroline thought Emmy looked more like a melting cake.

With each step, Emmy's tightly coiled blonde locks bounced. When she finally ended the dance, she swayed over to Caroline and tugged her wrist. "Come on, Cara. Your hair is fine. The guests will be here soon!" she whined. "Don't you want to dance with me?"

"You were doing fine without me," Caroline said, reaching up to her shorn hair, which her attendant had battled with a curling wand for over an hour earlier. Her stick-straight hair had finally submitted, and the tuffs bowed into each other in submission. At least she was still able to wear the silver rose pins her father had gifted her.

"Stop touching it. You're going to make it worse." Emmy swatted Caroline's hand away from her damaged mop.

"I think Alma singed the ends," Caroline groaned.

"I told you, you should have left it spiky. It was rather interesting that way at least."

"It looked like I'd been struck by lightning."

"Mother says I should apologize. She said a woman's hair is an important part of their identity." Emmy fingered a shiny blonde curl. "So, I guess I'm sorry. Forgive me?"

Emmy's eyes bulged and watered, and her lip gave a little practiced quiver. Caroline had seen her rehearse her apologies and the mock sweetness she delivered them with in the mirror loads of times. She still couldn't hold a grudge for long, though. Caroline always ended up forgiving Emmy. They were sisters, after all.

"It's fine, Emmy. It will grow back," she said, frowning.

"It will." A self-satisfied smirk crossed Emmy's face.

The way her sister could get away with anything grated on Caroline, but she did her best to plaster a fake smile across her face. It was just hair. She should brush it off as casually as Emmy did and not let it get to her.

Emmy perked up. "Good. Oh, see what they've made for us!" She dragged Caroline on the dais where two smaller thrones were sitting adjacent to the king and queens, the latter who'd entered from a discrete door behind the podium.

"Hello, girls," Queen Cerise greeted. "Are you excited about tonight, seeing all the guests in their finery?"

Caroline narrowed her eyes, not ignorant to the fact that the queen had said *girls,* but addressed her inquiry only to her daughter.

"Oh, Mother, do you think they'll love my dress?" Emmy made several twirls, and the cake dress took flight, turning around her in the air.

"No one will be lovelier," Queen Cerise praised her daughter, eyes shining with the pride only a mother could possess.

"What about Caroline?" Emmy prodded, pressing her lips into a prim smile, and gestured for Caroline to spin. Caroline didn't want to spin. She didn't want any more attention than necessary.

"Go on," the queen demanded, mimicking her daughter's circling hand gesture.

Caroline smoothed the simple grey silk that hung limply on her boyish figure and turned in a quick circle. Emmy had developed womanly curves by the time she was fourteen. Caroline had no shape to speak of and was still sprouting toward the sky. Every comparison made between her and Emmy was like a dagger twisting a little deeper into her wounded ego.

"She looks nice, doesn't she?" Emmy pushed. "Besides the hair, of course."

"Caroline looks..." The queen hesitated, wrinkling her brow, searching the room for an escape. "Oh, there you are, dear," she deflected as the king joined his family on the stage.

"What do you think of your thrones, my darlings?" he asked, motioning to the two custom made wooden chairs on either side of his and the queen's.

Emmy sashayed over to hers, surveying it. The king's artisans had carved elaborate blooming crimson roses and thorn-covered hunter vines which appeared to be sprouting from each plank of wood. Gold leaf topped the tip of every petal and thorn. Emmy plopped down, wiggling her butt to settle in the seat, and looked out to the empty room as if she were looking over an awaiting crowd of her subjects. "It's perfect!" She clapped her hands together excitedly.

"Caroline?" King Thom asked, eyebrows raised.

Caroline savored the texture of the smooth wood as she ran her delicate fingers across it. Her throne wasn't as ornate as her sister's. It was taller and narrower, like her, and it would take her years to grow into. Delicate vines crawled up the two three-sided posts, which supported a back panel that was shaped like a diamond.

Other angular shaped geometric patterns were carved into the surface reminiscent of thorns, and a single rose, painted an iridescent black, was carved into the face of the backrest. Silver trimmed the edge of the petals and the linear grooves which ran down the arms and legs of the chair.

It was less elaborate than Emmy's, and she might have thought less effort and cost had gone into making it, but her father had taken great care to instruct the craftsman of its every detail. A tear came to her eye and her heart didn't feel like it could fill any further. Never had she received such a gift.

"You don't like it?" He bent down eye level with his daughter, his heavy brow furrowed in concern, misinterpreting her reaction.

She shook her head. "No, Father, it's perf—"

"Your Majesty, something's not right." A voice echoed across the empty room as Torac, the head commander of Roskide entered with six heavily armed guards at his heels.

Caroline had known the stout commander since she was a child. She couldn't remember when she'd seen Torac so rattled.

"What is it, Torac?" King Thom's ruddy skin turned sallow, causing a chill to run up Caroline's spine.

"The guests seem to be... *missing*. At first, attendants couldn't find them in their rooms, or the gardens. They should have been getting ready for the festivities, but their belongings are gone, too. We spotted a caravan leaving the city." Torac flexed his hand over his short sword as he paced before his liege.

"And no one noticed?!" Queen Cerise demanded. She gathered her skirts in a white knuckled grip and turned toward her husband.

Swearing under his breath, King Thom rushed over to one of the lower, narrow windows in the Great Hall of Roskide. The castle was built into and atop a sagging mountain peak overlooking a wide bay and the harbor city to the south. To the north, rolling vineyards and farmland stretched to the river which separated the kingdoms.

The Dallimore family took advantage of the strategic hilltop location, carving caves and tunnels through the mountain under Roskide in a fashion that the deeper one ventured into its belly, the more lost they might become should they not know the way. The design had kept many Everstal royals safe over the years, and the king and queen had schooled the girls on its intricate, winding layout since they were children. In Roskide, hide and seek took on a whole other level of difficulty.

Caroline peeked over the ledge around her father's shoulder to see the dust being kicked up at the gates by a fleet of horses and carriages, leaving the city at a pace which suggested they were fleeing. How they'd been able to get outside of the sphere of the king's power without detection, she couldn't conceive. It had been the use of the Gift, the ability of the ruling

Dallimore to seize the will of another, which had stopped the war. By King Thom's actions alone, they had fifteen years of peace and prosperity between the kingdoms. To Caroline, her father was only second to the Gods. All powerful, undefeatable. To see him in a panic like this—

King Thom spun, grabbing Caroline by the arm, his grip wrenching a whimper from her lips. "Run, hide!" he commanded as he released her, shoving her toward Emmy.

Stomach flip flopping, Caroline followed her older sister across the room, and behind the dais toward a favorite escape tunnel they frequented during their games. A booming groan stopped them short. Caroline glanced back to see a ruby-toned dagger protruding from deep in her father's shoulder.

Rosenwood. Any other blade could wound a Dallimore, but with a weapon crafted from rosenwood, a wound would be fatal. Even if it didn't hit anything vital.

A chilly hand wrapped around Caroline's wrist, tugging. "Come on, Cara," Emmy pleaded as she ducked through the opening.

"But what about Father?" Caroline whispered as she followed Emmy into the tunnel.

"Don't worry about Father. He'll use his power to compel them to turn themselves in. This will be over soon." Emmy's voice shook, betraying her confidence, and silent tears flowed down Caroline's waxen face as she crawled after her sister through the narrowing passageway.

All Caroline could see was the red of that dagger as they ran, taking little used pitch-black corridors beneath Roskide in which even they became lost from time-to-time. Had Emmy not seen it?

"Ouch!" Emmy cried, as a thud sounded in the cramped space. Her sister ran headfirst into the underside of one of the many stairways that dipped over tunnel sections here and there. "It's the stair over the west passage. We missed the opening. Turn around. It must be close."

Caroline ran her fingers across the cool stones, searching for the insignificant crack which split the wall right above the alcove, a spot

Emmy defaulted to when she was being lazy at their little game. Hiding spots were bound to be repeated, but due to how difficult this one was to find, it was a favorite of Emmy's.

"It's here," Caroline whispered.

The girls squatted down and tucked in deep. Caroline leaned against Emmy, trying to stave off the chill of the subterranean passageway and her chattering teeth.

They sat for what felt like hours, unflinching, barely letting a breath escape. The silence would have been deafening if it weren't for Caroline's roaring heart. How could one be so cold, but sweat at the same time?

"We should probably split up," Emmy said, finally breathing.

"Shhhh..." Caroline hissed.

"Wouldn't Father have come to find us by now? Or at least sent Torac?" Emmy's voice was feebler than Caroline had ever heard it, causing the sick feeling twisting her insides to wring even tighter. "What if something happened to him? And I'm the only living Dallimore. You should go—to distract them."

"He'll come. We just need to stay here."

Footfalls sounded from the direction of the overhead stair. An ominous sense caused Caroline's trembling to begin anew. If the source of the sound were friendly, they wouldn't be taking such care to be silent. It wasn't her father.

Soon, breathing accompanied the steps, and as they approached the crack that the crevice laid beneath, they stilled. Caroline's heart jumped into her throat, and she swore the hammering was audible. She reached back to grab Emmy's hand, hoping for her sister's reassurance, but Emmy had tucked herself impossibly far back in the little cave, leaving Caroline between her in the opening.

"I can smell your fear, little princess. I can hear your breathing."

Caroline swallowed. Trying to still her pumping lungs, realizing the man only thought he'd found one of them. Emmy must be holding her breath. She should have done that, too. How stupid could she be?

"Come out, come out." The sound of steel dragging across the stones set Caroline's nerves alight. So much so that she didn't feel the toe of a boot land on the small of her back until it was too late.

No, Emmy wouldn't.

A scream tore from her lips as she burst from the cave with a thrust from behind.

How could Emmy do this? Give her own sister over without a fight. The betrayal stung harder than the smack of her cheek against the chilly stone as she hit the wall opposite the hiding spot. Hands swiped in the dark, grasping for her, as she scrambled with all her might to escape their clutch.

Getting to her feet, Caroline leaped in the opposite direction and started running. She was quick and nimble, she reminded herself as she sprinted. And she had the maze beneath Roskide memorized in the same way other children had the passages of sacred texts memorized in their mind. She had a chance.

Heavy thuds followed her down the tunnel, gaining on her. Caroline spun down a corridor, but the man whipped around just as fast behind her. A meaty hand smacked into the top of her head as he reached for her, trying to snatch a fist full of hair but coming up short, and she shrieked.

Caroline came upon a set of stairs descending to a lower level and she paced down them, taking two at a time until she came to a platform. She took off as soon as she hit the landing, keeping her hands in front so she wouldn't crash into a wall in the dark.

Her fist smashed into a corner, sending a jolt of pain up her arm, and a cry escaped before she could stifle it. The man chuckled from too close behind her.

Fingers grazed the back of her silver gown, and the next swing hit higher up, landing on the base of her neck. A strong hand gripped down hard, halting her course, and jerking her around to press her face first into a wall.

She was gasping from the running, or the fear, or both. The blood soaring in her ears echoed and drowned out all other sounds. Convulsions wracked her body. Wait, the rattling was coming from the man gripping her neck.

"Answer me!" he demanded, wrenching her away from the wall so he could shake her more thoroughly.

"I can't—" she eked out between shallow breaths.

"Where's your sister?" The man's voice was as gruff as his grip on Caroline, which tightened in emphasis. She was incapable of responding, so he dragged her down the passageway. As they made their way through the maze under Roskide, Caroline's panicked breathing evened, and clarity slowly cleared the mist of her fright clouded mind. She wouldn't make it easy for this man. *This assassin.*

He was going to kill her anyway, and if he had found them in the hidden tunnels, it meant the Ivanslohe's had uncovered Roskide's secrets or there was a traitor amongst them.

Caroline thrashed under the man's grip, swinging, and flailing her arms, connecting a few slaps against his solid flesh. He grunted as the back of her hand connected with what she assumed was his jaw.

"I see you've recovered," he said.

The assassin gripped the scruff atop Caroline's head, jerking back so hard a bolt of white-hot lightning shot down her neck. "Where is she?" he demanded again, breathing acrid air into her face. Caroline couldn't see him, but this assassin was a foul creature. "Show me her little hiding spot, bastard, and I may let you live."

"We separated," Caroline forced out, then gurgled a cry as the man's grip tightened on her hair, making fresh tears burst from her eyes. "I swear. She made me go this way."

Heavy breathing engulfed her as the man considered her answer. "Where did she run off to?" he growled, slamming her back into the wall and wrapping a hand around her throat before Caroline could suck in a breath.

She raked her claws down the assassin's arms, feeling skin and blood gather under her fingernails, but he didn't ease the vice-like grip he had on her throat. Her lungs burned, and she was becoming light-headed. He was going to kill her. That was the moment she understood her father was dead. Which meant the queen was dead too. She wasn't sure if the lack of air or the grief flooding through her would kill her first.

Her arms and legs slackened, and the assassin's meaty hand was the only thing keeping Caroline pinned to the wall.

King Thom should have been able to use the Gift to stop the assassins. That one of them was slowly suffocating her could only mean one thing. Emmy, her half-sister, who had shoved her out into the passageway as bait for their enemy, was now queen.

Upon the ruling Dallimore's death, the Gift, the ability to take another's will as your own—to compel, would pass to the succeeding ruler. It was the gift to the Dallimore's from the Gods, and the price they demanded was paid eagerly in exchange for such a power, though the king never shared with Caroline what the Gods demanded in return.

Surely Emmy would feel her new power and come save her. Caroline's eyes rolled back in her head, and she used the last bit of strength she had to reach up and tap her lips.

"Good girl," the man said, releasing her.

Caroline crumpled to the ground, gasping for breaths. *Time.* She had to buy herself some time, but her mind was a torrent of conflicting thoughts.

She pushed you into the hallway. She might as well have left you for dead.

No, Caroline, she chastised herself. If Emmy were queen, it would be Caroline's duty to sacrifice herself to save her sister.

But they could have stayed hidden in that alcove. They both could have lived, and the man towering above her would have eventually given up, or Emmy could have used her power against him. Even if he'd heard them, it was pitch black and sound reverberated in the tunnels, so it was a challenge to tell where the sounds originated from. He couldn't have known he was right above them.

The heel of his boot crashed into her side, making her cry out, interrupting the war raging inside her mind. "Talk, girl," he said. "I'm losing patience."

"She's gone to the treasury. It's the safest place."

"Take me there." Fabric ripped as he grabbed the bodice of her gown and yanked Caroline to her feet. "Move!"

Caroline's lip trembled as she stumbled to her feet. "I don't know the way," she lied. "I'm a bastard, remember?" She hoped he would find that plausible, though it would likely lead to her death. A Dallimore would live, though, and Everstal would have a ruler, even if it was her traitorous sister.

"I don't believe you. Take me to the treasury. Now!" he growled.

Metal scraped, the clang reverberating off the stones, seemingly a favorite scare tactic of his. The assassin tapped it twice when it didn't elicit the expected response and pressed a sharp point into Caroline's back. The stinging bite right below her shoulder blade caused an involuntary step forward.

Emmy could still come.

Something otherworldly crawled across Caroline's skin, and she gave a violent shiver, trying to shake the sensation off. She failed, and the hole bored into her core, and buried itself deep in the pit of her stomach where her deepest breath came from. It was an unfamiliar fullness that almost made her gag with its relentless churning. Was it some sort of twisted knowing that happened right before you died?

The assassin used the weapon to prod her along toward what he believed was Emmy's hiding spot. As she led him through the maze of Roskide, far away from the new queen, it occurred to Caroline that Emmy was not coming for her. The heaviness that inched up your throat right before you retched swirled upward from her gut. She didn't care if her sister would be queen. If the situation were reversed, she would have gone for Emmy. That's what sisters do.

Later, Caroline would look back on this moment and wonder if that was when her heart had turned black, or if it had been the second the heel of her sister's boot touched the small of her back. Caroline was on her own. There was no one coming to save her. Not her father, not Torac, commander of the guard, or her older sister who now carried the Gift, the Power of Kings—a gift to the Dallimore's from the Gods.

With a thought, Emmy could have forced her captor to impale himself on his own blade. Bitterness wrenched her insides as she took another turn through the labyrinth. Six more steps in the dark, then stairs. The thud of the assassin stubbing his foot against the first step sounded. He grunted in pain, momentarily letting his blade drop.

Caroline gritted her teeth. She could run. This was her chance while he was distracted. *Run.* Caroline flew up the stairs. The assassin didn't know the way through the tunnels. She would be faster this time. A streak of sunlight refracted around a corner ahead, one of the few places in the tunnels that snaked near the outside walls of Roskide, far away from the underground vault where the treasury of Everstal was hidden. Her captor would know she'd been leading him astray as soon as he saw the light.

There was a fork in the tunnel that laid ahead at the top of the stairs. The assassin's footsteps were falling behind as she chased up the narrow, winding staircase. She was small enough that she didn't need to duck, giving her an advantage over her assailant. Caroline's bare feet nimbly gripped the slick stones as she crested the last steps, taking two at a time.

A figure stepped out of the darkness, and she crashed into it, stumbling back, catching herself against a wall before she tumbled down the stairs.

"What do we have here?" a new voice slithered across her skin.

Caroline took in the second assassin, who stood before her in the reflected light. He was a narrow man, scars crisscrossing his neck and black paint covered his eyes, nose, and mouth, leaving the rest of his gaunt face in stark contrast. He wore a black tight-fitting one-piece which covered everything up to his neck. A black mask sat pulled up, resting on his forehead. The new assassin licked his lips and twirled a small dagger in his hand, and a shiver flittered up Caroline's neck.

"She's not for you, Servius. Hollis wants this one alive," the larger assassin, who wore the same black attire, huffed as he came up behind her, clamping down on the back of her neck once again.

He spun her around and pulled her toward him so they were eye to eye, and Caroline startled at the brilliant blue of his eyes. The royals from the northern kingdom of Veetula had vibrant blue eyes, like the clearest mountain lake, but up close, they almost glowed with their own innate light. She'd seen them from a distance, that defining characteristic, but she didn't realize even assassins might carry the trait, or a royal might be an assassin.

"You've been leading me in circles," he hissed.

Caroline clenched her jaw tightly, refusing to answer. They would not end her life after all, so why should she speak?

As if reading her thoughts, the first assassin said, "Just because I'm not going to kill you, doesn't mean I can't make you wish you were dead." A seedy grin crept across his blunt features, and any hope Caroline had melted away.

Grubby fingers dug into her skin, and he directed her toward the narrow window the light was filtering in through. She fought, kicking, flailing wildly as he picked her up and shoved her head-first through the opening. Screaming pain shot up her legs as her knees scraped over the exposed edges of the broken stones, and her stomach dropped as she free-fell over the edge.

At the last second, she jolted upward as the larger assassin's firm grip sealed around her ankles. Front-facing, she slammed into the rose-vine-covered wall. Dagger-like thorns of the historic rose bushes, a symbolic feature wrapping Roskide in a blanket of flowering vegetation year-round, dug into her flesh and her whole body sparked in agony.

Wind howled, whipping around over the turrets and across the rounded wall she dangled from. Her silver dress slipped down, bunching around her torso, and she had to grab the gown so it wouldn't slip entirely off her shapeless form.

"You will lead me to your sister. We will not leave this castle until we can deliver her lifeless body, along with that of King Thom and Queen Cerise, to our sovereign."

Tears streaked down Caroline's cheeks as fast as the hate filling her heart. The rage consumed her so fully she barely felt the tiny rivulets of blood trickling across her throbbing skin from the scratches inflicted upon her by the thorns. She peeled open her eyes and surveyed her options.

Directly beneath her, a crimson rose was splayed open in full bloom. She wrinkled her nose in disgust, the horrible flower causing the image of her sister and that hideous dress to flash through her mind. A single drop of her red blood dripped down onto its petals before sliding off to journey down the woody vines.

It was told the creeping vegetation was what kept the aging castle held together, but that was only a folktale. Still... Caroline reached out, grabbing ahold of a vine, testing it to see if it might hold her weight. If she could free her legs from the assassin's grip, she might be able to shimmy down the vines like a ladder and escape.

She squeezed her hands around the thick, crawling stalks, stifling a sob as the thorns pierced her palms. She yanked. They held firmly affixed to the wall. It was worth the risk, she assessed, so she began kicking anew, slapping her ankles together, hoping the man's knuckles would smack and he'd lose his grip.

"Haven't had enough?" he growled at her, shaking her up and down.

She couldn't repress the scream that ripped from her throat as fresh cuts and scrapes raked across her body. Then he was pulling her back up inside the window.

The first assassin planted her back on her feet, and she swayed, disoriented from hanging upside down for so long.

"If you don't cooperate, it will be Servius's turn." The larger guard, whose name she hadn't learned, patted his blade against the other assassin's chest.

Servius grinned, exposing a row of gleaming white teeth trimmed with metal brackets attaching somewhere in the shadowed cavern of his mouth, which added pointed edges to the six teeth across the top. The gesture was effective in its intent and Caroline could feel the color drain from her skin.

Servius tapped his foot anxiously as he waited for her to give him a reason to strike. His muddy eyes were hungry, though she wasn't sure for what. That prospective horror made her tremble, then step back. The assassin ran his palms down his black clad thighs, leaving a darkening trail of moisture behind them.

Caroline's heart seized up. She tried to move, but her body clung glued to the wall and her heavy, panic-filled limbs remained stationary. Opening her mouth, she tried to speak, tried to raise a hand to point. Hot shame battled with sticky dread. This was why she could never have been the heir. Her fear had frozen her.

Servius stepped forward, placing his hands on either side of Caroline, boxing her in. He leaned his head down and ran his nose across the exposed skin of her neck which the dress's tiny straps didn't cover, breathing her scent. With his next excruciatingly slow pass, hot metal grazed her skin and a wet tongue trailed it, tasting the sweat and blood dotting her flesh.

Caroline closed her eyes. If she could not escape, if she could not save herself, she would do so inside her mind. Lock herself away in her imagination. She would envision herself as the type of woman, powerful, like her father, who could have easily taken down these two assassins standing before her, well within the range of his power.

She imagined hurting them like they hurt her. Relished in the thought of exacting retribution on them. Caroline and Emmy had always giggled at the torments and pranks they inflicted on their attendants, the cooks and gardeners, their teachers, and tailors. They had never been truly cruel. Until now, Caroline wouldn't have understood what being truly cruel even meant.

Searing heat scored across her shoulder, bringing her out of her dream into the present. She gritted her teeth and squeezed her eyes tight, redoubling the effort. Caroline thought of that sharpened edge of the blade carried by the first assassin. How sweet it would feel to drag it across his throat and watch the warm blood flow out of his neck.

No. Her father would have compelled the other assassin to do the work for him. Then turn the blade against himself. Imagining their death might be the only way she'd survive this torture. The way the larger man would slip the blade out from its sheath, the sound the metal on metal would make—she could almost hear it.

So quietly, he would slip behind Servius while he was engrossed in marring her delicate skin. The assassin would wrap his hand across the other man's forehead, yank him backward, and run the weapon across Servius's exposed throat.

Hot liquid squirted across Caroline's face, and she opened her eyes to see the wide eyes of Servius clawing at the ruby gash on his neck. Caroline darted her gaze around the hallway, searching for her sister.

She had come. How had she known where to find her?

She almost started crying anew, relieved that she was no longer alone, but her sister was nowhere in sight. It was impossible. *Unless you had taken blood of the person you meant to command, your target must be within your line of sight.* It's how someone had thrown the rosenwood dagger which struck her father, from some carefully concealed location.

The first assassin took two startled steps back, trying to shake the blade free from his hand. Servius slumped to the floor, lifeless. Caroline gripped the wall for support, but weak knees buckled beneath her, and she slid down to rest in the blood pooling around the dead assassin.

She looked up and met the horrified gaze of her original captor.

It couldn't be. The man before her struggled to escape the force pinning him to the spot. She glanced down at the body in front of her, then back up at the man. And grinned.

Experimentally, she imagined him raising the weapon just a little. His jerky hand elevated. Caroline surveyed the cuts and scrapes across her tattered body, and reached a hand up, touching the torn skin at her neck. Her hand came away red.

The sour smell of piss brought her attention back to the first assassin. A dark stain covered the front of his pants, and he was visibly seething between bouts of shaking.

"If it makes you feel any better, I don't think either of us expected today to end this way." Caroline huffed a laugh, which grew in strength as she pushed herself up the wall and onto unsteady feet.

This time, when she imagined what she did with the knife, she did not close her eyes.

The assassin let out a forced breath as he pressed the blade deep into his belly. Caroline stepped out of the way, around the dead body to allow the man to climb up on the window ledge. He stole one last glance at her, fear blazing in his blue eyes, before he threw himself over.

Caroline reached a shaky hand down and picked up Servius's dagger, forcing her damaged palm around it. She clenched it to her breast as she made her way down the winding steps.

If this power had passed to her instead of Emmy, what did it mean? Was her sister still alive? Were there other assassins?

An emptiness, like hunger but far more corroding, pulsed at the space above her navel. Only a few steps taken, and she was out of breath. After she'd tripped for a third time, Caroline decided it would be safest to sit on the steps for a moment to make sense of what had happened and wait for her energy to renew. Just for a moment, she told herself.

CHAPTER 3

C AROLINE WINCED AS SHE blinked her eyes open. Blinding white light shone down upon her, and she raised her hand to shield her eyes while they adjusted.

"The new heir," an ethereal voice whispered.

"Indeed," another answered.

Caroline dusted herself off as she scrambled to her feet, assessing her gore covered body. Her silver dress was soiled with dirt, blood, and little tears from the rose thorns. And she was still oozing in places, which opened as she moved.

Wrinkling her brow, she touched the wound at her neck, then glanced up to the five figures sitting on simple stone benches in a semicircle around her. Could there have been something on Servius's metal teeth, a poison? Was that why she'd gotten so tired after she'd killed them both?

Her eyes peeled back as realization struck and she stumbled a few steps away from them. She surveyed the Gods, for that was surely who was before her. "Am I dead?"

They were eerily similar in appearance and appeared neither male nor female. All clad in white draping robes, pale ivory hair pulled back from their alabaster faces. Gaunt cheeks, pale pink lips, and small straight noses. The strangest thing was their eyes. Five pairs of the palest platinum pupiless eyes stared back at her, the irises so faint they almost blended in with the whites. Long ivory eyelashes surrounded them and fluttered as they blinked.

The only apparent difference between them was the amulet that hung on the silver chain around each of their necks, though she wasn't near enough to get a glimpse of the symbols on each. She had learned enough about the Gods to understand that they must represent the five orders: Life, Death, Justice, Pain, and Love.

One by one, they cocked their heads to the side, then glanced between themselves as if they did not understand her.

"Am I dead?" she repeated, a little more firmly.

The first one huffed a laugh under its breath. Another mimicked the sound, then a cacophony of flittering laughter filled the nearly vacant, colorless space.

Caroline narrowed her eyes and crossed her arms across her chest, not understanding what was so funny with her assumption. She was in an empty white space, like the center of a cloud—if a stone platform sat in the center of one, surrounded by deities. That seemed to her like what one might expect in the afterlife.

Was this the time for her judgement? As the thought occurred to her, she uncrossed her arms, and clasped them innocently in front of her stomach instead. If she was to be judged, there was no sense in angering the Gods.

Their laughter had her thoughts in motion, and she winced as they took flight. Images of Cook retching and the two murders she'd just committed flickered in her mind. Well, they weren't really murders and, they had killed her family as well, so surely the Gods wouldn't condemn her for that.

What happens next? Her hand slipped out of the other because of the sweat now coating her palms. Caroline raised a reluctant hand, intending to get the attention of the Gods. The whimsical sounds emanating from the beings stopped abruptly before she could pose her question again.

One cleared its throat. The God in the middle who she assumed was Death. "No, daughter, you live still."

"Then, where am I?" she asked, shifting between feet, allowing herself to survey the space. Her eyes strained to find the edges of the endless platform.

"Did your father teach you nothing of the Gift?" The God's eyes seemed to glow from within when it said *the Gift*.

"No," Caroline breathed. "I shouldn't have received it. My birth was not legitimate. It should have gone to my sister, Princess Emmaline." She didn't know why she was telling them this. Surely, they knew—they were Gods.

"Young Princess, you feel we have made a mistake?" the one she thought was Death boomed in a deceptively deep voice. Power flowed into her body, then her stomach rolled as she dropped to her knees from the God's invisible touch.

"*Justice*," the God who sat in the center said as it forced her face to turn upwards. Her assumption had been wrong.

Caroline trembled as she fought its control, then heaved, but swallowed the bile that was gurgling up her throat. Justice eased its grip, and she doubled over, spewing onto the stones. The contents of her stomach disappeared as fast as it splashed on the ground.

She regarded the Gods, wiping the back of her wrist across her mouth.

"Next time, don't fight. It will be better for you," Justice said.

She sniffed as she bowed her head in submission. It was told that compulsion often made the compelled ill if they resisted, but to be compelled by a God... Gooseflesh crawled up her arms. Many of the little cuts from the thorns were healing over and some were even pink with new skin.

She whipped her gaze back to them. She was alive.

"We are only here to help you, daughter. And we have conferred, because Thom did such a poor job in informing his child of the weightiness of this power, we shall be gentle this first time. But you should know, you may not wield such power without balance. When you use our Gift, you must pay what is due."

Caroline glanced between them. "I will pay," she said, standing more erect. If they deemed her worthy to carry this power—she shuddered to imagine the implications—but she would follow in her father's footsteps and use the Gift to protect her kingdom. *Her* kingdom? Did this mean Caroline was the true queen of Everstal?

"Very well, Your Highness." Justice gestured for the God to its right to rise. "Pain, make it swift."

Pain stepped forward, and its robes swished as it approached Caroline. Perhaps this wasn't such a clever idea. Her legs were shaking so hard she stumbled backward. An invisible strength wrapped around her, holding her in place.

"Remember," the one on the outside of where Pain had risen from said, "don't fight it." A serene smile crossed its face and a foreign warmth radiated through her. That one must be Love.

Pain was standing in front of her now and raised its hands to clasp either side of her cheeks. The God tilted its head, and pressed its mouth into a tight smile, as if it might be enjoying this.

Oh, no—

A flash cleaved between her eyebrows and slammed into the back of her skull. Her body tried to double over, to fold in on itself, but Love's power kept her upright. Her mouth opened, and a keening wail spouted from her throat, but her senses were so blinded by the pain she couldn't hear it.

Liquid energy ripped down her spine and shot out the tips of her toes before everything went dark.

✦

Caroline's eyes fluttered open, but she slammed them back closed. Keeping her lids clamped shut, as if that might somehow shield her from what she might discover, she reached out, running her hands over the fluffy bedding surrounding her. Her fingers traced the 'C' embroidered on her pillows. She was in her bed. Had it all been one horrible dream?

She'd never had night terrors before. Caroline opened her eyes and surveyed the room. It was indeed hers. She looked down at her body under the covers, only to discover she was completely naked, the silver dress she remembered wearing no longer there. Also gone was any sign of the abuse she'd endured.

Reaching up, Caroline ran a hand through her hair. That was as she expected. She threw the covers off, swung her legs out of bed, and wandered over to the tall mirror that leaned against a wall in her room. She turned this way and that, inspecting her body. The blood and grime, the evidence of what she'd experienced, still caked, dried, and cracked on her flesh, but she couldn't spot a single bruise or sign of a scrape.

She padded over to a pitcher of water and poured some into a basin. It seemed like a ridiculous thing to do considering what she'd just been through—what had happened to her family—what might still lurk in Roskide, but she needed to get the muck off her skin. Dipping the cloth into the cool water, she wrung it out, then scrubbed.

Dressed in the most practical attire she owned, which amounted to boots and a simple black sheath dress, Caroline stalked the castle halls, gripping a dagger she'd found in one of the rooms. She needed to know if she was alone in the castle and what had become of her family.

Her rooms were on the third floor, so she searched there first, climbing the floors of each spiraling tower as she passed through every wing. The first body had been a shock, but she'd passed half a dozen by now. And she hadn't come across a single living soul. Her footfalls echoed down the silence of the stairwell as she descended to the second floor. It was the same as the third floor. More bodies. More abandoned rooms.

They'd killed everyone, attendants, and guests in residence alike. It explained how the royals had been able to sneak away outside of her father's compulsion. His loving face flashed in her mind and grief hit her so hard she had to grip the wall.

She came to the Great Hall where her father had taken that first dagger. She debated entering to see what was left, but thinking of that rosenwood projectile which had come from out of nowhere, she decided she'd peek inside. As she approached the doorway, a pricking sensation skittered up her spine. She knew it. They were still here. She hadn't expected to have to defend herself so soon and so directly.

Caroline spun and flattened herself against the wall, shimmying behind a planter and rosebush that grew from it. She scanned the atrium, looking for the source of her heightened awareness. Her heart started as her gaze caught on a figure hiding in the shadow of the mirrored planter on the opposite side of the door. Wide gold eyes stared at her from the hiding place and the figure put a finger to its lips, shushing her. Then it waved a hand in a *follow me* motion.

Caroline narrowed her eyes at the figure, but he stepped from beside the planter into the light and started creeping down the hallway. He was only a boy around her age, fifteen at the most. He turned back toward her, widening his eyes in an insistent gesture.

She waited for a warning sensation, like the prickle she sensed before, for a long moment. When it never came, she slipped from behind the planter, and fell in line with him. His pace picked up and soon they were jogging light-footed through the servant's hallways on the ground floor. He led her to a small cupboard in the back of a dormitory and crouched down to crawl in. He fully disappeared inside it, gone for a few moments.

Whipping her head around, Caroline tried to repress the panic quickening her breath. He was still gone into the cupboard at her feet. Had he led her into a trap? But if that were the case, how would he know about this hiding place in Roskide? It made more sense that he was one of the castle worker's sons who'd survived the massacre outside the tunnels while she'd been fighting for her life.

It was a miracle an assassin hadn't found her while she'd been recovering in her bed—assuming they were still here. The boy poked his head out of the cabinet and gave her a quizzical expression before disappearing again. She released a breath, then knelt to follow him.

The cupboard opened into a small room that had a few cots which lined the walls. There was a basket with what appeared to be loaves of bread and cheese, and a pitcher, which she assumed he was using for water. In the far corner, there was another small door you'd have to crawl to pass through, created, so whoever sought this refuge would have a second way out.

"How long has it been?" Caroline whispered, walking over, and dropping on the bed. The springs gave a slight whine, and he winced. *Sorry*, she mouthed.

"Three days," the boy said in an equally quiet tone. "I think everyone who survived fled to the city. But I didn't have anywhere else to go."

"Are they all dead? The king and queen?" she asked, though she knew the answer.

The boy nodded, sniffing as his eyes glazed. That must mean he'd lost someone that night, too. Caroline's eyes burned and she blinked a few times, shoving down her own grief, which was attempting to rise at the confirmation of the truth she already knew.

Caroline envisioned her father's kind eyes one last time before she erased the image of the man who'd been her only lifeline from her memory. If she thought of him, she would let it overwhelm her.

After what she'd been through, after what the Gods had expected of her, she no longer felt like a fourteen-year-old girl, full of mirth and innocence. Her father was gone, her sister had betrayed her, men had tortured her and tried to murder her. She had no space or luxury for grief. She took a deep breath and hammered that unwelcome sensation behind an iron clad wall where it would stay indefinitely.

"What is your name, and who were your parents?" Caroline asked.

"Angus, Your Majesty. Mum passed ages ago. Torac is... *was* my father."

Another suspicion confirmed. If Torac was gone, most, if not all the guards would have perished with him. They'd be beginning from nothing. "And you know Roskide well, I assume?"

"Yes—"

"Then you shall be my eyes and ears. Congratulations on your new appointment."

"Your Majesty?" The boy's voice was a whimper, clearly unsure of Caroline's expectations.

Caroline snapped her head up. *Your Majesty*, he'd said. Reality struck her like a boulder. She was a queen now—*the queen*. The Gods had decreed it by passing the Gift to her and not her older sister. She didn't know what type of sick joke they were playing at, but she decided right then she wouldn't be one to waste the opportunity. And she wasn't one to forget, either. If the Gods were to demand punishment from her for the use of her power, then she would follow their image. Those who had hurt her, her family, her *kingdom,* would get their punishment too.

She thought of the Gods, the serenity in Love's face as Justice sentenced her and Pain exacted the payment. Then she remembered how satisfying it was to compel the assassins to end their lives. Had that been worth the pain, the payment to the Gods? The answer was clear. It had been clear for generations of rulers before her too.

Yes, and she would do it again gladly for this power—the Gift.

"Are they still here, our enemy? In Roskide?"

"I think so, Your Majesty." The boy wrung his hands, looking more sheepish than what she expected for his age.

"Was my sister among the dead?"

"I didn't see her."

Caroline narrowed her eyes, and the spot on her lower back blazed in her awareness. "Good," she said, and a grin crept across her face. "We'll have to find her then, won't we?"

Caroline and her fledgling commander spent the next several days lurking in the hallways, setting traps for the assassins. They used her presence to lure them out, then Caroline used the Gift. There had to be a reason they were still in Roskide. They were still searching for Emmy.

They picked them off one by one until they'd gone a week without sensing another living thing in the many hallways and rooms of Roskide aside from Red, the collection of identically named castle cats. And that included her elusive sister.

She made nine kills and so far, the Gods had not extracted their payment. Caroline's confidence was blooming, and she found the deaths she caused didn't weigh on her like she might have imagined they would. These murderers hadn't stopped at her family or the armed guard. Roskide was a wasteland, and she had a feeling she would fight an uphill battle to re-staff the castle after such a massacre.

Finally, Caroline and Angus mustered up enough bravery to enter the Great Hall. Eight bloated corpses laid in their own bloodstains across the room, in-between wilted flower sculptures and banquet tables. Caroline tucked her nose into the neck of her shirt to escape the scent of the rotting and foul food and the putrid smell of humans decomposing in the Everstal heat. An arrow protruded from the eye socket of a female guard she recognized, and her stomach churned so hard she had to turn away.

"They're not here," she called to Angus across the room. She remembered her first captor saying King Hollis wanted the bodies recovered.

Angus gasped and Caroline looked up to where he stood over the body of a large figure. Caroline approached and noted the man's sable skin and familiar strong jaw. Torac. Wrapping her arm around Angus's trembling shoulder, she said, "I'm so sorry."

Angus shook his head and stepped out of her embrace. "It's okay. He wasn't a good man." The grimace on his face contradicted his words. Good man or not, Torac was still his father. Angus gulped a quick breath crossing his arms over his stomach and fled from the room. Caroline found him throwing up behind a planter where they'd first met in the atrium.

"You okay, Angus?" She patted him on the back. Caroline vowed not to form any attachments, but poor Angus had slipped in right before she had made that mental decree.

He gagged, then heaved again.

"We'll restaff Roskide, and we'll have them take care of the bodies. Okay?"

Angus nodded. "How?"

"Well, first we'll try coin. If that doesn't work, I'll force them to serve me."

Angus looked up from where he was doubled over and gave Caroline a side-long glance. In the many hours they'd spent together, she'd shared how the power worked and that as her current most loyal subject, she might come back from a punishment incapacitated and he might need to take care of her.

There was also the fear that the subjects of Everstal would eventually come snooping around Roskide since their rulers hadn't been seen in weeks now and rumors were likely swirling out of control. But Caroline felt the need to locate and deal with her sister before she announced herself and her intentions to the people.

"Let's pay a visit to the treasury, shall we?" Caroline stormed down the hallway and slipped into the first opening to the tunnels she came across. A more confident Angus, slipped in right behind her.

It took about half an hour to make the winding passage down to the treasury vault beneath Roskide. "It's just in here. Help me with the door."

Putting both their weight into it barely made the door budge. "Shit, it must be barricaded from the inside," Angus said.

Emmaline. Caroline should have known she'd gone there. She'd even suggested as much to the assassin.

"Emmy!" she shouted. "It's me, Caroline. Open up!"

Nothing.

"Princess Emmaline," Angus shouted, his voice louder than Caroline's. He pounded on the door with his fists.

"Shhh... I hear something." The creaking and shifting of an object being moved stopped abruptly.

"Are they gone?" Emmy's voice sounded faintly through the thick door.

"They're gone, Emmy. Open up," Caroline yelled back.

"How has she survived in there this long?" Angus muttered.

"The vault is stocked with months' worth of rations and there's a makeshift toilet chamber that goes down to a deep well. There are barrels of wine and a small spring flows down one of the walls. It isn't much, but it is enough to keep one alive," Caroline explained, as more objects were wrenched across the floor.

Metal groaned loudly and clanged, sounding like it had fallen into the open resting position. Caroline nodded toward Angus and they both put a shoulder into the big door and heaved. The door swung open on creaking hinges, revealing the glow of several lanterns positioned around the room.

Emmy was standing, still clad in her red ball gown, though she had shorn most of the superfluous frills from it, so it was only a sheath. She shook her head, exhaling loudly. "Oh, Caroline, you have no idea how happy I am to see your face. It's been dreadful down here all alone."

Angus snorted and darted an incredulous glance at Caroline. She'd informed him of her sister's ways, so she couldn't trick him with her fake and manipulative utterings.

Emmy screwed up her face and looked Angus up and down. "Who are you?"

"He's my second in command," Caroline answered for him. She stomped into the room, surveying the space.

Emmy had dug through the treasury to find plush rugs and blankets which were laid out in a makeshift bed. A table had been set up with a lantern and a beautiful golden enameled plate was set out and a serving of half-eaten rations were sitting upon it as if she and Angus had interrupted a quaint private dinner.

She raised an eyebrow at her sister, whose mouth was agape at the commanding way Caroline was moving about the vault. "It hardly looks like you're roughing it."

"Father's gone?" Emmy asked, wringing her hands before her.

"And your mother," Caroline bit out.

Emmy put her fingers to her mouth and rested a shaky hand on the table.

"Your Majesty?" Angus interrupted.

"Yes?" both girls replied in unison.

"I was referring to the queen," he sneered at the princess.

Emmy stepped back. "Are you going to let your little friend talk to his sovereign like that? Or shall I deal with him? I should inherit Father's power any time now." She pressed her shoulders back and lifted a haughty chin.

Metal sang as Angus pulled an antique sword from a scabbard. He grinned at Caroline as he lifted it at her sister, whose mouth dropped open.

"Kneel before your queen," he commanded.

"I will not. What's the meaning of this?" Emmy barked, putting her hands on her hips, adding a foot stomp for emphasis.

Caroline closed her eyes, banishing any glimmer of a fond memory from her mind, replacing every single one with the feeling of that nudge Emmy gave her into the hallway. Into certain death. She opened them and glanced around, reminding herself of how easy her sister had been living, not giving much thought to what Caroline might be going through.

Then she looked Emmaline right in the eye, gave her the cruelest smile she could muster, and brought her to her knees.

꙰

"We're going to have to find some better options for food," Angus said.

He and Caroline sat on an open-air balcony, made from the same red striated stone the rest of Roskide was constructed from, at a plain wooden table overlooking the city. The moon was rising, and stars were just coming out. This balcony off the war room was a favorite of her father's. He could often be found in this exact chair ruminating on the day's decisions or meeting with Torac. The fact that she sat here with the young man she'd decided would be her commander wasn't lost on her.

"That will be the next order of business after I take my punishment. I don't want to be speaking to an audience and the Gods decide to whisk me away during the middle of it." Caroline gnawed on the chewy cake they'd retrieved from the vault after they'd locked her sister up in the dank prisons which were carved into the side of the mountain. Only the worst prisoners were there and, as she and Angus discovered, they'd all died from thirst or starvation in the weeks they'd been forgotten about. The smell was horrendous, and it was almost inhuman to leave Emmy there. *Almost.*

So, they found the least putrid smelling section, threw her in, then delivered her fancy bedding and table, suggesting she make herself at home. It had taken all the strength Caroline had not to rip every shred of hair out of Emmy's head as she grabbed her dirty blonde locks and dragged her inside the cell. When the lock clicked, Caroline didn't look back.

"How long are you going to leave her there?" Angus asked, sensing her drifting thoughts.

She studied him, but couldn't sense any judgement in his eyes. To Caroline, it only cemented his loyalty to her.

She shrugged. "Indefinitely? Why? Do you think I should let her out?"

"If it were me, I wouldn't. But I'm not a queen." They shared a glance, then a grin. As she built her guard and castle staff, she couldn't afford to be so informal with them. Somehow, with Angus, with what they'd been through together, the friendship had blossomed. And she supposed she was permitted one friend.

"Why haven't they summoned you yet?" Angus asked as he tore off a piece of hard cheese and stuffed it into his mouth.

"Oh, I'm sure they're waiting until I become complacent." Caroline threw her gaze to the heavens. "Come and get me. Exact your punishments. I've earned it," she called to the sky.

A tingling sensation bit up her calves and swirled around her. "Shit, Angus. They are respondi—"

⤛❧

Angus blinked as his queen dissolved into a fine mist that evaporated with the rays of the sun.

⤛❧

"Seems like someone's been busy," Death called down to Caroline as she appeared on the familiar white stones.

She glared up at the Gods, resentment of their power over her already bubbling up. And this was just the beginning. "Let's get on with it. I have a kingdom to restore."

"Already bored with us?" Justice shook his head, sighing. They were quiet for a while, appearing to confer between themselves through some sort of mental channel, then Justice motioned to Pain to rise.

Pain approached her without fanfare and leaned down to whisper in her ear, "Satisfying, isn't it?"

Her breath quickened as she braced for what was to come, and she shot a look at the placid Gods still on their benches. *They were enjoying this.* "Twisted fucks," she muttered.

"That's not very nice language for a young queen, daughter," the God she learned was Life chimed. Its face displayed a subtle grin, but otherwise showed no tension or facial flection at all. Just peace.

Caroline laughed. She wasn't sure what she was laughing at. Perhaps it was the irony, or Pain's secret admission. Maybe it was her devolving opinion of the Gods. She didn't know for sure, but she couldn't stop herself. She was only a fourteen-year-old girl, and these were eternal beings. She should prostrate herself before them, not laugh in their faces.

But she couldn't control herself. She had seen too much in the last week of her life. Caroline wasn't the same girl any longer.

Pain smiled so only she could see—as if they shared some sort of secret understanding—and placed its hands on her, cupping her head around her jaw. A cool, pervasive energy passed to her from its silky hands as they squeezed. The total control Pain embodied as it looked down into her eyes was almost a comfort. Caroline braced herself. Before she threw her head back, she caught Death wink as the first wave struck.

She would take this penance gladly, she reminded herself as she gritted her teeth coming down from a crest, the blinding pain ebbing long enough for a thought to slip through. When this was over, she and Angus would get to work rebuilding Everstal into a kingdom so powerful that none could challenge her. There would be no peace treaties or truces made during her reign. She would extract her wrath on Veetula, and its blue-eyed royals would cower before her. There was no price she wouldn't pay. Caroline would deliver their punishment, and it would make the anguish coursing through her veins feel like a mercy.

PART TWO -

THE CRIMSON REIGN

CHAPTER 1

TEN YEARS LATER

T ENSION FLOATED THROUGH THE air as Angus poked his head into the war room, eyeing the queen bent over a stack of letters at the long mahogany table. A map of Everstal was carved into its center and in the middle of that, there was a lifelike replication of Roskide, the rose-colored-and-covered castle which was the crown jewel of the kingdom. She ran a hand through her iridescent black hair releasing a sigh. Stomach clenching in response, Angus cleared his throat. He hated delivering unwelcome news to his queen. Especially following the most recent discovery of the whereabouts of her former lover, Felix, and the condition of his new bride.

Caroline looked up from the papers she was studying to her commander. She blinked as if trying to flutter away the strain from long hours of sorting through the correspondences. Inquisitive silver eyes studied him, waiting. Few men met the queen and weren't taken aback by her beauty. It wasn't that Angus didn't find her visually appealing. Romance and all it entailed wasn't something he was interested in.

He'd seen the consequences firsthand with his parents and enjoyed their relationship as it was. Besides, they'd grown up together. They were the only family each other had, and that suited Angus fine.

When they met at fourteen, they'd both been gangly teens, not grown into their adult bodies. Now, Caroline stood taller than most women and had lithe curves, long limbs, and the smoothest alabaster skin he'd ever seen. She typically wore her hair loose, a long sheet of black ice which reflected the light gleaming blue. But it was her intelligent silver eyes, hooded and slightly upturned, which always discerned too much that set her apart.

"Is now a good time?" Angus shifted on his feet feeling small in her presence.

The man standing before the queen was no longer the wiry boy she'd met, either, only days after all hell had broken loose in Roskide. And on the heels of the former king and queen's assassination. It had taken them five years to rebuild the guard, staff the castle, and reorganize the armies, but they'd done it growing up together. Then another five to become the smoothly operating unit they were now.

Angus understood he'd become an imposing figure, like his father, Torac, her father's own commander. Tall, broad shouldered, a stubborn square jaw that jutted out like an anvil, and intimidating deep gold eyes that could pin a person to a spot. But none of that mattered when he was standing before her. It didn't matter who you were—Queen Caroline Dallimore had molded herself into a figure many respected and even more feared.

"Where's Evran?" she asked, brow furrowing in concern.

Gripping the documents in a clammy hand, he ran his other across his cropped tight curls and down his tawny face, the gesture betraying his anxious energy. Caroline narrowed her eyes. She was fully aware of his nonverbal communication.

"He didn't report for duty this morning. I sent a courier to his family's home, and he wasn't there either." Angus pressed his lips into a hard line and dropped the documents on the table before her.

"He's gone... like the others, isn't he?" It was more a statement than a question. She knew.

Angus nodded. "That makes him the third guard this year to vanish."

꧁꧂

"Gods," Caroline swore, chucking a fountain pen across the room. It struck the wall, ink splattering. People went missing, but her *personal guards*... That was enough to make the hair on the back of her neck stand on end. "I don't like this."

"Neither do I," Angus said. "We're working on getting to the bottom of it, but so far, we don't have a viable lead. He was in the barracks last night, confirmed by several other guards. He must have disappeared in the night. His bed looked like he slept in it, but his boots were still under it. You need to choose an immediate replacement. Those are the top three candidates."

Caroline groaned and reached for the papers Angus pointed to, their ominous presence something she could no longer ignore. She scanned the first one and set it aside. She went through the next two and tossed them on the table and shrugged at Angus, who was waiting with his hands linked behind his back. "Does it matter? They all seem equally proficient." The poor condemned soul she selected was going to disappear anyway, like the others—if they didn't uncover what was happening to them first.

"They're outside the room if you'd like to meet them," he said.

"Very well, show them in." Caroline reclined back in her chair, gripping the armrests as if she could channel all the tension gripping her shoulders into the wood.

Angus poked his head out into the hallway, murmured something, then three guards followed him in and lined up as he directed for her inspection. As Caroline placed the papers beside each other, Angus reached down and shuffled the middle document to the outside. He waved a thick hand toward the guards. "Cole Harris, Brock Holzman and Johnneth Althorpe."

The men knelt before her, diverting their eyes to the floor. "Rise," she said.

❦

The queen studied the three men Angus had brought before her. Caroline's instinct was always so keen when it came to these matters and, often, she made the decision he would have. The queen and her commander were a formidable duo that way.

Caroline's face remained impassive, yet he caught the subtlest tick of her jaw as she ran her gaze over the three guards. That slight tell was the reason this choice would be one of the rare times they disagreed. Specialist Brock Holzman was senior to the other two men by a few months and a little gruffer and more direct, which would suit Caroline's temperament best. He was a square barrel of a man, with ruddy brown hair cropped close to his skull and a dense arrangement of freckles dappling his tan skin. But the documents outlined each of their personalities, strengths, weaknesses, and she had studied them.

"Johnneth is an unusual name," Caroline said, her voice taking on a decidedly smoother tone than it had when it had been the two of them.

"A family name, Your Majesty," Johnneth responded, his stare floating up from the floor to meet her gaze.

Angus did not miss the subtle glint in the man's eye, and he scolded himself for including him in the selection, having believed Holzman the obvious choice. Specialist Althorpe had been with the guard for five years this month, however, technically making him eligible and he'd been insistent on being presented as a candidate today. Serving as the queen's personal guard was his sole life ambition Althorpe claimed, which chipped at his normally sensible resolve.

Angus could only understand the sentiment all too well, so he'd given the man what he'd wanted thinking he would only be appeasing him. He didn't believe his queen would make such an impractical choice. While Althorpe was strong, skilled in all manner of weaponry, and unusually quick-witted, the man was a little too overconfident—too green—eager even, despite his qualifications, and her interest brought with it no small measure of concern. Granted, Caroline could take care of herself. She had proven that much.

Still, he needed to encourage his queen to find a new lover soon, so she wouldn't distract her fledgling guard out of boredom. Or better yet, they could finalize one of the *return blows* they'd been concocting against Veetula now that they'd stabilized the kingdom.

"Specialist Althorpe, you may stay. The rest of you report back to your stations," Angus commanded, wishing to get this over before his agitation seeped beneath Caroline's notice. Harris and Holzman shuffled toward the door, shoulders slumped—dejected.

Caroline whipped her body in his direction, and he mirrored her motion. "But I—"

Angus nodded at the table, and the queen stopped short as her eyes landed on Althorpe's dossier in her grip. Caroline sneered at him, and he raised his brows in a *that's what I thought* expression, the look exchanged between them blocked from the new guard's view. The last thing Angus needed was for the green specialist to think he could get away with such casual behavior toward the queen.

"If that is all, I'll leave you. I plan to leave tonight to personally fetch Felix and his bride. You sure you want them alive?" he asked, shooting her a conspiratorial grin over his shoulder as he turned to leave the room.

"Yes, alive," she responded, returning her eyes to the warrior-like man before her. "I have other plans for them." A cat-like smile widened Caroline's pink lips as she shifted her focus back to the documents she'd been reviewing.

Angus put a hand on Althorpe's shoulder as he walked from the room. "You know what is expected of you. I'll return as soon as I am able."

Over six and a half feet of Specialist Johnneth Althorpe towered over the opposite end of the mahogany table. Caroline swallowed, staring up at the imposing man Angus had left her alone with. Johnneth's dark hair was cut close to his head, how all guards were, which accentuated his high cheekbones and well-proportioned facial structure. Though he appeared about ten years older than her, his tan skin was stretched taut and only smile lines appeared on each side of his supple mouth and at the corners of his mischievous hazel eyes.

Where Felix's brawny muscles wrapped over his broad shoulders like a prized bull, Johnneth was more compact like a racehorse, lean and built for speed. Tight cut muscle peaked out of sleeves cuffed around his biceps and at the collar of his uniform. His sinewy thighs flexed, the cords outlined by the fitted fabric of his pants, as he shifted his weight, waiting for her command like a mountain cat poised to strike. Specialist Johnneth Althorpe appeared deadly, and that sent a little thrill tingling up her spine.

But he was beautiful, too. Breathtakingly so, and as she studied him, she wasn't certain she'd ever seen such beauty in the male form. Johnneth put Felix to shame—so much so that she questioned what she'd ever seen in the latter. She would still punish him, though. You couldn't wrong a queen and get away with it.

Caroline opened her mouth to speak, then darted her assessing eyes to his ringless hands before her cheeks flushed. Why did she have to do that? This guard belonged to her, regardless of whether he was attached or not. And here she was, acting as if she'd never seen a man before. *Honestly*, she scolded herself.

The corner of his mouth was kicked up ever so slightly, a hint of a smile playing on his lips like he read her every thought as plainly as if she'd spoken them aloud. *Cocky.* She'd seen that in his file. Caroline glanced back over at the papers in her hand wondering if she'd made the wrong decision.

"Character flaws," she read aloud. "Overconfident. Has been known to misjudge his own ability. I think I'll add prideful to the list." Caroline tapped a finger on her pout, then scratched a note on his record. She was done with overly self-assured men. She should take care of this now. "Shall I knock you down a level, Johnneth? I could compel you to crawl after me on your hands and knees until you learn your limitations. Would you like that?"

"No, Your Majesty." Muscles in Johnneth's neck flexed, but his face betrayed no emotion. He threaded his hands behind his back and continued to wait for her order.

"And you're also aware that my last three guards have vanished... POOF." Caroline made an explosion gesture with her hands. "Gone in a blink with no discernable clue left behind."

He nodded, the hint of a smirk twitching at the edge of his lips.

"I won't warn you again. Don't make me break you." Any trace of that fledgling grin slipped away, and Johnneth swallowed. Caroline savored it, knowing that she could make a man like that nervous. "Now, go take your position. I'll be another few hours here."

Johnneth averted his eyes downward as he took his position before his enemy. The rumors were true. That almost iridescent blue-black hair that hung in sheets over her slender shoulders, those full pink lips, knowingly quirked up at the corners. And her eyes were a mesmerizing shade of, not grey, but *silver*. Caroline the Cruel was staggeringly beautiful. It took all of his self-control not to openly gawk, to let his hungry eyes roam over her fine features and keep them glued to the pink stones surrounding them.

After all this time he'd failed to get close to her. She was at Roskide, he'd be stationed at Bowring. She was at the vineyard; he'd be training at Roskide. It was as if the Gods were intentionally keeping him away from her. In five years, as he'd worked his way up the ranks through their army, into the guard, and to the elite castle guard, he'd never even happened upon a chance encounter close enough to really take her in. And there she was, gripping a sheet of paper in her hand with his name on it.

Five years of his life. That's how long he had to serve to get his appointment and Johnneth finally figured out her commander's weakness. Used that weakness to his advantage. Angus truly lived to serve his queen. He had no partners, no family, hardly a possession in his sparse room. Angus was the queen's man. And Johnneth played to that. *If you'd just give me this opportunity*, he'd said, begging the commander, *it would mean the world to me*. It had almost made him cringe to speak the words, to prattle on adoringly about the queen and her kingdom, the enemy he'd come to Everstal to dispatch.

Years of practice told him his features were schooled into a blank stare as her hungry eyes tracked across his body, threatening to send unbidden shivers skipping across his skin. She *wanted* him. Of course, she did. He was more than aware of his looks, his robust form and how women responded to it. This young queen, down a lover, was no different. She felt desire when she looked at him. It was going better than he could have hoped.

"Of course, Your Majesty. I'll be here. Your wish is my command." Johnneth allowed his voice to deepen enough to encourage her wandering thoughts, but not enough to invoke her wrath.

As he stood near the door, he caught her glance up at him more than once from the corner of his vision. It had taken him years to get here, but now that he was in her presence, assassinating the unsatisfied woman before him was going to be easy.

CHAPTER 2

"A ND WHERE ARE WE off to this morning, Your Majesty?" Johnneth asked, as he placed a foot into a stirrup, swinging the other across the speckled blue-grey gelding that Angus gave him upon his appointment. The unused leather of the saddle creaked under his weight as he shifted forward, and he wished he had time to break it in before such a long ride. It was the first time since Angus had assigned him to her, they'd left the intimidating fortress of Roskide. Caroline had told him to be prepared to be gone for three nights, nothing more, which made him bristle.

"Oh, a favorite subject of mine is having an issue with his labor. We're going to go help him correct it." Caroline had already been there when he arrived at dawn and was now fussing with her own mount.

In the two weeks Angus had been gone, he was on double duty, but Angus instructed Specialist Holzman to share the burden and he took the overnight shift outside the queen's chambers so Johnneth could get a full night of sleep before their trip. Satisfied with his own adjustments, he dismounted and followed the queen back into the stable building to attempt to convince her to take a carriage, *again*.

"Your Majesty, it would be a lot easier to keep you safe if you would consider—"

Caroline held up a hand, silencing him as she, along with two servants, slipped behind a velvet covered screen. Moments later, the dress she'd been wearing appeared on top of the screen.

Fabric rustled, and the queen grunted. The two women dressing her were mumbling something to the effect of *hold still* under their breath.

"My people need to see me, Johnneth. I won't hide in Roskide, or in a carriage. I've done that and it isn't fun. Besides, I'll be protected," she said. A wispy, playful glint edged her voice.

"I won't be able to protect you—"

"I didn't mean you," she cut him off, huffing. "But it seems very *in character* to assume so."

Johnneth cursed the assessment Angus has written on his dossier—*cocky*. He let out his own huff and crossed his arms over his chest. If she only knew.

Metal clinked from behind the curtain, raising Johnneth's hackles. If someone attempted an assassination while he was mere feet from her, it would lose him his position, along with any opportunity he may have for his own attempt. And without rosenwood no less. She'd live, become more guarded than ever, and he'd be fired. Still—

Metal scraped louder now, and his hand shot forward on instinct, pulling a panel of the screen aside. Caroline held what looked to be metal fish scales against her chest over a hip length, sleeveless slip. Her feet were bare, and her bottom half was clad in matching cream leggings. She almost seemed less intimidating—*girlish*.

His mouth fell open, even as his head cocked to the side curiously. Her eyes flipped up toward him, a single eyebrow cocking. "May I help you?"

A servant pressed herself up from the little stool she was kneeling on, and wrenched the screen out of Johnneth's hand, closing it. "I forget, he's new," Caroline explained off-handedly to the women dressing her.

"Well, he should have better manners, Your Majesty," a servant replied.

"Indeed," Caroline said, though her playful voice didn't match her curt words. "Angus had this armor crafted for me. He says they tested it. Only a high velocity projectile could penetrate it, something more than an arrow."

"What about your head?" Johnneth grumbled, not pleased being admonished by a servant.

"You'll see."

He didn't need to see her grin to know a mischievous one lit her face. It was in her voice, which drew him in like the sweetest honey. She stepped out into the room and took a few steps across the stone floor, then held her arms out, allowing him to inspect the metal vest she was wearing. "Go on," she urged, and turned slowly so he could see.

Her amour was clever, he had to admit. And it was another mystery about the Queen of Everstal and how she operated unlocked. They crafted the suit from finely hammered metal scales linked in a pattern that fit her precise measurements, to be worn over her undergarments, but under her riding gear, which she hadn't put on yet. Johnneth couldn't stop his fingers from running across the smooth joints where the material seamlessly curved down her back.

"Satisfied?" She gave him a prim smile, then sauntered behind the screen to finish dressing.

"That still doesn't cover your head, and I would say the brain is the most vital organ of all."

Caroline laughed. "Some would say the heart."

The edges of his lips twitched up, even as he tried to cinch them down. When she came out, she performed the slow spin before him again. The armor added a little bulk to her, but the queen was so slim she appeared only a little more curvaceous beneath the silver bodysuit. It protected her vital organs, and for her head, there was a metal collar of linked plates that fanned around her neck and up the back of her skull. They didn't fit too closely and looked like gills opening for a fresh intake of water.

The women rolled her black hair in two twists on either side of her head, beginning at her temple and connecting in the back to resemble a sort of half-crown. Johnneth was holding his breath. He let his lungs burn before he finally exhaled. It was the second time she'd caused him to lose his composure. She was a twenty-four-year-old woman. He was over ten years her senior and *should not* be affected by her. His enemy, standing before him, and waiting for him to speak. Fully understanding the effect she had on others.

"You look..." Her eyebrows raised subtly, but he let his eyes drift past her shoulder and take on an impassive expression. "Safe."

"You look like perfection," the mouthy servant corrected as she attached a gauzy full skirt around her hips, leaving the front section open so the legs of the jumpsuit were visible.

Caroline didn't hide her smirk of displeasure and she paced out of the building and into the yard. A groomsman handed off the reins of the sleek black stallion to her. She'd stepped into the stirrup, swished up into her saddle, and was fanning out her skirt across the horse's rear before Johnneth could offer her a hand.

He took his own mount and sidled up next to her. Caroline waved a hand to the ten awaiting soldiers on horseback littering the yard, and the neatly ordered pairs of men and women sprang into motion, loosely encircling him and the queen. Her command was easy and absolute and he'd yet to see her exercise the Gift. Every moment that passed where she didn't use it made the anticipation so much worse and now his imaginings had taken on a life of their own.

But it was hard to reconcile that with the woman who rode next to him pointing out different estates which dotted the rolling countryside in the distance. It's hard to envision her transforming from this calm, intelligent, yet commanding presence into the monster he'd heard so much about. She was nothing like he expected.

The route down the mountain was long and twisting. When they rounded yet another bend, she said, "Tonight, we'll be staying with an old acquaintance of mine. Then it will be another day's ride to our destination." She pointed to an estate off in the distance. "That's his land there."

It wasn't long as the raven flies, but traversing through the winding roads more than doubled the ride time. Everstal had a different, softer kind of beauty than Veetula. The weather was temperate, and vegetation covered every bit of undulating land that wasn't built upon. Breathtaking views of distant mountains and the marine sea would surprise him every so often.

The land didn't mirror its steward, however. Caroline's beauty was harsh, cold even, like Veetula where the mountains had the jaggedness of newly formed earth. Dense coniferous forests teamed with wild game, and in the northern lands, fields of blue ice stretched out beyond the line of sight. It begged the question of her lineage. Who had been Caroline's mother, the woman, who King Thom Dallimore had become enamored with on a campaign on the eastern edge of the borderlands? The campaign which had claimed the final swath of land from the Manula, finally pushing them over the Maidenwall mountain range which separated Veetula and Everstal from the far away kingdoms. Now it was only them in the west with their endless border skirmishes.

Johnneth could sense Caroline's eyes on him. "You're deep in thought," she said.

"Only enjoying the view, Your Majesty." He hoped she'd leave it at that and not ask him any further questions. Because questions might lead—

"The view must be that much better from up there on his high horse," a soldier in front of them called over his shoulder, eliciting a chuckle from the others, including the queen.

"Yeah, Super Specialist Althorpe. What else can you see from way up there above the rest of us?" one of the others goaded.

"That's enough," he scolded, picking up the pace. Their teasing had been tolerable when they'd all been of equal rank, but now the ribbing was inappropriate. He'd always taken everything he'd done a little more seriously than most. Some people understood. His family understood. But common soldiers—his intense nature was a running joke with them. He was more like Angus, or even Caroline, in that. It was in his blood.

"I threatened to make him crawl on all fours, if that makes you all feel any better," Caroline chimed in, speaking loudly enough so everyone in their party could hear. "But I figured that would make our trip take significantly longer, and I know how whiney you all get if you don't get a hot dinner."

Caroline nudged her mount and rode up to the man who'd made the joke and the two fell into a familiar banter.

"Captain Vance, how's your wife and the new baby?" Caroline asked.

"They're well, Your Majesty. Little Gwen is sleeping through the night like a champ. Belle and I couldn't be prouder," Vance said, beaming from ear to ear.

"When you're ready to make a visit, I'd love to meet her."

"Truly?" Vance went stiff, but it wasn't with fright, Johnneth didn't think.

Caroline nodded eagerly. "Of course. I've seen your lovely wife. I'm sure Gwen is every bit as beautiful."

Vance nodded, and when his head quit bobbing Johnneth thought his chin rested a little higher. As their conversation trailed out of range of his hearing, he considered the woman he was meant to protect.

Since he'd been appointed, he'd seen her with many people. She gave the illusion of familiarity yet gave nothing of herself. Except with Angus. He was the only one that seemed to get behind the wall of ice he sensed she'd erected sometime in her past. But these people, she knew by name. She asked them about their families, remembered details of their lives. Allowed a certain level of camaraderie to exist within her regular escort, which inspired their loyalty and affection. But none of them saw the difference he saw.

Each time they stopped to rest, eat, and relieve themselves, the members of the escort relaxed, but not the queen. Impenetrable Caroline was just as rigid and aware as ever, spine straight and chin raised. The symbolic expression of Everstal's strength she intended to project. The assured smile across her cherry painted lips was a bonus, flaunting the invincibleness she seemed to feel. But she wasn't one of them no matter how well she faked it.

Caroline stood with a woman outside of a bakery where they'd stopped to get a snack and rest. Her brow was furrowed in concentration, and she was nodding intently as the woman spoke. She gestured for Vance to give the woman something. He reached in his pocket, and fished out a pouch of coins, handing them over to the woman. The queen ran a hand along the woman's shoulder, the gesture softer than he would have expected.

A queen who made herself available to her people was appealing and the woman didn't seem to fear her. Yet he couldn't help but notice for every adoring smile greeting her through an open door, another wary gaze peered through a window.

Caroline sauntered over to him clutching a white sack in her hands. She tossed it to him and he swiped it out of the air. "Got you something," she said.

Johnneth eyed the package, and pulled a braided pastry covered in a fine powdery chocolate sugar, wrinkling his nose at it. "What was that about?" he said, lifting his chin in the direction of the bakery. A few coins would have more than covered the dozen pastries they had.

The queen groaned, eyeing his unopened package. "Don't tell me you don't eat sweets? I'm sure one treat won't ruin that pretty physique." She winked and batted her eyelashes in mock sweetness as she walked over to him. She eyed his twist, tore off a piece, and stuffed it into her mouth.

"I eat sweets. Just not often. Didn't you just have one?" he asked, smirking down at her.

"So what if I did?" she said, when she finished chewing, then sucked the powder from her fingers. "And that was about getting more of that woman's delicious pastries delivered to Roskide. I think daily, don't you?"

Johnneth frowned at what he hoped was her teasing, but was transfixed by the motion of her fingers. He pulled off a piece of his twist and bit into it imagining what it would be like to have those pouty lips sucking the sugar off—*no, bad guard*. Caroline's eyes slid to him as she approached her mount, running her hand along the smooth black fur of the horse's neck. Had he missed some critical piece of intelligence, and she read minds too? No, she read people, and she was always observing, which was a whole other danger. His stomach jumped at the thought.

"We need to get moving. I feel exposed here." Johnneth nodded to her reins. He stuffed the rest of the pastry in his saddlebag and dusted his fingers off on his pants. He didn't offer the queen a hand as she mounted because the queen didn't need his help, which he was quickly learning applied to most things. In moments, their party was trotting away from the village with the sun beginning its descent.

CHAPTER 3

J OHNNETH COULDN'T HELP COMPARING himself against the Lord
Reginald Hastings of Galloway Manor. Regent of the surrounding
province and advisor to the queen. *Reg*, as Caroline referred to him.
About the same age, blond shoulder length hair, tied at the nape of his
neck. Green needling eyes, muscular, but not as muscular as him. Tall,
but not as tall as him. Rich, well, he surveyed the estate, the sprawling
collection of brick and timber buildings. The stables, the orchard, the
aviary, the guest house, the fountains, the peacock and peahen engaged
in a mating dance in front of them. Not as rich as him.

He grimaced. Gods, he was worse than the peacock. Why did he
all the sudden want to jump in front of the queen and say, look at
me, I'm better. I'm more than him and fan his feathers for her to see.
One moment he was trying to understand her, then she put her fingers
between those lips and his primal urges were singing, *Impress her*. Not
ideal, but he could ignore it. He *would* ignore it.

So instead of making a fool of himself, he trailed behind Caroline,
as the Lord led her, into the main building—by the arm, a possessive
gesture which made his teeth grind. He was only being protective for her
safety, he reminded himself. He didn't like Hastings the minute he saw
the man. He didn't trust him.

Dozens of candles lit the receiving hall, illuminating *leather paneled
walls*. And weapons, swords of all varieties and dead animals adorned the
burgundy panels, along with several portraits of Hastings or his relatives
standing over fresh kills like battle heroes. Bile rose in his throat. Men of

caliber didn't need such gaudy adornment. Johnneth didn't even try to hide the sneer which took root on his face.

"Caroline, you remember Ann, yes?" Hastings gestured to a servant and Caroline nodded. "She'll help you out of your traveling attire and get you ready for dinner. See you in an hour," he said, lifting Caroline's hand to his lips and giving her an overly suggestive stare.

Hastings turned to him. "I'll make sure you have a room near her."

Unable to stop himself, Johnneth stepped forward. "No need. I'll be keeping guard in her room tonight... to make sure she's safe." He shot the other man a *from predators like you* look.

The room the queen was appointed was spacious with overflowing opulent furniture and décor. Johnneth walked in and leaned against the wall inside the door, having to force himself not to take his head in his hands and shake it. Good Gods, what was he thinking?

Caroline followed Ann into the bathing chamber, and she turned before the door shut. "I'm safe here. Relax, okay?"

"Yes, Your Majesty," he said dutifully. Was he that transparent? He didn't feel relaxed. He felt on high alert. You've known her two weeks. You will be the one causing her harm before long, so get it together.

Johnneth stood against the wall behind the queen's right shoulder, so he had a good view of her and this Lord she dined with. The man had tried to wave him off, suggesting he go grab a bite in the kitchen. *Her Majesty is perfectly safe with me*, he'd said. Johnneth's jaw was beginning to ache.

"It's a shame about Felix," Hastings said. "Not a wise man, I take it? He didn't understand the gift he had." He raised a wine glass, held it to the candlelight, swirled it, then made an elaborate show of sipping and savoring. Johnneth's frown deepened. Did Hastings think the queen would find that appealing? He glanced around the excessively decorated room. That she would like any of this?

"What he lacked in brains, he made up for in other areas," Caroline said. "And don't worry, Reg. He'll pay." The expression that crossed her face oozed a tantalizing combination of sex and vengeance. Was she flirting with this Lord Hastings? No, she was toying with him. Still, he'd take the mountains of paperwork days over this.

Caroline took her last bite and placed her fork down on her plate, followed by the napkin in her lap. Johnneth stepped forward to pull out her chair, even offering her a hand which she took, sparing him the embarrassment of rejection.

"Is there anything else I can offer you, Your Majesty? How about a nightcap and some interesting conversation, somewhere we can speak," Hastings said, glancing at Johnneth, "*in private?*"

Caroline stood, yawning. "As much fun as that sounds, Lord Hastings, we need to be off early in the morning. Sleep is what I really need right now."

As she passed, she ran her nails teasingly across Hastings' scalp, and the man shut his eyes on an inhale. His napkin was clenched in his hand, like he was fighting the urge to jump up and follow the queen. Johnneth was beginning to understand the feeling.

He lingered in the hallway after Caroline went upstairs, agreeing with Hastings that the queen technically was safe in the manor. The Lord stepped through the door into the dimly lit space and Johnneth stepped in front of him. "You need to back off," Johnneth said, a little too firmly as he poked a finger at the other man's chest.

"She's quite mesmerizing, isn't she? A true prize." Hastings sighed, nonplussed that he was being threatened by the queen's personal guard. He scanned the stuffed beasts that lined the walls of the hallway, his trophies. What he wanted to make Caroline. "I've known the queen a lot longer than you, specialist. I was her first, and I'll be her last. She just needed to get a few years of fun out of her system. She's still so very young. And soon enough, I expect you'll disappear like her other missing guards, and I'll be here when she's ready to settle down."

Bloody, messy, deadly red flashed across his vision. Was he shaking? He was indeed shaking. Get it together. He took a long breath to slow his pulse. To calm the Gods' blessed blood roaring in his veins that occasionally turned him more animal than man.

"I may not know her that well, but even I can see she is far too good for you. So do as I say and back off." Johnneth turned, not waiting for a response before he stormed away. What was he going to say? *If anyone hurts her, it's going to be me.* Because that is what he was here for.

He stepped inside the queen's room without knocking and shut the door a little too firmly. "What do you see in him?" The question was inappropriate, but he didn't care.

Caroline, now clad in a silky hunter green nightgown and a matching thin robe, flicked her gaze to him. "At the moment, the owner of a convenient place to stay."

"You let him speak to you that way?"

Caroline snorted. "Hastings is harmless." Her eyes scanned over him then widened. "Oh, you threatened our host?"

Johnneth didn't answer. He couldn't answer, so he averted his gaze.

"I know you feel protective, and I appreciate that, but you can't go around threatening every man who comes onto me. Trust me, I can handle them."

"But you flirted with him, and that will only encourage the behavior. Do you know he thinks he's going to marry you?" He gave her a pleading look.

"This seems a little outside of your scope of work." Caroline raised an eyebrow at him and slipped out of the robe. She laughed as she climbed into the plush bed, and he frowned. Sitting up, she regarded him. Counting off fingers on her hand she got to eight, then she held them up for him. "That's how many times he's proposed, and I've rejected him. Hastings would never hurt me. We're old friends now."

"He mentioned that," Johnneth grumbled, understanding her implication. Unsure of why that information gave him such a queasy stomach.

"What's this about, Johnneth?"

It was a good question. What was this about? He ran his hand across his buzzed hair. "I don't know. I don't like it. I don't like him and the way he looks at you, the way he speaks to you, like he thinks he could own you like one of those disgusting trophies." He shook his head, but straightened, squaring his shoulders. "You're right. It's not my job and I'll mind my business. I know you can take care of yourself."

Caroline didn't reply. She nestled down between the blankets, letting her assessing eyes rest on him for a long moment before they slipped closed.

CHAPTER 4

J OHNNETH SURVEYED THE MEMBERS of the escort gathered in the manor's courtyard early the next morning, including the armor-clad queen. And of course, Hastings was there, lingering at Caroline's side. "I'd be honored if you stayed on your return, Your Majesty. Perhaps we could spend more time together. I could offer you a glimpse of the enjoyment a real man can provide."

"Yes, perhaps," she said, patting him on the chest, but her eyes strayed elsewhere, distracted. She accounted for the ten guards, then settled on him and he could have sworn her shoulders lowered a smidge. "Oh, good. Let's go," she said. "I'm eager to get to the vineyard."

Hastings leaned in to embrace her, but Johnneth stepped between them holding out his hand to the other man. "Appreciate the hospitality," he said, forcing the words out. Hastings gave him a brief shake and a sneer and stepped around him to follow the queen who was poised to mount her stallion.

The man was blatantly ignoring Johnneth's warning. Hastings' hands went forward to assist the queen and Johnneth didn't even try to stop himself from clamping a hand down on the Lord's shoulder tugging him backward. "Her Majesty doesn't need your help."

"You should take your own advice," Hastings said, jerking his shoulder out of Johnneth's grip.

"I would think eight failed proposals would be a clear enough message, but you don't strike me as perceptive so let me help you out, buddy. She doesn't want you. Get it now?" he said, keeping his voice low.

Hastings blanched, then shot a short, pained glance at the queen like he was shocked she'd shared as much with him. Good. He deserved the embarrassment for his presumptuousness. Hastings didn't step forward again, instead bowing low. "Send word if I can be of service, Your Majesty. I'll be ready and waiting." He stuffed his hands into his pockets, turned and strode back into the manor.

"What did you say to him, Specialist Althorpe?" the queen asked, narrowing her gaze in Johnneth's direction.

"Nothing he didn't need to hear. So, about these laborers?" he asked, changing the subject as they trotted away, Galloway Manor fading behind them in the distance. He tried to keep his voice neutral, curious even.

"You'll see, soon enough," she said. He hadn't answered her, so she wasn't going to answer him. Fair enough, so they rode on as the sun rose, hung overhead, then began its descent once again.

What they were about to do had been niggling at him for the better part of the day. The workers were on strike. Caroline had tried to set a fair wage range for the different manual trades, but he suspected many landowners skirted the requirement. How else would it explain the protestors they passed lined up in the streets of the bustling village nearest the estate and the sprawling lands surrounding it?

He'd been shocked when she freed them several years back around the time she'd taken Felix as a lover. The act was some sort of ploy to make herself appear more palatable to a restless people. None of it would have been necessary if they treated the servants like family how they did in Veetula.

Caroline surveyed the gathering crowd. "The harvest is coming. Will you work?" she called out to them.

A resounding *NO* along with a lot of other grumbling bounced across the buildings and through the alleys back to the determined queen.

She swept her hand out toward them, many flinching and lowering themselves in response. "There you have it, the answer to your question. Simple enough."

That didn't ease Johnneth's worry.

Caroline picked up the pace, galloping away from the town towards the arching iron gates of the estate. Her saddle weary guard kept pace until they were safely inside the stone walls and a squat, elderly man was loping out to meet her, followed by a menagerie of servants.

The queen was a blur of legs and skirts as she dismounted, handing off the mount. Fabric billowed behind her as she strode toward the man. "Dominique, my friend," she called. "How are my grapes?"

～⤙

"It's divine, as always." Caroline had her eyes closed as she took another sip of the swirling red liquid in her glass. She didn't partake often, but when she did, she'd have nothing less. The winery was, to her mind, one of the highlights of her kingdom. The centuries-old stone home was surrounded by undulating fields of vineyard. This time of year, the sun set at its latest point in the day and the view from atop the hill Dominique's ancestors built the estate upon was dreamlike. Red, orange, and magenta danced in a lightshow across the rolling green hills and glassy blue ponds as the sun stole its color behind the horizon.

They served dinner in a long open-air hall at a banquet table which comfortably seated all twelve of her party, Dominique, and several of his protégé. The members of the queen's party sat around enjoying the bounty served to them, including selections from the vineyard. When Caroline came here to visit, Johnneth learned that the soldiers who made up her normal escorts would draw straws for who was lucky enough to accompany her. And the regular patrol she'd assigned to the estate meant they were allowed to partake as well.

Each course Dominique's team of chefs served had been planted, selected, harvested, or hunted at the precise time of ripeness or age. The man was one of the few masters left in the world and she'd send a selection of trainees to him annually. The man had no children of his own and Caroline would ensure his life's work would not die with him.

"We passed protestors. They were angry," Caroline said between bites. Dominique let out an exaggerated sigh. "You know how it is. Every few years, the same ideas circulate. Now we pay them, and they still want more. Sometimes I think I ought to fire them all and train a whole new crew in the off-season who'd be grateful for their wage."

"You know what I think. You are far too lenient. You always have been."

Dominique tipped his head to the side, grumbling. "Some of these workers have been on this vineyard since my parents' time. Or their children have. This is as much their home as it is mine. They need to see your parents avenged, Caroline. You need to give them a cause to direct their energy at. You make substantial changes which have a far-reaching impact, but the people talk of vengeance. They think you mean to distract them."

"Never mind all that. They'll have their vengeance soon enough. How about you stick to making wine and I'll deal with my people?" When Dominique only frowned at her rebuke, she continued. "How long do we have?" Caroline swirled her glass, studying the garnet liquid.

"I'm sampling the vineyard every hour. I predict we'll harvest on the full moon, three days' time. Possibly two."

"And if they don't acquiesce?" she asked.

Dominique averted his gaze. Caroline knew what his lack of eye contact meant. He wouldn't allow her to force them. He would need almost fifty individuals to work the fields, then attend to the weeks-long refining and barreling process afterward.

"Fine. We'll get a sense tomorrow. See who's willing. You have us twelve here. I can have more come from Roskide."

"Caroline," Dominique said, voice cautioning. "You know this is a delicate process."

It was clear what the old man was saying, and she didn't want to hear it. "You can't have it both ways. Besides, if the queen takes part in harvesting your grapes, you can charge twice the price per bottle. You can even sell to Veetula, and they can drink it as they curse my name." She raised the glass in his direction as an attendant came in with a basket of this hour's sampling, offering the first taste to the queen, naturally.

Dutiful Johnneth, who'd been reluctant to join them at the table, chuckled. "They'd be more likely to pour it out."

"Sacrilege!" Dominique mashed the grape between his teeth, allowing the juices to play across his tongue. "Two days, Your Majesty. Two days."

Johnneth followed the queen up to her room, inspecting it first for anything amiss. She padded in behind him, removed the gauze skirt and was tugging at the laces at the back of her neck. They'd been ravenous, so she'd kept the scales on, claiming they weren't so cumbersome and would take too long to remove and re-dress. He suspected it was out of respect for the old man, who had the feast waiting. None of the other soldiers pressed her so he assumed it was a battle they'd lost many times before and he followed their lead.

"Just a minute. Let me get a servant," he said, watching her struggle.

"Attendant," Caroline corrected, with a slight slur.

"Yes, a servant—"

"Attendant," she said more forcefully.

"Same thing," he said, the agitation of five years of subservience peeking through his polished veneer. No doubt an effect of the single glass he'd allowed himself.

Caroline reached up on the tips of her toes and pressed a finger to his lips. It took all his control not to pucker them and place a kiss to her cool fingertip. That was concerning.

"You are wrong," she said. "Attendants are paid. Servants are owned. You should know that, Specialist Althorp, since you're such an enthusiastic fan of mine."

A girlish grin played at the edge of her lips, and he cursed Angus and the notes on his dossier. Caroline's self-assured manner, the way she spoke with such certainty, caused an uneasy sensation to pop into Johnneth's awareness. An idea, like the first bud of spring. Veetula was wrong, Everstal was right. And it wasn't the history between the two warring kingdoms, it was the way things were done, the laws and traditions she looked down upon. She could do it better. That was her fundamental stance.

Johnneth said a quick prayer of thanks to the Gods that Caroline was too tipsy to notice his slip up. "Of course, you're right," he said for good measure, even as he doused the bud with a frigid gust and cursed himself for not bringing the rosenwood dagger. What a perfect opportunity wasted.

A soft rapt sounded at the door and an *attendant* slipped her head inside. "Oh, perfect," he said, relieved that he wouldn't be stuck alone, undressing the queen. Johnneth gestured for the woman to come unravel Caroline and he went to take his position against the wall by the door, deciding not to worry about what his relief suggested.

The attendant swiftly pulled the laces through the first of the eyelets and the seam at the back eased open. Caroline's shoulders lowered ever so slightly. The protruding veins in her neck retreated below the surface of her smooth skin. Her breathing evened out as she released the tension she must feel all day packaged up as the Queen of Everstal.

Johnneth could almost feel empathy for her. He knew all too well what it was like keeping up a carefully constructed façade—it was something they had in common. But his mind quickly raced to the workers and how willing she had been to use that awful power her family line had inherited to force their hands. She was just another Dallimore.

"This explains why you took so long in the bathroom today," he teased despite himself as the attendant pulled the final lace free. *Don't. Keep it professional.* But it was so easy to get sucked in when he was around her, like her very presence charged the air drawing him in.

Both the attendant and Caroline shot him a smirk.

"Thank you, Silvie," Caroline said, and leaned forward so the woman could peel the material over her shoulders and down her hips as if he weren't standing there. "Some heated water would be nice. To wipe the dust from the road away."

"Of course, Your Majesty." *Silvie*, another attendant whose name she memorized, curtsied and scuttled to the adjoining chamber.

The fishlike scale rippled with her movement as she sunk into a high-backed chair and held a booted foot out to him without saying a word. A grin sparked from her lips to his as he obediently palmed its heel and tugged, slipping it off her foot. Then the other. He glanced after the attendant.

"You're nervous." Caroline's discerning gaze roved across his body, and he could feel her savoring his form like the wine she'd drank earlier. Her eyes hadn't lingered on Hastings that way.

His male pride surged, even as the corners of his mouth turned down. "Hardly," he said, scoffing. He wasn't the type of man who got nervous around women. Even ones as disarming as Caroline.

"Oh, that's right," she crooned. "*Overconfident*. Did Silvie ruin your plan to seduce me, then? Tempt, then ravish me Specialist Johnneth Althorpe?" she said, her tone smoothing out, licking across his awareness. Taunting. "I see the way you look at me. Think I couldn't have resisted you?"

Laughter burst from her lips. She didn't think it would have been possible and part of him, the male part that also had other ideas about what it wanted, was dying to prove her wrong. A voice in his head cautioned, *Dangerous territory*.

"No, Your Majesty." His own voice lowered into a grumble as she worked the little latch that held the armor in place along her sides. When she'd unsecured the last latch, she pulled the front piece off and stood, laying it atop the other that had slipped off into the chair behind her. A damp undershirt clung to her skin and the silver suit still hung half on her hips as she sauntered to the bathing chamber. Johnneth kept his eyes raised, but when she turned, he couldn't help but track each swish of her hips as she moved, arms raised, freeing hairpins, one by one, until all that beautiful hair fell in waves around her fine-boned shoulders.

"Good. Because, as you'll find out soon enough, I'm not one to be trifled with." She paused at the threshold and eyed him over her shoulder, silver iris's glinting in the candlelight.

Her gaze, which held all the authority of her position, struck him with a sudden clarity and he almost stumbled back. Caroline Dallimore was the type of fiercely self-assured woman he'd envisioned for a wife. Not her, obviously, but someone like her, who could heat his blood with a glance, get under his skin, and keep him guessing.

The problem was in his thirty-five years, he'd never met a woman quite like Everstal's queen. She might be twenty-four, but there was a timeless intelligence with a sensual undercurrent swirling in her eyes and he liked it. A lot. He needed to end her, complete his mission, and get out of here before he decided to do something stupid like claim her. The challenge in her eyes made him certain there was no other man up for the task.

"That will be all," she said, dismissing him.

Johnneth clenched his teeth, spun on his heel, and retreated to his own assigned room next to hers. He nodded to the guards outside the doors as he slipped inside, a whirlwind of conflicting sensations nipping at his heels.

Boards creaked as heavy footsteps traced out onto the balcony ruining the silence Caroline was relishing. "You're awake?" her guard asked, voice as abrupt as the bright morning sun.

"Couldn't sleep." Caroline waved a hand at the spread crowding the little table where she sat. "Feel free," she said, watching him survey the food, but opt to take a position leaning against the railing.

"Don't be insufferable. You're blocking the view."

Johnneth's chest flexed, and he ran a hand down his flat stomach, like he disagreed with her statement. Since he was more than willing to show it off, she let her eyes follow him as he paced around behind her, near enough at her shoulder she could hear his breathing. "They're already gathering," he said. At least twenty people stood outside the estate's gates and a lone rider was trotting out to open them.

"Seems my people are eager to have their opinions heard this morning." The sun was fully above the horizon when the final workers made their way up the drive and had lined up outside the entrance of the estate. Dominique walked out on the balcony to join them, along with several of the apprentices from the prior evening's dinner.

"Ready to get this over with?" Dominique asked.

Caroline shrugged. "It's bad timing. Normally I'd be more generous, but Angus got back a day ago and what he brought with him has soured my mood."

"He found Felix, then?" Dominique asked, his grey unruly eyebrows reaching toward the sky.

Angus didn't agree with what she'd done, elevating the man, though he didn't say more. She supposed he was right—it was a mistake of a young, inexperienced queen. That's why she'd enjoy the view this time, but not partake. She gave him a nod in confirmation, not wanting to say more, possibly to extend her denial a little longer.

"Let's go disappoint some farm workers," she said, pressing herself to her feet.

Caroline led the way around the wooden deck, which wrapped fully around the second story of the structure, in covered and uncovered sections. She stopped at a wide staircase and descended to midway. The crowd gathered around the base of it immediately began grumbling their dissatisfaction.

Caroline didn't wince as her nails dug into her palms. Dominique underestimated their entitlement. They egged each other on, their confidence bolstering each other's. Ever curious, Caroline was content to allow their flagrant disrespect to escalate to see how deeply ingrained it was. She could always learn something from each experience with her people.

Johnneth and Dominique, in contrast, were shifting agitatedly by her side. Johnneth's hand shot to the sword at his hip, but she reached out, halting him, keeping her eyes on the people below. "Unnecessary," she muttered so only he could hear. "You think he's going to throw that?"

The apple sailed across the crowd, aimed directly at her. She narrowly ducked. "Gods, Dominique. Are you still thinking we go with your plan?"

A few of them launched other projectiles before he could answer. Two firm hands gripped her shoulders and pulled her behind a wall of chest. Her hands immediately went to the barricade of man and muscle, putting himself between her and the angry mob. Sweet, but again, unnecessary. Fruit and rocks smacked into Johnneth's back. "Let's get inside." He was urging her up the stairs to protect her.

"Unhand me," she demanded, jerking her shoulders. She stared up into his hazel eyes as a larger rock caught the back of his head and he stumbled into her, taking them both down. Johnneth sprawled across her on the staircase, which gave her a perfect view of the workers over his shoulder, among the other sensations his heavy body pressing down against hers was causing. A thought and the crowd was motionless.

She narrowed her eyes at Dominique, who was crouched behind a column.

Sorry, he mouthed, shrugging innocently.

Caroline frowned at the vintner, then shifted her attention back to the sack of bone and muscle lying across her. Love save her, he smelled delicious. Sweat mingled with something else... woodsy. "Did they stun you?" she asked. "My elite guard?"

Johnneth grimaced as he pushed himself off her and got to his knees, throwing a glance over his shoulder at the still frozen crowd. "You could have done that earlier."

"I wanted to see how bad they'd be if I didn't stop them."

She leaned up and ran her fingers across the buzzed hair of the back of Johnneth's scalp. Her fingers came away smeared with warm blood, which she showed him. His eyes peeled back in alarm, and he scrambled off her. How odd. Did he think she'd take the opportunity to use his blood to gain power over him? Very deliberately, she wiped the red on the silver pant leg until all the smudged color was off her fingers, then held out her hand to him for his inspection.

It took the man an effort to extend his own hand to hers and help her up. Strange indeed. Perhaps fear mingled with his admiration of her. That wouldn't do with a guard at this level. She made a mental note to learn more about him.

Or perhaps she would switch him with Specialist Holzman, which would please Angus, and take Johnneth as a lover. He was certainly acting possessive enough, maybe even a little jealous. And he'd been giving her those lingering glances that made heat stir in her lower belly. The way he'd stepped in between her and Hastings, it was a little roguish, but if she were being honest, it made her feel things. Johnneth was trying to be a good guard, but he'd be willing. And even if he did fear her a little, maybe it was part of the allure. Some men liked women who could challenge them.

But he hadn't disappeared yet after a full month, which was a good sign. She supposed that was reason enough to keep him on for a while longer. Feeling better about that, Caroline stood and squared her shoulders. "Bow," she said. The crowd collectively dropped to their knees.

"Let's start with this. If you threw a single thing in the direction of the staircase, stand." Exactly ten people rose to their feet. Caroline pointed to a nearby wall. "Go, stand there until I tell you not to." The seven men and three women obeyed.

She turned to the remaining workers. "Rise." They shuffled to their feet.

"I understand you are trying to extort my dear friend Dominique simply because I prefer his product. You are paid ten silver a week, are you not? Twice what any other farm labor makes in this region."

"Everybody knows what he gets per bottle from the royal coffer. We want our share."

Caroline motioned for Dominique to approach her side. "Very well," she called. "Dominique, pay the workers the weekly rate they are requesting." Gasps reverberated through the crowd. At the queen's command, apprentices fetched a basket of coin from a nearby room and began passing out the sum. When they'd finished, she asked the workers, "Satisfied?"

Some voices in the crowd made sounds that rang like, *Yes.* Still other voices were laced with distrust. Those were the ones who understood her. "Dominique," she said, still projecting her voice. The knowing among the crowd braced. "I'll have four units sent immediately to aid you in the harvest. Then, over the winter, you may rebuild your workforce."

Dominique bowed. "Thank you, Your Majesty."

Caroline turned, ever-so-slowly, back to the crowd. "I'll oversee it from here. You're dismissed."

The crowd erupted into a mess of confusion for a few moments before the queen marched down the rest of the staircase, her skirt billowing behind her, and toward the protestors stuck at the wall. Johnneth didn't follow her immediately, still a little stunned from the moment he thought she was going to take his blood. Something in the grumbling crowd had caught his attention. A woman was pushing her way through toward where Dominique was speaking with the apprentices.

His hand flew to his waist, where a throwing knife was hidden. He had it in hand when the glint of metal drew his eye. The woman was turning a gold coin between her fingers, staring at it intently. Then she said something to the vintner he couldn't hear, but he got the impression it was about keeping her job. They appeared to converse for a moment, then she gave the coin back and walked around the crowd, heading back to the gate. Surely Dominique wasn't foolish enough to re-hire someone who'd stood by as their fellow workers assaulted the queen. He had a soft spot for them, though, as he'd already shown.

As another approached, Johnneth sheathed the knife and turned to catch up to Caroline. She was standing near a guard she'd installed at the vineyard years ago. "Days?" the man asked. Caroline eyed the workers against the wall like a hawk homing in on its prey.

"Days, weeks. I don't care. Let them soil themselves. Bread and water only. When they can no longer stand, they may be released. I think Justice would appreciate this one." The self-satisfied gleam in the queen's eye sent an uneasy tickle through Johnneth's awareness. "No cheating," she said, tapping her temple, then sauntered back into the estate, glancing back once to see if her ever-present shadow trailed her. When her eyes met his, a mischievous grin brightened her beautiful face.

She was *her* in that single expression. Not the façade she wore. Not the woman he'd just witnessed use her Gift for the first time, compelling several dozen people to their knees, which hadn't been *that* terrible, he admitted. It was the woman under the figurehead *Queen Caroline Dallimore,* and she was pleased to see him. Only a few weeks and it was working. The only problem was the elated surge it gave him knowing it. And it wasn't because of the mission.

His mind flashed to how perfectly her supple body had felt for the few seconds she'd been beneath him. To the unforgivable thoughts he'd had about her after that glass of wine the night before. Johnneth slammed the door on the memories. *Shit.*

CHAPTER 5

R AVENS SCATTERED AS CAROLINE stormed across the square. The onyx scavenger's shed black silken feathers danced in the wake of her trailing skirts before settling once again on the rust-colored cobblestones. The birds seemed to know when to flee.

Angus stood outside the door she was headed toward, which opened to an elevated courtyard on one of the lower levels of Roskide. He wrung his hands as she approached. "They're in there." He jerked his head to the door. "What are you going to do?"

Caroline narrowed her eyes and tossed her chin to the sky making her hair dance like the feathers. "Don't worry. I have something planned. Something perfectly and uniquely suited to our friends in there. If I've learned anything from the Gods, it's that pain comes in all shapes and sizes."

Gritting her teeth, Caroline tamped her rage down and opened the door.

Felix, the man standing rigid before Caroline and drawing her full ire, had come from nothing. Everything he now had was because of her generosity. His trading business, his position among the merchants, even the self-possessed confidence he wore so flippantly, as if he had been born to his gifted position.

He had hoped for something more from their arrangement, but that was his own damn fault. She never made him any promises.

To be the lover of a queen should have been enough. It had taken them months to find him. He had stolen his new bride away to a sleepy town in the foothills of the old mountain range at the edge of her kingdom.

If Felix were a smart man, he would have whisked the girl far away into Veetula, the cold kingdom to the North—enemy territory. King Hollis would have taken the man in. Felix probably would even have been celebrated for scorning the queen. But there was nowhere in her kingdom she couldn't find him.

And Felix wasn't a smart man. That's not why she'd been interested. Caroline thought of the first time she'd seen him, sweat trickling down his muscled back as he toiled away on the Karper's farm. He was leaned over a plow and had removed his shirt to soak up the sweat from his brow.

Maybe it was the way the sun glinted off his golden skin, the way he brushed his ash hair out of his eyes. Or maybe it was the way he adjusted himself after he boldly drank in the shape of her, not realizing the identity of the beauty who'd exited her halted carriage to stand before him. She had to have him. Caroline was practically salivating, watching his body flex and heave. She approached the farmer and bought his indenture at once. Made him a free man.

She introduced him to trading in the luxury items coveted in Everstal and soon after, she took him to her bed. She taught him how to touch a woman. Please her. He had been serving her nicely until one night he failed to arrive at her room. At first Caroline had thought a deal had gone foul, but after a week's worth of lonely nights, the rumors drifted her way. Angus had been afraid to tell her. Rightly so. She'd even threatened to compel him—she had never done it before. Not to him, her commander.

She had been betrayed. Again. And how had Hastings known? Did that mean everyone knew? How embarrassing.

Felix ran off with some woman—the daughter of another merchant because she could give him something the queen could not. *A wife.*

"Hello, Felix," she purred.

Felix raked a thick hand through his hair. Hair she'd pulled on as she'd directed him toward her pleasure. She shivered at the thought. To think he'd been with some other woman while he'd been with her. The man's stupidity was endless.

"Caro—" he started.

"You don't get to call me that anymore, darling." She smiled grimly.

"Your Majesty, if I may ask—"

"No, you may not ask." Caroline loosened the grip on her skirts before Felix could catch the motion. She had a role to play here, and she would do it.

She cleared her throat. "If you had wished to have a wife, a child..." She watched the dirty blonde standing behind Felix, sniffling. The woman was clearly showing, the bump at her stomach which she cradled poked forward of her ample breasts.

Caroline cocked her head to the side, addressing the woman. "What's your name?"

"Her name is—"

Caroline cut him off again. "She was bold enough to steal the lover of a queen. She'll be strong enough to speak for herself."

The woman's wide eyes darted between her husband and the other woman. "I—my name's Jaine, Your Majesty," she said, voice wobbling.

Caroline sauntered over to Jaine and reached her hands out toward the woman's swollen belly. "May I?"

Jaine brought a trembling hand up to her mouth and she shot Felix a pleading look. Tears tracked down her cheeks, no doubt thinking of the terrible things the queen was about to do.

"Caroline, I won't let you hurt her." Felix thrust a hand out to grab the queen and pull her back, but he froze as he fell under Caroline's power.

Felix's body vibrated as he fought against the invisible restraint, color sapping from his tan skin.

Caroline huffed a laugh. "I wouldn't physically harm a pregnant woman. What type of monster do you think I am?" She shook her head and motioned her hands forward, urging Jaine to give her permission.

The woman squeaked, "*Yes.*"

"Has it started moving yet?" she asked, placing her hands on Jaine's stomach.

"He has, Your Majesty. Kicks most often in the mornings, like he's waking up with me."

"You're calling it *he*?" She raised an eyebrow at Jaine in question.

The woman flashed a loving glance at her virile husband. "Well," she stammered. "Felix is so strong, such a man. I thought he must produce a boy."

Caroline snorted. How could he have chosen such a pathetically smitten woman over her? It was ridiculous.

"Very well. You could name him Angus." She patted their robust captor on his chest, to which Angus half grumbled, half laughed.

As the couple stood, antsy, nervous energy radiated off them.

"If you aren't going to kill us, then why are we here?" Felix asked, clenching his fists at his sides as Caroline released him.

He was sweating now. The perspiration, a sign of his nausea, the result of him fighting her hold. "You need to learn better manners."

"Please, Felix," Jaine pleaded.

"Your Majesty, may I please ask why we are here?" Felix kept his tone neutral and lowered his eyes to the floor.

"Better." Caroline smiled. "Because I'd like to offer you and your new bride a home and assistance with the birth, of course."

The couple's heads whipped toward each other.

"You wouldn't refuse me, would you?" They didn't answer, so she continued. "You see, Felix. I've grown rather attached to you. Made you, so to speak. And now you've made a baby. I'm interested to see how it all turns out. I wish you would have come to me with this." She ran a hand across her forehead in mock frustration. She wasn't frustrated. She was livid. But they didn't need to know that yet.

"Please, make yourself at home. Angus has had your things moved. Felix..." she said, walking back out the door, expecting him to follow. She gestured at four trunks which had been placed outside. "Take your time, unpack, then I'll see you both at dinner."

She took a few steps across the courtyard, but turned around and sashayed to where Felix stood outside the door. She dragged her eyes up his muscled chest and placed a hand over his heart. Caroline eyed her ex-lover from beneath heavy lids, giving them a flutter in emphasis. "I wish you would have told me what you needed. We could have worked something out. You'd want that, wouldn't you?"

Before he could answer, she looked away and hurried back the way she came. Angus's loud footsteps pounding the stones as he trailed after her.

A satisfied smirk took residence on Caroline's face. He'd taken the first seed she'd planted. The glimmer in his eye all the evidence she needed. His overconfidence was her least favorite thing about him. A brimming confidence was sexy, but Felix thought he was invincible. That fact evidenced by his recent actions.

She hoped she wouldn't need to plant too many more before she could act. Her skin crawled as she thought of the time she'd need to spend with them in order to enact her plan. She'd have to rely on that confidence of his, then she'd strike.

CHAPTER 6

J OHNNETH FOLLOWED CAROLINE ON the long winding path from her wing to the section of Roskide housing the main kitchens and dining hall where she'd been meeting with the doomed couple. If only he could tell them to run and never look back. But saving them whatever misery she had planned wasn't why he was here. He must maintain a singular focus, despite how hard that was around her. Still, his curiosity and her relentless drive toward whatever goal she'd set for their punishment drew him in, like how the crowd in Veetula gathered to watch the monthly executioner swing his axe.

"It's been almost two months now that you've been dining with them, Your Majesty. What are you up to?" he asked, knowing each question, each time they spoke, was another crack in his effort to bring down the wall she kept up between her and everyone but Angus. And it was a dangerous line to walk.

It wasn't the same with Felix since she hated him. This was about punishment, and while he didn't agree with her methods, something had to be done to send a message.

She chortled. "What would you have me do—forgive and forget? You saw where leniency got my father. He should have taken Veetula when he had the chance. He wasn't ruthless enough, that's what I learned from him in the end."

Johnneth was glad he was a step behind the queen so she couldn't see the strain sprout across his features. Caroline stopped abruptly and turned as if she sensed his betraying thoughts. He fixed his face as a blank slate and lowered his eyes to meet hers.

"Shall I release them, Johnneth? Is that what you think would be *just*?" Caroline blinked up at him as she studied his face.

"Of course not. I'm still learning the... sacrifices it takes to rule, Your Majesty." It's only that Johnneth didn't see why she needed to drag it out. He understood she was waiting for them to become complacent, and whatever she aimed to do would be far worse than any physical punishment.

Caroline patted his chest, like she'd done to Hastings, and he bristled not wanting to be lumped into the same category as that man. "Good," she said. "You don't have to approve of every choice I make. You only must abide by them, uphold my rulings, and of course keep me safe." Her fingers had traveled to the leather ties which hung loose from the top of his tunic, and she was twisting one around a dainty finger. So not like Hastings, then? No, he remembered her hand raking through the man's hair.

Still, unable to find the words, Johnneth nodded. She was standing too near him, as if drawn by the electricity sparking between them. That was real. And he felt so tall, so male hovering over her and couldn't step away. Didn't want to.

The corridor where she'd stopped them was a windowless section, with torches sporadically placed, dimly illuminating it. The nearest flame's flickering reflection danced across her bright silver eyes, and, for a moment, she was only a woman standing before him and he only a man. The glowing light softened her sharp contrasts, and as he stood towering over her, he sensed how young the queen truly was. If he didn't know better, he could almost see earnestness in her stare, like she wanted something she could never have, but couldn't stop the dreaming.

Johnneth's eyes tracked to her fidgeting hands, and his own reached out curving around her waist. Her breath caught, parting her lips. And like a doomed moth, he glided into her flame.

He sensed the exact moment she became the queen again. Dropping her hands, she spun on her heel and continued her path toward her awaiting guests. Johnneth trailed after her admonishing himself for his momentary lapse. He should really learn to keep his mouth closed and his hands to himself.

Caroline shut out the drifting thoughts of her looming guard, the way his mouth opened slightly like he had something to say, but couldn't find the words. The way his strong hand had slid around her waist. The spot still burned warm from the touch. It was moments like that which made her consider abandoning this mission to punish Felix and veer in an entirely different direction. She glanced back at Johnneth, letting her eyes linger, and he stood a little more erect under the scrutiny of her gaze. Then his eyes flicked to her for the briefest second, and her heart skipped.

Giving into this momentary craving would be easy. But she never did what was easy. She did what was necessary.

Shaking off the vision of the man behind her, she focused her full attention on her guests. She found their affection sickening, but she permitted it. Encouraged it, even. For a fool, Felix did seem somewhat committed to his wife, who was looking like she was ready to burst. He flirted with Caroline occasionally when he thought no one was looking, but she was struggling to get him alone, which was why her plan was taking much longer than she'd anticipated.

Jaine had even confessed to Caroline that Felix had been pushing her for sex, but she was so uncomfortable as her size swelled that she was never in the mood. Did Jaine even know what she was doing, confiding in the vengeful queen? She learned the woman was naïve, but this was beyond being overly trusting. And of course, Caroline had encouraged the other woman to deny him, citing she should be taking care of herself and the baby. Felix could use his hand, she suggested.

It had been a month since that conversation, and she cherished every new line of tension that appeared on Felix's thick jaw. Any day now.

"I have a surprise for you," she said, twirling her fork between her fingers. "Can you guess what it is?"

Jaine's eyes brightened as she looked at the queen. "Gosh, I don't know. You've already done so much for us." She reached over and squeezed Felix's hand.

"I've had a cradle crafted for the baby. I've designed it myself. There are a few last details I didn't feel comfortable finalizing without your consent. You'll meet me in the Rose Room to meet the artist tomorrow before lunch?" She waited for the other woman's response.

Jaine clapped her hands in front of her chest and squealed. "Yes, Your Majesty. That is so wonderful!"

Caroline reached over and patted her hand. She almost felt guilty. The woman was living in a fairytale. She hoped Jaine enjoyed it while it lasted because it was all about to come crashing down.

Felix's eyes skimmed across the Rose Room as he walked in the next afternoon, sighing as they snagged on Caroline. "Aren't you supposed to be meeting with Jaine?" he asked, tone grumpy.

Being the husband of a near birth pregnant woman didn't seem to be something the man was too fond of, as it turned out. Caroline gave him a sympathetic pout. "We met before lunch. She went with the designer to your room to see how the colors would go with some bedding she'd gotten. They'll be occupied for hours."

A platter of food was laid out on the oval table in the informal space Caroline preferred for her lunch meal. The way the sun came in through the balcony and reflected off the mirrors and the red stones gave the room a warm, seductive feel. Perfect for what she had planned. Other than the table, there were two hutches on each side of the room, normally filled with porcelain dishes, linens, and serving ware. She flicked her eyes toward one, then back to the spread before her. Picking up an orange slice, she put it between her lips, sucking the juice from it before she plopped it in her mouth.

"Have lunch with me?" she asked sweetly. "I know you must be starved." Caroline licked the sweet liquid from the orange off her bottom lip, then took it in her mouth, biting.

Felix's eyes followed the motion, and his mouth fell open. She caught his neck muscles flex as he swallowed, his gaze trailing down the length of her form.

"What are you wearing?" he asked, his dark eyes lingering on the black fabric cinched around her hips, which splayed open right in the center below the highest point of her thighs.

"Oh, only a fresh style I wanted to try. Do you like it?" She plucked another orange slice and leaned against the table. The motion caused the fabric to fall away, exposing her long creamy legs.

It was like she'd compelled him, the way he walked toward her. They were a hand's length apart and his pupils had dilated. She wanted to check his other anatomy to see if it was responding as well, but she refrained. Slow down, Caroline, she reprimanded herself, but anticipatory jitters fluttered in her belly. She had waited months for this moment, the spring coiling tighter and tighter.

"What are you doing, Caroline?" he asked her, his voice a low growl that once would have sent shivers down her spine.

"I thought I'd been giving you little hints, but you don't seem to have recognized them." She batted her lashes for effect and ran a manicured nail down the length of her neck. "You remember what it was like, don't you, Felix?"

Felix gripped the table on either side of her and leaned down so they were at eye level. His desire for her was palpable. Perfect.

She gently pressed her hands into his chest, running them up around his neck, burying them in his hair the way he liked. He groaned. "I would have allowed you to have her if you'd asked. A mother for your child. I still would if you wanted me. You didn't have to choose," she said, making her voice breathy as she played to his ego.

He gave a deep, throaty chuckle. "You think I stopped wanting you?"

She nodded, widening her eyes.

"Caroline, a man could never stop wanting you."

"Then what are you doing, Felix? Have me. Take me right here."

"What about Jaine? I don't think she'd approve."

Caroline leaned her head up, tracing her nose up his neck, stopping when her lips were against his ear. She licked, pulling the lobe into her mouth. "I'm her queen. Who is she to deny me? Besides, she doesn't need to know."

That snapped his control. Hands went to her hips and trailed up to her breasts. She leaned back, and he caught her mouth in a crushing kiss. He pulled away and ran his hands up the center slit of her gown, slipping his thumbs under the band of her undergarments. Tugging, he had them free and at her ankles. "I've been dreaming of this," Felix moaned, pushing a hand between her legs, testing her readiness.

"Me, too," she breathed. He'd know why soon enough.

His muscled arm swept dishes off the table, and they clattered to the floor. Lifting her up, he seated her on the cleared surface as he continued to trail steamy kisses down her throat and on the breast he'd tugged free of her bodice.

"Felix," Caroline ground out. "You never stopped wanting me?"

"Never," he growled.

She tossed her head back as he worked his fingers inside her. Gods, if it didn't still feel good. She hated him, but that didn't change the sex, apparently.

"Then what are you waiting for? Take me," she commanded.

Felix pulled his hand from her and popped open the laces of his trousers, springing his angry erection free. By the looks of his seized-up balls, it had been a while.

He pressed into her without hesitation, filling her. "So good. I needed this. Needed you, Caroline."

He claimed her mouth as he pumped into her, gently at first, then with increasing urgency. She pulled away again, squeezing her thighs around him, encouraging him to keep going.

They watched each other as he worked, building their rhythmic pleasure. "I needed this too, Felix." Caroline moaned as her body approached its climax. Not yet, she urged her body to settle. She hadn't been with anyone since Felix. Taking another to bed hadn't felt right until she settled her score.

A satisfied glint shone in Felix's eye, and she suspected his ego was relishing in the thought of a queen as *his* lover. It likely made him feel powerful, like a god. They were panting with the effort now, and she looped an arm around his neck to hold herself in place as he ground into her. "Did you ever think of me when you're with her?" she asked between breaths.

"Yes," he groaned.

"How often?" Caroline cried out as the first burst of pleasure swept through her. It wasn't as electric as it had been before the betrayal, but the sensation was enjoyable nonetheless.

"Every. Fucking. Time," he answered, hammering his last strokes before he stiffened over her, convulsing with his own waves of pleasure which she imagined were much more satisfying than her own.

She leaned back, resting her elbows on the table, and smiled up at Felix standing between her legs, imagining himself to be king. This was going to be so much better than the orgasm.

She released her hold on Jaine.

The hutch's double doors flew open, slamming with a crack against the wall. The pregnant woman stumbled down from her enclosure, tripping over the items from the table that were scattered about the floor. Caroline had removed the shelves normally inside and compelled the woman into the cabinet, silencing her with a thought.

An expression of horror was etched across Jaine's features. She'd heard every word. Jaine put a hand to her mouth and gagged, as she gaped at her husband. The rage directed toward Felix made Caroline wonder if the other woman was capable of murder. Had she'd misjudged the wife and they should have disposed of Felix together and become friends?

No. She huffed a laugh, shaking her head. "Please move, Felix."

His limp cock slid from her entrance as she shoved him away. He was dumbstruck and jolted back, as if only now realizing what had happened. Caroline's grin was so wide it hurt as he took her in.

"Did you really think you could scorn a queen, especially one with my penchant for consequences, and get away with it, Felix?"

Retching drew both their attention. Jaine had one hand on the wall, the other holding her own hair back and was bent over, spewing foul bile on the floor.

Felix darted his eyes between the two women, seeming unable to decide whether to lash out at Caroline or help his wife. Attacking the queen would be of no use, so he rushed to his wife's side.

"Don't. Touch. Me," she bit out between heaves. Felix's hands paused in mid-air hovering around his wife. He turned and stared daggers back at Caroline, who'd grabbed a linen napkin and was cleaning herself off as if she hadn't just shattered their marriage.

Jaine pushed herself away from the wall, taking care to step around the items on the floor and Felix. Her lips were peeled back in a hideous sort of craze, and she bolted toward the table, wrapping her fingers around a carving knife.

Caroline tilted her head as she studied the woman. This was providing much more entertainment than she expected. She set the cum stained napkin aside and met Jaine as she approached her. Felix wrapped his hands around his wife's waist, trying to pull her back, but Caroline stilled him, curious to see what Jaine would do. The women took two paces toward each other, and Jaine lifted the tip of the blade to Caroline's throat swifter than she might have expected.

Caroline leaned forward, letting the tip of the knife pierce her skin. "Why is your anger directed toward me, sweet one? He's the one we both should feel murderous toward."

"He was mine," Jaine sobbed. "We're having a baby."

"Ah, well, technically, he was mine first—and my rights supersede yours. Or have you forgotten to whom you are speaking?" Caroline snarled.

Jaine's skin drained of color and the knife she released clattered to the ground between them. A single sob escaped her trembling lips before Jaine fled from the room. Caroline released Felix. He ran to the door, chasing her. Before he made it to the hallway, Caroline called his name, and he paused, looking back—a glare shot in her direction.

"You are no longer welcome in Everstal. Take your pregnant wife, whatever you can carry and leave my kingdom. If I ever see your face again, you'll die, she will die, and I'll take your child and raise it as my own. And I will teach them to adore me and be my perfect mirror. Is there anything about that you don't understand?" Caroline arched an eyebrow.

"Understood, Your Majesty," he snapped.

"One more thing." She walked over and pulled a ring from her pocket, slipping it on her thumb. Felix flinched as she grabbed his wrist. A quick swipe with the little blade that was fashioned onto the silver ring which lined up with her own pointed nail but longer, and a line of blood welled up where it'd passed. She eyed the blade, pricking her pointer finger on its tip, and the blood collected on its surface mingled with hers. A chilly energy zipped through her, and the connection was made.

"I will give you one more command as my final parting gift. You are not allowed to bed another woman for as long as you live. You made your choice in Jaine. Now you live with it."

His eyes said *I hate you*, but his head only nodded a single time before he turned and raced after his wife.

CHAPTER 7

T HE CLICK OF HER heels sounded as Caroline stepped out into the hallway to watch Felix round the corner in a jog. She flicked her eyes up at Johnneth, who was waiting in the hallway. He'd heard everything too, and his striking face was scrunched up in disapproval. Johnneth grimaced as he searched her eyes. The silver must be duller, more muted because of what she'd done.

"Come, I need to get out of this awful dress," she said, shifting the bodice as if it was what made her uncomfortable.

"Was that not the result you intended?" Johnneth asked, stepping from his position on the wall, falling in line behind her.

"It was a perfectly executed punishment." A dribble of Felix's seed traced down her inner thigh, eliciting an involuntary shiver, which shook her entire frame. "Gods, that man had a lot of cum. I guess that's what happens when it's been a while. You, guards, wouldn't know anything about that, would you?" she teased, flashing a half-hearted wink back at him. Caroline grabbed a handful of her dress and used it to wipe her thigh, then picked up her pace, eager to get to her room.

❦

Johnneth's jaw ticked at the thought of Felix's seed on her, and he cursed the protective instinct that the queen's presence constantly triggered. Since those first few weeks he'd gotten better at wrestling it under control and thank the Gods he had. Every sound she'd made had passed through the door. Caroline had intentionally not been subtle. The sound of her moans and the slapping of flesh were too much. He wasn't sure if he should plug his ears or go in, execute the man, and take over for him.

Caroline stormed into her suite. As he passed an attendant dusting in the sitting room, he ordered them to draw the queen a bath before he followed her into the bedroom.

Caroline was wrenching around her back, clawing, trying to get at the lacing of her gown. "Johnneth, get it off me," she hissed, having no success.

He approached her. "Here... be still." She was wrestling with the garment, like she might break out of it, so he grabbed her shoulders, stabilizing her with a firm grip.

"I can't help you unless you be still." He got ahold of the bow—more like a knot—at the top. She must have caused the tangle with all her thrashing or when she was with... never mind.

"Get it off," she demanded. "Johnneth. Please." His name was a plea on her lips, and he could see sweat gathering along her blotched neck. Caroline tugged at the top of her bodice. The queen was imploding.

"Stop," he said, voice raised. It came out a little harsher than he planned, but she froze. It was long enough for him to get his fingers inside the upper seam at the top of her shoulder-blades and rip.

The sound of shredding fabric blew through the room. The silk split down to the small of her back, exposing the two divots on either side of the base of her spine. Caroline caught the front of the dress before it fell to the floor, holding it against her bare chest. Then, as if remembering what she held to her, she let it drop.

It took a moment to make sure the queen's rapid breathing settled before he turned away. She was slim, but her hips flared out enough that she wasn't boyish at all. Her curves were fluid sweeping down her tall frame—what was he thinking? The last thing Johnneth should be pondering was the queen's shapely physique.

Especially after she'd been with another man moments earlier. Especially considering his mission and that damn smile. Specialist Brock Holzman, Angus's choice, wouldn't be staring at the queen's ass. He'd be doing his job. It was bad enough he'd touched her waist the day before.

"Are you okay?" he asked, voice soft, testing the water.

"Burn it," she answered in a flat tone, then made her way to the bathing chamber.

After he'd taken care of the dress in the enormous fireplace in the sitting room, and gone to fetch Caroline a drink, he tapped on the bathroom door.

"Come in," she said, voice lighter than it had been before.

He slipped inside the steamy room. Dragging a stool over he sat a cool beverage on it without a word, and returned to his position, pressing his back against the wall right inside the door.

Caroline eyed the glass. "What's this?" She picked it up and gave it a sniff.

"A cocktail I thought you might like. It has lavender, lemon, a drop of honey, and of course a shot of liquor." How much should he divulge? Best to keep it minimal. "I used to have one of these when I was feeling stressed. I think it's the lavender," he said, and chuckled. "*Or the liquor.*"

The queen huffed a laugh and took a tentative sip, raising her eyebrows. She took a longer sip. "You made this?"

"I can make it, but no, not this exact cocktail," he said. "I asked your attendant to make it while I was taking care of your dress. I didn't want to leave you."

"It's fresh and not too sweet," she said, and placed the half empty glass back on the stool. "Do I seem stressed?"

Gods, this woman. She always had to dive right into the heart of everything. "You seem affected," he said, figuring that was a fairly safe thing to say.

Her fingers, which were lifting the glass from the stool, tensed putting the bones and tendons in her delicate hand on display. Did she not like seeming affected, or *him* seeing her affected?

Caroline snorted. "I'm a queen. Queens don't get affected."

"But you're also a woman. You're allowed to admit things rattle you. That doesn't make you weak." His voice dropped an octave as he spoke. Why, why, why? he asked himself.

The water sloshed and Caroline dipped under, submerging her head fully. Johnneth leaned over, peeking into the sudsy water of the tub. How long was she going to stay down there?

When she finally popped up, she sucked in a long breath, and exhaled it slowly. "I will always do what I must, and I will not allow my choices to shake me. My responsibility will always come first, and my subjects will not get away with treating their queen with so little respect. I think I made that quite clear to Felix and his bride today, don't you?"

Something about the somber way she spoke made Johnneth long for the times when she wasn't acting out the role of queen. The brief glimpses of the observant, inquisitive, disciplined, yet fun and flirty woman she could be. He shouldn't, but he enjoyed that version of the calculating creature soaking in the tub before him. But right now, she was the woman who was capable the total mind-fuck she'd delivered Felix today. A gust licked across the back of his neck making his hairs stand on end.

"You took his blood?" He'd seen the little ring-knife she used and witnessed her threaten to use it during the petitions, but she hadn't actually taken the blood yet. He suspected that was exactly what she'd done. If a Dallimore had your blood, they had total control of you, and now she owned Felix.

"Yes," she replied, as if she thought nothing of it.

"How many people's blood have you taken?"

She shrugged. "I've lost count."

"How can you keep track of who you're trying to manage?" he stammered.

"I don't. With most of the threads, I have a sense of who they belong to, or a face. Usually, the threat is enough. Can you imagine, one day you're going about your business, and a mad queen decides to bring you to your knees out of nowhere because she's having a bad day. Or forces you to jump in front of the next carriage or off a bridge. It sounds awful, I know, but it works to keep them inline. Outside of Dominique's people, obviously. The sweet old man spoiled them."

She sighed as she sank deeper into the water so that her mouth was right above the surface. Some of Caroline's black hair floated at the top, thankfully obscuring the body below which the fizzled-out bubbles no longer covered.

He'd seen the consequences of getting tangled up with the queen.

"You'll let them live, really?" He couldn't help himself, all the questions and she was tolerating it. If she didn't want to talk, she usually shut him down immediately.

She flipped over in the tub and hooked her hands over the edge. Her chin rested on its porcelain edge as she faced him directly. "*Really*. I always do what I say. You're awfully curious today."

He wasn't sure if it was a question, so he said nothing. Johnneth looked toward the opposite wall but couldn't help catching the mirror that leaned against the wall to the side of the tub. He also caught the arch of her back and the two rounded cheeks that bobbed above the surface. Opening, then closing his mouth, he suppressed the deluge of warmth that the glimpse of her unleashed.

"See something you like?"

Though his eyes were directed to the ceiling, he could feel her grinning over the fact that she was getting to him. "I'll be right outside."

～❧

Caroline lay there in the tub until the water had lost its heat. When Johnneth left, she'd scrubbed her skin until it was bright pink. She was glad of what she'd done, truly, but she couldn't shake the icky feeling on her skin everywhere Felix had touched her.

When she finally dragged herself from the bath, she gave herself a long, hard look in the mirror. She was a queen and would always do what she had to do to ensure no one would escape her wrath, but Caroline deserved better. Deserved loyalty and love. A man that looked at her like—

Her thoughts drifted to the guard outside. *Looked at her the way Johnneth did.* Like she was a sought-after prize, or a forbidden treat he was dying to get his mouth on. Men in her kingdom wanted to marry her. There were a dozen Lord Hastings who falsely believed they had a chance. That wasn't the problem. And Caroline would send her dismissals to their requests for an audience with her, their lavish gifts, letters, and poems—all sorts of flamboyant gestures designed to get her attention. They didn't even know her, only of her beauty and position.

Even with the ones she'd met, there was never a hint of passion there. The closest had been with Felix. They had chemistry, but he wasn't clever enough to make her equal. To challenge her. A king to rule beside her. At some point, she'd need to choose. Twenty-four was still young, but eventually, as Angus constantly nudged her, she'd have to decide. A marriage showed stability, and the people would be more settled with a pair of rulers on the throne. And then there was the matter of an heir to pass the Gift on to one day. Still, she held out hope.

Gooseflesh traced up her arms as she imagined the guard's supple lips making their way so slowly across her skin, erasing the memory of anyone who'd come before him. Sometimes when you looked at a man, you could tell what type of lover they'd be.

They'd been flirting since she'd selected him, the attraction between them obvious, but she hadn't considered acting upon it. Caroline hardly knew anything about the man, except that every time they spoke, the instant lust that was between them was undeniable. He seemed intelligent, and he certainly cared deeply for others, which he demonstrated every time his face betrayed his disapproval of one of her punishments.

There was something about him that made her think he might be more than just a guard one day. Something about his countenance, his commanding presence, which stood out to her, but she couldn't quite put her finger on what it was. And Gods, the man was handsome, in a timeless, regal way. He'd be dashing in a crown, and when their eyes met, her world shifted.

Somewhere buried under the extinguished coals of her black heart, an ember remained. And Johnneth was primed to stoke a flame from the ashes. Maybe all he needed was a little spark.

An hour later, the queen emerged from the bathing chamber. Johnneth was about to go in to make sure she hadn't fallen asleep in the tub when she'd finally slipped out, wearing an uncharacteristically fluffy robe. It was black still. He had to laugh.

He followed Caroline into the sitting room and stood by the doorway as she curled up on the end of the tufted red couch and eyed the plate of little sandwiches which had been placed on the side table.

"I thought you might be hungry. You should eat." Johnneth gestured to the plate. "Would you like wine or water?"

She raised a suspicious eyebrow at him. "Both."

Picking up a sandwich, she sniffed it, then took a tentative bite, setting the uneaten portion back on the plate. She picked up the wine instead, and Johnneth frowned at the half-discarded sandwich.

"Do you ever get to see your family?" she asked before he could tell her to finish it.

Johnneth froze. "I..."

"Come, stand in front of me so I can see you while you speak."

He obeyed, pulse pounding in his ears. All she had to do was sense that he was lying and she would compel him to spill his secrets, which would earn him nothing less than death. And he would fail. Johnneth considered how much of the truth he could spin into his tale.

"I haven't seen them in five years," he answered.

"Since you joined the service to the crown? Is that right?"

"Yes," Johnneth said, leaning back against the mantel beside the roaring fire, trying to appear more casual than he felt. He was curious about where this line of questioning was headed. The queen reclined, sipping her wine, and fidgeting with the tie of her robe. She didn't seem suspicious of him. The distant look in her eye made him think she wasn't entirely present.

"Do you miss them?" she asked, staring not at him, but at the flames.

"Every day," he answered, considering how much to share. "My older brother and I are close. He even saved my life once when I got into a situation which was a little over my head. I idolized him as a child."

"But you still chose to come here, to serve me?" She was looking at him now. "What made you want to do that?"

Stick to the truth. "My duty called to me. One day my brother and I were bedding women, drinking, and carrying on, driving his wife crazy with our antics." Johnneth chuckled at the memory. "The next I was heading to enlist. Honestly, it was getting old. I needed a purpose, so that's when I decided to join the guard. I set myself a goal to make it as your personal guard. I wanted nothing more, and I worked every day to earn my way up in the ranks."

Caroline's eyes gleamed as he spoke passionately about his desires. If she only knew his true meaning. Her throat bobbed as she took another sip of the berry liquid she was swirling in her glass.

"How noble. So here you are. Is it everything you thought it would be?"

Was she everything he thought she would be, was the better question. Johnneth sensed the hidden question beneath. Caroline Dallimore was more than the Cruel Queen from the stories that circulated of her. He let the corner of his mouth twist up, knowing a dimple would appear in his cheek, and allowed himself to let his gaze slip across her face, memorizing her perfect features. Johnneth would know her so well, that when he struck, she wouldn't see it coming.

She eyed him, still waiting for an answer.

"No, Your Majesty," he said. "You are so much more."

CHAPTER 8

"CAN YOU BELIEVE THIS?" The queen held a slip of parchment she received from the vintner that morning overhead. Angus snapped it out of her hand and quickly read it, chuckling at the contents.

"Four days," Caroline continued. "One of those traitors lasted four days."

It is what Angus had been cautioning her about for the last year. The people were becoming restless, waiting for ten years for their queen to strike Veetula. Deliver the blow as retribution King Thom's death demanded. Some were even questioning why she hadn't done it yet as Dominique had suggested—as everyone seemed to keep reminding her. Still, the queen hadn't struck. He had certainly gotten their armies up to speed. Even presented several covert plans to eliminate the Veetula royals.

"They're becoming more defiant, Caroline," Angus said.

"You warned me this would happen. Yes, yes—I know." Caroline fluttered a hand through the air, waving him off.

"They want blood, Your Majesty." Angus braced his hands on the table and leaned over giving her a stern look he hoped would convey the urgency weighing on him. Dominique was right. She needed to act.

"And I will give it to them. But not until you can convince me it will be a decisive victory. I want every single person in that frozen wasteland to understand the fear I felt running through those tunnels, knowing my father was dead, expecting at any moment my life to bleed out of me from a knife in the back. I want to be the monster under their bed, their waking nightmare. If I must take the blood of every person under Hollis's rule,

I will do it until they willingly fall to their knees at my feet. I'll accept nothing less."

Angus couldn't suppress a sigh. He glanced up at Althorpe who was grinding his teeth. Instinct told him he should send the man out of the room, which was strange. Specialist Johnneth Althorpe was getting a little too comfortable with the queen and being privy to conversations like this didn't help. Angus was more than capable of looking out for her safety during these meetings between him and Caroline.

He pressed on, pulling a folded letter out of his pocket, and tossed it on the table before her. The queen knew what it was without reading it and groaned.

"Another skirmish. Where this time?" she asked.

"On the border. I sent troops to clean up and establish order. Hollis did too, but the survivors are angry. Tensions between our people are escalating. Even the merchants who normally operate in the neutral trading towns have reported an increase in raids and street fights. The magistrate in Bowring said the cases of theft are up two-fold from this time a year ago."

"Then we'll have to work harder," Caroline said.

Angus's mouth pinched into a frown. He didn't know if they had the capacity to work harder. There was only so much a ruler could oversee themselves. A king would solve the problem, which Caroline was still determined to put off. Taking over Veetula would also solve the problem. Sure, at first it would be more work, but eventually, as one kingdom, one people under Caroline's rule, things would smooth out. He just needed to get her to do *something*.

Right when Johnneth started to soften to her, she reminded him of why they were enemies. Caroline hadn't blinked when she'd spoken about annihilating his family. It took every bit of self-control not to let his face slip into the rage that was churning inside him. But he was glad she'd said it. Hearing the truth of who she was from her own mouth was exactly what he needed.

Caroline chewed on the end of a peppermint stick as she studied the map carved into the table. Gods, watching her lips work... Her vitriol didn't change the fact that he wanted to bed her. How could you be aroused by someone you hated in the depth of your very being? Someone who represented that blasphemous power that her ancestors had the gall to request from the Gods. And what her father had used it for. For what he'd witnessed as a child, a memory which dragged him from sleep many nights. He could almost hate the Gods for giving that unholy power to the Dallimore's.

"What do you think, Johnneth?" Caroline's voice drew him out of the rage filled stupor his mind had spiraled into.

Angus, leaning over the table, stiffened. "Specialist Althorpe is here to keep you alive, Your Majesty. Not give his opinion on political matters."

Johnneth gave a curt nod to the commander. He completely agreed and had no desire to speak because speaking might betray his roiling emotions.

Caroline placed the end of the candy which she'd sucked down into a point between her teeth. She eyed him, then snapped the end off, crunching as she chewed. When she swallowed, still watching him, she said, "I think Johnneth has something to say, and I'd like to hear it."

She always had a way of keeping him on his toes, whether she intended it or not. Who was he kidding? She definitely intended it.

He stepped forward, splaying his hands out on the table, and leaned over the carved map. "Warrik is on the other side of the border from Bowring." Caroline shot him a look like she didn't need a geography lesson from him. "I'm going somewhere with this. Warrik is a logging town. Its primary source of income is the milling of timber from the surrounding forests and the ones up the river. The different mills employ most of the townsfolk. Bowring, on the other side of the river, has access to all the farmland of Everstal."

Johnneth waved a hand at the blush stone surrounding them on all four walls. "Everstal has other resources for building and enough timber to get by. Veetula on the other hand, particularly the small borderland villages—"

"Need the supplementation that travels through the river towns," Caroline finished for him.

"Right. And when you freed the indentures and the new pricing structure went into effect in your kingdom, it affected—" Johnneth caught himself. "It affected theirs. The price of grain almost doubled. Everstal citizens could afford it with the new wages, but in Veetula, where families may have only had one or two members not in an indenture bringing home income, put simple things like grain out of their range."

Johnneth sighed as he took a seat, ignoring the thin line Angus's lips were pressed into. "In a good year, they can live off the game and winter crop, but reports say the last few winters have been harsher, so I expect the tensions result from that. They need the supplement, but can't afford it."

Caroline blinked at him. It made perfect sense. Of course, there would be ramifications from her releasing the indentures, but none this extensive. Merchants and landowners had been angry, but she'd encouraged them to put a new pricing structure in place and within a few years, it appeared to work. A prickle, like the touch of Justice's icy hand, slid up the back of her neck. She would not sit here and be blamed for this.

"That sounds like the problem of that bastard Hollis Ivanslohe. It doesn't give his subjects the right to raid mine," Caroline said, fuming.

Johnneth shot to his feet before he could stop himself, his chair grating across the floor behind him in a burst. How dare she bring up Hollis's name like that?

He banged his fists on the table once, the sound echoing off the solid walls. His frustration did not ease as he stared at the unmoved queen. Out of the corner of his eye, Angus was swiftly making his way around the table.

"Those are innocent people going hungry, Caroline," he said, keeping his eye trained on her, his shaking hands rumbling the table. *Cruel Queen indeed.* But he kept that to himself.

Angus wrapped his fists into the fabric of his tunic, gripping tightly, and spun him so he was staring into angry gold eyes. "You do not have the privilege of speaking the queen's name. You will address her as Your Majesty. And you certainly don't have the privilege of raising your voice to the queen."

Johnneth jerked like he would yank himself out of Angus's grip as the rose-colored walls encroached into his vision. But the commander held firm. "You are dangerously close to losing your position. Do you understand me, Specialist Althorpe?"

That snapped him out of it. If Angus dismissed him, he'd be back to the start. "Yes, sir," he ground out, forcing his eyes to lower. Angus released him and he took a step back.

Angus's jaw was working as he ran a hand across his head. "You're suspended for one week. Go train with the new recruits and try to remember your place."

He couldn't help but glance between the queen and the commander. Angus radiated his agitation as he paced, but Caroline only stared between the two men with an amused glint in her eye. He shot her a pleading look, which she dismissed with a subtle shake of her head. She wouldn't intervene on his behalf. *Fine.* He bowed. "As you wish, commander." He barely had the wherewithal to un-grit his teeth as he said it, then marched from the room.

After Felix had been exiled, several more weeks had gone by uneventfully… outside Johnneth's minor altercation with Angus and the subsequent suspension. He'd been itching to get back to the queen's side.

A breeze drifted through the room and Caroline twitched, raising her chin slightly like she was waiting for something, all while keeping her eyes glued to the document in her hand. Johnneth picked up on her anxious mannerisms, taking them for paranoia, which was reasonable considering how her father had been killed and why he was there. Angus said the odd, but subtle behavior was her waiting for the

Gods' summoning, whatever that meant. And now she expected this summoning after what she'd done to Felix and his bride.

Caroline released a breath then her shoulders lowered. The breeze wasn't them. Her uncanny ability to always be alert was making this a challenge. He could kill her in her sleep, but even then, her eyes flashed open at the slightest movement. But Caroline was tired and lonely. Surely, he could use that to his advantage.

Signs of tension and fatigue would spring up in subtle ways he suspected only he and Angus caught. She was wary, constantly on guard, and he begrudgingly admired her constant vigilance. She and Angus had even gone as far as rebuilding the areas in Roskide which she frequented, so there was no chance of someone hiding in the room without her having a direct line of sight. The woman took no chances.

But Johnneth would succeed. There was no choice. Only more time to bide, he reminded himself. The queen had waited months to get her revenge on a lover. He could wait years for the perfect opportunity if he had to. His success must be absolute. The rosenwood dagger, which he always had on him, burned hot in the concealed pocket of his pants.

Caroline flicked her gaze to the window, listening as the vining rose bushes outside rustled, then went back to work. Her paranoia didn't stop her from tending to her duties as monarch. For a queen, Caroline had an uncommonly small administrative staff. While Johnneth loathed every fiber of her being, he was coming to respect her work ethic. He wasn't sure he knew a royal who put in such long hours or who liked to deal with so many things personally. It was as if she enjoyed it, which he didn't believe. She loved the control.

Since Angus had returned from fetching her former lover, he was constantly around. He was her commander and her second personal guard, all in one. Couldn't she send him away on another task? He needed to get some uninterrupted time alone with the queen.

Caroline sighed, drawing Johnneth's attention. Her delicate hands kneaded the base of her neck, which had been craned over papers all day, again. These days were the most mind-numbing. He wasn't sure how she did it.

At least the Petitions, the biweekly events at which the queen permitted the public of the kingdom to bring their concerns before the crown, created some interest. In Veetula they'd of course heard of the infamous proceedings. They were the primary setting of the stories of Everstal's wicked queen.

It was true, she ruled swiftly and without regret, leaving no room for interpretation of her supreme authority, but so far, her *punishments*, as she called them, were relatively reasonable. *Compared with the stories.* Outside of poor Felix and Jaine, of course. That was savage.

Johnneth coughed, and Caroline regarded him. He held his hands in the air and made a squeezing gesture. It had been months, and he was making no progress. Time to up the odds.

"What? Now you're my personal masseuse too?" she asked, a wry grin dancing across her lips.

"I live to serve," he dared, his returning smile almost asking for permission.

Caroline beckoned, giving him the go ahead. She threatened him with punishments on a daily basis, but he sensed that secretly she liked his confident demeanor. For that, he added a trace of swagger to his steps as he approached her.

Johnneth moved aside the edges of her silk blouse, so the pale skin of her neck was exposed, and wrapped his nimble fingers around her shoulders, working the tense tissue. *They're just shoulders. Focus,* he cautioned himself. Caroline shattered the thought with a groan, leaning back into his hands as his thumbs worked their way up her neck.

This was the closest physically she'd permitted him, and he really needed to find something else to fill his mind with. Like how this would be the perfect place to strike from, and he could feel her relaxing with every rub. *Perfect* if it weren't for the mirrors strategically placed around the sitting area she'd chosen to work in today. The second she sensed something was awry, she'd be in control, and it would be his life. A chance he'd fought for five years to gain, wasted.

The room was smaller than the war room, and informal. But it was no more comfortable and had an identical wooden chair to the other ones she used in the different rooms she frequented to do her work. There was a patterned lack of routine to her movements about Roskide. The way she sprinkled her presence about the castle would be impossible to track, much less catalogue. Every action the queen took was designed to keep herself alive.

Caroline cleared her throat, and Johnneth glanced at the mirror connecting their gaze. "You stopped," she said, raising a brow. Caroline held the eye contact, assessing him. "What is going through your mind, Johnneth?"

"Nothing. My apologies," he muttered, chastising himself for getting lost in his thoughts. Touching the queen had the opposite effect than what he'd intended—he was the one losing focus.

"I can compel you to tell the truth, or you can tell me on your own, because I know *nothing* is not what's distracted my personal guard, Specialist Althorpe." Caroline smiled in mock sweetness at his reaction.

Johnneth admonished himself for the vulnerable position he found himself in. He had to say something believable. If he couldn't, she'd force him to tell her he'd been contemplating how easy it would be to kill her if it weren't for the mirrors.

"I was having inappropriate thoughts, Your Majesty. I'm ashamed to say." That was enough of the truth. Let her take it as she likes." Johnneth darted his eyes away as if he were embarrassed to be caught, then flicked them back to see if she'd bought it. "I can stop if it makes you uncomfortable," he attempted, hoping she wouldn't ask him to stop. And only because this physical contact was a step in getting her to let her guard down with him. No other reason.

As if sensing his thoughts, Caroline wetted her lips with her pink tongue and gave a little moan on the next squeeze, which shot straight to his cock. He should have gotten laid before going to the selection. He hated the way his body was drawn to the animal attraction between them. How was it you could have despised someone your whole life, yet want to fuck them still? Thank the Gods, Caroline's head was between his hips and the mirror.

A toothy smirk crossed her face, knowing her motion had its intended effect. "What I wouldn't give to be inside your mind."

He was having a similar thought, though her mind wasn't the body part in question. Johnneth ran his fingertips across the tops of her collarbones and up her neck. She gave a little shiver and gooseflesh trailed behind. He made to retrace the motion the other direction, but Caroline was gone. The queen had disappeared, and his tempted fingers were met with air where her smooth flesh had been a half-second before.

The Gods had summoned her. And not a moment too soon. If that had continued any longer, Johnneth couldn't honestly say that he would have stopped whatever that massage was leading up to.

He surveyed the vacant room. Angus had warned him about the inevitability of her being whisked away by the vengeful Gods to pay the price for using the Gift. He'd been watching her use it for months now, with no consequence. The stunt she pulled with her former lover and his new wife had pushed them over their limit.

How long did he have before she returned? Surely it was long enough to find one of the castle girls who offered sex for coin and deal with his condition. He preferred the brothels or the women his appearance attracted in the taverns, but a castle attendant would have to do.

Johnneth stormed down the hallway toward the lower levels of Roskide, shifting his still firm erection in search of relief.

CHAPTER 9

T HE LINEN CLOSET THEY'D found was a tight fit. There was enough space for two bodies and some jerky movement. The petite blonde castle girl had been all too willing when he'd asked, not so subtly, if she knew any ladies willing to help a lonely guard out.

She giggled as they shut the door and sticky hands roved up his chest, trying to wrap around his neck, before he pulled them off and spun the girl around, bending her over a stack of crates.

"What did you say your name was?" He grunted as he reached around to unclasp the trousers she wore and yank them down.

"Kelsey," she sighed as he rubbed his cupped fingers slick with spit across her opening to ease his entry. He always liked to at least know their names.

"You ready for me, Kelsey?" Johnneth didn't wait for her to respond before he buried himself in her. Gods, he needed this.

Kelsey let out a loud moan at the intrusion, which she followed up with satisfied, rhythmic whimpering as he pounded into her. Her breathing hitched and after a bit, he could feel she was getting close, so he reached his hand around to her front to encourage her pleasure.

"That's it," he breathed, as the girl's tight core muscles gripped around his cock when her first orgasm hit. It was always better for him when they came, too, and thank the Gods Kelsey didn't need much because it had been a while. Johnneth moved a hand from her hip up to her shoulder so he could hold her in place as he pushed even deeper, taking her relentlessly.

A vision of his rough hands on Caroline's silken skin in the same place flooded into his mind. The image of her from behind as he followed her up the winding staircases of Roskide made his cock strain even harder. He shouldn't be thinking of her, but he couldn't stop himself. He was hoping he'd be able to drag out the pleasure a little longer, but thoughts of what the queen's body would feel like writhing under his like that day at the winery, shred what little control he was clinging to.

The girl cried out again, and her clenching and his visions of Caroline were enough to cause him to erupt. Johnneth gasped and jerked a few more times as he spent himself within the girl.

Banging on the closet door snapped him back to reality.

"Althorpe, is that you in there?" Angus yelled.

Shit. "Give me a minute," he croaked out. It had been quick for them both, but hopefully it had been enough to take the edge off.

"Sorry, Kelsey," he whispered, pulling his softening cock from her entrance. "I hate to fuck and run, but we've been caught."

Kelsey snickered as Johnneth patted her on the backside. He buttoned his pants and fished out the coins she was promised, finding a hand in the dark to slip them into. "You'll remember to take something for prevention, right?"

"Of course. This isn't my first dalliance, lover," Kelsey purred. "Maybe we'll bump into each other again?"

"Maybe," Johnneth murmured as he slipped out the door, giving her some privacy to take care of herself. When his eyes adjusted, he was standing toe to toe with Angus's formidable form. His brown skin stretched taught across his tense features, and the gold of the man's eyes darkened a shade. He was pissed.

"What in the hell do you think you're doing and where the fuck is the queen?" Angus seethed.

"Relax, commander. She was summoned about half an hour ago. I figured I had a minute to ease some tension, okay? Men have needs. *Some* men have needs," he clarified.

"Save it and report to the queen's chambers immediately. You Gods damned guards, always thinking with your dicks. I ought to have you all castrated, so you'll think with a different part of your anatomy."

Angus stormed off down the hallway in the opposite direction, leaving Johnneth to obey.

Johnneth had been pacing in Caroline's rooms for hours when the queen finally appeared. She landed on her feet, but her knees gave out and she sobbed as she dropped to the floor. Johnneth darted forward, driven by his instinct to catch the falling woman. As he gathered her in his arms, she cried out at the contact. Rivulets of blood ran down her back, now bare and stripped of the fabric that had been shredded around it.

"Gods," he swore.

Caroline's head lolled, and her eyes rolled back in her head. He took her chin in his hand and turned her face toward him. She was taking slow labored breaths and looked like she was about to lose consciousness.

"Caroline, stay with me."

What was he thinking? He wasn't going to get a better opportunity than this. The queen was unresponsive. Johnneth fished around in one of the hidden pockets he'd sewn into the seam of his pant leg, searching for the rosenwood dagger. *Shit*, the pocket must have flipped to the back of his leg during his romp with the castle girl.

Caroline went limp in his arms, and he had to adjust her to keep her from slipping out of his hold. "Easy there. It will all be over soon." If he could get his fingers a little deeper. Cool wood brushed against his fingertips. He flicked them, trying to wrap around the hilt of the blade. *Got it.*

His heart was hammering as he tugged, pulling the weapon free. This was it. Bury the dagger deep, then Caroline would be the Cruel Queen no more. He could even escape Roskide with his life. The dagger caught on the lip of the pocket right before it came free. Johnneth wiggled and twisted it as Caroline stirred.

"Angus?" she muttered.

"Gods damn it," he cursed.

The door whined on its hinges and crashed against the wall as Angus gusted into the room. Johnneth stuffed the dagger back into his pocket, concealing it. He hoped Angus hadn't glimpsed the distinct red wood that was characteristic of the only known substance that could mortally wound a Dallimore.

"Don't worry, Johnneth. We've got her," Angus soothed, thankfully misinterpreting the meaning of Johnneth's curse. "I'm here, Caroline. Easy." He placed firm hands under her armpits, taking her weight from Johnneth and motioning to her four-poster bed. "Go place a pile of pillows in the middle. We'll need to lay her across it and get these wounds cleaned before they heal over."

Once he had a mound of pillows on the bed, he and Angus carefully laid the semi-conscious queen across them, face down.

"You doing okay?" Angus leaned down and asked her tenderly, brushing a knuckle across her cheek.

Johnneth's mouth fell open as she grinned.

"Still worth it," she uttered between clenched teeth. "Completely. Fucking. Worth it."

"We're going to get you cleaned up. I'll show Specialist Althorpe what to do in case I'm not here next time. Then you can rest. I won't leave you until you're healed," Angus assured her.

It was an arduous task, picking out bits of fabric and the queen's long hair from the wounds already trying to scab over.

"How is she healing so fast?" Johnneth asked, smoothing a section of hair along with the others.

"The wounds created by the Gods are imbued with their power, which speeds the healing. Sometimes it's blood, sometimes bruised or broken bones. Others, the pain is only mental or internal, and she complains of blinding headaches. She'll be good as new by the morning." Angus angled his head to observe the other man. "I know the first time it is startling. But it's a price she is willing to pay. All the Dallimore's were, though I think the Gods have it out for Caroline. I gather she can be pretty defiant with them."

Caroline's torso rumbled under Johnneth's fingers, and he winced, hoping he wasn't causing her any more pain. He'd had no idea what the Dallimore's had gone through to use their cursed power. No one outside of Roskide did. His family endured no such suffering for the gift they'd received from the Gods. But his ancestors hadn't thought to make such a bold request. He and Caroline winced in sync as he pulled a fiber from a deep lash. The humanity in him couldn't help but feel for her pain. Not that it changed anything, did it?

"I hate them," Caroline ground out.

As they finished getting her cleaned up, the mixed feelings Johnneth was experiencing toward the woman they had sent him to execute danced through his mind. He volunteered, really. It was how much he hated her, the Dallimore family, and everything she represented. But when he was in her orbit, he wasn't quite himself. It was like her draw pulled him in and his blood took on a new vibration as it drifted through his veins. *Protect her, take her, claim her*, it said. *Marry her.*

Angus smoothed back her hair, finger combing it and it took all Johnneth's self-control not to grab his hand and push him away from her despite the fact Angus was more like a brother to her than anything. And it didn't matter that he'd been moments away from being the one to hurt her—*kill her*—himself. He wanted to lean over her limp, damaged body and shield her from the world like some kind of fucking animal. Gods, what had gotten into him?

She was a pretty woman. Nothing more. *Liar*, the voice said. Okay, she was smart, and pretty. *And interesting, resilient, willful*, the voice continued. He wanted to groan. If only there were some sort of switch that could shut his inner monologue up until he could get out of her presence, but he was stuck until Angus released him.

Could he have finished her if he'd gotten the dagger free? He liked to think he would have. But her damaged body had been so soft in his arms, so vulnerable, and his hands so very shaky. Even as he'd massaged her neck before, she'd become so pliant for him, melting into his touch. Arousing things within him, he ought not to be feeling toward this woman.

Caroline's eyes twitched and her breathing evened. She was sleeping and Angus instructed Johnneth to go get some rest as well. *Finally.* He also gave him another scolding about shirking his duties for a quick lay which he dutifully took.

Johnneth looked over at the queen one last time before he obeyed. Then images of Veetula and his family sprouted in his mind. A sword buried in a king's belly and the vibrant life draining from his sapphire eyes. Yes, he would have done it. Defeated, Johnneth left the room, determined not to replay his past mistake at the next opportunity.

CHAPTER 10

"**B**RING IN THE NEXT petitioner," Caroline called. She leaned over and whispered to Angus, "Who's next?"

Her commander studied the roster he was holding, then regarded Caroline. "Looks like it's a hunger case, then a murder. After that is an abuse allegation. Another one came in saying it was urgent, something about spousal misconduct and I figured you'd want to see them, so I added them to the list last minute."

"Perfect," she said. She would never admit it, but her body still ached from their vengeance the night before. Nothing a trip to the underground springs couldn't cure. And maybe another massage from her very masculine, very attentive personal guard. The way his calluses brushed over her skin so gently liquified her. She couldn't help but wonder what else those hands were capable of. She stole a glance at him behind her left shoulder. A shiver stole across her skin as she greedily raked her eyes across his towering form. *Mine.* The word popped into her mind before she could stop it. He shifted, as if sensing her attention, but never lowered his eyes to her, keeping them fixed on the room before them.

It would irritate Angus if she bedded him, but there were perks to being queen. And why should she deny herself if he was someone who might resurrect her no-good heart? Angus would have to... *Angus*, that's right. Caroline brought her attention out of her fantasy and back to her commander.

"Can't they all be simple tax evasion cases?" She'd swiftly dealt with three this morning. The people always had excuses, but either they confessed if their hardship was real in the end, or she compelled them. Simple.

The cases where the humans of Everstal wronged each other were exhausting, but her hands-on approach and swift punishments were how she kept the populace in check. Yes, there were smaller courts in the outlying towns of her kingdom, but she oversaw the worst cases herself, and those within the boundary of Roskide and the surrounding city.

Caroline sat on the altar in the Oratory of Roskide. When she'd begun the petitions she held them in the Great Hall, the very one where her father had presented her the throne she now sat upon. The very location where he'd been murdered—taken from her. But she'd blocked all that out and barred the doors to the expansive room. The Oratory was the practical choice for these proceedings. Especially since she and Angus had re-decorated after she'd decided she had little use for a room for prayer to the Gods.

The oratory, which was on Roskide's first floor, another perk as it kept the public at a distance, had minimal furnishings. The rose-colored stone, like everything else in the castle, made up the walls, the ceiling, and the floor. It was like being in a pink room. She had taken the hanging tapestries down depicting each of the five Gods and replaced them with hand-painted murals. Like everything, she'd taken great care to explain her vision to the artists. They'd turned out better than she'd expected, and she paid the artists handsomely.

The one on the expansive wall to her right showed Roskide resting on the old mountain peak, its signature scarlet roses crawling up the hillside and over the castle. The mural to the left was of roses in every color, not only red. The vines snaked around the many small windows, which illuminated the space and up toward the ceiling. Her favorite was the mural behind her, though. It was a larger version of the single iridescent black rose her father had ordered carved and painted on the back of her throne. The vines which it bloomed atop grew up from the gold and ruby crown she never deigned to wear. It was too big, and gold clashed with her skin. The painting crowned the queen sufficiently, anyway.

She glanced over at Johnneth who always seemed a little worried during the petitions. "Having fun?"

He pressed his mouth into an anxious line. Most often, only Angus attended the Petitions, giving Johnneth a break from his duty, but Angus had wanted Johnneth to stand in today. Directly after the proceedings, her commander was leaving to conduct a military training which pulled him away from her occasionally.

"Next," Caroline called.

Angus motioned to guards at the door who led a bedraggled-looking woman and four ratty children all under the age of ten. The woman's clothes were in tatters, as were the children's, and their little gaunt faces pinched her black heart.

When they'd made their way to the foot of the dais, Caroline leaned down, inspecting them. "Explain."

The woman trembled and glanced back toward the door longingly. She did not want to be there. Caroline clicked her nails on her armrest impatiently.

"Your Majesty." The woman knelt, tugging her children toward the floor to do the same.

"Rise and explain why your children appear like they haven't seen bread in weeks." Caroline had no patience for neglect. This woman should have come to the crown sooner. Perhaps it was a substance abuse problem she battled with or an abusive spouse. She cautioned herself not to make a judgement too quickly. She had a sense about these things, though.

The woman stood, placing hands on the shoulders of her two youngest children. "We're starving, Your Majesty. My husband has been sick for months. We've run out of money."

Her face heated, flushing a deep crimson. Pride. Caroline knew it. A little fear too, based on the woman's still rattling hands, which twisted in her skirts.

"How long since these children have had a proper meal?" Her voice was becoming a snarl.

"We begged for a loaf yesterday." Her eyes went to her feet. "Another a few days before."

Her knuckles had turned white around the ebony wood of her throne. "Why did you not come to me sooner? And I suggest you divulge the truth."

"Didn't want to disturb you, Your Majesty. You must have much more important things to do—We know your reputation. It's been told all over the land the way you are ruthless in these *petitions*." Spite drenched the woman's words. Caroline pushed the compulsion, and the woman continued. "Me and my husband didn't want your tainted help."

Caroline met the woman's sneer, releasing her. "So, it was preferable to let your children starve?"

The woman's skin took on a pasty sheen, an effect of the compulsion mixing with her fear of Caroline. "I was going to, but..." She glanced down at her youngest one, its belly beginning the swell of starvation, and her voice cracked. "But I couldn't. If my husband knew I was here..."

"How do you think it makes me look when my people are begging in the streets, their children teetering skeletal at their feet?"

The woman rested her eyes anywhere but on her.

"Answer me!" Caroline shouted.

"Please, Your Majesty. Please help us." Fat tears were dripping down the woman's face and her children were clinging to her skirts.

The oldest boy stepped forward and peeled a cap off his matted, sand-colored hair. He placed his hand on his stomach. His mother tried to pull him back, but Caroline raised a hand to stay her. "Please forgive my mum. Da's sick and hasn't been able to work. They're good people."

"They let their fear and their pride get in the way of taking care of their children. I should not let their choices go unpunished." She addressed the ten-year-old in a matter-of-fact way. He was brave enough to do what their foolish mother was not.

The boy twisted the tweed cap in his hand and blinked the most innocent pale blue eyes up at her. "Mum has learned, haven't ya, Mum?" He turned his plea toward his mother.

She began nodding furiously, the predicament she was in sinking in. The woman fell to her knees. "Please, Your Majesty. Forgive us our folly."

⁓

Johnneth narrowed his eyes at the queen. A glimpse of a smile crossed her lips as she stared at the boy. She'd been so harsh on the woman. He feared the punishment he sensed Caroline was about to bestow. If only he could intercede and make her see reason. This poor family had been through enough.

"Very well." Caroline raised a hand, waving them off. "Reporter—" She turned to a scribe sitting at a simple desk to her left. He grabbed a fresh sheet of paper, dipping the fountain pen in the inkpot in anticipation. "Please transcribe the verdict as follows. This woman—" Caroline waited for someone to supply her name, which the scribe jotted down. "—will be required to visit the royal pantry once a week to gather a provision of food for her children and a plan to ease them from starvation. In two weeks, if their cheeks are rosy, they may be allowed food for the entire family and a healer to aid the father."

Caroline glared at the woman who'd risen from her pleading position on the floor. "You may continue to beg for you and your husband's food as your punishment. If I find out you've taken a single ounce of your children's rations, I promise you, I will live up to my reputation. Now go. Take your children's order to the pantry and let this be your warning. I won't be as forgiving a second time."

The queen flashed a glance back at Johnneth. "I can feel your disapproval seeping off you, Johnneth. You should learn to hide your emotions better."

Johnneth blinked. Angus was giving him a wry grin. The commander seemed to approve of her every action. The punishment hadn't been that horrible, he supposed. At least the children would be fed. It was a small mercy.

"Next!" Her voice echoed across the room.

Two men shuffled in, both in common attire, but it was crisp and clean, unlike the poor family. They were glaring daggers at each other, and a group of guards were around them keeping a distance between them.

"Which one of you is the murderer?" Caroline brushed her sheets of black hair over her shoulders and leaned forward to study the men.

The taller, dark-haired one thrust a wiry finger toward the stocky blond man next to him, who held both hands up in supplication. Caroline didn't force them to bow. She seemed eager to get on with it, like something was eating at her nerves.

"Who did he murder?" she asked with a sigh.

"My brother, Your Majesty. A business dealing gone wrong." The tall man's voice rang full of conviction.

"Did you do it?" she asked, simply.

"I didn't kill anybody, Majesty. I swear. Otto slipped. I tried to stop him. When I pulled his body from the river, he was already gone."

"You bashed his skull in," the other man seethed.

"I told you, he hit it on the rocks."

Caroline was watching their interchange through squinted eyes. It was like she was trying to gauge which one was lying without using her power. He suspected she had a guess already.

"Quiet," Caroline said. The men silenced and directed their attention toward her. "Will the accused please step forward?"

The stocky man's mouth dropped open as he obeyed. Guards stepped up, readying their weapons in case he tried to bolt. "I didn't do it, Majesty. Please—"

"How many other people have you killed?" She looked over at a paper being extended to her by Angus. "Samuel?" His name was a lulling melody on her tongue.

He shook his head, eyes wide with fear.

"I've been doing this since I was fourteen, Samuel. I know when a man is lying. So, will you confess, or shall I make you?"

A dark stain spread from the front of his trousers and Johnneth darted a glance between Samuel and the queen. He was almost certain that Samuel hadn't been lying. That it had truly been an accident and the pitiful man was innocent.

"Go on," she prodded, voice dripping with mock sweetness.

Samuel was unable to speak. His terror had gripped him into silence.

"As it suits you." Caroline shrugged.

Shaking, trying to fight off her control and failing, Samuel talked, confessing to a string of murders. After the first one, he couldn't stop. Killing had become his solution for when he didn't get what he wanted. It had made him feel powerful, taking what he'd believed was owed to him, from man and woman alike. When he'd gotten to what he'd taken from the women before he'd killed them, Caroline stopped him.

"I've heard enough from your vile mouth. Angus?" With a flick of her fingers, Angus brought forth a burgundy velvet pillow from a pedestal he stood behind. Atop it sat a looming threat.

This was the punishment which fed much of the gossip and Johnneth was about to witness it firsthand. Though he tried, he wasn't strong enough to shield the cringe that overtook his features. The man had destroyed the lives of a sizable number of people, he reminded himself. He would get a death sentence in either kingdom.

"Are you ready for your punishment, killer?" Caroline rose from the throne and sauntered over to the pillow Angus held, picking up the long dagger by the blade. At a dramatic pace, she stepped down the stairs toward Samuel, and he followed a step behind. Johnneth turned to Angus for a clue, but an amused grin was playing across his face. *Gods.* Was he the only rational one in this room? This was madness.

Caroline extended the blade to Samuel. "Since you like killing so much, I figure you'd prefer to do it yourself."

Samuel's body was convulsing, his fear etched into the deepening worry lines of his face as he stared down at his fate.

"Go on, take it." Caroline thought Samuel's hand up, wrapping his stubby fingers around the hilt of the weapon. All anyone could do was watch.

"Do it over there." She gestured to the side of the room opposite the windows where benches had been cleared away. "I have more petitioners today and I don't want them to have to stand in a pool of your blood." She compelled the man to walk to the spot where an old rust-colored stain darkened the stones.

Caroline positioned him right over it and took her time, drawing it out, making the man raise the blade and point it toward his own heart. This was a part of the punishment, too. The sheer dread the anticipation created.

Samuel impaled himself with sick fascination, the sharp tip sliding in easily. Caroline had done this before, *many times*, knowing right where to aim the blade so it wouldn't become obstructed on a rib. Thinking of his father, his stomach turned as sweat beaded on his upper lip. He struggled with the memories until they became a distant flicker in his mind once again.

The killer slumped lifelessly to the floor, his skull cracking as it smashed against the rock. Blood spread from both wounds, mirroring the old smear.

"Git rid of the body," Angus commanded. Guards hurried to grab the body under his shoulders and drag him from the room, leaving a bloody trail behind his boots.

Caroline didn't address the accuser or glance back at him again before she called, "Next."

The case following the murder was a child abuse allegation. Johnneth had never seen her quite so shaken as when the mother had shown her the little girl's battered arms and back. Before the mother could tell her more of the horrors the girl had endured at the hands of the man who was supposed to be her greatest protector, Caroline had swiftly issued the sentence.

By all outward appearances, the queen made it look like she wanted to get on with the proceedings, but Johnneth was beginning to suspect that the well-being of children was the cruel queen's one soft spot. She had spared the child the horror of having to relive the abuse, immediately reading the situation.

She promised support for the teary mother until she was able to get on her feet, the mother, who was profusely grateful to the queen for believing her. So, the scribe had handed the mother the order, and they left the oratory. The husband would never see the light of day again, but the mother had glanced at the spill of blood to her left more times than Johnneth could count and begged Caroline to punish, but not *kill* the child's father. Caroline had complied with the woman's wishes.

"One more, right?" she addressed Angus, who nodded. "Next."

A burly black-haired man with a thick mustache stormed into the Great Hall, dragging a petite sable haired woman, his fat hand gripped around her bicep.

Caroline raised a single eyebrow. "I would suggest you release her, your wife, is it?"

The man's upper lip curled up, but he let go of the woman.

"It's been a long day, so I don't suggest you try my patience." Her head drifted toward a rose-vine surrounded window. A raven was perched on the ledge, waiting for an opportunity to inspect the scent of death for a meal.

"By your not-so-subtle behavior, I assume you are the accuser, and she is the accused?"

"That's right, Your Majesty." The man sank to his knees, lowering his eyes to the ground.

"Rise and explain." Caroline leaned forward, resting an elbow on her crossed knees, then her chin on her fist, her other mindlessly rubbed her lower back.

"My wife has a lover. And she refused my advances. That's how I knew. She's been visiting another man's house when I'm not home, so I followed her."

"Accused, step forward." The fatigue had settled in Caroline's voice and the woman obeyed. She scanned the woman. A faded yellow and green mark showed on her cheekbone, and Johnneth could see red marks around the woman's neck. The queen had seen them, too, because her jaw had clenched as her eyes traveled over them.

"You believed your wife was having an affair, so instead of approaching the crown with your petition for a divorce, you stole my job from me. Is that it? You've decided the verdict and punished your wife on my behalf?" Venom was in her gaze toward the man.

"No, Your Majesty, I would never." He waved his hands in front of his chest as he proclaimed his innocence.

"If you were going to lie about it, you should have at least waited until your wife's body could no longer tell the truth." Caroline stood once again and marched down to the woman, stopping when she was a foot from her. Being her personal guard, he again mirrored her coming up feet behind her left shoulder. Only the three of them could hear the hushed conversation.

"Tell me what is going on," Caroline urged. "Speak freely."

The woman's lip trembled, and she fidgeted with a loose lock of her hair. "I was sneaking food to a neighbor. My husband wouldn't approve of giving our food away, and I didn't think I'd get caught. See, my neighbor, he's old and fell. He hurt his back and was having trouble getting around. So, I brought over some ingredients and would cook him lunch. Just soup mostly, and I'd bring bread sometimes, too. But one day, the day Al followed me, my neighbor's younger son had come while I was there. I didn't do anything, I swear. We're both married and he was only checking on his father. But when Al burst through the door—" Tears streaked down her face, and she raised a hand to her throat, hiding the marks.

"I believe you."

Johnneth struggled to stare straight ahead. The gravity of the queen pulled his head in her direction. She wasn't compelling the woman, which meant she really did believe her.

"Al, step forward and join your wife," the queen commanded.

The man confidently strode up to meet Caroline. He raised a justified chin, ready to hear his wife's sentence.

"Let me see your hand." His brow furrowed in confusion, but he obeyed, placing his thick hand on her outstretched palm.

Caroline squeezed. "Your wife was not lying, and she did not soil your wedding vows."

Relief and regret flashed across Al's face. "But—"

"So, you will be the one receiving my punishment."

Al gasped as the queen slashed the little knife she wore on her thumb across the back of his hand. His eyes peeled back in shock, and he stumbled a step back, cradling his injured fist to his chest.

Caroline grinned as she pricked her finger with the blade, mingling their blood. "If you ever lay a hand on your wife again, for a real or imagined wrong, I will hurt you, and you won't see it coming. Do you understand me?"

She lifted her hand, a long black sleeve of the gown she wore draping in an arch from her body, making an impressive silhouette. The flapping of wings drew his attention and the raven which had been perched on the window was swooping down toward the queen.

Johnneth started to draw a sword to protect her from the crazed bird, but she placed her other hand on his, stilling him. Warmth tingled where their skin connected, and he swallowed the knot it had caused.

The raven landed on her forearm, and she brought it down below her breast, stroking the glossy feathers. He didn't know what to think of what he was witnessing. She was just and terrifying, and so much worse than he'd imagined, yet somehow so much better. Johnneth shook his head, trying to clear his confounding thoughts.

"If you harm her, I will know. My pets will watch you. There is nowhere you can go where I won't know. And I will come for you. Do you understand?"

A speechless Al nodded, eyes bulging wide as he took in the queen and the raven perched on her arm. His wife had plastered a hand across her gaping mouth and was taking barely notable steps backward away from the queen.

"If I was you, I'd spend the rest of your life begging your wife's forgiveness. Now leave me."

Caroline raised her arm in a swift motion and the raven darted for the nearest window, escaping into the approaching night.

CHAPTER 11

"**I** COULDN'T HAVE HAD the attendants make your bath extra hot?" Johnneth grumbled as he followed the queen down yet another staircase, having to bend low to keep from bumping his head. They'd walked together through the bowels of Roskide many times before, but never this deep. Absently, he wondered if this was where the vault of the treasury was, too. Only Caroline and Angus knew that location.

"Trust me, it will be worth it," she said, and took another turn. "Here we are."

Caroline pushed the wooden door open, and he followed her inside. The cavern looked natural, hewn by the flow of water from the mountain. It was hard to know in the tunnels under the castle what was carved by man versus the Gods.

Johnneth sat the satchel he'd been carrying down on one of four stone benches that were clearly hand hewn. He put the torch in a metal holder affixed to the wall, then pulled out the items Caroline had requested.

There was a small alcove to the side of the space which Caroline headed toward after she'd snatched a towel. "Don't set the wine on the bench. It will heat it and ruin it," she instructed and slipped behind the rock lip. Her shoes plopped to the floor as she took them off.

Johnneth touched his hand to the stone bench. Sure enough, it was hot, but not enough to burn. The perfect temperature to soothe tense muscles and he understood why she'd wanted to visit the spring. She still ached from the payment the Gods had extracted from her the night before. He couldn't believe it when she didn't cancel the Petitions which began early that morning.

Opening the wine, Johnneth poured her a glass, then corked it and set it on top of an extra towel.

"Through here," her smooth voice echoed across the stones. He followed it around a corner, which opened into a slightly bigger space, tall enough so he could stand at full height.

"Gods, Caroline," he swore, almost jumping back at the shred of a towel that was flimsily secured around the queen. She smiled over her shoulder at him, a devious glint to her eye, then dropped the towel, tossing it to the side, but keeping her back toward him. Her hips swayed, commanding his attention as she moved closer to the little pool, the curving silhouette of her body better than any dream he might have had.

"What are you doing?" He swallowed, thankful that he wasn't being admonished for using her name.

Caroline moaned as she dipped a toe in the steaming pool in front of her. The metallic liquid rippled, rings of water reflecting the light for the torch she'd moved into the room, reverberating away from where she'd entered the water.

The small pool wasn't big enough for more than two or three people. He was transfixed as Caroline fully submerged herself in the dark water, then rose, pushing her soaked black locks away from her face.

"It's not like you haven't seen a woman before, Johnneth. Angus told me about your little romp with the castle girl."

He repressed a groan. Angus had told on him. And he had been with other women. Plenty of them. But he'd never seen a woman who controlled the heat of his blood with the slightest effort like Caroline did.

Resting her elbows on the warm stones, she beckoned for him to hand the glass of wine to her. "There's no one down here to protect me from, Johnneth. Feel free to join me." Caroline splashed the water beside her. "I promise I won't look." A feral grin crossed her face.

Just because she is inviting you into the water doesn't mean she wants anything more. You don't want anything more either. How did she always get the upper hand in these situations? His visit to Kelsey wasn't paying off nearly as much as he'd hoped it would, and he clamped down on the male urges trickling into his awareness.

Sweat beaded on Johnneth's skin, and he glanced down to see the dampness collecting on his loose tunic and trousers as it ran down his body. Damn this steamy room. The rosenwood dagger was tucked inside his pants in the hidden pocket he'd fixed, but if his clothing clung to his skin any more, it might expose the weapon's location. He could pass it off as something for her protection, but what if she asked to see it?

"Fine," he said, then went to the other room to strip and collect his own towel. And of course, hide the dagger in the satchel he'd brought.

"More wine," she called.

He ran a hand across his buzzed head. This was completely inappropriate, which on one hand was ideal for his plan to up the odds, but if Angus hadn't left and somehow found out, his ruse would be over. Johnneth tucked his towel around his waist and grabbed the bottle, resigned to his soak with the queen. He set the bottle on the folded-up towel next to her as he poured her another glass.

To his surprise, Caroline bobbed over to the other side of the pool with her glass and turned to the wall. Johnneth narrowed his eyes at her, fully expecting her to turn around. But she never did as he dropped the towel and slipped into the water.

"You didn't peek," he said, not sure if he should be offended that the glimpse of his torso hadn't tempted her.

"You're disappointed," she said, turning around to face him, leaning against the opposite wall. The tops of her breasts were visible right above the surface, and like a bad guard, his eyes strayed toward them. He had to mechanically raise his eyes to meet hers.

"No, I only thought you might."

"One thing you'll learn about me, Johnneth, is I'm not a liar. You can count on what I tell you to be true, and I will always hold to my word. Even if it isn't what you'd think. No matter how *tempting* it might be."

The scorching heat in her gaze made him glad his lower half was beneath the water, as the queen seemed content not to act upon their mutual desires. Being with her this close and unclothed was too much of a temptation, and she knew it. He could see the amusement that played in her eyes. For now, he could play along, and perhaps have a little fun too.

Caroline ran her fingers through the water, watching the little waves she created, letting the heat between them dissipate. "I've been thinking. I could grant you time off to visit your family when Angus gets back."

If he weren't leaning against the lip of the pool, he surely would have fallen back at the generous gesture. "But I haven't been serving you for long enough," he stuttered, trying to think of any excuse for her not to grant him leave.

"Not directly, but five years is a long time to go without a visit. You seemed like you missed them."

Shit. That was more thoughtful than he expected from her and not at all what he'd intended. "I'd love to see them, and I appreciate your kindness, but I'm getting the hang of my rotation. Maybe after a year, I'll be more comfortable." Then a thought occurred to him, and he let a sensual grin play across his face. "If I were to leave so soon, I wouldn't want you to replace me."

Caroline nodded. "Very well." Perhaps it was a good sign that this man who clearly missed his family preferred to stay near her. Watching Johnneth walk into the stone cavern wearing a towel and carrying a bottle of wine was a sight she could get used to. His muscles flexed across his towering frame with every stalking step he took. The man moved like an animal, and she could see how he'd passed Angus's tests with such ease.

Johnneth scratched his nose, which was a perfect pyramid, straight, regal and a little square down the ridge. It made his sharp cheekbones and his deep-set eyes staring at her beneath a strong brow stand out. What would his hair be like if he let it grow out from the tight cut all the guards wore? Straight, wavy?

"Can I ask you a question?" Johnneth said, eyeing her as she studied him.

"Have I ever denied your curiosity?" she answered. His inquisitive nature was one of the many things she found appealing about him. And he was always asking her questions.

He lowered beneath the water, then rose and shook the water from his scalp, like he was stalling to consider his words. "That thing you did with the raven..."

Caroline raised her eyebrows, waiting.

"You don't actually communicate with them, right?"

She had taken a sip of her wine and promptly spit it out as a laugh expelled itself from her belly. Johnneth grinned, then he laughed too. Once they'd started, they didn't stop until tears were streaming from Caroline's eyes. Gods, he was attractive when he laughed. His smile lines deepened, and she wanted to run her fingers across them. Wanted to kiss that mirthful, parted mouth and swallow the happy sound that came out of it.

"I've never actually done that before... Wasn't even sure it would work. I don't know what I was thinking. Can you imagine what the rumors will be now?"

"Everstal's Cruel Queen controls man and beast alike," Johnneth announced, egging on her giggle fit. The carefree way she laughed made her look like a woman, more human in a way, not like the storied queen she was. The radiance on her face lit by the sconce on the wall drew him in. He wanted to thread his hands through all that hair and pull her to him. *Mine.* As the thought came and went, he wasn't entirely sure he'd had it. Like a fading memory of a dream briefly remembered after waking but burned away with the rising sun.

"You know, I got a scolding by Angus after that, too. Somehow, I'm the queen, but my commander never hesitates to reprimand me." Caroline shrugged and narrowed her eyes in his direction, catching the change in his expression. The queen had learned his mannerisms in the few months he'd been with her, like now, how the space between his brows pinched as he considered what he wanted to ask her.

"Go on. Ask," she said.

"You and Angus, you never, you know..." Johnneth started.

"Had sex? Got involved romantically? Is that what you mean to ask?"

"I'm sorry if that is too personal." He shifted uncomfortably and eyed the exit as he awaited her response.

"No, it was never like that between us. Angus found me when I was fourteen, after my father and his wife had been assassinated. He'd been following me through the halls as I snuck my way around, trying to assess the damage they'd done. Then one day decided to make his presence known. He was the grounding force that gave me the strength to rebuild. Everyone had abandoned the castle or been murdered. His father was among the dead, Torac, my father's commander, so we bonded over that. But that is all. He's my dearest friend." Her only friend was the truth he suspected.

"The only thing that was left of my father was a bloodstain." Caroline shook her head. "I don't like to relive the memories."

"No, of course not. Thank you for sharing what you did." Johnneth's eyes burned as he imagined the pain the adolescent princess must have experienced. His mission became harder when he thought of the child she once was.

A bolt of fear struck through him, and he turned away. He pressed himself up out of the water, not worrying about hiding his body from her. Snatching his discarded towel, he rushed to the entry room and dried himself off. "I'll be waiting whenever you're ready to leave. Take your time, Your Majesty."

He quickly got dressed and fished the drops from his bag, placing two in each of his eyes. The familiar sting faded in a few seconds, and he breathed a sigh of relief. Johnneth wrapped the dagger in the used towel, stuffing it into the satchel and assumed his position by the door to wait for the queen.

⟡

With Angus gone, Caroline was more at ease to 'misbehave' as she deemed it. Unfortunately, this only served to make her more appealing over the past two weeks. He needed to do this before she had him any deeper under her spell. He shifted the rosenwood dagger around to his back pocket and gave a little wish to the heavens, to his ancestors they would guide his hand and his tongue. It was the latter he would need to lull this queen into a state of vulnerability.

"Close your eyes," she demanded, her flirtatious voice more tempting than required. He was days, if not minutes, from being hers. From claiming her for himself like an uncharted territory conquered and relishing in the spoils. Johnneth exhaled and shut his eyes. Her soft fingertip traced across his lips sending gooseflesh across his skin. "Open."

His body responded, eager to obey her command. She slipped a round sugary object into his mouth, which caused his mouth to salivate. He chewed and swallowed whatever she'd fed him.

"You can open now and guess what that was!" Her voice was excited like a child's might have been on their birthday.

"You really love sweets, don't you?" She nodded. "Well, let's see," he played along. "Carmel, and the flavor of an apple, but rounded, and the inside was creamier than the outside. We must not have those where I'm from."

"It's a truffle. Isn't it divine?" She held up a tray of the toffee-colored treats to him, and he picked one up and gestured for her to open her mouth. He placed it between her parted lips, letting his pointer finger linger. She closed them around it and the evil creature sighed as she sucked the sugar off the tip.

He knew exactly the little game Caroline was playing. She was toying with him. He was going to play along and see how far it could get him.

The dagger burned hot in his pocket as she fed him another treat. Angus was due back tonight. His stomach flipped as he replayed what he needed to do in his mind.

He took the tray of sweets from her and set it to the side. Johnneth couldn't remove his eyes from her mouth and without thinking he raised his hand, cupping her cheek and a thumb was brushing against it. Her breath caught, but she leaned into his touch.

Johnneth could hardly breathe, his lungs seizing as he leaned his head dangerously close to hers. Caroline didn't pull away, though. He prayed to the Gods he wasn't about to foil everything and ate the last bit of distance between them, bringing their lips together in the gentlest way possible.

He wasn't sure if she'd shuddered or if it was him, but her mouth was so soft and inviting. He leaned in to deepen the kiss ever so slightly, terrified of scaring her off.

Caroline jerked back and covered her lips with her hand. A deep flush had taken root on her cheeks and a wave of horror flashed through him.

Oh no, she'd only been taunting him. The queen had never had any intention of taking anything further with him—he'd misplayed his hand. Five years of his life, and in a blink, he'd messed up everything.

"Caroline—I mean Your Majesty, I'm so sorry," he begged.

"Shhh, Johnneth. Not here, okay? Roskide is full of prying eyes." Caroline grabbed his hand, dragging him from the room.

Caroline knew it. The spark was there. Whatever was building between them had been the same for him, too, and when his lips had touched hers, it was like nothing she'd ever felt before. He'd been so gentle, timid even. Like his greatest concern in the world was her reaction. Gods, he was so beautiful and caring. Maybe those five ethereal demons didn't hate her after all, and the gift of this man was going to make up for all her suffering. She could only hope. Her heart squeezed, then thundered as she dragged him in the direction of her suite.

It was only chemistry, but with time, their banter might become so much more. She'd never felt such attraction and easy companionship with anyone. And she believed he felt it, too. When they were alone in her suite, away from the eyes of Roskide, she was hoping he'd kiss her again, igniting the wildfire that had eclipsed all reason.

Johnneth could barely center his thoughts as he followed her back to her rooms. *Now.* He had to do it now. He didn't know what he was deathly close to—he just knew it was something he'd never felt before and that it was looming before him for the taking. In the darkened hallways, he slipped the dagger from the hidden compartment and into his back pocket.

They were both breathless as they slipped through her doors, and she turned to him giddy, like she'd found out the juiciest secret. The joy on her face only made her that much more beautiful. And it wasn't only desire in her eyes. That on a woman, he would easily recognize. There was something else in her that was urging to be discovered.

It was a delicate balance he was waging now between his body and his mind. Firelight illuminated the woman before him, and he had to kiss her again. Not fuck her, or make love to her, just kiss her. That would be enough.

She stood still, watching him through wide-open eyes, waiting, giving him space to decide where to take this next. Her chest pumped up and down, betraying any calm she hoped to project.

Every step toward her was an eternity, like wading through thick mud, his legs becoming jelly with each step. Johnneth didn't know what was coming over him as he stared down at the queen, but it was so overwhelming it was almost painful.

Silver rimmed eyes with a faint glow at the edges beamed up at him, beckoning him to her. An image flashed through his mind, turning his blood to ice, and he had to use every ounce of his self-control not to let it slide across his features. The only other eyes that glowed from within like that were those of his family. The image of his father taking his own life, forced by her own father's power, sprung to the front of his mind. Gripping on to the memory like his life hung in the balance, he lowered his mouth to hers.

Caroline sensed the briefest moment of hesitation before his lips touched hers. Warmth flooded through her body, radiating not from below her belly, but from her chest. This was it, the spark she'd been waiting for. As Johnneth gave her the gentlest of kisses she thanked the Gods she'd never given into Angus's prescription that she should find a husband. Had she followed his advice, she'd have never found this, whatever was blooming between her and the most sinfully gorgeous man she'd ever laid her eyes upon.

His hand slid around her waist and ran slowly up her back, eliciting the best tingling sensations. Caroline was getting lost in every touch, every drawn-out nibble he placed on her lips. Johnneth nudged her mouth open with his tongue and her lips parted. Rapturous vibrations clouded every thought as she let him fully consume her, knowing his trembling meant that every sensation of hers was the mirror to his.

It was... *painful.* A sharp shooting pain tore her from the fantasy she was lost in. Someone attacked them while they were distracted. No, this was not how this was supposed to happen. Caroline peeled her eyes open and darted her awareness around the room, searching for the assassin. If she could get her awareness on them, this would be over.

But no one was there. Prickly panic flared, momentarily blurring her vision. It was only her and Johnneth. It couldn't be. Caroline's eyes flew to his. They were as wide as hers. Their heads simultaneously tracked down to her waist where a ruby-colored wooden dagger protruded, his nimble hand wrapped around its hilt. *Rosenwood.* A full blade made from the material was lodged in her flesh, right beneath her ribs.

Everything was a burning agony lashing out from her chest cavity. She wasn't sure what hurt more, her heart or the deadly wound inflicted upon her by the man who she thought might be the one.

He staggered back as if he were unable to believe he'd done it. Her eyes narrowed and she bared her teeth. She grabbed the dagger he'd embedded within her wincing as she gave it a testing tug. It was too painful to rip out. Red flashed across her vision, and she lunged forward, unleashing her rage. The tips of her nails dug into his forearms, dragging bloody red lines behind them. Johnneth shoved her back, and she slipped on a puddle of her own blood and her hip cracked on the stones.

As Caroline scrambled to her feet, two sensations hit her. The tingling that came on the wind before the Gods took her away and the chill that zipped through her when she'd mingled her blood with another's.

She had seconds before she was gone. Caroline would be back. She'd get the Gods to heal her, to save her life. Then she'd be back to deal with this traitor.

Her lips drew into a cruel slash as she felt the compulsion take hold.

CHAPTER 12

T HERE WAS SOMETHING ABOUT the look on the queen's face
that had made all his instincts scream, *Flee!* He couldn't believe
Caroline had vanished. He couldn't believe he'd done it. He'd killed her.
She would have been dead within moments, but they'd taken her before
he could confirm it.

Her face as she'd realized what he'd done, the horror, was an image he
would see on repeat, burned into the deepest recesses of his mind for
the rest of his life. He should be feeling grateful that he didn't even have
a body to clean up. If he ran into Angus, before he fled Roskide, he'd
be able to explain her disappearance easily. As he stood there trying to
calm his aggravated heart, he couldn't bring himself to feel thankful for
his stroke of luck. Instead, a trembling hollow ache was blooming in his
chest around the fear.

Johnneth's heart thundered, and he was hardly able to draw in a breath
as he surveyed the room. Step one, ignore the conflicting sensations at
war within his mind. Step two, take care of this mess—*her blood* which
pooled in a small circle at his feet. He rushed to clean the still warm liquid
from his hands and the floor, and threw the rags into the fireplace, which
they kept burning in her rooms at all hours this time of year. A dread he
couldn't shake soaked his mind as he watched to make sure there wasn't
a crimson stained fiber left in the hearth.

Satisfied, he'd filled a glass goblet with wine, then dropped it on the
floor, allowing it to splash his trousers, staining them for an alibi. He
sniffed the air, hoping it had masked the metallic scent of her blood,
which still lingered. Once he was convinced he covered his tracks, he

slipped from her room and hurried down the corridor heading in the direction of the attendant's section of the castle.

He threw together a quick pack of rations and stole a cloak which had been discarded in a storeroom. A few more flights of stairs and he'd made it to the entrance on the lowest level the attendants used reporting for duty. He nodded to the guards, who recognized him immediately. "Night off," he said, and passed through the door.

He made it across the yard, to the outer wall. The man stationed there, recognizing him, pushed the iron grate outward, and it swung open. "Thanks," he murmured, blood racing. He'd done it—killed the queen and got out of the castle alive.

A wave of nausea rolled over him, and he staggered. He turned back to the guard and tried to give him a reassuring grimace. She'd compelled him. That was what the icy energy zipping through his blood had been. He forced his body into the first alley he came across and fell to his knees. He could almost laugh that a punishment had been her final act.

Johnneth could hardly think as he stumbled down the alley, her shocked glowing silver eyes a haunt in his mind obscuring the path before him. A few more steps and he was on his knees again. The further he got from Roskide, the sicker he became. Still, he crawled forward. He'd crawl all the way to Veetula if that's what it took to get away from here. His stomach clenched, then he was spewing up its contents. Bile and the remnants of the sugary truffles splashed on the worn stones beneath his palms.

He scrambled back a few feet, and the nausea eased. Testing the limit, he advanced, and again he was vomiting on the alley floor. Gasping in giant breaths, he pushed himself backward and pressed his back against the building right inside the alley. He couldn't get more than a few yards beyond the castle walls without illness incapacitating him. Caroline had confined him to Roskide. She probably had faith Angus would eventually sniff him out. Deliver the punishment she hadn't had time to do.

Wait. She could have compelled him to throw himself from the nearest window. Take the dagger and end his life right then, but in the split second before she vanished, she'd decided to keep him there, *alive.*

He shuddered. It was like she sensed she'd be back and wanted to deal with him herself.

Dread lanced through his mind, almost making him need to hurl again.

He didn't know how long he stood in that alleyway collecting his thoughts, but eventually, he peeled himself off the wall and made his way back to Roskide.

"Back so soon?" the guard said, eyeing him.

"Changed my mind," he answered, hoping the man couldn't see his sallow skin, the telltale sign of fighting the queen's compulsion. He supposed he could chalk it up to food poisoning. He'd certainly retched enough.

"Angus made it back yet?" he asked the man as he approached the attendant's entry.

"I believe he's due within the hour." The guard stepped aside, allowing Johnneth to pass through unhindered.

Good. He sighed internally. That would give him time to get his composure before he needed to inform Angus of her visit to the Gods. He had to keep up the ruse, since he was confined to this castle.

If she never returned, Angus couldn't suspect him, and maybe he could have some influence over the fate of the kingdom in limbo without its queen. She had trusted him, and her commander might too. A guilty twang bit at his conscience. The worst case he could envision was being sent from Roskide by Angus on some mission and being discovered when he was unable to leave the confines of its walls.

Once back to the relative security of his room, he pulled his shirt off, tossed it aside, and surveyed the scratch marks on his forearms. They were shallow but had drawn enough blood for Caroline's compulsion to take hold.

A few inches of water was in the basin on his dresser. Scooping up a handful, he splashed it on his face. The crisp water cleared his head immediately. His eyes shot to himself in the mirror. Could a Dallimore's compulsion survive them? If Caroline was dead, how was he still resigned to the castle? He watched his reflection as the color slowly drained from his cheeks.

PART THREE –

THE IVORY ROSE

CHAPTER 1

C AROLINE BLINKED AWAY WHAT were the last moments of her
life. For surely this was the end. She still wrapped her slim fingers
around the rosenwood dagger. Her hand was too pale and red poisoned
veins spidered out from where Johnneth had driven it into her.

Johnneth. She shook her head. Anything that beautiful had to be a
fiction. She should have known. That kiss couldn't have been real either,
though it had cracked that obsidian wall that kept her safe.

The dagger would kill her. They'd won. Veetula would take her
kingdom, even if Angus freed Emmy and let her reign. Her sister wasn't
clever enough to keep them at bay. When she died, would her imprisoned
sister inherit the Gift, or would it die with her and Everstal would be no
more? A part of her preferred the Gift to die than go to that traitor. Even
after ten years, she still resented her sister.

A scream bit from her lips as she wrenched the dagger free. The
gnawing chasm where the blade had been seared and the wound's fiery
edges curled outward. Caroline's knees hit the white marble floor with
a crack she didn't feel. Her awareness, too, consumed with the death
creeping through her body to feel a minor stab of pain.

White marble.

Her gaze shot up to the five Gods who sat on their benches around
her in a semicircle, watching her life slowly seeping away. Caroline forced
herself to get to her feet. She hated them in that moment more than
she hated anything. Even the man who'd killed her. He at least believed
he served some sort of loyal purpose. The Gods were just voyeurs who

found their satisfaction in the misery of humans like her. She refused to let them see her so defeated.

"You're going to just watch me die? You could heal me." Caroline hated the pleading in her voice. Hated that she needed what only the Gods could give. She longed to be back in Everstal. She'd sit through days of Petitions, fight through the mountains of paperwork that ruling required if she had the chance. She never balked at it. It was what she lived to do.

"Why do you think we brought you here, daughter?" Life said, her ethereal voice as low as Caroline had ever heard it. They weren't pleased. *Good*, she wasn't pleased either.

A chill swept across Caroline's skin, a thread of power from Life sent to stall her death.

Fury reddened her vision as she studied the unmoving beings. Only Death sat glowering. The others had impassive blankness scrawled across their androgynous features. If they planned to save her, they sure weren't acting like it.

Caroline was used to pain. It had become a friend, a constant in a strange way. Dying, or it was the reaction her body had with the rosenwood—this pain was unlike anything she'd experienced before. Every thread of her being vibrated with lightning-fast shocks of electricity, so hot they eclipsed fire, as they danced through her insides. It was like burning alive with the power of a thunderclap.

She reached up and touched her wet cheek. Caroline pulled her sleeve up, cursing the silken fabric that would be a poor tool to soak up the tears that sprung unbidden from her eyes. The sultry gown she'd worn to tempt him. Her mind kept drifting back to her murderer. Something about it didn't sit right with her. Aside from the obvious.

"Daughter, what a mess you've found yourself in." Justice's robes rustled as their arms crossed.

"I don't need your sympathy. Either heal me or put me back in Everstal and let me die." Every word Caroline ground out was a new misery.

"We can't let you die. It would offset the delicate balance we've worked so hard to *encourage*."

Caroline regarded them through her glassy eyes and staggered to the ground next to the fallen weapon, unable to command her legs to function.

Justice frowned down at the struggling queen. "To be honest, we thought you'd eventually sniff the prince out. You are still so young."

"I hoped you'd bed him," Love cooed.

"Well, I was trying to bed him, and you see how that worked out." Pain chuckled.

Caroline's mind caught on something they'd said. She sifted through the conversation between claps of agony. "Wait, what? The prince?" she bit out.

"See, I told you she didn't know." Justice smirked in Love's direction.

"Oh, but her heart did. I knew the moment she was born they were the perfect match. They just needed to collide. Like two roaring rivers merging."

"You did predict it, Love. Though I would say it was more like a tsunami overtaking a village. I didn't expect it to get so exciting so quickly," Life chimed in.

Caroline supposed she was the village in this scenario, considering her current position. She hated that they were gossiping about her while she lay there in the throes of death. She was powerless to stop them. Or stop the face that appeared in her mind.

A prince. She ran through the list of the men of Veetula's royal line.

A name traipsed across the long-forgotten visage in her mind. The man she'd seen only glimpses of as a child during the last peace celebration, which had ended in bloodshed. He'd been there, the one from afar, standing next to his older brother, King Hollis. She'd barely gotten enough of a look at him for his image to stick in her memory. Especially after the trauma she'd experienced that night. And anyone in the castle who might identify him, dead.

The name floated like a cloud on her last dregs of consciousness before the darkness consumed her.

Prince Breicher Ivanslohe.

Violent coughing wracked Caroline's body. Her hands snapped to her throat, nails clawing at the liquid metal that was being poured down her throat. Firm hands gripped hers and pulled them down to her sides.

She wasn't dead. Not yet. Pale, hollow faces came into view as her vision cleared. She must have passed out. It was the first time she'd ever seen them all leave their perches on the benches. All five were kneeling around her body, pouring their energy into her.

Caroline had thought the healing might feel like a crisp, gentle stream flowing through her. Instead, lava poured down her windpipe, spreading beneath her ribs, then fanning out to her extremities. Her back involuntarily bowed off the ground on a scream before she slammed back into it.

"Can you not do something? I need her still." It was Life snapping at Pain. She'd never seen them have such emotion.

"Even if I could ease her suffering, I wouldn't. She's a vile creature." Pain paused, then flicked his eyes to Love. "You do something."

Love, who'd been staring mindlessly into the distance, with only a hand on Caroline, sighed. "I'll see what I can do. Are we sure we wouldn't prefer to let her die and give the power to the other girl?"

Caroline tilted her neck back, straining her eyes to get a look at Justice, who was chuckling above her head. "I think we'd miss this one. She's proven to be far more enjoyable to watch than the ones before her. She's very... creative. I think I've become inspired."

"Then Love, please," Life beckoned.

Love shrugged and crawled across Caroline's convulsing body. "We didn't have to make the rosenwood so strong. I cautioned you against that." Love shot a glare at Pain. The Gods must not understand that Caroline was not only awake, but conscious and privy to their lapse in protocol. She was seeing behind the carefully constructed façade, which was the only view they'd allowed her to see when she visited them to receive her punishments.

The God Love lowered themselves down onto Caroline's body, their slight weight, and the gentle power that was fighting her pain enough to ease the worst of the tremors. Love cupped her hands around Caroline's face. Leaning on her elbows, she looked down into the queen's eyes.

"Daughter, are you in there? You must fight this. I'm going to do what I can to help you."

Caroline fluttered her lashes, making a show of her incoherence.

"She's lost in her mind. I told you if you wanted her to live, we shouldn't have let it go on as long as we did."

Love didn't seem to care one way or the other whether Everstal's queen lived or died. The annoyance temporarily distracted Caroline from the blistering pain. An idea slipped through the break.

The God's power floating through her body felt terribly similar to the Gift. If she could take just a little of that power, compel Love to give some up, she could heal herself. Maybe even prevent the Gods from stealing her way to punish her for using the Gift they themselves had granted her family line.

Caroline sensed Love was the easiest target, perched across her like she was. Pitiless pale eyes stared down over, only a foot from her face. This close she could see they weren't pupilless. White centers, nearly the color of the pale irises around them, pulsed with an inhuman glow.

Another scalding wave crashed through her. She had to get ahold of the pain. As she fought, more of Love's power flooded into her, a chill against the scorching heat. Seizing the moment, Caroline pulled on her own threads, heaving them up from the depths of her core and unleashed everything she had at Love. What the Gods didn't know was the will the steely woman they had helped create possessed. No one would be so bold as to attack a God. But Caroline was.

Give it to me.

A new agony rocketed through her, whiting out her vision. It was Love's power. Her compulsion had worked. And it wasn't the trickle she'd intended to take. It was a flood.

Love stiffened, fighting against Caroline's desire, but it was too late. The queen had caught her off guard, had her compulsion sunk deep into the God's mind and was forcing her to expel all their power out. Caroline was becoming stronger with each drop. When she had taken everything, she released the pale creature. Love's eyes had lost that unearthly glow, and they raised a hand to their mouth, scrambling off Caroline.

A fearful Love would alert the others to her newly formulating scheme. A thought, and Caroline froze Love and forced the powerless God to re-approach the others still kneeling over healing her and speak.

Love's voice quavered. "She's no longer in pain. Our daughter will rest now."

Caroline kept her hold on Love, as she used her power to send a compulsion to Pain and Justice.

Feed me your power. Release it into me.

Their arrogance shielded her from their suspicion. They stiffened, shock bleeding from their features as she slipped in unnoticed. Justice rattled as he fought her control, teeth clenched. Seething. With Love's power, and the energy she was siphoning in from Pain, it was too late. Like it had happened with Love, excruciating seconds of white-hot energy licked through her, and she relished it. Holding on, she drained them to a husk. The power funneling into her was making her heady, and she moaned at the sensation.

Life and Death looked up at their fellow Gods in alarm right as Love slumped to the ground. Or her white robes did. The two remaining Gods and Caroline stared as Justice and Pain shriveled up and disintegrated before their eyes, drifting through a swirling breath of air to the edges of the vacant space until they were no more.

Before, the Gods had suffered no consequences for their torments. They would pay the ultimate price for it now, at Caroline's hand.

Armed with her new power, she came to her feet and turned her attention to the remaining two.

"How could you?" Life breathed.

A wicked grin tore across Caroline's face. Life was all too easy to take. She batted Death's hold away as she accepted what Life unwillingly gave her, reveling in the anguish. "You've earned this. For hundreds of years, you tortured my ancestors, my father, for using the power you gave us."

"What you asked for was too great," Life spit between gasps.

"Then why did you allow us to have it?"

"We were bound to give it to you. When the kingdoms were separated, we vowed to arm each with one power, anything of their choosing. What the first King Ivanslohe chose wasn't an overreach. Your ancestors were too bold. There had to be a balance."

"And your family accepted the bargain willingly, daughter," Death cut Life off. "Still, it wasn't enough. Your ancestors used it, accepting the consequences far too easily. We feared we'd created a monster too powerful to tame. You needed a leash."

"So, you created the rosenwood tree and gave it to the Veetula royals." Caroline swallowed, looking at the crumpled white robes at their feet.

"We did. It was the threat they needed to keep your ancestors at bay." Death's jaw flexed as they ground their teeth. "Now I see you've become the monster we were afraid of."

Caroline laughed. "You have no idea."

Life thudded to the striated white stones, then followed the others into oblivion as dust.

Death studied his fallen companion's robes. "I won't be so easy to claim, daughter."

A wind whipped around Caroline, and a new torment rode on its wake. Her chest drew to the sky, feet lifting off the ground as Death's power ripped through her. A scream unleashed itself. She fought back, willing him to stop the onslaught. As their powers clashed, his hold on her was released and she crashed to the ground.

Glancing up from her hands and knees at the God looming before her, she shot out a new web, trying to wrangle control of every cavern of their mind. A thought occurred to her. Caroline narrowed her eyes as she stared up at the God.

"You said when our 'kingdoms were separated.' They weren't always separated? Who separated them?" Her mind raced alongside her aching heart. Caroline brought both hands over her mouth, unable to hide her shock. "It was you. The Gods created the rift between our kingdoms. The hate, the distrust that have existed through the generations. That was you who sowed it?"

Death sneered, not denying it. "Sometimes endless time is not a gift."

"You started a war, endless bloodshed, because you were bored?!" Caroline was enraged. She had known their ways, how they toyed with her. But she'd been so shortsighted to their duplicity. And no one, until her—right now, knew the fate they had set in motion. She had to make it out of this hellscape. She couldn't allow Death to rule the heavens alone. Caroline didn't know how, but she would right their wrongs. And if Prince Breicher knew this, *maybe*—she yanked that seed before it could take and let her rage overtake her anew.

Her hands shot out and wrapped themselves around the pale throat in front of her. Death swung spindly arms, pinwheeling backward at the attack. Caroline and Death tumbled backward, the God's head a wet smack against the hard stones.

Caroline straddled the last of the Gods, wringing the life from their body. Death clawed down her arms as they battled, but her fury fueled her power. She hit them with another charge of compulsion and savored the pain as it burst into her awareness as Death relinquished the last inkling.

The Queen of Everstal beamed as she extinguished Death.

Caroline awoke sprawled across a craggy hillside, which met a small plateau at the base of a mountain. She recognized the terrain as Everstal. The old mountain range ran for endless miles through the kingdom near the coast. Even as high as she was, she couldn't see the small summit on which Roskide sat from her vantage point.

A vague memory of stumbling down from the peak in the middle of the night, getting bruises and cuts from the ragged terrain, flashed through her memory. Caroline had been so exhausted she must have collapsed where she currently rested. She didn't know how much time had passed since she arrived dying at the feet of the Gods.

That was the funny thing about time when she was with them—it seemed to distort and sway. Sometimes when she returned, it had been hours, sometimes days. And that was by far the longest she'd been in their realm. A realm she wasn't sure still existed, as it spit her out somewhere above the clouds.

Her chest rumbled at the vision of herself appearing in a blink, like a hero in the old stories, reborn upon the zenith of a mountain. She would not be a God who would save them, though, gracefully delivering them from themselves. But she wouldn't be the monster they thought she was, either.

She could sense the new energy thrumming through her veins. The mighty power she had taken from the wicked Gods as she'd brought each of them under her will, compelling them to transfer their power to her. Their power and their life drained from them in an achingly slow procedure, though only moments had elapsed.

Caroline had been done with their punishments, their games. She'd hated them for years now. Without their power, the Gods were withered husks of entities. One by one, they dried up and floated away on the breeze. She didn't regret it.

Tiny knives stabbed a thousand pricks across her skin. Caroline tried to jerk upright at the sensation, but it only made the pain louder. She was lying on her back and out of the corner of her eye the low-lying shrubs surrounding her came into her vision. This close, the sharp spines which decorated the plant were angled toward her in attack mode.

Hadn't she been through enough? She couldn't shake it. The spines had driven into her body when she'd passed out and her flesh had healed around them. A cry bit from her lips as she pulled herself free, dragging herself to her feet.

Caroline twisted and took account of her torn back, which was rapidly healing. Her black silk gown was in tatters, and she grabbed a handful of her long hair. It was stark white. Not cream or silver, but colorless white, like the clouds she stared up at. She pulled the rest of her locks around her shoulders, assessing. It was all that way.

What had she done? Caroline surveyed her hands. They were still the same creamy color she was used to. What had she turned herself into?

The queen surveyed the land before her. There was a small village nestled into the hillside which she guessed was only a few hours' walk away. A little church steeple stood above the roofline, the five-pointed star, the symbol of the five Gods proudly reaching to the heavens.

Caroline rolled her eyes and took tentative steps across the rocks as she began her journey home.

CHAPTER 2

THE VILLAGERS GAVE CAROLINE the white gelding she was riding and the flowing robes she wore, along with a pack full of rations. They'd offered to send a messenger for a carriage for their queen. The rumor was that the queen had been missing for a month now. No Petitions had been held, and no one had laid eyes on her since.

A holy man had recognized her immediately when she entered the church and fell to his knees before her, murmuring something about a goddess walking before him. She'd accepted the man's reverence, and took his and the other villager's offerings, knowing word of her would travel fast. She needed to get back to Roskide faster, so she allowed the guide now escorting her through the mountain passes.

When they arrived at her home, she would award the man handsomely, along with the loyalty shown to her by the villagers. Caroline let a grin slip across her face, hidden beneath the white hood of the robes, staving off the crisp mountain wind. *If they only knew she'd destroyed their precious Gods.*

And she wasn't done. There was a certain prince who she had a score to settle with. Only a few more days. Then she could seek her retribution.

The gelding halted its trot as Caroline tugged on the reins right outside the city. She suspected she could vanish and reappear into Roskide, because the ability was how the Gods had brought her into their domain. But she was still gaining her strength back and was leery to use the power before she fully had control over it. And she needed this time to clear her mind.

She rode over to a rose-vine-covered wall. As she neared, each flower faded from a dark crimson to blush, then stark white. Caroline had been noticing the shift in the roses as they'd traveled, understanding it was her presence that was causing the bleaching. No other flowers had changed color, however. Only the flower that was the symbol of her heritage.

Caroline snapped off a rose, then shed its thorns with her nails. She pulled several more off the wall, then quickly wove them into a coronet, using flowers in every state of bloom. When she was pleased with the result, she placed it upon her head and entered the city.

Gasps and whispers erupted as the queen passed through the streets, as she intended. Caroline kept her hood thrown back so the people of Everstal could look upon her. They fell to their knees as she passed, staying there long after, and the rosebush plantings that littered window boxes and hedges washed-out as she wound her way up the mountain to Roskide.

The news of her return made it to the castle faster than she did. Angus burst from the two outermost doors, the hinges screaming as they bore the impact. The exhausted animal she rode upon whined as her broad commander approached.

Warmth flooded her as she stared down at the man.

The feeling was erased as the man who'd called himself Johnneth gushed out the door on Angus's heel. Her compulsion had worked. In her last moments in her bedroom with him, she'd taken his blood, then compelled him to stay in the castle until she returned, in effect, trapping him there. It seemed he'd been able to convince Angus he'd had nothing to do with her disappearance.

"Your Majesty." Angus dropped to his knees. His shadow didn't bother, only stood behind him smirking, with his arms crossed over his chest. The Prince Breicher Ivanslohe's cocky stance couldn't hide the drained pallor of his skin, however. The towering man was at her mercy now, and that filled the queen with glee. Caroline wasn't sure how she wanted to carry out his punishment yet, but seeing him brought the eagerness to do so to the forefront of her emotional landscape.

Shifting her robes so they wouldn't impede her, Caroline dismounted, handing the road-worn animal off to a groomsman who'd followed her in. She shifted her weight from side to side, trying to bring life back into her dead legs while still looking queenly.

"Angus," she beckoned. He arose and approached her. Caroline threw her arms around the big man's neck, eliciting an intake of breath from the crowd which had chased her up the hill. "There were times I thought I'd never see your stubborn face again."

"Your Majesty, Johnneth said the Gods had whisked you away." Angus couldn't seem to stop himself from taking a handful of her white locks into his fist. "What happened?" His voice was full of foreboding.

Caroline whispered the answer so quietly only she, Angus, and the prince could hear. "We have a traitor in our mists."

Angus stiffened, and Breicher glared down at her.

"Come. We'll speak of it in private," she commanded, and entered the castle. Both Angus and Breicher trailed. When the door slammed shut behind her, she finally exhaled. She was home.

They wound their way through the twisting halls and staircases upward into the belly of Roskide in silence. They made it to the war room. Caroline ushered them inside and shut and barred the door. Spinning on her heel, she thrust the rosenwood dagger out, catching Breicher by surprise. She pressed the blade into his taut stomach. A small stain of red the size of a grape blossomed where the point pierced his skin.

"You got the blood cleaned up that fast? I'm impressed."

Angus's eyes went wide, and he froze for a moment before a thick hand thrust out, wrapping around the other man's neck, slamming him back against the wall. Caroline slipped out of the way just in time. The two men clashed, and Angus, though robust in his own right, was no match for the power blessed royal, and went flying back, hitting, and flipping over the heavy table in its center.

Caroline raised a hand, and Breicher froze under her will. "That wasn't necessary. If you've hurt him, I will hurt someone you love. You need to gain an understanding of me and what I am capable of with the same supernatural speed."

Angus had got to his feet and picked up the dagger she'd dropped in the commotion up off the floor, turning it in his hands. "He tried to assassinate you?" Realization striking, her commander collapsed to the floor. Angus placed his forehead to the stones. "Forgive me, Your Majesty. This is all my fault."

"Angus, rise."

He obeyed, and she clapped a hand on her oldest and only friend's shoulder. "Your Majesty," he stammered.

"Caroline," she clarified, not liking his new formal tone. A punishment he was evidently delivering himself. "You couldn't have known, Angus. There is nothing to forgive. And our Prince here knows not what he has unleashed."

"Of course, *Caroline*." Her name was a hesitant request in Angus's voice.

She nodded at him approvingly. "All is forgiven. What has transpired was all fated in the stars. We have much to discuss."

Caroline turned to the man who was still frozen in place. "Prince, in the meantime, please sequester yourself to the prison while I decide what to do with you."

She waved him off, ushering Angus to join her at the table, not watching to see Breicher shudder as he obeyed her will.

Breicher scrawled another mark into the stone wall he leaned against, marking the eighty-fifth day. Guards came and went, delivering him meals and disposing of his chamber pot. They didn't even bother to lock the cell he'd let himself into. Probably on instruction from Caroline, a taunt displaying her power, though he hadn't once heard mention of her.

Caroline, the queen who'd returned an otherworldly creature. Had she died and come back to life? And why did seeing her alive make him so achingly glad?

A shiver shook down his spine as images of her flashed through his mind. She was his waking nightmare and dream all at once and he startled awake many nights, her name a haunt on his lips. Maybe they were the same?

Cool stone greeted Breicher's aching head as he leaned against the wall and stretched out his long legs. He didn't know how much longer he could endure this cramped prison cell. His warrior body needed to move—to work. It was the Gift of the Gods and they meant him to use it.

How could he have failed so miserably? He'd struck her deep with the rosenwood dagger. She should have been dead.

Gods. Breicher ran a hand through his chestnut hair, which had grown out since he'd been imprisoned. What havoc was the queen wreaking?

As if he'd summoned her, her velvet voice drifted toward him. It was so smooth—had he'd fallen asleep?

"Come," she commanded, though he could not see her.

Breicher sprung to his feet, eager for whatever change of pace Caroline had planned. Even if it meant his death. It's what he deserved. He failed. The weight of his guilt churned just below the surface of his conscience. He let his brother down, he let his people down.

He pushed the metal door of his cell open and followed the sound of the queen's light footsteps down the hallway. He caught a glimpse of her white hair as she turned a corner. She was a ghost he followed, through twisting passageways, up countless stairs until they stopped before a doorway. It wasn't hers. But it was in the wing she claimed as her own.

She glanced back at him for the first time, then pushed the door open. Breicher followed her into the space, transfixed and not fully understanding what plan the queen was hatching.

The first room was a sitting area, much like hers. A deep blue velvet couch sat in the center with black and navy brocade chairs on either side of it. Ebony wooden tables were positioned on either side of them and a larger one was in the center.

Caroline passed through the room, and he followed her into the next, a bedroom fit for a king. The enormous four-poster bed was an ominous thing, deep black wood spiraling toward the arched ceiling. A deep navy silk quilt lay across it and a wrought iron grate twisted in sharp lines covering the massive fireplace.

He racked his memory, but he couldn't remember such a room being present in this castle before.

Caroline paused, stealing him from his thoughts. She pointed to another, smaller door. "Go bathe. You're foul." Her nose wrinkled, and she turned away.

Still under her will, Breicher marched toward the door, stealing a glance backward at the queen as he let himself into the chamber. What was she up to?

He lowered himself in the steaming water the queen had pre-prepared for him, relishing the bite of the heat, almost too hot. Filth, from almost ninety days in the prisons of Roskide floated to the surface as he quickly scrubbed. All vanity aside, he was glad to be clean. If he had to confront her, he'd rather it be when he was feeling his best. Looking his best, and he'd take every advantage she gave him. He swished the water so the little islands of grime wouldn't catch on his skin as he exited the tub.

A black towel was placed next to the sandalwood scented soaps on a teak bench. He snatched it, toweled off, then shaved away the dense hair concealing the hard line of his jaw. Quickly donning the loose silk pants and slinky velvet smoking jacket, which had been laid out for him, he assessed himself in the mirror. His reflection made his skin crawl. He despised the luxurious material given to him by his enemy. Sighing, Breicher conceded to the relaxed, sensual image before him, no doubt part of some scheme of the young queen.

Breicher cracked the door to the sitting room, and caught sight of Caroline draped across the couch, a book in one hand and a glass of wine in the other. In the time he'd taken to clean himself she'd also slipped into some nightwear.

A floor-length black satin robe was cinched around a gown in a matching material. Her long color-drained locks cascaded over her shoulders, and though the queen wore no extra color on her freshly washed skin, her beauty radiated on full display. She was stunning. His throat tightened as he took her in.

"I thought we could share a drink, catch up, *prince*." Caroline didn't look at him as she gestured to a glass of wine, which was sitting on the ebony table next to the chair nearest her.

He wanted to grab her, shake her, demand to know what she was going to do with him. Instead, he barely restrained his own shaking as he took a seat and picked up the goblet, noting her control absent. Freely, he brought the red liquid to his lips, half hoping it was a quick acting poison. It's what he deserved. The wine burned as it bit down his throat. It was woody and full-bodied, the way he preferred it.

"What are we doing, Caroline?" he asked, keeping his voice as calm as possible.

Caroline huffed. "You no longer prefer my company?"

Her body shifted toward his, and she lifted her attention from the book, which she folded closed, to him. The onyx fabric of her robe slipped off her shoulder, exposing her delicate skin and his eyes trained on it like a target. *Stop it, you animal.*

"I tried to kill you, Caroline. I know how much you like your punishments. What do you want with me?" He forced the words out and his eyes up to meet hers, not masking the anger he felt toward her. Anger for her living and this horrible guilty churning he couldn't escape from.

She leaned forward and took a long slow sip of her wine, then set it on the dark table in front of the couch. Her movement caused more of her garments to slip to the side, sliding off her legs, displaying her skin from her thighs to her bare feet.

Breicher locked his gaze on hers, refusing to let it stray. And not because he was a gentleman.

"I want many things, Breicher. Tell me, did you kill my guards who went missing or were they simply abducted?"

His blood turned to shards of glass in his veins. It was the first time she'd said his name and he simultaneously loved and hated the way it rolled off her tongue. Or he hated that he loved it so much, which scared him, but what really terrified him was what she would do with the knowledge of who stood before her. He needed to be very careful. "They're safe. I had my brother arrange to take them away and in exchange for their silence, they'd keep their lives. How did you know?"

"I've had a long while to think about things. I put it together when I realized how long it had been since one went missing. You were next in line to disappear, but there you were, months and months, like the culprits had given up. Unfortunately, I saw that a bit too late. I want them returned to me."

The expression on the queen's face was commanding, severe and it gave him a thrill, though it made him cringe to admit it. "You mean to kill them?" he asked.

"What I choose to do with my people isn't your concern. *For now.*"

The words *for now* clung to him, and he struggled to decipher their meaning. He tried to school his features into neutrality, but it was hopeless. He was perplexed and it was painted across his face.

"I've also thought a lot about how I want to punish you. About what I want from you, prince. And how I want to go about getting it."

Caroline bent her leg and placed a bare foot on her other calf, sliding it back and forth gently like a lover's caress. The movement caused his blood to heat even as his fingertips itched for the touch. Get ahold of yourself.

He ignored her seduction. Tried anyway. When she'd come back, bleached, it was strange at first. But the more that he stared at her, the more he became enchanted by the visual. He had to get out of this room quickly. "You're more of a fool than I thought you were. If you think you'll get anything from me, you're mistaken."

"I don't think that's true." She gave him a once over, her eyes leaving a trail of warmth across his skin. "Maybe I'm a fool. But I don't suppose that matters now, does it?" She shrugged. The rest of the robe which was clinging on slipped lower. "As you can see, you've failed and now you belong to me." Her mouth pressed into a grim line that didn't conceal the heady gleam in her silver eyes.

"What happened to you?" he dared to ask.

"You haven't yet earned the right to know." Caroline's voice was nonchalant, with a cutting edge. As if she might have let him in if he hadn't done what he'd done.

Breicher couldn't help but scrutinize her every move. He took a long pull from his glass then let his eyes rove over her body, consuming what she was baring before him and she shivered beneath his gaze. He'd used their terrible chemistry against her before. He could do it again, though he didn't know what force was powerful enough to destroy the thing that sat before him.

Beneath all her bluster, she was a woman who'd been hurt... by him. He needed to remember that. A heady combination of vulnerability and strength rippled off her. It was so similar to his own conflicted emotional state he couldn't help but breathe it in.

Did she know the transparency of her own emotions? The anger, sure that made sense, but the desire? It was a palpable force in the room, surging in time with each flicker of the nearby fire. He'd tried to kill her—drove a dagger into the soft flesh of her stomach, yet that electricity that zipped between them seemed even stronger than before. The problem was he wasn't entirely sure what her desire was for—his death or his body—either way he was confident thoughts of him had consumed her much like his own mind was held captive by her.

The way she followed his movements as he stood to tend the fire sent satisfied waves of warmth to his stomach which clenched in response as if it had been her fingers to touch him. He was aware of his body, its robustness, health, and vigor, which wasn't average to put it mildly. It was a Gift from the Gods. The young queen appreciated the male form. He'd use his physique to his advantage. Allowing the tie on his jacket to slip open, Breicher turned to her and he felt the warm firelight dance across his exposed muscle, which he flexed under the heat of her gaze. He was adept at the art of seduction as well and knew how to make a woman feel good.

He gulped down the rest of the wine, savoring it as it warmed the back of his throat in the most delicious way on the way down. Walking over to the decanter, Breicher refilled his glass. Caroline tracked his every move—calculating, her pupils enlarging at the sight of his stalking form. He was a prince, not a peasant like Felix. His mind was as sharp as his body, and he could play the game and find out whatever punishment she had planned. Maybe even get out of this thing alive if he played his hand right.

Ever so slowly, he approached her, leaning down to set his glass on the table. Her breathing caught as he pivoted, putting his hands on the couch on either side of her head. Eighty-five days in prison and she hadn't executed him. He'd seen her kill a man for far less than the crime he committed. Breicher was beginning to understand that he was this Cruel Queen's weakness as much as she was his. But he was an assassin and a warrior. He could hone his emotions like a blade which would be so much easier now that his identity was revealed.

Caroline leaned back as Breicher lowered himself over her, bringing them inches apart. Leaning on one arm, he brought the other to run his fingertips along her jawline. The queen had all but stopped breathing. "You still want me," he said, in a low whisper.

She sucked in a quick breath. "Get off."

He waited for a stab of compulsion, but he got nothing from her except her refusal. The chill of her words prickling across his skin shattered the moment even as an unfamiliar wave of rejection struck him. It had to be another taunt. He wanted to bury himself deeper under her skin.

"I tried to kill you and you still want me." His voice was a husky tease as he moved off the queen obediently.

She snorted. "You're the last thing I could possibly want."

Caroline pushed to her feet, tugging her robe up on her shoulders, and stormed toward the door. Had he read the situation wrong? *No.* She claimed she always told the truth, but Caroline Dallimore was lying.

"Why haven't you killed me?" It was the question which had been gnawing at him. There was no doubt in his mind that his brother would have executed any would be assassin with haste. He couldn't figure her out.

She stopped her charge forward. "Is that what you want?" she asked, voice shaking. Her shoulders were rising and falling in swift movements.

"You couldn't do it," he blurted before he could stop himself.

Breicher barely tracked her as she spun in a blur of movement. He caught the rosenwood dagger a split second before it pierced his throat. The woman before him was fury unbound, and the force of her struck him like an anvil and he wanted it to. Wanted her. The traitor that he was.

"You don't want to die," she whispered, noting the dagger clasped in his hand.

She was right. It could have been over then if his self-preservation instincts hadn't kicked in. They stared at each other for long moments, their chests rising and falling in unison.

Control, that's what she needed. The corner of his mouth kicked up, and he looked at her from lowered lashes. "You've never wanted anything more." He didn't know if it was her truth or his, and he hated himself for it.

Caroline stepped back, and he threw the dagger so it sank deep in the wooden door right behind the queen. Incensed, she darted forward as if she wanted to choke him, but he picked her up mid-stride and crushed her against the door. If it hurt, she didn't cry out. The wood creaked, however, and whatever horrible, invincible thing she'd become was unaffected. She only seemed hungrier, shifting, and writhing against his excitement. "I hate you," Caroline growled, as she dug her nails into his biceps.

He lowered her to the floor, communicating all the darkness he felt back through their connected gaze. Breicher fell to his knees before the queen and ripped the slit of her nightgown wide open. *Gods*, she was bare before him. He pressed a hand to her stomach, holding her back against the door.

She might hate him, but she wanted him, too. He was certain. All he needed to do was confirm the truth of it. Breicher grabbed one of her thighs and swung it over his shoulder, and she let him.

"Liar," he growled, then lapped at the moisture pooling between her thighs.

⌇❦

So much for foreplay, though Caroline supposed their banter had been foreplay enough for tonight. *Dead Gods*, nothing had ever felt like the warmth her would-be murderer was delivering her. Caroline rocked her head back against the door as Prince Breicher Ivanslohe worked her, using his greedy mouth and hand to send peaks and valleys of pleasure cascading through her body.

Right when she didn't think she could take anymore, he'd give it to her with renewed enthusiasm, thrusting his tongue inside her and thumbing her most sensitive spot with perfect rhythm. All her pent-up frustration combined with the man's skill released much too soon and the most glorious rapture cracked through her. Her fingers wound through his chestnut hair, holding him in place as the last of it ebbed. She tugged his head back, so he was looking up at her from his knees. There was nothing more beautiful. Her moisture glistened across his lips in the firelight, and he looked ready to pounce right then and take her. And part of her wanted him to.

It would be so easy to give into the swamp of thick emotions they were wading through. But she wouldn't. They both needed time if this were to turn into something real.

His hair, which had been threatening to fall over his eyes, wasn't the only thing different about him. The ocean of gleaming sapphire which lit his eyes from within stared up at her, beating in time with her heart. Love had been right. They were the opposite side of the same coin, and if they strayed too close to the forge, she was sure they would melt.

She'd played to his warrior nature. His male urge to dominate. To win after he'd lost. He must be aching with the need to take her. Dominate her.

Caroline would give him that chance, eventually. But not until she'd fully bent him to her will. "You want me?" she asked, pulling her full lower lip between her teeth.

"Yes," he breathed.

"Good." She chuckled. "You'll make a fine king, Breicher."

The grin shriveled off his face, as if she'd dunked him into a pool of icy water. Caroline released his hair and shimmied out from between him and the splintered door.

"What did you just say?" he seethed, face reddening. Veins in his neck popped, not due to pleasure she suspected, but because of the complicated emotions she was prodding along. The first stage of her punishment.

"Oh, did I fail to mention it? You're to be my king. Make yourself at home in your new suite. Roam as you like. We'll be taking a trip in a month's time to inform your brother of our upcoming nuptials, along with my other plans for him and his kingdom."

Caroline crossed the sitting room and snatched up her robe, slipping it on, covering her ruined gown. She approached where the prince knelt in shock and ran her thumb across his glistening mouth. "I'll be just down the hall if you need anything. We'll talk more soon." She patted his cheek for effect. "Oh, and thank you for that. I can see why you are so confident. You are *very* skilled." Then she left him in silence.

CHAPTER 3

"**O**H, DON'T BE PETULANT, Breicher. You failed your mission. I'm still alive and worse than ever. *And* I'm making you have breakfast with me. Awful indeed." The queen bit an apple to emphasize the point and wiggled her eyebrows at Breicher.

He glared at her. She shouldn't have lived. Breicher understood nothing of what was happening to him now and the woman across the table carried on like the same Cruel Queen she was before whatever had happened to her. And her taste, last night. Fuck, he was getting hard just thinking about it.

"You're taking your failure a little worse than I would have expected."

"You're going to force me to marry you," Breicher grumbled out, regretting how much control he'd already let her have. "I'd rather be dead."

"I think you rather like me. And besides, it's not like I'm making you sleep beside me, although I imagine you'll be begging me for that before too long. I'd like to share a few meals, get to know the prince who will be my king a little better. You should eat." Caroline jabbed her fork in the direction of his plate, then took a sip of piping hot tea.

"I've lost my appetite," he said and pushed the plate away, crossing his arms across his chest.

Caroline shrugged and took a piece of bacon from the discarded breakfast and popped it into her mouth. "You know, I've been so much hungrier since I've been back. It's like all this power needs fuel."

When she'd picked off the best selections from his plate, Caroline pushed off from the table. "Come, I have things to discuss with you."

He followed her from the sitting room into her bedroom, where an attendant had set out a fresh gown. She walked over to it, running her fingers across the smooth grey silk, and flipped it over, ensuring the clasps in the back were loosened.

Breicher stared at her as she dropped the robe. The queen was bare underneath, and his breath drew in on its own accord. She turned regarding him, and his eyes remained fixed on her.

"What are you doing?" he asked.

"Getting dressed. Afraid of seeing me naked?"

He huffed.

"I'm going to be your wife, so you might as well get used to it." She paced over to him, carrying the gown. "Here, hold this."

Breicher complied, and Caroline stepped into it. She held it up to her waist as she faced him, the nipples crowning her perky breasts hardening beneath his stare. Then his eyes tracked lower to the spot he'd driven the dagger under her ribs.

Breicher's hand reached out as if it had a mind of its own, and he ran callused fingers along the soft flesh that had healed over what should have been a life ending injury. She didn't pull away. Just watched him thumb over the spot.

"My only regret is that it made you into whatever you've become. If I hadn't done it, you'd have still been the enemy we understood. Now you're something else entirely, aren't you?"

His hand moved from her ribs to the white hair cascading over her shoulders. It was soft, like the satin of her bedding, and he wanted to run his fingers through it. He wanted to get a fist full of it and tilt her head back and... No. That's what she wanted, for him to be helpless under her spell. She'd had the upper hand until now. He needed to figure out how to take it from her. If he was her weakness, that might be the only way.

Her mouth parted as she stared up at him and it would be so easy to lean down. He wanted to tell her he hated her, and he'd stab her all over again.

But that kiss and how ready she'd been for him... The queen had transformed beneath his touch and the memories already held too much space in his mind. Kissing her was the last thing he needed to be thinking about, especially with the half-dressed woman standing in front of him and his body responding the way it always did with her. And it's all he could think about. He forced an image of his father into his mind and let the ice bath the memory brought with it wash over him.

His fate was sealed. Breicher didn't see any way out, so he'd focus his efforts on tempering her. Making sure she didn't abuse the power he suspected she'd somehow stolen from the Gods. Rule beside her in Everstal for the rest of his days if that's what it took.

"I'm the same woman I was before, Breicher. Just a lot more powerful." She stepped away from him and slipped her arms into the sleeves of the gown. Caroline turned, giving her back to him, gesturing to the clasps, and he took to fastening them one by one. "I should have been dead," she said, turning to look at him after he'd finished. "But you all underestimated my will to live."

Her bare feet padded across the cool stones, and that familiar attraction welled inside him. Caroline had been bare before him moments before, but it was her steely will that drew him this time.

She was fastening on an onyx earring, and he came up behind her, gripping her hips. He studied her in the mirror. "I'm glad you lived. But I wish you would have died." The truth of it startled him, and he glanced up to see the odd look in his own eyes.

Caroline's stare narrowed in the reflection at his contradictory statement. "Liar."

"That's the trick, isn't it? Who am I lying to? You or me?"

The briefest look of sorrow flashed across her features before it was gone. "I wish you would have come to me instead of trying to kill me. But what you did has set off a chain of events that I cannot halt. As Life poured their healing energy into my body, the Gods told me things. Vile, selfish things that they'd done which separated our kingdoms, pitted them against each other, causing all the bloodshed between our people. They toyed with us, Breicher." Her silver eyes held such pleading as they met his in the mirror.

"It's not possible," he said, hands involuntarily squeezing her hips.

"It is. And I killed them for it."

Breicher's eyes flared, and Caroline spun in his arms, so she was facing him, leaning against the vanity. "You killed the Gods?"

Instead of answering, she said, "I know how deeply ingrained your hatred of Everstal, of my family is. But everything we've been taught is a lie. If you would believe that we could change things for this world. Together."

"What are you saying, Caroline?" A sick sinking feeling rooted in his gut, and he stepped back.

She took a ginger step forward and placed her outstretched palms on his stomach. "Yes, I made the monsters who created the rift between our kingdoms pay. They are no more and I'm not sorry. I know you're conflicted about me. Trust me, I feel the same about you, but we could set all that aside."

"So what? You're planning on being some type of savior now?" Breicher scoffed. "I know what you're up to and I won't be another pawn in one of your games."

Breicher's rebuff was practically a growl and Caroline started at the aggressive tone. She had to make one more effort, for her own sake. She didn't like the weak sound of her own voice as she practically begged him, but if there was anyone she'd lower herself for, she supposed it should be him. The man she would make her king.

"I know it isn't what you want. That they're your family, but as long as they want me dead and continue to keep our kingdoms at odds, then I must do this."

"What you are suggesting is a worse betrayal than marrying you. You're crazy if you think I'd agree to it."

Caroline ran her hands up his chest and threaded them through the hair at his neck, which had grown out since she imprisoned him. The deep, rich brown a juxtaposition against her cool skin. His pulse throbbed under his warm skin as he warred with himself. If the fates had charted a different course for them, they'd have been so good together. She craned her neck up toward him and stood on the tips of her toes to press a soft kiss into his chiseled jaw and he sucked in a breath. "Please, Breicher. For me? For what could be?"

He wrapped his long fingers around her wrists and yanked her hands from around his neck, shoving them at her. "As if I'd do anything for you."

The hopeful facade melted from her gaze, and she let her ire replace it, free for him to see. And by the narrowing of his eyes, he did see it. "Fine. Have it your way. You should have been smart enough to know I'd take Veetula anyway, with or without your consent. I guess how gentle I'll be doing it is the only thing to be decided now."

Her future king's wheels turned, expression flipping from disgust, to fear, regret, then rage as the opportunity drifted away from him. At least if he'd allied with her, she'd have let him have some say. Storming over to her wardrobe, she grabbed a pair of low heels, slung them on and headed out the door, not waiting to see if he followed.

Once in her war room, she stole a glance back to see the man trailing after her. Angus was already inside and a few other advisors. "Prince Breicher has elected not to have any say in this council meeting in favor of loyalty. He is here to provide us with information only. Shall we begin?" She jerked a hand toward the seat next to the one she'd taken, urging Breicher to sit. He obliged.

Angus had a barely concealed, *I told you so*, scrawled across his serious features. Rarely were she and her commander at odds, but the subtle expression made her blood churn almost as much as the indolent man next to her. Breicher was still reeling from the vindictive way she'd thrown their engagement at him, but he had tried to kill her. Why did the men in her life have to be so impossible? Though she supposed being surrounded by a bunch of *YES men* wouldn't have pleased her either.

"This would be a lot smoother if I'd have been right, *commander*," she hissed, and Angus flinched. She wasn't sorry. "Now I'm going to have to either use threats of violence or compulsion to get my future husband to talk. Which shall it be, my love?"

It wasn't how she'd wanted it to go, but that didn't stop her from the giddy elated feeling that chittered up her spine as all the eyes in the room focused on the blanched prince.

He glared at her. "You wouldn't..."

She huffed a laugh. "You know I would," she lied. But he didn't need to know her bluff. And she'd rather not compel him. Keeping the Veetula royal family alive served two purposes. A wedding gift to her husband to be, and an offering of good faith to the people. The Ivanslohe's were well liked enough, certainly more than her though she didn't see why, and she'd use their surrender. The way she planned to make it seem like they were working together would endear her to Veetula's citizens.

He crossed his arms, and for a moment, she thought she was going to have to do it. "Breicher, stop being tiresome." She shoved a stack of drawing paper and a few pieces of charcoal over to him. "The first thing we need to know is the layout of the entire castle. When you're finished and Angus is satisfied, you'll detail the location of every last Rosenwood tree."

Her prince leaned forward and picked up a stick of charcoal, studying it. "What do you plan to do with the information?"

"Pity, Breicher. You've lost the right to that knowledge, too. And I gave you a choice. Now draw."

Angus repressed a grin. The man had it coming. Prince Breicher had frozen, waiting for the compulsion to trickle across his flesh. But none came. In her own way, his queen was giving the man a choice now still. The prince's face was screwed up into a calculating expression. He thought there was still a chance for him to change the tide. To get Caroline to change her mind. He obviously didn't know her that well. Once she decided something, she didn't alter her course. Angus shook his head, looking between the two royals—at the battle of wills they were engaged in. It was futile. Caroline would win. She'd beaten the Gods. The foolhardy Johnneth didn't truly understand what he was up against.

Breicher, Angus corrected himself. He should have known the character *Johnneth's* motives weren't true. Particularly when he'd seemed a little dissenting and weak in the knees at that last Petition. But Caroline wouldn't listen. If he'd never presented the man as an option for her selection, none of this would have happened. But maybe it was a good thing. He didn't know if the god-like woman sitting before him was invincible, but he figured she was as close as a human could get. And she was on some mission to join the two kingdoms after what she'd learned. At least they didn't have to take the threats against her life as seriously anymore. But the truth was his queen's entanglement with this foreign prince was his fault, regardless of whether what had happened to her had been a good thing, and now he'd bear the consequences of this guard, this assassin prince, being elevated to be her king.

Breicher leaned over to her, and Angus perked up. What sure to fail request was he going to make? "Caroline, can I talk to you in private?" he asked.

"Draw, I said," Caroline demanded, and Angus grinned, loving his friend's ruthlessness. Her hands were white knuckled around the wooden arms of the chair she occupied.

"Caroline, please. We can work something out," Breicher whispered, flicking an annoyed glance his way. Then the prince reached for Caroline's wrist, but she batted his hand away.

This was getting old already. "Just compel him and let's get this over with," Angus groaned, running his hand down his face, squeezing his eyes shut with the gesture.

"Promise me you won't kill them?" Breicher asked, and Angus almost felt sorry for the man.

The queen smirked and flitted a hand through the air, waving the idea off. "I don't *currently* have any plans to kill your brother, his wife, or any of their children. So, please draw and don't give me any reason to create them."

Breicher let out a long sigh and began to draw. Caroline excused herself and Angus sat with the other advisors for long hours while the prince laid out the plans for Kierengaard. The castle was an elegant building topped with spires, different sections and wings abounded, but it was not the impenetrable maze of Roskide. Its location was what made it a challenge to sack. But now that Caroline had the power of the Gods, that was surmountable too.

Angus tapped a finger on the open ballroom in the compound's heart. "When is the solstice?" he asked to anyone who'd supply the information.

"Three days shy of a fortnight, sir," Seb, the trade advisor, answered. As the man's small head nodded vigorously, his crisp black hair didn't budge. Angus wrinkled his nose. What did the slight man put in it that made it so stiff?

"Wonderful," he answered, shifting his focus. "Our intelligence says their annual festival is planned to go on as scheduled. The queen, Breicher and I will arrive before the feast is opened. Once she has control of the room, we'll send soldiers to open the gates of the city and beyond, instructing any forces stationed between Kierengaard's walls and the border to stand down. Soon, Veetula's army will be our own."

Angus rose, folding a stack of papers in front of him, tucking them beneath his arm. "Oh, and let's keep an eye on our prince. We don't want him to get a message out to his brother and spoil the surprise." He gave Breicher an angry frown. "The queen's forgiveness only extends so far."

Breicher was on his heels as he left the room.

"She's unleashing her army on Veetula?" Breicher said, unbridled panic lacing his voice.

"You should make an effort to get to know her. Understand her motives, at least. But you don't know her at all." Angus shook his head, disgust coated his skin and pulled his face into a grimace. "Your queen does not engage in meaningless bloodshed. Why would she kill the people she intends to unite?"

Granted, whatever the Gods had said that had made her so intent on this mission of hers, he did not fully understand. He suspected defying their games was motivation enough. When she'd first presented the idea to him, it had seemed unreal. But as she spoke, a new sense of purpose had lit her eyes and he had to give it to her. Using the Veetula prince as a tool, making him her king was as ruthless as it was clever. And it might even work. It was the fact that before that idea had blossomed, she'd been unwilling to execute him. That made Angus uneasy.

Breicher's fingers wrapped around his forearm, and Angus whipped around, grasping the other man's throat, slamming him into the wall. Angus's anger and catching the stronger Ivanslohe off guard gave him the slight advantage. The prince hadn't fought back. *Yet.*

"Have a little faith in the woman who somehow deems you worth marrying. You have an opportunity here whether or not you see it, and I'd suggest you not squander it," Angus reprimanded before Breicher got a word out. Then he relaxed his grip and stomped off down the hall, leaving Breicher to ponder his words.

CHAPTER 4

"I THOUGHT YOU'D BE here," Breicher said as he slipped into the steam-filled room deep under Roskide. The coquettish energy of his first visit to the hot spring so different from the somber tone the cavern now held.

He poked his head around the corner. Caroline's head was leaned back on the tepid stones surrounding the pool and her naked body bobbed just below the surface. Her white hair was soaked and fanned out around her, floating in the water, and draping across the stones. Only her eyes tracked over to him.

Breicher held out the bottle of wine and two glasses. "I brought a peace offering."

"It's going to take a lot more than wine to get anything out of me." Caroline's voice was flat, bored even.

"Can I join you?" he asked, even as he slipped his shoes off.

She sat up, eyeing the wine. "I don't care."

"Better than a no." Breicher shrugged and tugged his shirt up and over his head. He tossed it aside and began unlacing his trousers, letting them drop to the floor. He figured it was only fair. Making quick work of the cork, he poured them two glasses and sauntered over to her making sure he was on full display.

She only raised her eyebrows as she took him in. If he were being honest with himself, he'd been hoping for more of a reaction.

"You wouldn't care if I took a lover, would you? Someone who I found more palatable?" she asked.

Breicher almost slipped on the slick stones, but righted himself before the wine sloshed from the glasses. He bent down, handing her a glass, then lowered himself into the pool. The warmth filled him, lessening the tension he'd been holding onto that not even the luxurious bed she'd put in his room eased. Or it was the proximity to her that let his shoulders lower. There was some assurance in knowing where the queen was. If he was with her, she couldn't be hurting anyone.

"I know. It seems I've made yet another mistake. And you're upset with me." When she didn't respond, he continued. "Angus says I don't know you. I misjudge your intentions. That I should try harder."

He tried to gauge her response. A slight downturn of her lips was all she gave him before she took a sip of the ruby liquid.

"Are you not going to speak to me?"

"Why should I? Speaking to you doesn't do any good. I don't take part in meritless activities. You could always offer to entertain me with your mouth in other ways?" Her eyes creased at the edges and a sly glint brightened them.

"You already know what I have to offer in that department. Besides, you might as well take a lover. I don't think becoming romantically involved would be a wise choice for us. Too much is at stake to have our judgement clouded."

"Feel free to leave." The bite in her tone was unmistakable as she turned her head to stare at the wall. "And for the record, I'll permit you no lover. I won't have my king spreading his seed throughout the kingdoms. Understood?"

"That seems like a bit of a double standard." Breicher swirled his glass of wine, downing it and reached for the bottle. He felt her eyes crawling across his torso as he moved. "Caroline, I think we both know I'm not dead because you want me." It wasn't his looks or plain lust. It was that spark when they kissed. That stupid, haunting, delicious kiss. The spark that had blurred her senses, creating the opening for what he'd done. Never had a kiss affected him like hers had. Sure, kissing was a nice precursor to sex, but unnecessary.

"You're not dead because you're useful," she said.

He chuckled and swam over to her. He'd use that spark to get an edge on her again.

An involuntary shudder rippled across Caroline's skin as Breicher approached. She didn't push him away, curious to see what he was going to do. He framed her in with long arms positioned on the stones on either side of her and she edged up a little taller in the water. His face was so near they were breathing the same air and static charges seemed to jump back and forth between them. Caroline thought of the control she'd had when she lulled the Gods into complacency before she stole their power. She fixed her features into the same inanimate gaze.

"May I kiss you?" he breathed, and her pulse threatened to drown out all other sounds.

"What for?" she said, trying to make her voice as apathetic as possible.

His brow creased as if he didn't understand the question. "Why do people normally kiss?"

"Usually because they *like* each other." The words tumbled out before she could craft them.

Breicher grinned. "I think we definitely *like* each other. That isn't the problem."

He had a point, though she wouldn't admit it. "The problem is that I'm not feeling anything, Breicher. No chemistry. I guess when someone tries to murder you, whatever spark that might have been there fizzles out. But I'll let you kiss me..."

His grin changed to a full toothy smile, like he'd finally won something. He leaned down and rubbed their noses together in the smoothest gesture, and an impossible heat surged through her. He met her eyes, leaning in, but they narrowed as his lips met the fingertip she'd slipped between them. It pressed into his puckered mouth and pushed him away.

"Cocky as ever, I see. You didn't let me finish. I'll let you kiss me the day we marry, after we take our vows. If you want to make any sort of inroads with me, you have a month to do it. Then the kiss you deliver better set the sky alight. Now go back to your side of the tub, or I'm leaving."

Breicher peeled himself away from the queen, trying to slow his heart throbbing in time with his cock, which was fully aware of the naked woman only a few inches from it. As if reading his thoughts, she said, "Paid women count as lovers, too, Breicher. I expect fidelity if you want to prove yourself to me."

He gritted his teeth. She didn't understand that the vitality of the Ivanslohe line wasn't only about physical robustness—it also enhanced his appetite, his primal needs. It was like an animal instinct, the need to mate, at times clouding all other thoughts from his mind until he'd found a release. It's how all the Ivanslohe's were, women included. A blessing or curse, depending on how you looked at it. Thank the Gods they'd got his nieces married off when they did. He laughed internally at the thought. But how could he explain that to her? Especially when being around her sent it into overdrive. "It's the Gift, Caroline. I have needs."

"I'll still permit you your hand, if you're a good boy." Caroline, ever in control, blinked across the tub at him, ready to savor his reaction.

It was bullshit. She was lying. Or her game was longer than his. He should take a lesson from her playbook, thinking back to what she'd done to Felix. But he'd been in a prison cell alone for almost three months. Now that he was out and around the most seductive woman he'd ever seen, his body was trying to show both him and her just how much vigor it had, like a prancing rooster. Still, he tamped it down.

"Very well," he obliged. "Then let's talk."

"Tell me the story of the rosenwood tree. I know it was a gift from the Gods designed to be my weakness, but I want to hear the lore," she said.

"If you want to hear a story about your weakness, shouldn't you be asking to hear a story about me?" Breicher let a wolfish smile loose as he cocked his head to the side.

"Keep dreaming, Prince." Caroline pushed herself up from the water, letting the steaming rivulets drip off her bare flesh as she wrung out her hair.

Breicher swallowed a heavy breath and looked away. Seeing her like this and being forbidden from a woman was nearly unbearable. When he looked back, she had wrapped herself in a towel, and sat on the ledge, her back leaned up against the wall and feet dangling in the water. She'd poured the rest of the bottle into her glass and was twirling it in her hand, waiting for him.

"I'm surprised you've never heard it."

"I have. I want to hear your version."

Breicher sighed. He knew what she wanted. Or at least he thought he did. He'd get to the heart of it. She was going to spare his family, and he guessed part of the reason was the same as why she'd spared him. This he could give her. Besides, he guessed the wood would have no effect on her now, anyway.

"In Veetula, they teach every male of the Ivanslohe lineage to cultivate rosenwood from an early age. The Gods chose rosenwood because it is notoriously hard to grow. I had ten trees total when I selected and fell the one I used to carve the dagger I stabbed you with."

Caroline's eyes widened, and she leaned forward, setting her wine aside.

"When we get there, I'll show you my grove. I'm sure you'd enjoy seeing it." She chuckled, shaking her head, but kept silent. "We should have struck sooner, but after our assassins killed your father, we didn't know what had happened to you and your sister. We knew there were assassins, my cousins and others, who never returned. Then, when rumors circulated that you'd taken the throne, you didn't seem like much of a threat. Hollis and I were busy celebrating our victory."

"For five years?" she asked, incredulous.

"You were learning the rigors of ruling, and we knew we'd have to deal with you, eventually. So, one day Hollis called a group of the surviving men in our family into a council and put out the call. I answered and harvested the largest of my trees to begin working on my dagger. The wood is only malleable for a few days before it dries and becomes hard as stone. And the trunks, it takes them years and years to gain diameter, especially enough to carve a dagger from. So, my hate for you drove me to work day and night to perfect the blade I'd kill you with. When I'd completed it, I thought it was a work of art. I was younger then. I hadn't gone through Angus's training yet. I rushed to show Hollis what I'd made. He's a good man, Caroline. He praised me like an older brother should. We had one last night of glory before I left."

"And it took you over five years to get to me?" she asked, clearly trying to keep her features schooled in neutrality.

"You were the last of your lineage. Ten years would have been worth the wait. The Ivanslohe line has had rosenwood for almost eight hundred years and we'd yet to rid the world of your bloodline. And they'd only given it to us after we'd spent the first two hundred years of recorded history, mostly under your family's rule. Your ancestors were too powerful. What they'd asked for had been too much and we didn't even know the price you paid to use the Gift. My ancestors had begged the Gods for something to even the scales. Every male in my family got one sorry seed. They struck the rest of the trees in the wild with disease, so we had the only known rosenwood in existence. It took almost twenty years for a tree that was even viable to grow large enough to carve into a weapon. You've heard of Magda, right?"

Caroline nodded.

"She convinced her husband to give her a small piece, and she whittled what looked like ten sewing needles. King Karis used those as darts to deliver a commanding blow to Everstal decimating its royal family so only a few survivors were left. Of course, they didn't know rosenwood was only required to kill the Dallimore who held the power. When they felled the Dallimore King, the power transferred to the youngest daughter, Morine who was in hiding. The Kingdom fell into chaos for years until she was old enough to wrestle control back and push us out, like you did. The rest is history. When I got assigned to your guard, it was one of the closest chances we'd had. And had you not been saved by the Gods, I'd have achieved the impossible. But you lived and here we are." Breicher drained the rest of his glass as she did the same.

"I think I could love you if my death weren't the intended end to your tale." The look in her eyes clearly showed her pain, and she got up, not bothering to dress before she exited the chamber in her towel.

Breicher gathered their things and carried them back to their adjoined rooms, her words replaying in a rhythm in his mind. She could love him? Surely, he hadn't heard that right. And why did the thought of her affection make his skin heat? He rubbed at the tight spot on his chest as he stalked in front of the connecting door between their bedrooms, but the light was dim beneath, suggesting she'd retired for the evening.

It wasn't until her soft panting floated through the door, followed by a subtle cry that caught her falsehood. Caroline was a good liar and Gods, that little sound was so very sexy. He deposited her things beside the door and rubbed at the renewed stiffness at his groin. She'd been thinking of him, so he'd do the same, drawing out his pleasure, a vision of her a phantom in his mind.

CHAPTER 5

H E TOLD HER THE exact location. It was only a small betrayal to explain the layout of Veetula's white stone castle, Kierengaard, and Caroline grasped the floor plan easily. Her keen mind was another thing striking about the queen. It was like a razor she constantly sharpened. Nothing escaped her notice. Still, as he'd drawn each level, each passageway, and spire of his towering home, his stomach rolled.

Breicher had to swallow this betrayal down because she had his blood. There was no escaping her or her wishes. And she wouldn't hesitate to use her power on him. If he didn't comply, the situation would only become worse. She would have brought them into the city with the power she'd stolen from the Gods and made a terrible scene as she wreaked havoc through the streets. He had no doubt. He grimaced at the thought of her disrupting the peaceful way of life in Veetula and creating unnecessary fear which never led to anything but suffering. It hadn't escaped his notice that she'd slipped the little blade ring on her thumb while they'd been talking, so he was certain she was prepared to do whatever it took to take the northern kingdom.

"Ready?" Caroline wrapped her fine, icy hands around both his and Angus's wrists. A warm, tingling energy vibrated across his skin—the Gods stolen power—and a floating sensation overtook him. Breicher suspected he was no longer present in his own body as the queen whisked them away.

Tonight was the winter solstice, the coldest time of the year in his frozen homeland. Each season, the night the sun was at the furthest point in its orbit, Veetula held an elaborate celebration that went on well into the night, celebrating the sun's rebirth. The Ivanslohe's encouraged guests to dress in bright oranges and yellows, which created a lively atmosphere and made the Great Hall, which was usually decorated in icy blues and whites, feel like a sunny winter sky. He remembered the last one he'd attended, only a few short months before he'd left to infiltrate Everstal.

He and Hollis had gotten so drunk that his brother's wife, Queen Agna, had admonished them, demanding they leave the hall for all the ruckus they were causing. So, what had they done? Invited the rowdiest party guests to join them in the archery range, then asked for volunteers to test their aim. Even spitting drunk, the two of them were an ace of a shot. Of course, the next day, Agna had sent healthy purses of silver to the contestants for their little games with her apologies.

This joyous festival was when Caroline decided to strike.

Gasps and whispers sounded across the Great Room as their party apparated on a breeze landing in the center of the vacant sky blue and white mosaic dance floor.

Five years had passed since he stood in this room. It was the same. Breicher took in the velvet panels hanging from the wooden rafters, sheets of blue ice, the color of the winter sky in the kingdom where he'd grown up. Embroidered on the panels was his family crest—a navy mountain elk surrounded by doves weaving snow-colored ribbons around the king of the forest's antlers.

The first time Hollis had taken him hunting, he had only been fifteen, and barely able to muscle the string of the bow in position. It had taken them days of tracking, but finally they found a massive buck with a rack sizable enough to rival the one on the crest. His heart ratcheted so high his vision blurred. It must've been the adrenaline, but that time when he had drawn the string it had been effortless. But he hadn't expected it and wrenched it back so hard in his excitement, the bow had wined, scaring off the cautious animal. Hollis hadn't stopped laughing until they were both in tears.

He didn't want to think about him, feel the pain the happy memories caused, but he scanned the long room for his brother still. Hollis was going to kill him for this betrayal, but there wasn't a choice. Surely, he'd see that. The dais sat at the opposite end of the entry. Along the two linear walls were long dining tables covered in ice sculptures, elaborate silver candleholders, and tiered platters stacked with decadent offerings. Guests were taking their seats, while others were still walking about the open space in the middle, mingling.

His brother perched on his throne, casually leaning over, flirting with a pretty serving girl delivering his wine to a bedizened goblet, which he lazily held in between two fingers of his outstretched hand, and Breicher shook his head. His auburn-haired Queen was engaged in similar behavior with a young male seated at her side, openly twirling a lock of his sand-colored hair.

It wasn't a love match. The fact that Breicher had been the second-born son had been a relief to him. It had meant he might find love with whomever he chose to spend the rest of his life with. Because divorce was not an option in Veetula. Especially for his family, so the choice had been a point of gratitude for him. But the calling of duty had stirred, so he volunteered to take the mission to infiltrate Everstal and assassinate its queen and now he was poised to marry her.

He could almost laugh at the turn of events.

The crowd quieted as they took account of his, Caroline, and Angus's presence, the screeching of instruments halting their song echoed across the vast space.

"Oh, don't stop," Caroline commanded. The musicians looked from her to the Royals on the dais, then back. "Your playing was so lovely." She clapped her hands in mock encouragement.

A wicked toothy grin opened across her face, exposing her flawless teeth. "You know who I am?" she addressed them. It wasn't really a question and several of the musicians flinched, expecting to feel her power slither across their skin.

After several moments of thick silence, a single player ran their tentative bow across the strings of a violin and light music filled the air again, encouraging other players to re-join the chorus.

"No, not that. Play something darker. More triumphant." She didn't even look their way as she waited for them to obey her command.

A conductor murmured something to the band that Breicher couldn't make out. The musicians flipped a few pages, and a deep, foreboding melody misted through the hall.

Caroline sighed. "Much better. Angus?"

To the crowd, there was no mistaking who Caroline was and what she was there for. Her white locks were falling over themselves atop her head, piling inside and securing the too big crown she never wore, which was her family heirloom and symbol of their power. He'd learned how she hated the gold against her cool, milky skin, but she was wearing it tonight, so there was no question of her supremacy. A rose made from rubies sat at the center of the gilded coronet, the only part not partially obscured by her hair. Between golden spikes, each was tipped with an enormous diamond which pierced the full circumference through the mounds of white.

His intended had chosen a loose gown in the perfect ivory, like a bride on her wedding day, and it was trimmed with a fine woven rope of finely spun gold. All the warmth cloaking her made her glowing silver eyes that much more a striking contrast. His gaze caught on her lips as he studied her, painted the deepest scarlet, almost black. Her finishing touch was the sash she wore across her chest made from a garland of handwoven, fresh white roses.

If one didn't know better, they might think she was one of the Gods she had destroyed.

"Bow before your new queen," Angus commanded.

Murmurs erupted across the crowd and his brother staggered to his feet, rushing across the dais, pointing a finger, and barking orders at alarmed guards while raising the other hand protectively to shield his wife behind him. Breicher would give it to the pair. They may not be faithful to each other, but they were loyal.

A flood of guards burst into motion, scrambling to get to the unwelcome visitors.

Caroline didn't move, but every individual in that room which held over three hundred dropped to their knees in unison. She cocked her head and the corner of her garnet lips ticked up. Breicher couldn't tear his eyes away from the woman who would be his wife. He'd never seen anything more terrifyingly beautiful. Powerful, self-assured. Dominant.

He wanted to possess her in that moment with every fiber of his being. Fully and completely consume the woman standing before him. Take her into him like a fine wine, swallowing the burn down until it scorched the deepest part of him. He was becoming lightheaded at the intoxicating thought. If they weren't in a room, surrounded by hundreds of people, he would have taken her right then, unable to resist her lure.

As if sensing his smoldering thoughts, her gaze drifted to his. Platinum on the outside of her irises were lit from within. He'd only ever seen them do that once—moments before their first kiss.

Hollis's raging voice slashed through the memory.

His brother was at the foot of the dais on his knees, trembling as he tried to look up at the queen who sauntered in his direction.

It was like Breicher's whole body had been dipped in a frozen lake, shattering any illusion he might have. Caroline was here to take the crown from his brother. The very fact that he was standing next to her and had not completed his mission was betrayal enough.

The war inside him blazed exactly as she'd intended with her punishment. In that moment, he knew if he ever acted on his desires, he would be done for. Hers completely, body and soul. So, he resolved he would never enjoy his wife, the way a husband should. She may be able to force him to marry her, but he didn't believe she was sick enough to force him to bed her.

Hollis glowered up at Breicher then. "You've failed us," Hollis said and the dagger in his brother's gaze twisted in his chest. When Hollis learned what Caroline had planned, whenever she told him they were to be married, it would break his heart.

Caroline stared down at her soon-to-be brother-in-law, the *former* King of Veetula. "Enough. Rise," she commanded and released the power from him and him only.

Hollis shot to his feet and jolted toward Caroline. To her surprise, Breicher stepped between them, placing his palms on his brother's chest. "Don't, Hollis. We can't stop her."

Caroline snorted. It was true enough. She'd been assessing the limits of her new power since she'd stolen it from the Gods and left them withering husks in their cold marble home. Prince Breicher was right.

They were at her mercy, and the sooner they came to terms with that, the better.

Breicher stepped back into place beside her, and she got her first full look at the man she'd come to dethrone. He was fifteen or twenty years older than his brother, but still as robust, and shredded with rippling muscle. Standing beside each other, she saw the resemblance between them, the hard planes and angles of their faces, their towering height, a foot taller than most men, and their striking luminescent jewel toned eyes. His tan skin and dark ochre hair popped from the dazzling mustard suit that hugged his unyielding form.

Faint lines traced across Hollis's face, especially pronounced between his eyebrows and jutting out from his frown. She stared at him unabashedly, thinking of the Gift the Ivanslohe's had chosen from the Gods.

"What is it you want, Cruel Queen?" he hissed between clenched teeth.

"*Strength*," she mused.

Both he and Breicher said, "What?" at the same time.

"Your family chose strength. When the Gods made their offerings to the divided kingdoms all those years ago. That is what your family had asked them for, wasn't it?"

"Not just strength," Breicher corrected. "Vitality, health. It is why children of royal birth have such a low mortality rate."

"And how the sons have the physiques of storied warrior gods and the sex drive to go with it?" Caroline raised an eyebrow at Breicher and ran a possessive fingertip from his shoulder to his elbow and he shivered under her touch. The twitch of his cheek told her he was repressing a prideful grin. "Interesting how the threads of fate have unwound."

"The people of Veetula will never submit to a usurper. A woman who is their very definition of terror. An Ivanslohe will die on this throne or Veetula will be no more. The people will not stand for anything less."

Caroline lifted her chin and walked up the steps of the dais. When she approached the silver throne carved from knotty ash trees, she paused and ran her hands across the sleek wood, like she'd first done with her own throne in the Great Hall of Roskide. Her ivory gown swished around as she positioned herself right in front of it. It was so quiet it was as if the entire crowd was holding a collective breath. Then she sat.

The Ivanslohe throne wasn't like the one her father had made her. The assassins had overlooked the smaller thrones when they'd come, only destroying her father and his wife's elaborate chairs, two relics of a different time, much like the one she sat in.

Caroline made to evaluate the chair, leaning back, and shifting her weight around in it. "No, you're right, Prince Hollis. This throne won't do at all."

His eyes peeled back in horror at what he believed she was suggesting. He had no idea what she was capable of. "I'll have to have something more suitable made, of course, for my time here, but I would never let such fine craftsmanship, such an important family heirloom, go to waste."

The air in the room seemed to deflate. She eyed Breicher, whose face was narrowly holding in the shock she expected he was feeling. Caroline hadn't told him about her plans. It would be a long while, if ever, before she relied on or even trusted him. The scales of his heart were too heavily weighted in favor of Veetula. But he would see, and eventually, *soon* she vowed to herself, he would be hers. Truly hers. He'd been right. She'd never wanted something so much before.

That he'd tried to take her life—almost succeeded was a strange aphrodisiac. Perhaps she had met her equal. A partner to rule with her and unite the kingdoms again.

"Prince Breicher," Caroline called, waving her refined hand toward the seat she'd vacated. "Please. I think it will suit you much better than it does me. We'll have something uniquely crafted for my needs.

She'd told him she wouldn't make him kill his family if he'd cooperated. They were still in the punishment phase of the relationship. Caroline just hoped he wouldn't test her. It wouldn't do to kill off the royal family before she addressed the people.

And she'd convinced herself a peaceful takeover would be the first step into Breicher's heart. She'd make his people love her, and he'd be her king, ruling beside her, reinforcing the union of their kingdoms. A feat no one believed was possible. But a creature who was practically a God themselves had never attempted it. Caroline would achieve the impossible. She knew it, like she knew the sun would rise.

Several stiff steps later, Breicher approached his brother's throne. He positioned himself in front of it and threw an apologetic look at Hollis, the demoted prince. The look of his brother's eyes was unreadable. The moment they were alone he'd explain everything, he promised himself.

There had to be some way out of this.

Breicher looked to the vacant heavens, then sat himself upon the throne of Veetula. The fates were funny indeed.

"Yes, I think it is much better suited to you, my love." Caroline's voice was unnecessarily loud as the crowd sat in stunned silence. Gasps sounded here and there over the room as the implication sunk in. Her heels clicked across the dais as she passed in front of him and approached Agnes, still on her knees.

Caroline held out an upturned hand to the other woman. Shit, he'd seen where this had gone before. His future wife didn't know how to make friends. Only enemies, or wary acquaintances. "You may rise."

She must have lifted her compulsion, because Agnes gingerly rose to her feet smoothing out her sunshine-yellow silk gown, shifting her narrow hips, appearing to move away the stiffness. Her red lower lip quivered as she raised her eyes to meet Caroline's. Though Agna looked like she wanted to be anywhere other than here losing her crown, she won the battle for control she was wrestling and took Caroline's hand.

Agnes wasn't an Ivanslohe, so she didn't have the benefit of the vitality the line possessed. She bore Hollis four darling children, and one, Cecily, who thank the dead Gods wasn't here, when she wasn't exactly early in her youth. He expected her legs must have ached from kneeling through Caroline's production.

It took everything in him not to interfere, knowing it would only be worse for them if he did. An injury or worse bestowed upon them, which was really intended as a punishment for him.

His breath caught as Agnes's knuckles went white around the queen's grip. He burst from the throne and made two bounding steps toward the women, but stopped short when Agnes released a shuddering sigh.

Agnes's big green eyes blinked at Caroline. "How did you do that?"

Breicher glanced at Hollis, who was being held back by Caroline's power. His tan skin becoming wan and slick with sweat as he fought to get to his wife.

"It's something I've been working on since I took it from the Gods. They were always able to heal me, so I figured if I had their power, I might be able to do the same. How do you feel now?"

"I've learned to endure the needles in my hips years ago. But the pain is gone."

"I don't wish us to be enemies, Princess Agnes. I'm not here to destroy you, or your husband, as our families have done to each other for hundreds of years. I want your strength beside me. I will give you two weeks to consider my offer of friendship. I will expect your answer before the ceremony."

Caroline turned to the crowd and raised her voice. "In two weeks, Prince Breicher and I will wed on this very stage. I expect full attendance. You do not want me to interpret your absence as dissention because there is one thing that's painfully true about my reputation. I will not hesitate to punish you."

She surveyed them as murmurs erupted. His brother rushed over to Agnes, throwing defensive arms around her. Their son Jaden, his nephew, who was about Caroline's age, ran forward to join their embrace, eyeing Caroline warily. The boy had become a man in the years since he'd seen him. Clearly an Ivanslohe, but he had a finer bone structure and a slightly upturned nose, like his mother. Same deep-set sapphire eyes, deep brown hair, and broad shoulders though. His lips, which were wide, somewhere between the fullness of his father's and the thinness of his mother's, were quirked up at the edges as if this unexpected turn of events might amuse him. Even as a boy, Jaden was different, always seeming to have another script playing out inside that calculating head of his.

The queen looked over at the family, and Breicher swore there was a longing glint in her eye. She exhaled loudly. "You're dismissed." The crowd rose and hastily made their way out of the Great Hall. She cocked her head at a quizzical angle as the mashup of bodies fled. Angus stepped up beside her and was standing at her right like the dutiful commander he was.

"That went well," Angus said. "You'd think with as many waxen faces, we had a mass execution."

"They believed they were safe, Angus. Can you imagine how difficult it would be to take this stronghold with brute force?" Caroline absently rubbed the spot under her ribs where he'd driven the rosenwood dagger.

"I don't think they'll work on me anymore, but we better not leave it to chance. Burn all the rosenwood trees. I want every single tree, seeds, saplings, burned. Anything made for the gods awful wood, in the fire."

The guards stood, clearly unsure of what to do.

"You heard your queen," Angus snapped.

The one who held the highest rank shot a wary look toward Hollis, then started barking orders to the men.

Hollis was smart enough not to signal the man his approval of the order and trigger Caroline's ire.

Caroline scanned the room, her brow creasing. "Agnes, don't you have a little daughter? She'd be about ten now, right? Where is she?"

Agnes blanched. "She's away, visiting cousins, Your Majesty."

His sister-in-law was lying, probably hoping to shield the girl from the queen there were so many frightful rumors about. The truth was children were never permitted to attend the solstice party. They had activities planned for them throughout the day, then they were sent to early beds. Solstice was for the adults and the type of entertainment they liked to engage in wasn't appropriate for kids.

"Well, call her back. She can be my flower girl." She turned to him, nostrils flaring. "Come, Prince Breicher. I'd like the tour you promised."

Caroline waved a hand, and the remaining crowd parted. She strode through the center toward the doors, not looking back to see if he followed. Breicher shot an apologetic look to his brother, then chased his future wife out of the room.

CHAPTER 6

HOLLIS TOSSED BACK A finger of the smooth clear liquid called winter's sin. Breicher used to drink it with him, but since he'd spent years in Everstal with the stuff out of his system, he had no tolerance. Evidence of that fact had his head swimming with the first pour. Hollis slammed the glass down on the table and reached for the bottle. He'd avoided his brother for two full days before he finally cornered him.

"When I saw her, I thought we were done, brother," Hollis said. "You know they say your life flashes before your eyes? It's nearly just like that."

Was that what happened to his future bride when he drove the dagger under her ribs? No, she'd had enough wits about her to get his blood and curse him.

"Breicher, focus." Hollis shoved another glass toward him. The brothers downed the liquid. "You really haven't fucked her?"

"No," he chuckled. "I'm not so sure that's a good thing. You see her, right? She's terrifying and clever too." Breicher hiccupped.

Hollis's rough hands wrapped around his jaw, giving him pats that felt more like slaps trying to hold his attention. "You almost sound like you like her?"

He shook his head in defiance. "Obviously not."

Hollis huffed. "I can see the appeal. It's just that if you fuck her—if you let her think she has any power over you—Breicher, if you fall for her," he said, an angry edge lacing his voice, "it will be a betrayal of your family and your kingdom. It is up to us to do whatever we have to, to take Veetula back from that abomination."

Breicher growled, his hackles raising. *Shit.*

"I was so close," he said, hoping Hollis would take his instinctual defensiveness about Caroline for his desire for revenge.

Hollis patted him on the back in consolation. "Don't worry, we'll take care of her. And in the meantime, you go up to your room and I'll send you a distraction."

An hour later, Breicher was sprawled across his bed with his cock in his hand when a knock sounded at the door. *Hollis's distraction.* His brother was going to get him killed. "Go away," he yelled.

The knock sound again more insistently. "Fuck off, whoever you are. I don't want whatever you're offering."

The handle turned, unlatching the pin, and a female strode into the room. No, an angel. Breicher blinked a few times to clear his vision, making a mental note not to let his brother pressure him into drinking winter's sin with him again. "Go away, angel," he growled.

"You think I'm an angel?" A silken voice tip-toed across his skin. *Caroline.*

Relief that made him immediately uneasy washed over him. What Hollis didn't know was that she was already getting to him. Then he remembered he had his throbbing cock in his hand. He tried to suppress his embarrassment and stuff it back in his pants, when she said, "No need to stop on my account."

He hesitated.

"Go ahead," she continued. "I'd love to watch."

His hand moved involuntarily, retreading the familiar motion as she crawled on the bed beside him for a better view. "Who did you think was at the door, Breicher?"

Gods, she asked it in such a sweet way he couldn't help but let her voice warm his heated skin. "Someone Hollis sent. Someone that wasn't you." He shouldn't be saying that. This was the exact betrayal his brother had been cautioning him against.

She gave a sultry chuckle. "Hollis doesn't want us to be together. He's wrong, you know," she said, tracing a finger from her neck down to the satin trim curving over the swells of her breasts, fingering it idly.

"You should go," he grumbled, but didn't cease stroking. She was like a fantasy come to life.

Caroline took his other hand in hers and brought it up to her mouth. "You sure about that, Prince Breicher?" A second later, her hot tongue was flicking the pad of his finger, then it was sliding into her mouth. Right as she sucked, his balls seized and a sharp wave of pleasure rushed through him, spilling itself on his taut stomach. He'd been too quick, and she'd think him inexperienced, another reason to justify the embarrassment creeping up his neck.

When the tremors subsided, he looked up at the queen, whose eyes were heavy lidded. She moved to get off the bed. "What about you?" he asked, regretting it the moment he did.

"Some other time when you're not drunk," she said, walking back into the bedroom with a hand towel. Gently, she wiped the mess he'd made on his stomach away, then went and unlaced his boots, pulling them off like he'd done once for her.

"Agnes told me Hollis probably was getting you wasted, and you might be a bit of a lightweight." She helped him get his pants down over his hips, then the covers up over them both.

"You're staying?" he asked, unable to resist combing through her white locks, which spread across her pillow.

"It wouldn't do if my future king died from alcohol poisoning before I crowned him, now, would it?" Caroline curled up on her side with her back facing him and in a few moments her breathing fell into the rhythm of sleep.

Hollis would kill him if he knew what just transpired. But in his inebriated state, he didn't care. Her pretty face lacked all its usual tension. He wanted to hold her. Would she let him pull her close or wake and push him away? He envisioned himself as a hunter then. Slowly, he reached a hand under the covers toward her waist, like he'd catch her unaware and then she'd be happily nestled in his arms before she could protest. His fingers crept forward another few inches.

Breicher awoke with his hand still reaching for her, but she was gone. Had it been a dream? The winter sun and booming headache splitting his brain in two jolted him back to reality. That and the ruined towel on the nightstand. It was like he'd been dipped in a vat of shame, the way it coated his insides. He'd wanted her and let her see exactly how much.

He groaned, turning over. Why did it have to be this way? Couldn't they have been two normal people who'd met in a chance encounter and fallen for each other naturally? Instead, here they were, historic enemies pitted against each other since birth. Maybe she was right—they were inevitable. The thought came and went in a flash, replaced by his brother's voice. *They were a betrayal.* And he knew what Hollis did with traitors.

At least he'd been coherent enough to send the woman Hollis had sent away. Oh shit, that had been Caroline at his door. Did Hollis send her? Or had his future wife caught the woman traipsing the hallway toward his room? Dread released the soggy shame gripping him, the stale sensation replaced by a new, more foreboding feeling.

It took an effort of will to call for an attendant, eat his breakfast, clean up and make his way down to the study, where he'd agreed to meet Caroline to discuss the wedding.

The scene he happened on when he arrived rattled his already rattled nerves. Part of him wanted to burst into the room before the queen did any more damage, but the part that won out was Angus's. *You don't know her at all.* He wanted to see what she'd do, so Breicher tucked himself behind a bookshelf, peering over the neatly rowed volumes and observing.

Caroline knelt in front of his youngest niece, Cecily, fingering a bouncy auburn curl. Agnes had hoped to shield the girl from the queen for as long as possible. They'd been in the wrong place at the wrong time.

"Well, aren't you precious? I remember when I was your age. Ten years old, if I'm not mistaken. My sister and I would... Well, never mind that. Do you know who I am?" Caroline asked.

The little girl's blue eyes were bright with curiosity. Cecily put a finger to her lips. "You're Queen Caroline, and I'm ten and a half."

"You're a clever young lady. What is your mother making you study?" she asked, eyeing the stack of books on the nearest table. Agnes shifted uncomfortably and placed a hand on top of the nearest one, obscuring the title. The other hand went to the top of Cecily's head.

Before Agnes could quiet her daughter up, Cecily said, "Mother's teaching me about the war where your daddy killed Grandpa."

Caroline's jaw clenched. She shot a glare up at the former queen. "What a dreadful thing to expose a child to. I sure hope that doesn't give you nightmares. One day you and I can do a lesson and we can learn something fun. Have you ever heard of an octopus?"

Cecily's eyes widened and her curls bounced as she shook her head.

"It's a type of fish with a jelly head and eight legs called tentacles." Caroline held up her fingers, wiggling them as she tickled the girl. Cecily burst into giggles, but Agnes pulled Cecily in closer to her side, glancing a warning shot at Caroline.

"One day, I'll bring you a book from Everstal that shows you all the sea creatures we've ever identified. Pink and purple ones, yellow and blue. Would you like that?"

Cecily nodded vigorously. "Oh yes, please, Your Majesty."

Agnes cleared her throat, clearly having had enough. "We'll be going now." She scooped the stack of books up and ushered her daughter out the door.

As Agnes and Cecily left, Breicher stepped out from the stacks and sauntered over to his intended, as if he hadn't been spying on her. Papers from Agnes's lesson were still scattered on one of the desks in the center of the library and she was eyeing them angrily.

"What's got you all ruffled?" he asked, leaning against the edge of the desk, picking up a loose sheet looking over it as if he didn't know.

"Oh, your sister-in-law is trying to mold the mind of a child against me. My future brother-in-law, who I so graciously spared, is trying to lure my future king into the arms of another woman. And honestly, will I sound crazy if I say I think your nephew, Prince Jaden, is spying on me? So, nothing has me ruffled, Breicher. Queens don't get ruffled. My leniency is being blatantly disrespected and it's making me angry."

Well, at least she knew about Hollis's attempted gift and didn't seem upset at him about it. "I doubt Jaden is spying on you. Why would he do that?"

"My guess is your delightful brother has him up to it. He can't just accept that I'm being reasonable."

Caroline raised a hand to her pursed lips. *Shhh*, she mouthed. With a few long strides, she was rounding the corner to one of the furthest rows where Jaden was swiftly making his way around the corner.

"Jaden," he called, letting his voice carry the authority of an older relative.

The young prince turned on his heel, and paced toward him and the simmering queen, as if he were merely looking for a good book. One of which he held in his hands and was mindlessly flipping the pages as he turned his gaze upward. "I'm not spying for my father."

Breicher crossed his arms over his chest. "But you are spying?"

"I was looking for something to read." Jaden's smug face made him nervous. Did he not understand Caroline would compel him to tell the truth? Having that icy power shock through your veins wasn't a sensation he'd wish on the young man, or the queasy sensation her grip on your will gave you.

Instead, Caroline shot Jaden an amused smile. "And what did you find, prince?"

"It's an anthology of reasonable queens." Jaden turned the book, more like a pamphlet, in his hands. "Surprisingly thin."

Caroline snorted and Breicher caught the true name of the title Jaded had snagged off the shelf as he'd been caught: *The Complete Handbook of Stone Masonry*. He shook his head, hoping his nephew didn't invoke the queen's wrath. "Jaden, don't you have some love-sick bed partner to be tormenting?"

Footsteps announced Angus's presence. He walked a little too assertively for such a relative newcomer to their world, past the rows of books following their voices. *Like Breicher was the only overconfident one.*

"Caroline, I thought we were meeting about the logistics of the wedding." Angus frowned when he saw Jaden, the object of their scrutiny, at the end of the passageway. "Jaden," he said in greeting, then went back to ignoring the man. Breicher thought he noticed the glint in his nephew that suggested he'd found a new object of his interest and moaned internally. That was not what they'd needed now, and for Jaden's sake, it was futile, though he supposed Jaden would figure that out soon enough on his own.

"To answer your question, Your Majesties, I am actually in-between bed partners at the moment," Jaden interjected. "I plan to open applications any day now, so if you know anyone who would be interested, please send them my way."

Breicher knew the look Jaden shot Angus as he prowled by. Predator and prey because he'd been that man on the hunt before, too.

He left the study, turning as her eyes tracked him. "I was wrong. Hollis doesn't have him up to it... he's too irreverent. Agnes?"

He didn't want to speculate on the young prince's motives and Angus seemed more than happy to pass over any conversation that had to do with the man, thankfully. The rattling of porcelain drew their attention. "Sounds like the tea has arrived. Let's have a cup and get on with the charade," he announced, earning a glare from Caroline as he made his way back to a larger table beside the orderly row of desks. Never would he'd imagined he'd be sitting with the woman he'd tried to assassinate, planning their wedding.

⁊⟋⟍

Breicher shoved the winter's sin away. "I tried, Hollis. I'll see if we can make it her coronation instead of a wedding, but she won't agree. You don't get it. Attention or glory isn't what makes her tick."

"Then what makes her tick, Breicher, since you seem to know her so well?" Wrinkling his nose at the drink Breicher had rejected, he snatched it, tossing it back in a single swallow.

Had his brother's face always gotten that red when he drank? "She wants two grand public weddings because she believes our marriage symbolizes the joining of the kingdoms."

As he finished, a glass flew across the room, shattering against the stone wall. Grabbing a new glass from beside the decanter, Hollis poured himself another finger. "That is exactly why we can't let it happen."

Shaking his head, Breicher pushed up from the plush chair he'd sunk into in Hollis's solar. "You seem to forget if we don't do what she's asking, we're all dead. Starting with me since she has my blood. She could make me kill you, Hollis, and I'd be powerless to stop her. And she hasn't. Can't you be grateful for that?"

Jaden's uncle released a deep sigh and stormed out of the room. He'd never seen such a conflicted man. Breicher clearly wanted the queen, but his love for his brother, Jaden's father, who was clearly in deep denial about his situation, was preventing him from giving in to his true feelings. Maybe he'd write a story about it one day, or a play perhaps.

Slipping into the room, he made his way to the bar cart, gesturing to the broken glass along the way. "What a mess."

His father looked up from where he'd buried his head in his hands. Deep red, almost purple fine veins etched their way down his puffy cheeks. A ring of pink surrounded the deep blue of his eyes. "No kidding," the older Ivanslohe said, waving his glass in the air at his son.

Jaden picked up the decanter, pouring himself a glass, then another for his father. "I meant the glass. I don't think you can prevent this... them, I mean."

Hollis growled and threw back the drink. "You'd have me give up my throne so easily?"

Eying the empty glass clutched in the former king's white-knuckled fingers, he said, "It was just an observation. I'm not suggesting anything." Jaden sipped, the clear liquid burning a path down his throat.

"Sit down, son. We need to talk about the fate of this kingdom. If your uncle won't do what must be done, then it will be up to us."

Jaden set his half empty glass down on the side table. "Actually, I have a date to get to." He was out the door, and it was snapping shut behind him before his father replied.

CHAPTER 7

"How many petitions do we have, commander?" Caroline had seated herself on her newly carved throne on the dais of Kierengaard's Great Hall. Breicher, as her intended, sat to her right on Hollis's old throne beside her. Angus had arranged benches for the rest of the royal family directly below the lowest step. She'd demanded the former king and queen be in attendance and was determined to show a unified front.

"Only five today, Your Majesty." Angus stood at a podium and was reading a tally handed to him by a reporter. She'd opened the hall so any subjects who were interested may observe.

"Very well." She fidgeted with the sash she wore around her gown. "Where are they?" she grumbled under her breath to Breicher. She'd stalled as long as she could. Movement at the back of the room caught her eye. The four missing Veetula royals slipped into the room. Jaden dipped to the side as soon as they'd passed the threshold. He leaned on the wall opposite the benches, with his knee bent and foot rested on the stones. He lazily hooked his thumbs in his pockets, and the casual smirk he wore gave Caroline the impression he was up to something.

A gust of cool air breezed through the room as Agnes nudged Cecily forward. Had *she* done that? The child seemed to read the foreboding charge in the space and was pressing back against her mother's palms as Agnes shoved her forward. Every urge in Caroline's body screamed for her to wrap her hands around Agnes's throat and let her know exactly how she felt about that smug look as she seated Cecily next to her. She'd even dressed the child in a somber grey frock and twisted her pretty auburn curls into a tight knot at the base of her skull.

Letting her eyes bore into the woman, she said, "Approach."

Agnes sat unmoving and Caroline swore the world had turned scarlet for a moment. A thought and the defiant woman was on her feet, scuttling to the queen, wide-eyed. Bringing her within an arm's length of her feet, Caroline forced her to her knees and leaned down to whisper, "What type of monster brings a child to these sorts of proceedings? And that outfit, Gods, you'd think this was going to be a funeral. Are you trying to draw my ire?"

Agnes trembled even as she sat tight-lipped. Caroline hadn't intended for her to speak because she knew the answer. The defiance in Agnes's eyes was enough to loosen the tight control Caroline held on her power and, before she could stop herself, she'd seized control of the woman's lungs, catching her breath.

Agnes's eyes bulged and Caroline said, "I didn't want things to be like this between us, but it seems I need to make myself clear and you need to understand the threat that I am."

Caroline wasn't sure if it was the nervous glance from Cecily or the gentle hand Breicher laid upon her forearm that made her release the compulsion. She shook Breicher's hand off. Agnes sucked in a breath, but Caroline kept her kneeling. Cupping her cool fingers around the other woman's cheeks, she tilted her face up to meet her own, then she kissed her forehead. Let it look like she was blessing this audacious woman.

"Rise," she commanded loud enough for the whole room to hear. Agnes scrambled to her feet and glanced around like she was unsure of what to do with herself. "Thank you for coming, Princess Agnes and bringing Princess Cecily, but I'm afraid I promised the young lady a pony ride. Isn't that right, Cecily?"

The child's innocent wide eyes darted between the two women. "But mother said I must attend the.... umm." She paused like she was trying to remember the word her mother had used, then her eyes brightened. "The spectacle."

Caroline allowed herself to laugh. The nerve of this woman. She'd deal with her later. "Yes, but she didn't know I'd already promised, right, Agnes?"

Agnes paled and eyed the bench like she wanted to crawl under it and die, but she said, "That's right. Let's go and find your pony, dear."

Caroline cleared her throat and with a nod, Angus approached the little girl. He knelt, offering her one of Caroline's peppermint sticks he dutifully kept handy. "My commander will escort Cecily to the stables. I'd be honored if you'd stay, *Your Majesty.*"

Breicher knew the sardonic slash that had cut a path across the queen's face, exposing her gleaming teeth all too well. A sympathy pang squeezed his chest for his former queen. Agnes was on her own. He and his brother were smart enough to stand by and let Caroline deal with Agnes's boldness as she saw fit. Hollis had warned his wife that they should leave the girl out of it, but Agnes seemed to want to use her as a weapon against the queen. Agnes had said if she had to be there, might as well use the opportunity. It was a good life experience, she said, for the turbulent world Cecily would be married off into one day.

He'd seen the adoring glimmer in Cecily's eye when she'd seen the beautiful woman in the library, though. The instant spell Caroline had unknowingly cast over the girl, and the way her mother had gone rigid as a board as she'd realized it. Agnes had been working daily to instill the same hatred his father had instilled in him as a boy toward anything to do with the southern kingdom. It didn't seem to be working.

Caroline tapped her foot impatiently as her eyes redirected to the podium Angus had vacated. Reading her thoughts, he started to rise, but her grip stilled him.

"Jaden," Caroline called across the room. "Please." she pointed to the podium. "Time to get your feet wet, since you seem so *interested.*"

Breicher had to suppress a groan, but even across the room, he sensed his nephew perking up. The extra briskness in his usually languid motion, or the intelligent glimmer brought to life he was trying to hide from his father. Breicher had spent years learning how to read people. He doubted anyone else noticed.

Gods, the prince was all legs and arms, so much taller than when he'd left five years earlier. He stood as high above the podium as Angus, but he was gangly by comparison. Jaden flipped through the papers, tapping his long fingers against the wood as he reviewed them. It only took a few minutes, then he nodded back to Caroline. The couple minutes' delay making the petitioners antsy.

"Very well," she said. "Proceed Prince Jaden Ivanslohe."

That voice, which was like an unpleasant memory Angus couldn't shake, resounded through the room as he entered. He'd figured Caroline would stall for as long as needed. She was the queen, and they could wait all day if needed. Still, he'd hurried back as soon as he'd deposited the little princess with the awaiting female handler, a reigning champion from the south Caroline was a fan of. Angus thought it was an absurd length to go to for a child, and he'd told her as much when she'd whisked the woman in this morning for the lesson. But that was how Caroline did everything.

"Petitioner, please come forward," Jaden said, erupting a flurry of movement from the audience. Two men pushed through and bowed before Caroline. "Stand and state your case."

Angus stopped short. Caroline was allowing Prince Jaden to run the petitions. And he wasn't supposed to be the one to release them from their knees. He waited for Caroline to reprimand the prince, but the men began speaking, and all Angus could do was try to seal his mouth shut.

He caught Caroline's eye as she listened to the men. She gave a subtle jerk of her chin, indicating he stood aside. That didn't bother him, her will was his own. It was that she seemed amused, which meant she was likely viewing this as some sort of punishment for the flippant man. But the more he watched the young Prince, the less he believed that's what was happening in his mind.

No, this wouldn't do at all.

It was nightfall again in this ever-waking nightmare that comprised Breicher's life now. A few moments earlier, Caroline had sauntered into his rooms, poured herself and him a glass of wine and walked out onto the balcony expecting him to follow. It was the same thing she'd done every night since they'd arrived in Veetula—after the night he'd embarrassed himself. They were establishing a pattern, and he caught himself looking forward to her arrival, another source of his shame. Grabbing a throw blanket, he wrapped it around his shoulders and followed her outside to where she'd taken a seat on the plush chaise he'd relocated for her.

"I didn't expect Kierengaard to be so beautiful. It was supposed to be a place where nightmares came to life and your family acted out all the atrocities we hated you for," Caroline said.

Breicher glanced out at what he could see of his family home from the balcony. Rugged snow-covered mountains rose to the east beyond the sprawling town which lit the valley with the lamplight that illuminated its many homes and businesses. The white stone multilayered castle rose up from the plateau it was built upon, similar to how Roskide was atop a hill. But where Roskide seemed to drape itself over the hill, weighing it down, Kierengaard felt spindly, reaching up toward the empty heavens.

Caroline's spire was visible where it rose from a sheer wall that met the face of the rock rise and the slate roof tiles almost lifted into the clouds. The spire had been abandoned, but after he'd given her a tour of the castle, she told him she'd fallen in love with the view and immediately commissioned the wing renovated. It had been done precisely to her detailed specifications in a few short days.

"Both of our homes are beautiful in their own right," he said, hating the need he felt to maintain a neutral stance, or else anger the queen.

"That went well, don't you think?" she asked, ignoring his diplomatic response, and took a long drink. She gestured to his glass, then the side of the chaise opposite her.

He stared at the drink warily but took a seat. Had she worn that silk robe through the halls to get from her spire to his? He'd offered her a blanket before, but she didn't want one, claiming she liked the way the chill bit at her skin.

"You think that went well?" he asked.

She huffed. "I didn't have to kill anyone. I figured I might with it being the first one. But I'm thinking my subjects here are timider. Or they're unfamiliar with the process, but I expect in time that will change. Our little spy did well."

"I'm not so sure about having Jaden lead the petitions, especially considering that fact."

Caroline shrugged and took a sip. "You believe me now? I guess we caught him outright, so even you can't deny it." She winked at him. "He needs something to do besides bedding half the kingdom. You know the saying about *idle hands*..." As she said it, her own hands slid along the silky material adorning her thighs, to emphasize the point.

Why was she here, tormenting him like this? He'd sided with two of her judgments against his brother, and Hollis had berated him for an hour afterward. He'd called it a hairline betrayal and issued him a warning. A full crack, as he described it, and Breicher would be stripped of the family name. He didn't even want to know the tongue-lashing Jaden was getting. "I can't do this with you, Caroline."

Her teeth clenched, but her eyes remained impassive. "Hollis is going to have to accept that we're going to rule as a team." When he didn't respond, she said, "I imagined you had more backbone."

He snorted, his thoughts flickering back to his finger in her mouth. "Yeah, me too." Breicher stood and walked across the sitting room into his bedroom, shutting the door behind him. She was too prideful to follow. He leaned back on the door in case he was wrong, waiting. Glass crashed against the old timber vibrating through his shoulders and when he looked down, red wine was seeping beneath the door. A second later, another goblet, presumably his glass this time, smashed against the door. He chuckled, shaking his head. He could almost see the fury on her beautiful face.

After the door slammed, he glanced at his bed longingly. The soft linens beckoned him, like they'd erase the struggles of the day and whisk him away to a simpler place. But when he nestled himself beneath the covers and allowed his eyes to drift shut, being the traitor he was, all he saw was her face.

"We need to talk," Breicher said, leaning against the timber door frame in the queen's Veetula room the next morning. His stomach had fluttered as he'd climbed each step up the winding staircase.

Caroline, who was trailing a brush through her unbound hair, stilled. "Getting cold feet?" She turned to face him on her little stool, the silk of her nightgown slipping away to reveal bare feet, and smooth limber limbs beneath. Seeing her like that, so comfortable in his family home, it was all he could do not to fall to his knees before her, bury his head in her lap and beg her for forgiveness. Instead, he was here to make a request she would not grant.

"I shouldn't have walked away from you last night."

"No, you shouldn't have."

"Listen, I think we can work together." That piqued her attention.

"That's good news, since that is the plan."

"Yes, and perhaps you could call off the wedding and instead have an official crowning."

"Not a chance, Prince. You may leave." The chill that radiated off her sent tremors down his spine.

Four nights had gone by and Breicher kept his eyes glued to his door, waiting for the queen's nightly arrival. For the fourth night, she hadn't arrived. Even though she left every night, she'd spent a glass of wine's worth of time with him discussing the events of the day. It had become a comforting routine once he'd understood her intention hadn't been to seduce him. But perhaps that was worse.

An hour went past, and then another. Breicher crawled into bed, but his eyes wouldn't shut. He'd laid there squeezing them until he had half a headache. Had something happened? Concern for her safety immediately sprung to the forefront of his mind. No, he shook it off. She was fine. Caroline had chosen not to come to him tonight, again.

Fine. He would go to her.

Caroline perched on her window ledge, the shutters blown open. She leaned forward with her arms wrapped around her knees and stared out at the full moon rising, which framed her delicate figure in a glowing orb.

She looked so peaceful, like a dream, her white hair glimmering in the moonlight. How was she not freezing? The power she'd stolen from the Gods must have made her impervious to the blistering air that was lifting the ends of her hair.

If she heard him, she didn't acknowledge it. Glued to the spot, he watched the woman who would become his wife in a few days.

Eventually, the moon rose above the top of the window frame, so it was longer visible and he stirred from his spot on the wall, watching her. It was a few hours like it had been when he was her guard, as if for a second, they were back in that moment in time.

Like she felt his eyes on her, she said, "I'm a fool, aren't I?" Her voice was soft, barely audible.

This was the worst it'd been, his desire to go scoop her out of the window, take her to bed and make sure she knew exactly how he felt about her. Even if it was only to pull her into his warmth, shield her from the cold. Protect her. But how would he do that—he didn't even know what these foreign swirling emotions were.

He needed to run from this place. Leave and never come back, regardless of the cost to himself. He didn't know how long he stood there warring with himself. Breicher tried to speak. Tried to tell her she wasn't a fool, but his throat squeezed, and he couldn't edge a word out. Instead, he slipped out the door and fled into the night.

CHAPTER 8

"WHERE'S CAROLINE?" HE ASKED anyone who would answer as he strode into the Great Hall, noticing that of the royals, she was the only one missing. He'd hardly spoken to him since he'd suggested she call off the wedding except for those damning words. *I'm a fool, aren't I?* Her silence made it easier and harder at the same time.

He surveyed again. Angus was absent, too. Hollis only sneered and wrapped his arms around the back of the bench in his normal spot. Agnes darted her glance around like if the queen didn't appear at any moment, she was going to ditch the petitions.

Jaden stepped forward. "Angus caught me in the hall. There was another skirmish. This time in Avondale. Her Majesty and the commander went to address it themselves. She said we should see the petitioners today."

"You and me?" Breicher asked, incredulous. Since word of the petitions had spread, more requests had come in and Caroline had suggested doing as needed until the people of Veetula were *caught up.*

"Angus said you sat in on them in Everstal and would know what to do. Ten today." Jaden shrugged, nonplussed about the whole ordeal and only shot a defiant glare toward his father before he assumed his post at the podium.

As Breicher seated himself, he envied the prince's easy confidence. He hadn't seen the queen in action, so his naivety was benefiting him. Jaden must have already reviewed them because he shouted, "Open the doors! Petitions may begin."

Jaden introduced the first group, a few merchants, with a boundary dispute on some farmland, a precious and rare commodity in Veetula. As he listened to the men, his mind wandered to where Caroline might be. Was she in danger? Was she being respected? Was she harming anyone?

Jaden cleared his throat. *Shit.* He hadn't caught the last of that. He glanced at his brother, who was smirking. "We have a land registry, correct?"

Hollis shrugged and fingered one of his wife's auburn curls.

"Yes, Your Majesty," Jaden answered. "Kept in the hall of records, managed by the bookkeepers. We could send out a surveyor, perhaps, if Your Majesty thinks it would be wise."

Clever young prince, indeed. One he had a feeling he was going to owe big time after this. "Yes," he said. "Exactly what I had in mind. Make it so," he said to the court reporter, who was furiously scratching down notes. "We will send one within the week. They will rule on behalf of the crown. You're dismissed." The men, both probably hoping the queen had validated their claim, left grumbling.

He and Jaden made quick work of the rest of the petitioners, and he was a little thankful Caroline hadn't been in attendance today. The client who'd beaten up the prostitute for demanding payment had been particularly grisly. The moment he'd seen her blue-and-purple eye, his blood had heated. That was the type of thing that made Caroline go on the offensive.

She was eager to put in place the many new laws she'd enacted in Everstal in Veetula, but she'd done it over ten years. Change took time. He and Jaden crafted a punishment that would have made Caroline proud and hit the man where it hurt. The woman left with a promissory note that had her beaming, and Breicher imagined she was headed straight to the treasury to transfer her debt to her wealthy abuser, plus a little extra for her trouble. His name would be sent to the brothels, and he'd be banned for one year. At that time, his behavior would be reassessed by the queen.

When they'd finished, he left the chapel through a corridor behind the dais. Footsteps he recognized as Jaden caught up to him. "How much trouble do you think we're going to be in with father this time?"

He huffed a laugh. "Well, *she* wasn't here, so hopefully, not that much."

"I don't see why he cares. It's not like he ever enjoyed ruling, or was any good at it," Jaden said.

"You forget, it was your father's plan that brought down King Thom. Hollis has a mind for strategy."

Jaden snorted. "Military prowess and an ability to plot a successful string of murders doesn't make you a good king."

"Awfully high handed for one so young, don't you think, Prince Jaden?" Breicher raised a brow at the younger man as they walked along.

"Your future wife is my age and took the crown at fourteen if the stories are to be believed. Built back her kingdom, pushed us out and enacted a slew of new laws by the time she was my age."

Breicher shook his head. "Fair point. Still, Hollis has lived his whole life being groomed to be king. Taught that loyalty should be valued above all else and that his word was the law. I don't know if he'll ever be able to see things differently."

Jaden paused and wrinkled his brow at his uncle. Why did his uncle care so much about what his father thought? Breicher stopped to face him and waited patiently for the thought that was brewing in his mind. Jaden squared his shoulders and said, "Then what are you going to do about it?"

Breicher's mouth turned down into a half-frown. "Nothing, Jaden. There's nothing we can do. You did well out there today, you know." His uncle patted him on the back and kept walking.

"We made a good team, uncle," Jaden said, before he took the next hallway he came to. Gods, it was disappointing. Though his uncle was only ten years older, after everything he'd experienced, he'd expected more from him. Granted, he'd made an assassination attempt on a notoriously brutal queen and survived. That would understandably shake a man's confidence. It didn't excuse his complacency, though. They had a duty to their people. Jaden was also an heir and a prince. If his uncle was going to ignore him and be content to live in a state of denial, he'd find a way to make things happen himself.

Jaden was about to pull his hair out, it was all so futile, when a crisp wind blew through the war room the four Veetula royals were arguing in. Angus and Caroline materialized in a swirl of angry air right in front of the door.

"You're in pants," Jaden said, cocking his head to the side, then immediately zeroing in on the injured commander.

"Caroline—" Breicher gasped. "Whose blood is that?"

"I was ambushed!" Caroline said, holding up her hands to keep him away. Surveying the room, she locked on Hollis, who was repressing a grin, and Agnes, inching toward the door, ready to flee.

"Did you do this?" she demanded, storming over, and getting into Hollis's face, blocking Agnes's path.

"Nooo—I may have had a little too much winter's sin and suggested that it would be possible to some old, very loyal subjects. But..." His father wrestled for control against Caroline's compulsion. "I did not order them to act. And I warned them of the consequences, *Your Majesty.*"

His father's eyes peeled open as her hand flew lightning fast through the air and struck his cheek. Agnes screamed and plastered herself against the nearest wall.

"Get out," Caroline yelled. "Before I kill you both."

"Me too?" Jaden asked, his voice a little sheepish.

Caroline whipped her head in his direction, and he swallowed a nervous lump in his throat. "Stay for all I care," she hissed. "I know you'll be listening through the door if I don't allow it. At least this way you'll get the story right."

Using the distraction, his mother and father fled from the room, the door snapping closed behind them.

She spun and charged toward Breicher, shoving a finger in his face. "I will end your brother, I swear to all that is holy, if you don't get a handle on him."

Breicher's skin went ashen, but the queen wasn't finished.

"I am this close—" She held up two fingers. "—to driving a dagger into his heart myself. People unnecessarily died today because of the seeds he's been planting. If it happens again, I will hold the entire Ivanslohe line responsible, starting with you."

The future king didn't speak or move. Was she compelling him? Then, as if it pained him, Breicher's hands went to her cheeks, smoothing out the hair that was still sticky with blood with such care. He nodded. "I'm sorry this happened, Caroline." Were his eyes glowing? An Ivanslohe's eyes only glowed when their power was thrumming through them at full strength, either in the heat of battle or when they were—ew! Then, as if responding to Breicher's, rings of luminescent silver reflected back. *Get a room* is what he wanted to say.

Instead, Jaden circled nearer to get a better view of this fury driven queen. This was the cruel, unleashed woman he'd heard so much about. "I'll deal with him," he said, surprising himself. It took everything he had to still himself as Caroline turned to him, her eyes glinting in a way that was all at once a challenge and a threat.

"Are you sure you're up for it, prince?" she asked, a taunt dripping from her voice making his insides quiver.

She liked this, being feared. Was that what it was with her? The thought made him question how many things he'd heard about her were actually true and how many falsehoods she'd allow to run wild for the sake of creating the larger-than-life figure she was. Breicher had told him about the raven, as unbelievable as it was. He supposed if he'd been king at fourteen, he might have employed a similar tactic.

"I'm not promising perfect results, but I think I can manage it."

Caroline huffed. "Then it's your job."

Fine. He had a plan.

Angus grunted. "Are you sure we can't just kill him, Your Majesty?" Angus was still gripping the back of the chair he'd been leaning against since they'd gotten back to Kierengaard. His dark skin was waxen, and he looked ready to pass out at any moment.

Caroline started toward him when Breicher wrapped his fingers around her bicep and pulled her toward him. "Jaden, take Angus to a healer and make sure he's taken care of. I'm going to deal with the queen," he growled. Gods, to be on the receiving end of that kind of ferocity, the possessive urge filling his uncle. He only hoped the queen understood what she'd gotten herself into.

A moment later, Caroline was being carried out of the room in his uncle's arms. He slowly turned toward Angus, who was injured, bleeding—a little ragged looking if he were being honest. But those shoulders never seemed broader. The question was, would he want to be the one doing the carrying or being carried?

As if Angus read the untoward notions rolling around in his mind, he started edging toward the door.

Jaden rolled his eyes. "Oh, stop it. You're disgusting, all covered in blood and Gods know what else. I'd prefer not to get my hands dirty." He paused, brushing off invisible dirt from his palms. "You're not still bleeding anywhere, are you?"

Angus slipped his hand inside, a tear in his shirt, feeling around for something. An open wound, broken rib? "No, she healed the worst of it. Just some minor cuts, I believe."

Angus staggered toward the door, keeping his hand rubbing at his side. "Lead the way."

After the third time he'd scuffed the toe of his boot and almost tripped, Angus allowed Jaden to hook an arm around his shoulders and lean some of his weight on him. "You sure it's not too much for you?" Angus asked.

Jaden almost choked. Was Angus intentionally joking with him? Maybe he had a head injury, he thought, and made a mental note to have Caroline try to sense if there had been any lasting damage. "I may not be as excessively large as you, but I'm more than capable of bearing a small portion of your weight."

The healer hadn't been able to hide the grimace she'd made when they shuffled into the healing center. "Don't worry, Ambeth," Jaden assured the portly woman. "The queen has healed his more dire injuries. He needs a little patching up and something for the pain."

"Get that sword belt off him," Ambeth demanded, pinning a cap over her cropped orange locks. While Angus fumbled with the buckle, she poured a basin of heated water and mixed some extracts into it, setting it on the examination table.

"Prince, we'll be here all day if you wait on him." Angus grumbled something to the effect of *I've got it*, but the healer intervened. "Give me your hand."

Reluctantly, the hulking man let go of the belt and put a quivering hand on the healer's and she started working, starting with his bloodied knuckles. Jaden recognized that tremble for what it was. *Fatigue*. His body was spent.

"How does this thing even stay on you, you wear it so low?" he asked. Jaden's eyes trailed down to the other man's waist, where he himself was struggling with the intricate clasps. He was so close Angus's hot breath warmed his face as he worked. It wasn't foul, though, considering what he'd been through. It was minty and mingled with the metallic blood and earthy sweat coming off him. *Primal*.

"It's that butt," Ambeth suggested with a giggle. He'd almost forgotten his question; he'd been so focused on his other senses and figured he ought to cut the queen and his uncle a little slack. There was something alluring about a battle-weary hero. Angus let out a frustrated exhale, drawing his focus.

"Sorry," Jaden said. "The leather safety tie is knotted."

"Just cut it."

"No, I've about got it." He didn't know if he did it because it would drive the other man mad, but he dropped to his knees so he could see the knot better.

"Hold still," Ambeth scolded when Angus jerked.

Jaden stared straight ahead as he rubbed the knot between his fingers, loosening it enough that he was able to get it free. Then pulled back the strap and released the buckle, catching the belt with the sheathed sword as it slipped off Angus's hips. He looked up, grinning. "See? I told you."

"You can go," Angus muttered, glaring at him before he looked away.

Jaden couldn't be sure, but through the splatters of blood on his cheeks, was that a flush?

"I was charged with making sure you stayed alive, so I'll stay, thanks." Jaden pulled a stool over to the corner and took his watchful perch. Caroline's poor commander—he had no idea the trouble he was in.

One moment Caroline had brought to heel an entire village's worth of dissenters and returned her longest friend back from the brink. Now she was being carried through the halls pressed into the hard chest of a man unable to fight his possessive instinct. What a day.

"Are you hurt anywhere?" Breicher asked, brilliant blue eyes glued to her.

"I'm fine. I swear." She ran her hand across the solid wall of his chest, up to his neck, tracing the veins throbbing below the surface with the tips of her fingers. Her other arm slipped around his neck and teased his hair at the base of his head. Even though she was a mess, that she killed men today, her mouth watered, drawn to that tan flesh below his ear.

First, she tasted him with her tongue, then her lips, then her teeth. When she lightly bit down, he groaned, squeezing her tight against him. "Easy, Caroline, or I'll take you right here in this busy corridor."

As if to emphasize his point, two attendants passed by them in a flurry, giggling. Breicher entered the stairway leading up to her rooms in the spire, putting his warrior's body to use, taking her up the stairs two at a time like the climb was nothing. He kicked the door open and charged through, letting it snap closed behind them.

The moment he'd set her down, he drew her into him, threading his fingers into her hair, and kissing his way down her soiled neck. When he pulled away, a pink smear was across his lips. He leaned forward to kiss her, but she pulled away. Gods, she was aching for him.

"Caroline," he growled, pawing at her, touching, and squeezing every part of her he got his hands on. "I need you."

The desperation in his voice almost melted her. "I'm so ready for you, Breicher, but I'm not going to be covered in blood the first time we're together. I'll be a few moments." She had to clamp her thighs together to ease the ache.

Breicher grabbed her hand, dragging her into the bathing chamber. He positioned her in front of the mirror on the vanity and tugged her hips back so he'd have access to her front. A second later, he had the laces on her trousers undone. Matching intensity glowed in their eyes as he said, "I need to feel you."

The muscles rippled and flexed in his exposed forearms as he snaked one up her chest to cup her jaw. The other pressed beneath her underwear, rough fingers dipping into the silken heat that pooled there. She didn't know which one of them gasped as he pressed a finger inside, then another. Her boneless body wanted to collapse forward with pleasure, but he held her firm to him, grinding his erection into her backside.

"Please, Caroline, don't make me wait."

Dead gods, she really didn't want to. "I want your mouth to trail over every inch of my skin, and that can't happen when I'm covered in gore." He was going to protest, but she cut him off. "You can wait five minutes."

He grimaced as if it hurt to pull his fingers from inside her. "Hurry up," he said in a low, guttural voice. "I'll be right outside."

The water was freezing, but she hardly felt it. She'd never cleaned herself so fast in her life. Four minutes and she was wrapped in a towel and sauntering out for him. Her heart started when she found him on the edge of her bed with his head in his hands. Had he changed his mind?

"That was the hardest four minutes of my life," he said, lifting his head to display a hungry grin.

Blessed angels, Caroline thought, and dropped the towel, trying not to look too eager as she paced over to him. Greedy hands latched on her hips, pulling her into his lap. He was as ready as he'd been five minutes before. "Why aren't you undressed?" she asked, voice breathy.

He chuckled as he took a firm pink nipple into his mouth, causing her to toss her hair back, moaning. "You requested my mouth over every inch of your flesh, so I'm keeping my clothes on long enough to do that." He found her other breast, giving it equal attention, and she pressed down on him. "So I don't accidentally slip and impale you before I've accomplished my task."

Her mind was swirling and a haze of lust and some other chest squeezing emotion. "Kiss me," she demanded.

Obediently, Breicher's hands reached for her face to pull her mouth to his. But before they crossed that chasm, bells rang out across the castle, and Breicher froze. "Fuck," he yelled.

Urgently, she smoothed his mussed hair. "What is it?"

The gong strikes were deafening, each chime clapping unfettered through the open windows of the tower room. "An emergency. The sequence—three long bells is a call to convene in the war room."

His future wife's lower lip trembled and those watery silver eyes—she was about to burst into tears. Breicher had never seen her look so... fragile. Pulling her forward, he gave her a chaste kiss, which sparked with static charge, before he eased her off his lap. He ran his thumb across her full lower lip. "I know you've been through a lot today. Let's go see what it is, then we can come back here, and I'll spend all night making you feel good. Okay?"

His entire body screamed in protest as he wrenched himself off the bed.

Caroline paced over to the wardrobe and reeled back and punched it, splitting the wood with a crack.

"Don't do that," he rushed over to her, unable to resist running his hands down her still naked hips.

"Why not?" she breathed, leaning back into him.

"Because I'll bend you over and fuck you right here against this wardrobe while the world is burning down around us," he snarled into her ear, placing a trail of wet kisses down her neck. The bell rang three more times, as if everyone in the surrounding towns didn't hear it the first time.

The Queen of the Joined Kingdoms whimpered when he pulled away, and he could only laugh to himself. He may be damned, but what a sweet hell.

The queen's face was still deliciously flushed when they arrived at the war room. His brother, Angus, and Jaden were already there.

Hollis glared between them. "What were you two doing that took you so long to get down here?" *Traitor* was the word he didn't need to say.

"None of your business," Breicher said, placing his hand on the small of the queen's back, ushering her past his brother so she wouldn't pounce on him with that pent up frustration. He pulled out a chair, and she took a seat. He took the one next to her, only now realizing the shift in his reluctance. Something about seeing all the blood on her had changed something in him, the worry that it had been hers punched through his gut had struck him silent. He really looked at her then and it occurred to him that if this was his life, it wouldn't be so bad. He could be king.

With that thought, he said, "So what is so urgent that you had to call us away from far more entertaining activities? We don't seem to be under siege. No new blood unless I'm missing something?"

The command in Breicher's voice gave Caroline a thrill. And he wasn't trying to hide what had happened between them. Warmth flooded into her awareness, and like Breicher sensed it, he draped his arm across the back of her chair.

Hollis's upper lips curled at the action exposing the top row of his teeth.

Jaden shot his father a murderous look, which pleased Caroline, then huffed. "My mother has taken Princess Cecily and fled. She was seen leaving the castle in traveling cloaks in one of the fastest carriages less than an hour ago."

"Shit," Breicher said. "She must have been planning to get her away before the wedding." An expression dripping with condemnation was exchanged between the two men. "*You* obviously weren't in the loop."

Hollis puffed out his chest, chuffing. "I'm surrounded by traitors."

"You're a sorry loser," Caroline said. "Either say something productive or don't speak." She tapped her nails on the table. "How far could they have gotten?"

"In an hour?" Breicher answered. "Depending on how congested the streets are, and which route they're taking, possibly to the edge of the city."

The captain of the Veetula royal guard, a man named Victor Carl, walked into the room along with three other top tier captains.

"Princess Agnes and Princess Cecily are missing," Breicher explained. "The official story is they've been abducted, but we fear they've fled for fear of the repercussions from the recent raids. It's an unfortunate judgment on Agnes's part because the queen's intention is to be a merciful ruler."

Caroline bristled beside him, but he reached a hand over and threaded it through hers. Her rising tension subsided. Merciful wasn't the exact word she would use, but she supposed it was close enough. Word would spread of how she'd expeditiously handled the men who were all but martyrs today. Her only regret was how close it had come with her commander's life.

"Send out your fastest riders and canvas the area. I want them brought in, unharmed before lunchtime tomorrow. Your discretion is appreciated," Breicher said, voice deep and commanding.

Captain Carl bowed to the man who would be her king in a matter of days. "It will be done."

"Victor," Caroline said, halting him using his given name. Personal requests always went better when she employed a bit of familiarity. "Cecily's a child. Should you or your team find her first, I expect you and your men to shield her from any unpleasantness. She should not have to suffer for Agnes's lack of wisdom. Understood?"

"Yes, Your Majesty," the men recited in unison, lowering their heads. Breicher didn't fail to notice the subtle softening in their eyes before they charged from the room, released on their mission.

Caroline and Breicher exchanged a look, then rose from their seats.

"Where are you two going?" Hollis hissed.

"We're going to find my niece," Caroline said without hesitation.

Breicher held the door open for his queen, placing a hand on her shoulder as they passed into the hallway. His heart twisted when she'd said *niece*, placing the girl under her protection without flinching. That she'd thought it was more important to find the girl than to see to her own abandoned needs.

But he should have known that about her. Angus hadn't scoffed when Caroline had said it, knowing she'd expect him to stay and manage reports from Kierengaard. But he'd seen how protective she was when it came to those who couldn't fend for themselves and how she took a direct approach to everything she did.

Maybe his plight could be good. Wonderful even. It enthralled him, the determination of the woman beside him. A little ember of pride swelled in his chest as they mounted their horses and raced off into the night.

Caroline and her soon-to-be husband searched all night and found nothing. Not a trace of the midnight carriage and the riders inside.

"I didn't expect this was how I'd be spending the days before my wedding," Breicher said.

Caroline chuckled. "What did you expect?" Her eyes were as heavy as his, and she was holding back a yawn.

"Well, before Hollis got married, I arranged for all our cousins and a bunch of paid girls to meet at a cabin to the west of here our family owns. We spent two days in debauchery. Hollis was so hungover the night of his wedding, he had to lean against the pulpit in the royal chapel. Agnes kept glaring at him and me, but I could only laugh. At least she knew what she was getting herself into with my brother and the notorious Ivanslohe *appetite*." Breicher shook his head like he was reliving the memory.

Her lips pressed into a frown, and she nudged her horse forward again. "I guess it's good that Agnes has provided us this little distraction, then. And no need to worry. I can keep up with your *appetite*." She shot him a wink.

Breicher's sharp jaw clenched and the way his eyes slid to her under that strong brow suggested he'd be ready for her on a moment's notice despite their exhaustion. "There's no sign of them," he said, breezing past her comment. "Should you zip back to Kierengaard and see if any of the others have found them? Or we could stop somewhere to get a few hours of *sleep*?"

They'd made it to the first, and largest village, past the perimeter of the city surrounding the castle. They'd peaked in every stable for that elusive carriage. They weren't here.

"I'll go," she said, dismounting and handing him the reins. In a flash, she was gone and standing in the war room. Her commander's head limp on the parchment map spread across the table in front of him. He snored lightly and jerked as she approached, but fell back into the peaceful rhythm of sleep. The map of the northern territory had an intricate pattern of lines drawn across it, including the path she and Breicher had taken. A smudged circle, about the size of a silver coin, was drawn around an inn at the edge of the city to the east, right next to a small puddle of drool still dripping from Angus's cracked mouth.

Sensing a presence, she turned to find Jaden, who casually leaned against the door frame. He waved her out into the hallway. "Carl found them a few hours ago. They're due back to the castle at noon." Caroline wrinkled her brow, but Jaden shook his head. "I advised him to not appear hurried for Cecily's sake, at your request," he said, inclining his head, a self-assured grin playing at the edges of his lips.

Were all Ivanslohe men so overconfident?

"Good." Caroline trailed her eyes up and down his lean form. Not a hair was out of place and his attire looked as pressed as if he'd just put it on. Even the sapphire in his eyes had an unwearied glimmer in the firelight bouncing through the hallway from the several nearby sconces. He was definitely up to something.

"The night shift suits you," she said, running a hand over the smooth fabric of his lapel. His breath caught as the scales in the power dynamic shifted back to her. These royal men were too easy.

She chuffed, brushing past him.

"Where are you going?" Jaden asked, trailing after the queen. *Gods.* A little vibration walked down his spine as she swayed down the hall. If she were fair game, he might have been up for the challenge. But that was his blood talking. That constant annoying urge.

Like she knew what he was thinking, Caroline flipped her white locks and over her shoulder, she said, "To fetch your uncle in the village where I left him."

Then she was gone.

"What is your face doing, Agnes?" Caroline peered at the woman Captain Victor Carl had deposited a few minutes before. "The skin around your eye is twitching, just here." She pointed to the corner of her eye for emphasis.

Jaden had seen to his sister, taking her riding, but Caroline had been eager to deal with the flight risk that was Agnes Ivanslohe.

Agnes only sneered, averting her eyes.

"It seems you have misjudged me yet again." Caroline paced back-and-forth in front of Agnes's chair, her heavy velvet skirt rustling as she walked. She'd taken to wearing heavier clothing the last week. The chill in the air didn't affect her, but seeing her in her traditional Everstal warm weather attire unnerved the castle staff. She didn't think it was concern for her comfort, more a fear she would blame them for the lack of it.

Caroline paused in front of Agnes, tapping her finger to her lips. "Well, I'll be needing a wedding present for my husband, so I suppose your life will do." This was getting boring, sparing these enemies of hers.

Angus seemed to have the same feeling. "I thought the first time we spared them was the gift?"

She would have grumbled if it wouldn't have made her look unqueenly. Instead, she shot him a frown, then leaned down into Agnes's face. "I take it you've decided to decline my offer of friendship?"

"You wouldn't know what a friend was," Agnes hissed, and the dart landed as intended and Caroline felt her upper lip curl. That was a lie. She had friends... look at Angus.

Turning her back to Agnes, she addressed Carl. "Confine her to her apartment until I release her. She may be escorted to the wedding because I have a job for her, but afterward, take her back."

"Yes, Your Majesty." Carl bowed his head. "And Princess Cecily?"

"The girl will have no restrictions on her privileges. If she asks why her mother isn't permitted outside her rooms, then tell her I said her mother is not well."

With a mocking pat on the other woman's head, Caroline left, making a beeline for her chamber. She had friends, right? The thought nagged her all the way up the winding stairs. No, she decided. Queens didn't need friends.

Brushing the thought aside, locking it away with all the other daggers in her heart, she crawled into bed. There was time for a few hours' sleep, then she had a wedding to get ready for.

CHAPTER 9

B REICHER STOOD AT THE altar, unable to keep his feet planted. He'd worn the official regalia of the Veetula royalty, long navy slacks, with a fine sky-blue pinstripe woven into the fabric running up his legs, which only made his height more imposing. A cropped double-breasted jacket in the same material was secured with gleaming silver buttons, a white button up and tie peaked out from beneath. Across it was an icy blue satin sash with the coat of arms for his family name and the Veetula insignia of the Stag and Doves, along with any moons showing the recognitions he'd received in service to his kingdom. Wearing it had been another fight with his brother. Hollis had finally relented and was wearing his own sash, reluctantly standing beside him as Breicher had once done for him.

He scanned the crowd. So many familiar faces, some creased with worry, others wide-eyed, probably hoping for a scene. Caroline had selected the music, traditional sounds from his kingdom meant to endear her to its people. Typical calculating Caroline. So far, it was a conventional Veetula wedding.

The song the musicians were playing came to its natural end, and the murmuring guest silenced as the arching doors to the hall cracked open. He shot a hand out steadying himself on his brother's arm as Caroline stepped into the room.

Of course, Caroline wouldn't have worn white, as was tradition in his homeland. Among the pale and frozen colors of the guests, the hanging panels, ice sculptures, and bleached roses, the queen stood out like a black hare on a field of virgin snow. A charcoal metallic dress sat off her shoulders, the only skin exposed, and hugged her curves until, low on her hips, it flared out like the petals of a lily. It seemed they had woven each layer with a different precious metal, giving the gauzy material a molten effect when she moved. She wore no jewelry and unbound white hair flowed down her back, almost reaching her waist.

A soft drum beat with the gentle chiming of bells, timed with each of her footsteps.

Caroline stilled before turning to Agnes, who was seated in the front row, hugging onto a mid-sized gift box like it was the last parcel of food in existence. "Agnes," the queen said, motioning her to rise.

Agnes blinked a few times like she was coming out of a haze, then rose obediently, approaching the queen and placing the box on the altar. Her hands shook as she opened the lid and reached inside.

Caroline faced the crowd. "It is time for a new crown to represent the Joined Kingdoms," she said. One of the first things she'd done was make him take her to the treasury to get the largest five black diamonds in their possession. The diamonds, along with several smaller stones, numerous natural grey pearls, and square cut hematite now adorned the platinum tiara gripped in what he imagined were sweaty palms.

He wasn't sure if the crowd noticed the moment Agnes steeled herself, but steady hands brought the crown up to Caroline's head, placing the onyx and iridescent masterpiece on the queen's flowing white locks. Breicher was glad he wasn't the object of either of the women's stares as they wordlessly battled. "Kneel," Caroline said, and his heart skipped.

Agnes sniffed, then lowered her eyes, and brought herself to her knees before the queen. Breicher flicked his gaze toward his brother searching for any sign of aggression, but Agnes's flight had caused a rift between them. Hollis wouldn't intervene. Agnes was at the queen's mercy.

"Rise," she said. When Agnes stood before her once again eye to eye, Caroline reached out a hand, cupping her cheek and mouthed something that looked like *it's a step, sister*.

Caroline, now crowned, began her ascent to the dais, and the drums started their procession once again. The closer she came, the more active the little flutters in his chest. Was it getting louder? The drumbeats had to be coming in closer succession.

He swallowed deeply. "Caroline," he said, voice barely a breath, bringing her outstretched hand to his lips. She terrified him and made his blood race. Another woman would have never been enough. He was ready to give himself to her.

Caroline finished repeating her fifth line and her feet were starting to ache. Veetula ceremonies were a tedious thing. In Everstal it would be fifteen minutes tops. She studied the man across from her, who seemed quite glad to be standing through the excessive ceremony. His grin jumped over to her and her lips tugged upward.

Damn, he was stunning. Over six and a half feet of pure lean muscle, accentuated by the pale blue lines running the length of his suit, all hers. His hair had grown even longer, and she'd been pleased he'd left it a little messy. Her palms itched as she imagined how in a few short hours she'd be running her fingers through it. She couldn't wait to have those glowing eyes rove over every inch of the woman who was now his. She bit her lower lip at the thought.

"Are you even listening?" he whispered, and her face flamed.

She discreetly shook her head like a naughty child.

"I figured you might have caught that last part." The mischievous glint in his eyes made the dragon that lived in her chest beat its wings relentlessly. "No, nothing?" he teased when she didn't respond.

Breicher leaned forward, his stubble tickling her neck as he murmured, "His holiness has said I may kiss you now."

Her mouth fell open as she tilted her head up to him. Was she salivating? She was nodding eagerly, and she didn't care who saw.

His lips pressed into hers. Not soft like the first time, but intentional, as if he'd been thinking about exactly what he'd wanted the kiss to say. His hand made its way around the small of her back and the other threaded into her hair, and he deepened the kiss. Finally.

It wasn't the type of chaste kiss shared between a couple at an Everstal wedding ceremony. The way his lips moved against hers had heat, passion. She'd told him he'd better set the sky alight. But this wasn't bright like fireworks—it was deep and soulful like being dragged to the depths of the ocean and surrendering willingly. Her mouth opened to moan, and his tongue swept in capturing the sound and her mind emptied, becoming as vast as the sky at night. There was only them in that moment, spinning in time like a lost star held in the gravity of something so much larger than itself. His kiss was generous and demanding, all-consuming.

She was breathless when he pulled away.

"If I kiss you anymore, I'm going to spring free from my pants in front of all these people." He grabbed her by the arms and pulled her in front of him, and they shared a giggle. He leaned down. "I hope that was sufficient, wife?"

Wife. The word made her stomach jump. She edged up to steal another kiss.

"You're going to kill me," he said in a growl, and he turned her so her back was toward him. The holy man was saying something about presenting the Queen and King of the Joined Kingdoms and Jaden presented the matching crown she had made to Breicher.

Caroline snaked her hand between them, finding the hardness nudging into her back, and gave it a rub. Breicher jerked his hips backward, almost tipping his new crown off his head.

"Please join the happy couple in the Great Hall for drinks and dancing," the holy man proclaimed.

With the announcement, and the distracted guests, Breicher grabbed her and pulled her into a hallway behind the dais. He slammed her into the wall and had her dress halfway up her hips and was tugging a leg around his waist. "I want you so bad," he breathed into her neck. "Caroline, it's painful how much I need this."

She gasped as his teeth grazed down her decolletage and onto the swell of her breast he was working to free. "Breicher, the door is right there. Hundreds of people, right there," she said.

He didn't seem to hear her. Her husband was so consumed worshiping her peaked nipple and his other hand was creeping dangerously close to her undergarments. *Fuck it*, she thought. She was queen, and she'd have him wherever she wanted. His fingers slipped beneath her lacy ruined panties, nudging at her entrance, and she tossed her head back into the stone wall so hard a small crack sounded through the corridor.

"Hundreds of people are waiting on you two." Hollis's voice followed the sound. How had she not heard him slip through the door?

Breicher released her underwear and gripped her thigh like he was fighting for control. "They can wait all night for all I care," Breicher said, and an agitated protest rumbled through her. Gods, she was like a fawn beneath a mountain cat the way he was keeping her between himself and the wall, like he wouldn't share his fresh kill.

Then it occurred to her. He was really going to fuck her in this hallway if she didn't redirect him. She was going to let him, but Hollis had broken the lust addled haze. That wouldn't do. "Hey," she said, softening her voice, "your brother's right. Let's go to the party." When he grumbled, she grabbed his cheeks and gave him a sweet kiss. "Think of how much better it will be after all this waiting?"

Breicher released her leg and brought his fingers up to his mouth, sucking the taste of her off them, keeping the smoldering eye contact. She almost slid to the floor, the way her knees went jelly, but he helped her up, putting her clothing back together.

"Should I go touch up my make-up?" she asked, smoothing back her hair.

Breicher pinched her chin between his thumb and forefinger and assessed her face. "No, I want them to see you like this. You look deliciously ravished, my bride."

There was the predator she'd married. Breicher grabbed her hand and he and Hollis led them away.

Two mind-numbing hours later, Breicher's wife asked, "Can't we end this and go somewhere, husband?" Her thighs clenched beneath his palm, which was possessively splayed across them.

His deep, satisfied male chuckle vibrated through the bench they were both sitting on. Breicher had never felt luckier. It was a miracle the shift and he no longer felt the guilt.

There was still a line of guests waiting to give their congratulations. She'd made him wait in the hallway. Now it was his turn.

Breicher leaned over, tugging her chin toward him, pressing a slow kiss to her swollen pink lips. It didn't matter who saw them and this building volcano between them. Ivanslohe men were known for being generous with the objects of their affection in both public and private. He may only be judged for the object itself, but it didn't make him blink like it might have once had. They'd been wrong about her, and he basked in the warmth resonating between them.

"Care for a drink?" Hollis asked, holding out a glass of wine. He'd tried with winter's sin earlier.

"No, thanks. You take it. I want to be fully present tonight," he said, stealing a glance at his wife who was making small talk with two Veetula nobles. The line of her jaw, the poised way she sat and carried herself, stole his breath.

"Nah," Hollis said, passing the glass off to the nearest guest who took it, unsure of what else to do but take it from the former king. "I've already had enough."

That was strange. Hollis didn't believe in enough. "Not wanting to make a fool of yourself in front of the entire kingdom?"

"Something like that," his brother said.

Breicher raised an eyebrow. "What did my wife threaten you with that has you so spooked?"

"House arrest," Hollis confessed. "I don't know if I can handle being stuck in those apartments with Agnes for however long the queen decides to keep us there."

Breicher chuckled, clapping his brother on the shoulder. "Thanks for being here today. It means a lot. I know you and Caroline have your differences," he hesitated, assessing Hollis's mood, and continued, "and she stole your crown."

"There's that," Hollis said, eyeing the drink he'd handed off.

"But it means a lot, brother."

"There's nothing I wouldn't do for you, Breicher." Hollis scratched his head. "Hey, do you think I could steal you away for a minute to sneak a drink with the men where she won't see us? We missed our family tradition."

Breicher considered his wife. He was loath to leave her for even a minute, but it was his brother and he'd been so cooperative the entire evening. He nodded. "Yeah, but let's make it quick, okay?"

"Yeah, sure. Let me get the other Ivanslohe's and I'll wave to you when we're ready." His brother leaned into Jaden's ear and said something he couldn't read. They separated, Jaden heading for the bar, and Hollis found each of the other cousins. When they'd all slipped out a side door, Hollis waved.

Breicher's pulse picked up as he leaned over to Caroline. "I'll be right back, okay?" She wrinkled her brow, but he placed a quick kiss on her lips. "Guys want to have a toast. Five minutes, okay? Hollis has been particularly good. Just one drink."

Her face softened, and she wouldn't deny him.

Another longer kiss. "Thank you, my queen."

The pink lighting up her cheeks when he'd said it made him want to scratch the drink and the rest of the evening and go bury himself in her heat.

Breicher slipped out the door he'd seen Hollis exit. "Down here, Breicher," his cousin Jamison called.

"Did you guys have to pick such a dank corridor?" he asked but took the glass Jaden proffered to him.

He surveyed the Gods' blessed men of his family, pride welling in his chest, and raised his glass. "Thank you all for being here. I know the last month has been confusing, but I believe we can end the strife and centuries long conflict together. Your presence means the Ivanslohe line will endure."

A unified "Cheers!" rang through the hallway, and all nine men tossed the drink back.

Hollis grabbed the empty bottle from Jaden. "Go fetch another," Hollis demanded, and an uneasy, warning sensation had his heart skipping in his throat.

"Actually, I told Caroline I'd just be a few minutes. And one was plenty," he said, but Jaden had already skated out of the corridor. Breicher took a step backward to follow his nephew back into the Great Hall. This had been a mistake. The last thing he wanted was to get rounded up into a wild night of partying with the raucous men of his family. He wanted to spend the evening, and the rest of his life, bedding his wife.

"Come 'on, Breicher," Jamison wrapped a large arm around his shoulder, preventing his retreat. "You used to be so much more fun before that bitch wife of yours."

That made his hackles rise. He jerked his shoulder backward, violently throwing Jamison's arm off. "What did you say about my wife?" he hissed, as he charged forward, grabbing Jamison's collar, pinning him against the wall.

Scuffling in his periphery drew his attention. Four of his cousins surrounded them, and latched on his arms, pulling them off Jamison and pinning them to his sides. He gasped as a hand fisted in his hair and his head whipped backward. Hollis's face appeared inches from his own.

"I told you I would do whatever it took. You're my brother, and it's time someone did what's best for you and show you what kind of monster you're so smitten with."

A blinding crack and stars replaced Hollis as his vision swirled. Was that his skull? Then it was dark.

CHAPTER 10

"**I** FOUND HIM IN the hallway with two broken bottles of winter's sin. He claims he saw nothing." Angus led the two soldiers, dragging Jaden between them.

"Release him," Caroline commanded. She'd waited ten minutes before she'd sent Angus after her husband. The guards shoved Jaden to his knees in front of her and the guests were all turned toward the commotion. "Where is he?" she hissed through gritted teeth.

Jaden shook his head, rubbing his palms against his thighs. Blood was trickling from a cut at his temple and Agnes kept jerking forward like she wanted to race to her son, but was too afraid of Caroline to do it.

Caroline surveyed the room. She would not be their spectacle tonight.

"Bring him to the war room." She pointed at Agnes. "Take her back to her rooms and question her. Keep everyone else here until the king is found." Then she turned and stormed out of her wedding celebration without her husband.

Jaden had never seen the queen so furious in the month he'd known her. He kept peeking down at where her fingers were splintering the wooden arms of the chair they lashed him to as she leaned over him. Did she realize she was a hair's breadth away from losing control? He shuddered to think of what that would be like.

"Where is my husband?" she hissed.

"I don't know, Your Majesty. My father sent me back into the Great Hall to get another bottle. When I returned, they were gone. I tried to go after them, but this happened." Jaden lifted his head at an angle to indicate the split skin across his brow. Out of the corner of his eye Angus paced, looking ready to strike. "Obviously, I wasn't invited wherever they were going."

"Hollis must have told you something," Caroline insisted.

"Ask my mother," Jaden said, keeping his steely eye contact.

"Do you think Hollis told her anything after the stunt she pulled with Cecily?"

He unclenched his teeth. "If you don't believe me, compel me. Otherwise, you're wasting valuable time."

"I believe you." Caroline pressed the blood vessel throbbing in her forehead.

"I could help you look for him." He lightly jerked at the ropes Angus had used to tie his arms to the chair.

"I've had enough assistance to last a lifetime from you Ivanslohe's, so I'll pass." She sneered at him, but he only tracked her as she methodically paced around the room, the visual of a trapped wolf coming to mind. Those were the most dangerous ones.

Caroline had to give the prince credit. He held his chin high, and he hadn't flinched. His composure was more than most men facing her wrath, and she believed he wasn't lying. Jaden and Hollis were such a contrast. It would be hard to believe they were plotting together, even though they were family. But what did she know? Everyone here was a snake.

"I hate this place," she screamed, rattling the window panes. Never had she wanted to be surrounded with roses-and-pink stone so badly. That's what she would do. Once she found her husband, she'd whisk them back to Roskide, and she'd have her night with him in her own bed. Then they would rule the Joined Kingdoms together.

"Release him," she said.

Angus moved to protest, but Jaden slammed his arms down on the arms of the chair and the weakened wood snapped. Caroline started, but he only stood, staring at her, then slid a sly look to Angus. "Next time, use more rope."

On his way out, he stopped at the door as if thinking of what he wanted to say.

"Spit it out, prince," Angus growled.

"If I find him, I'll let you know." He tapped his fingers three times, then was gone.

⬩

"Where am I?" Breicher demanded, spitting out hay as the sun rose, illuminating his surroundings.

"I know you probably don't recognize it, what with all the blood," Hollis said, leaning against the wagon. His other cousins stood around him with their arms crossed over their chest, all just watching, waiting.

Breicher surveyed the town square where the wagon that he'd woken up in was parked. "Avondale?" He shook his head clear, wondering what Hollis meant when he'd said *blood*. And like it had summoned him, the pools of dried crimson staining the weathered marble stones of the courtyard sprang to the front of his attention. Realizing he was unbound, Breicher climbed down from the wagon. Stumbling, he whipped his head around. Blood was splattered everywhere. There wasn't a single unmarred surface.

"What happened here?" he asked, raising a hand to his mouth as nausea rolled. He tripped on an uneven paver, but Hollis and Jamison grabbed him under the arms, urging him to his feet.

"Your wife is what happened here, Breicher," Jamison said.

"Come, there's more to see." Hollis led them to a shop that had the word Delicatessen scrawled on a pane of glass. The shop wasn't open, but when his brother stepped through the door, Jamison shoved him in after. A woman was waiting behind the counter as if she'd been expecting them.

"Where's your husband?" Hollis asked, a little too gruffly for Breicher's taste.

"Dead, Sir."

"Who killed him?" Hollis asked.

The woman's eyes went wide, then shot to Breicher's, then to the floor. "The queen did, sir."

Before the woman said anything else, Hollis grabbed the collar of his jacket and dragged him to another shop a few doors down. This one had a few patrons starting to trickle in and baking bread wafted through the air, reigniting the queasy feeling in his stomach.

When Hollis had shoved him through the door and in front of the line, he put his meaty hands on the counter, leaning across it. "I need to see your son and your husband."

A delicate woman stuck her head up from a counter she was squatting behind. When she came up, she had two rolls in her hands and promptly dropped them and began shaking her head slowly as tears welled. "They're gone."

They left without a thank you, storming off to the next establishment. What was the meaning of this? Caroline had told him what had happened. They'd ambushed her. Why was his brother doing this? Then he understood. Hollis had watched as Breicher let down his guard and fell for the woman—no *monster*—who brought so much horror upon all these innocent people. It was clear there had been a skirmish, but the vengeance the queen had enacted upon the innocent people of Veetula was a massacre. He covered his mouth as his stomach heaved. To think he'd been ready to surrender to whatever was building between them made him break out in a cold sweat.

"Come, brother. There's more." Hollis waved him to the next stop. Then the next. Finally, after a short walk out of town, he brought him to a little cemetery. Well, it would have been small if it weren't for the fresh graves that littered the terrain.

A dark-haired woman, wrapped in a black shawl, approached with a bouquet. "I saw it all. She slaughtered them, Your Majesty, without mercy. Her face grew darker and darker with each new kill." She gripped his sleeve urging him to hear her. "I didn't think I could become more frightened, but then she made them turn their weapons against themselves and killed them all."

That's not how Caroline had said it happened. She said only five or six people had died before her and Angus fled. Breicher turned to the woman, who had tears streaking down her pale cheeks. Tight ringlets were pinned demurely against her head, and soft green eyes blinked up at him as she dabbed away a fresh tear. Did she look familiar? "Do we know each other?" he asked.

She shook her head. "I'm sure if we'd met, you'd remember." She gave him a tender smile, then walked over and knelt beside a new grave. "My brother," she called back to him, and he thought he sensed an underlying intention to her words.

"You don't know her," Hollis said and dragged him down a line of graves. "You haven't had your needs met in so long you're seeing things."

He and Hollis climbed to the top of the hill and turned to stare down upon the cemetery. Hollis allowed him to drop to his knees and joined him on the frozen ground. "There's so many of them."

"I thought you'd want to know before you did something you'd regret." Hollis put a gentle hand on Breicher's shoulder and gave a sympathetic squeeze.

"How did you know?" he asked, holding back his own tears, which were threatening to fall.

Hollis patted the hard ground. "I came after I'd heard what had happened. I was horrified that our people had done this to her, but they told me their stories. I dug graves with them, and they told me everything."

"I need a minute," he said to his brother, patting his comforting hand.

"We'll be at the wagon when you're ready," Hollis said, and got up to walk down the hill. He'd never been more grateful for his brother. Family was everything.

When Hollis was out of earshot, he doubled over and released a sob. How could she do this to him? Made it seem like they'd hurt her when she'd been the one wreaking havoc. He'd been so outraged, so ready to fold into her like the coward he was. Hollis was right, and he'd been trying to warn him. She was playing him. Another sick revenge fantasy she was playing out in slow motion.

She lied to him the whole time, all the while knowing she was drawing him in closer and closer. Like a spider, luring in her prey for the kill. The memory of a few hours ago flashed through his mind, of her on the altar, saying her vows. She hadn't even been listening. But when she'd looked up at him, blushing, he'd believed her, eagerly crawling into her web.

He should have known better than to fall for a woman who'd taken out the Gods. The warmth drained from his face at the thought of her power. What would she do to his family now that he'd found out about her punishment before she landed the final blow? His heartbeat picked up. He needed to play along, stall, and try to reason with her. She'd let him rule beside her as a figurehead if he played his cards right and spared his family.

He had to buy some time.

Breicher took his time on the way back to the wagon. His cousins were catching up around the fountain in the center when he arrived. "Where's Hollis?" he asked, noticing the man who he owed so much to was missing.

Jamison stood. "Hollis needed to pay a visit to an old friend really quickly. He shouldn't be too long."

Breicher chuckled, knowing what *old friend* was code for. Where he had found someone eager so early in the morning was anyone's guess, but he chalked it up to his brother, who had a lover in practically every town in Veetula.

As Hollis sauntered back into the square a few minutes later, beaming like a man who'd just had a good round on the mattress, a niggle of envy crept up inside him. He'd been abstaining for Caroline. She'd still kill him if she found out, but if he were careful, he could pull off a tiny fraction of the enjoyment Hollis got from their lineage.

"We have to go back," Breicher said, as Hollis approached.

Hollis ran a hand over his face. "You still want that demon?"

Breicher shook his head. "You were right, Hollis. But she has your family and we've seen what she's capable of."

❦

Every step was like treading through wet sand as he walked up the stairs to the main entrance of Kierengaard. As soon as he'd explained himself to his brother, Hollis understood they'd had no other choice.

They'd come up with an alibi and send his cousins on their way. The wound Jamison had given him would serve a purpose, after all.

Before he got to the first step, the doors flew open, and Caroline was running across the landing. She jumped into his arms, throwing her arms around his neck. For a second his heart leapt, but he wrestled it down. He pulled her arms off him, holding her wrists between them. Her brow creased, and she scanned him, noticing the cut and blackened eye.

"What happened?" she asked, voice full of fake concern. Her *act*.

Breicher raked a hand through his hair as the knot in his stomach tightened. "Hollis was pissed I missed the wedding ritual I told you about, so he abducted me." He put his hand on the small of her back and ushered her inside.

They made it a couple of steps, Hollis trailing behind when Caroline demanded they go in an anteroom. "Caroline, let's go upstairs, okay?" He made sure to keep his voice neutral. He had a fine line to walk now.

"No, both of you in, now," she demanded. "I deserve to know what happened on my wedding night."

"Your Majesty, it's my fault and I know the consequence, though I'm sure Agnes will throw herself out the window within the week if you lock me in there with her." Hollis leaned casually against the wall, arms crossed over his chest and a triumphant smirk barely concealed. His brother was going to get them killed.

At Hollis's voice, Caroline's face pinched like the sound grated on her last reserve of patience.

She spun toward him. "Shut up. Your apartments are the kindest place I'm considering sending you for ruining my wedding night. Me and Angus have been up all-night listening to countless reports from our guards who are exhausted from searching for missing royals for the second night straight." Caroline was clenching and unclenching her fists and eyeing Hollis's throat.

"Easy, Caroline," Breicher said, coming up behind her, rubbing her arms soothingly. Her rigid body softened at his touch.

"I know I shouldn't be jealous. That it is a family tradition, but the thought of you with another woman, especially after where last night was headed makes me see red. How many women was it, Breicher?" The queen held her breath.

"None." Breicher turned her so he could see her eyes. If he didn't know better, she was actually jealous. Probably because she considered him her property. "I didn't sleep with anyone, I promise," he said for emphasis.

"Then why didn't you come back till this afternoon? I've been sick worrying for you."

Breicher smoothed her hair, and impressively, a tear trickled down her cheek.

"I'm sorry I have to do this," she said, turning to Hollis, but not stepping toward him. Breicher searched the room for anything she might be about to use as a weapon, ready to pounce. Forfeit his own life to save his brothers. He was the one who'd failed in his mission, so he deserved to die.

"Hollis, how many?" she asked.

"One," Hollis said, and Caroline clutched her stomach and the top of the nearest chair at the same time. "One for me. None for Breicher. Now let go of me," he demanded, shaking against her power.

He smelled subtly of sex, horse, and the road. Caroline probably smelled it too.

She stared at the ground for a long moment, sucking in quick, panicked breaths. "Did you want to?"

"What?" he asked, shock jolting him. He placed an arm around her shoulder. "No, I didn't. Come on, you need sleep, okay?"

She reluctantly allowed him to lead her to her room in the top of the spire. He helped her undress, acting as any caring husband might, and tucked her into bed. "I'm not too tired, if you still want to," she said, unable to suppress a yawn.

What would happen if he called her bluff? She let Felix in between her legs after he'd betrayed her. He'd do well to remember that. "No," he said, and leaned down to kiss her forehead, then made it halfway to the door. "I'm not really interested in fucking a half-asleep woman. Besides, I smell like a stable."

When he glanced back, her eyes were closed.

CHAPTER 11

S OMETHING WAS AMISS. CAROLINE'S gut was rarely wrong about these things. He was one man when he'd left, and another when he'd returned to her in less than a day. She had to find the underlying cause of it, because as embarrassing as it was, she craved the man who'd been abducted more than any revenge she'd ever plotted or kingdom or power she'd coveted, and she wasn't going to lose him without a fight.

As soon as the door clicked shut, she was on her feet. Caroline ran to her bathroom, splashing enough frigid water on her face to turn her pale cheeks pink. The silver of her eyes had an ominous glint as she assessed herself in the mirror. She wouldn't want to be on the receiving end of the man she was after. She pulled the little knife-ring from the box of jewelry on her vanity, slipped it on her thumb, then swiftly threw on something she wouldn't mind getting dirty. Heart thumping angrily, she flew out the door.

Angus met her at the bottom of the stairs and gave her an approving once over. "Where is he?" she asked.

"The king went directly to his chambers. Hollis took a little detour by the cellar. I think we'll catch him on his way up."

They hurried along the corridors to the one that led up from the cellars and perched a few yards down from the door. It opened and Hollis stepped out, carrying two sealed bottles of winter's sin. He froze as he caught sight of her and Angus lingering in the hallway, triumphant ease draining from his features. Dread cinched up his face as Caroline squeezed the dagger and threw, like she'd once done to her husband.

The bottles crashed to the ground and Hollis's hand shot up to catch the blade before it pierced his chest. "I'd be impressed, but when I did that to your brother, he was much faster," she said.

"You tried to kill me." Hollis frowned down at the spilled liquor at his feet.

"Did you not hear what I just said? I knew you'd catch it. But I think I may have tried to kill your brother once. Only fair, I'm sure you understand." She pushed off the wall and stalked over to him. His fingers twitched and she sensed he wanted to turn that dagger around and use it on her. Instead, she held out a hand, and he placed it in her palm willingly.

"Go plant yourself in a prison cell and keep quiet. Number fourteen, I think?"

"Fifteen," Angus corrected her.

"Oh yes, that was the nicer one. Angus, escort him and see that he doesn't get distracted along the way. I'll be along shortly." Caroline stared at Hollis as she slipped past, tsk tsking him before she headed down the stairs to the cellar.

Angus had the former King's wrists in chains above his head when she arrived with the bottle she'd collected. Angus moved a little table inside the cell, and she set the liquor there with two glasses, pouring a finger in each.

She picked them up and crossed the space to him, feeling his gaze crawl all over her body like he couldn't help himself. Holding the drink to his mouth, she said, "Bottom's up."

Hollis drank the glass in one pull. She sipped on hers, then shook her head, wrinkling her nose as it burned down her throat. Hollis lifted his chin toward the glass and raised an eyebrow, as if to imply she couldn't handle it. Laughing, she downed the rest of what was in her cup. He was staring at her ass when she turned back to him. How had she not noticed that before? Or was he planning to distract her from his brother? That he thought he could was laughable.

"You like what I'm wearing, Hollis?" she purred, picking up the dagger, twirling it in her hand. "Were you jealous that I wanted your brother and not you?" Leaning a shoulder against the doorframe, she stretched out her long legs, crossing them at the ankle.

Her fitted top, the snug riding pants and knee-high boots showed off her svelte curves. For a queen, every action was an offense. Like how she'd left the top three buttons undone. And she was coming to understand one of the few things that motivated the Ivanslohe men.

"You've dreamed of me, *Everstal's Cruel Queen*, haven't you? Thought if it had been you and not Breicher, you'd already have me tamed? Is that it? After all, you were already a king."

Caroline sauntered over to him, releasing the compulsion keeping him quiet. "I loathe you," he said.

With the dagger, she gently ran it across his clothing, up his arms, down his chest, and stopped to tap the dead, semi-hard giveaway in his pants. "You may loathe me, but I think you find me equally as appealing."

"Just because I'd fuck you doesn't mean I find you appealing," he said.

Angus picked up the bottle and refilled the glasses. "Don't lie to your queen."

"We're going to play a little game, Prince Hollis. It's a lot like strip poker," she hesitated, and his eyes brightened a smidge. "That got your interest. Good. This is how it goes. I ask you a question, you answer truthfully, and I don't kill you. You lie and I cut off a favorite body part. And since I know you only have one, I think you'd better stick to the truth."

"That's nothing like strip poker." Hollis grimaced as he jerked around in his chains.

"Well, I will have to disrobe you to collect your debt should you lie, so similar enough."

"What do you want, Caroline?"

"Oh, I guess since we're drinking buddies, you think it's acceptable to drop the formalities? Very well, since you are probably never leaving this cell." She pointed to the window. "That's why I made sure you had a good view. Anything for family."

Behind her, Angus chuckled. Bringing in a little stool, he perched on it so he would be ready should she require him.

Caroline handed Angus the dagger, then took the two refilled drinks, feeding one to Hollis, then downing the other one herself.

"I assure you my tolerance is far higher than yours, *queen*."

Caroline tipped her head back, and deep belly laughed. "I'm practically a god, Hollis. I can heal the intoxication out of my system."

"Why haven't you compelled me yet?" Hollis asked suddenly, like the thought was only now occurring to him.

She approached him, spinning her hair in her fingers. "I will, if necessary." Wiggling her thumb in his face, she showed him the ring that had a set of swirling rumors of its own. Breicher would be upset about it, but she didn't care. She savored the blanched pallor of his skin, the control it would give her over the former king. And it wasn't her fault. He'd brought this upon himself.

A trickle of blood welled behind the blade as she thumbed his jaw. Holding her thumb and forefinger together, she pricked her skin, mingling his blood with hers. "Did you feel that?" she whispered, as a delightfully chilly shiver raced up her arm.

His eyes went wide, and he began struggling anew, as if his Ivanslohe warrior's body might break the chains free from the wall. "I hate you," he seethed, but finally went slack against the stones once more.

Caroline wiped the blood on her pants and retrieved the dagger. "You're going to tell me everything I want to know one way or another. And I'm the type that likes to play with their food."

"That could have gone worse," Angus said, rinsing his hands in a basin in Caroline's room in Roskide, staining the water red. She'd taken him there to discuss the implications of what they'd learned from Hollis somewhere that would be private. Hollis would be out for a while, and he was compelled not to speak to anyone about their conversation and to stay put. Considering Caroline now had his blood, Angus wasn't worried the man would try to fight the compulsion.

She'd been right. He'd underestimated the comfort of the familiar dusty pink stones. As soon as they'd arrived, attendants, after having a month-long break, were eager for the activity the queen's residence provided them.

Attendants delivered wine, along with food, and had a bath drawn. One attendant even offered to fetch the tailor or ready her horse. Roskide had missed its queen.

Caroline allowed an attendant to slip her boots off and take them to be polished. He'd followed her into the bathing chamber. She peeled the sweat slick clothes from her body and slipped into the bath. He'd seen her naked so many times it didn't faze him. Her figure did nothing to him like it seemed to for the men she drove crazy and that he was glad for.

"I think you should have killed him." Angus slumped down on a bench positioned against the wall under the little window. A warm breeze drifted in, and he let his shoulders sag as he scented the blooming roses right outside the opening.

"If I killed him, Breicher really would think I was a monster." Caroline dipped under the water, holding her breath for a long moment before she finally emerged. "What should I do?"

Angus wrinkled his brow. It wasn't often that the queen was at a loss. "I fear what I think you should do and what you want to do are completely different things."

Caroline smiled at her commander. "Let me guess. Kill Hollis, annul the marriage, banish the rest of the Ivanslohe's." She tapped her finger on her lips like she was considering. "Oh, and get a different husband. Did I get it right?"

"Hardly," he scoffed. "I think you should have killed them all already. They've been nothing but defiant towards you in the face of your mercy. Your husband stabbed you, for the Gods' sake."

"The dead Gods' sake," she interjected. "I don't think he wanted to, though. I think he's waging a battle between his feelings for me and his ideals, old beliefs, and misplaced loyalty." A serious expression crossed her face, and he sat up. "I plan to win, Angus. I will have him."

Angus sighed. In as long as he'd known her, he'd never seen her go back on something she'd decided. Once she'd made up her mind, she was as immovable as a mountain.

"Very well," he said. "We probably need to get back before the king goes in search of his brother."

Caroline took greater care dressing than she normally did. She wanted to appear sticky sweet, but irresistibly alluring and the dress she had chosen was perfect. Pale pink chiffon overlapped across her chest, held up by two delicate straps. A flouncy flowing skirt reached her ankles, and a slit that almost reached her hip lay closed except for when she was striding forward. She wrapped a string of natural pearls once close to her neck, and the second wrap dipping between the fabric of her bodice and her skin, leading the eye suggestively. Her aesthetic was the exact combination of a virginal princess and an adept seductress.

"I didn't think you owned anything pink," Angus said, giving her a quizzical look as she sauntered into her sitting room. "You look... pretty?"

She tapped a finger on his nose. "Precisely. Change of plans. I'm going to go fetch him under the guise that we have some work to do here."

"Who are you going to leave in charge in Veetula?"

Caroline frowned. "Jaden?" Her voice sounded a little unsure even to her.

"I don't trust him."

"Fine, you then, since you're volunteering. Come," she said, clasping his hand. Then they were gone.

CHAPTER 12

"I DON'T SEE WHY you are shadowing me," Breicher grumbled to the soldier on his heels. The lad was no more than a boy in his mind, the scrawny thing struggling to keep up with his long strides.

"Queen's orders, sir," the soldier said, practically jogging to keep up.

"And where is our illustrious queen this hour?"

"In her rooms?" the *man* asked. Clearly, he didn't know where the queen was and was offering up a guess.

"We just checked there." Breicher was going to punch something. He glanced back at his tail, the current and most likely candidate. He spun around a corner, crashing into someone charging just as fast as he was. Breicher narrowed his eyes, then reached a hand down to help his nephew up.

Jaden eyed Breicher's appearance, gesturing at his half-tucked shirt and his two days' worth of stubble. "You've seen better days."

"Thanks," Breicher said, frowning. His nephew was pristine, as usual. Pressed, tucked, and smooth. Where had the young prince been going in such a hurry?

Before he could ask, Jaden said, "What's he doing?" and pointed to the hovering soldier.

"Caroline has him *escorting* me. She's worried I might get abducted again, or so she says." Breicher scraped a hand over his rough jaw.

"Oh," Jaden said, perking up in surprise. "I thought his shift was over. Car—her Grace sent me. I'm to escort you the rest of the afternoon."

The soldier darted his eyes between the two royals, unsure of what to do.

Jaden heaved an annoyed breath and gave the man a look that questioned his competency. Waving a lazy hand, he said, "What are you waiting for? Scram."

The fraying soldier backed away from them, then turned and hurried down the hallway in the other direction. Breicher assessed his nephew. "Thanks."

"No problem. Try to stay out of trouble, Your Highness." Jaden gave him a mocking smile before he resumed whatever mission he'd been on, leaving Breicher to continue searching for the queen.

Caroline draped herself across a chaise, positioning the fabric of her gown so the right amount of her legs would peek out. Lying her head against a pillow, she shut her eyes. Footsteps sounded, then her husband cleared his throat. She started, then made to stretch further, exposing her skin. Between her fluttering lashes, she caught his eyes lock on her legs, but his arms were still firmly secured across his chest.

"You were fast asleep when I left you last night." Breicher smirked, eyeing her suspiciously. "How are you still tired?"

The truth was, she was tired. She hadn't slept a wink in two days. Caroline supposed she could have left the dark circles that were forming under her eyes, but that wasn't sexy, and she had the power to remove them, making herself look as fresh as a babe.

"I'm not used to worrying so much about someone else, husband. It's exhausting." Did he just flinch?

"Thanks for the shadow," he said, changing the topic.

"Where is he, by the way?" Caroline asked, blinking as she surveyed the wary man.

"Jaden rescued me." He gave her a sly smile.

"Of course, he did." Caroline sat up, digging her toes into the plush carpet. She leaned forward on her hands so her slight chest would swell against the silky fabric covering it. Everything between them would be a seduction until he was hers again. "You could lock the door and come sit down and tell me what happened." Her fingers slid over the smooth velvet of the chaise in a lazy circle.

Breicher's mind and body were at odds. Every impulse in him was screaming, begging him to take what was so plainly being offered before him. His traitorous eyes marched the path of her pearls down her chest and into her cleavage. The taste of her skin as he'd kissed her there a few days earlier was fresh in his mind.

A little voice urged him to calm down. Get ahold of himself. But images of raw earth in mounds scattered across the expanded cemetery wouldn't leave him. And he didn't want them to—ever. He clung to them, trying to see that instead of the picture of innocence the queen was painting for him. The picture was a lie.

In his mind, it was her first miscalculation. He'd have to be an idiot not to see what she was trying to do, how she was trying to manipulate him. He wouldn't have it and he'd make sure she knew he would not be toyed with.

"Fine," Caroline said, standing, oblivious to his racing thoughts. "If you won't come to me, then I'll come to you."

Watching her sway across the carpet snapped something in him. If she wanted to play the lamb, then he'd play the wolf.

Caroline winced as he slid his hand into her hair and gripped, jerking her head backward, exposing her neck to him. Her hands flew to his chest, and his mouth dragged a line of fire from her earlobe to her collarbone, kissing, biting, and sucking. Grabbing the dainty little strap with his free hand, he tugged it off her shoulder so hard the fabric ripped down her breastbone, exposing one of her peaked nibbles. He fisted her breast, squeezing and pinching until she gave a pleasured cry.

That's it. You like this. What a waste. He tore himself away from her long enough to grab the slit of the dress and tear it across her front, exposing the sheer panties she was wearing. His arm wrapped around her waist before she could protest, and he gripped her thigh, pulling it around his waist. Her eyes were triumphant balls of fire, and he experienced enough of her to know she was drenched for him.

Edging over to the chaise, he tossed her on it none too gently, then climbed over her, pressing himself onto her, pawing at every bit of flesh he got his hands on. He was going to get her so worked up, then douse her flame with an artic blast. Maybe then she'd think twice before she put on that pretty little act of hers, trying to lure him in again. Caroline let out a moan, pulling his hips into her own, and he relished the sound. It had gone on long enough to have the desired effect. Time to rip the bandage off.

He was aggressive and rough, and Caroline relished in it, greedily running her hands up his firm chest. Never had she imagined being handled like this and liking it, but it turned her blood into a fiery chariot, blazing through her, desperate to be extinguished by what only he could give her. "Take me," she cried into his neck. She didn't think she could stand another moment without him inside her.

"You'd like that, wouldn't you?" he asked, his lip raising in a snarl as he ground into her most sensitive area.

Her body arched toward him on its own accord, even as a fearful thrill sent her heart skipping. "Yes," she said. "Gods, yes!"

"Too bad," he growled. "I'll be your king. Nothing more, so don't expect it."

Breicher pushed off her and stormed out of the room, not sparing her a glance, and muttering something about a she-devil. The door clapped loudly behind him. Caroline laid there for a long moment, thunderstruck. Her clothing was in tatters, and she was trembling, trying to catch her breath. Dead gods, her need for him was becoming goliath, and she had felt his own. *What just happened?*

"Am I interrupting something?" Jaden asked, searching the room for whoever had the queen in such a state. Her dress was torn down the front, and a rosy nipple stood at attention. Someone had partially ripped away the skirting, exposing her scant undergarments. She didn't even budge as he approached, a leg still dangling off the chaise, putting her on full display.

Caroline opened her eyes and stared blankly at the ceiling. "I'm going to murder your father."

Jaden didn't blink. He shrugged, then picked a blanket from a nearby basket and tossed it to the queen.

He practically smelled her arousal. How could a man walk away from that and all that pink and heaving skin? The Gods had crafted his uncle from stone. Caroline took the blanket and wrapped it around herself, covering the ruined dress. Thank the Gods she did, because he was about ready to finish whatever somebody else had started—consequences be damned. Instead, he asked, "What happened?"

"Go ask your father. Cell fifteen. I care not to relive it."

Jaden raised a brow. "I see."

The queen was unmoving, and she was clearly done talking.

Angus passed through the door. One look at the disheveled woman, and he was snarling in Jaden's direction. *That could be interesting.* Jaden waved a hand at Caroline. "I didn't do this, if that is what you were thinking."

"Caroline, I thought you were taking the king back to Roskide," Angus said, shifting his focus.

Caroline smirked. "Didn't go as planned."

Angus and the queen were glowering at each other, which seemed like the perfect time for him to slip from the room and go discover the state his father was in.

Right as he was about to cross the threshold, Caroline said, "Oh, Jaden?" He paused at the door, not turning back. "You warned me not to expect perfect results, but this is far below perfection, wouldn't you agree?"

"Yes, Your Majesty," he said, gritting his teeth. He sensed whatever his father had done was narrowly close to getting them all killed. His muscles tensed as he stood there waiting to be dismissed.

"My patience is waning."

"I know," he said, closing his eyes, taking in a deep, steadying breath. "I'll do better, Your Majesty."

"You may go," she said, finally.

He let out a long exhale and rolled his shoulders as he stomped down the hallway in the prison's direction. Veetula's former king would talk, and then Jaden would figure out a way to deal with the repercussions.

⋆

"Have you seen your father?" His uncle's voice bounced off the marble walls, catching up with him, and he winced. Jaden had been hoping to avoid this conversation, but he had to tell his uncle what he'd learned. *What the queen, his wife, had learned.*

Caroline had released her compulsion on his father, allowing him to speak freely to his son, though he didn't understand why she would do that. Surely, she would know that his father would tell Jaden how she'd coaxed the information out of him. Jaden shivered at the memory, though if he were being honest, the man was only getting a taste of what he'd never hesitated to do himself.

"We need to talk," was all he said to Breicher, then kept pace as he led his uncle to a little used room where they might have a private conversation.

He ushered Breicher in, then closed the door, latching it behind him. He grabbed a stale pitcher of water and poured it in two glasses, shoving one across a side table. As the cool water flooded his chest, chilling the air in his heated lungs, he cursed the dead Gods.

"What is it, Jaden?" Breicher demanded, ignoring his glass.

"She knows." Jaden raked a hand through his hair, tugging at the ends.

Breicher started pacing. "Shit."

"Exactly. And that little stunt you just pulled is like poking a hungry bear. How much do you think she's going to take before she starts executing us?" Jaden shot his uncle a scolding look. He didn't care that he was his elder, or the king. Someone who didn't have their vision blurred with revenge, or their emotions in a knot, needed to get a hold of the situation before it was too late.

Breicher sat with his head in his hands as Jaden explained what his father had told him, careful to leave out the parts that would enrage the king. Particularly that Caroline had another Ivanslohe's blood.

"I didn't find her with the intention of doing that. When I saw that dress, I lost it." Breicher let out a hopeless sigh. "What am I supposed to do, Jaden? I can hardly stomach the thought of being with her after what she did to all those innocent people."

"And you trust my father painted an accurate picture of what happened?"

Breicher shook his head and Jaden watched him wrestle with his thoughts. He was sure what had happened was gruesome. He'd seen her and Angus when they'd come back, but he was also familiar with the type of shit his father pulled. He wasn't ready to make a judgement yet and planned to do his own digging to find out what had really happened.

"I spoke with countless witnesses, Jaden. Caroline had said only five or six people had died, but there were over thirty fresh graves."

Jaden wasn't here to argue with the King of the Joined Kingdoms. He was here to talk some sense into him. "Either way, you need to play nice. Work with her. Buy us some time so I can figure out what to do, okay?"

"Fine," Breicher said, groaning.

"Starting now." Jaden squared off against the arguments bubbling up in his uncle's mind. "Go to her now. Apologize. Tell her you need some time to digest what happened. Tell her you think you can still work together. Lie to her if you must. I don't care but go." Jaden pointed at the door and stood there until Breicher conceded and left in search of the queen.

❧

"What do you want?" the queen said, wrenching back and letting another dagger sail. It spun end over end until it sank dead center in the target almost twenty paces away. Breicher halted, in awe. She picked another up from the pile and positioned herself, ready to hurl it.

"I'm sorry," he said, forcing the words out. "I shouldn't have done that. I was angry and in shock. I *know* you *know*, Caroline."

Caroline lowered the weapon, turning ever so slowly toward him, and his pulse raced like a rabbit who knew a fox had caught its scent. "You *know* because I have allowed you to *know*. Because I don't wish for there to be anything between us. But I too am in shock, husband. I thought you might have taken my word for it. Especially considering your brother is not only lying, but trying to do whatever it takes to keep us apart. I felt that was quite obvious."

Spinning in a flash, she launched the dagger. It landed in the red rectangle at the top, the only space around the perimeter empty. Picking up another one, she said, "Go get them for me."

Breicher was sure she was going to kill him and had to fist his hands to stop them from giving away his trepidation. He waited for the sting of a blade piercing his back as he made his way to the target. Grabbing the first dagger, he rocked it back and forth until it came loose. He stole a glimpse over his shoulder. Caroline stood, twirling the one she'd picked up in her hand.

"You're fond of throwing. Can you use any other weapons?" he asked, genuinely curious.

"I find throwing knives helps center me. Especially when I'm angry." She gave him a mocking smile. "I haven't found the need to learn to wield other weapons. Physical prowess was never impressed upon us Dallimores, considering the nature of our power."

He gathered the weapons, careful not to slice his hands open. He wasn't sure she'd heal him. When he was about halfway back, she said, "Do you trust me?"

A muffled *pfft* burst from him before he could stop it. "No."

"I don't like your answer, but I appreciate your honesty." In a blink, her arm lifted, then sprung forward. He had a split second to decide if she genuinely wanted him dead. Repressing the instincts screaming *move*, he froze, breath catching in his lungs. Air stirred near his ear as the blade zipped by. He spun to the target right as it dug into the center. "Maybe you trust me more than you realize," she said.

How did she get under his skin like this? He wanted to grab her by the shoulders and shake her until she realized what a thorn in his side she was. Or force her under him and take out his frustrations on her with his body, like he was so close to doing only a few hours earlier. Knowing she'd only like that, he brushed away the thought. *Take me*, she'd said. A chill worked its way from his mind to his cock. He had to get out of here. He walked past her toward the door. "Let's try to work together—"

"I have been trying to work with you people. You're impossible," she yelled, chucking another dagger at the target. This time it went wide by a foot.

Breicher remembered the words of his nephew. "Please, give me time. I need to process what I saw, okay? Please?"

"Just leave," she hissed.

"Caroline, please?" For his family, he would beg.

"Fine. Take all the time you need. The result will be the same." *You'll be mine* was what she didn't need to say.

Fear of her wrath and concern for his brother warred in his mind. Finally, getting up the nerve, he asked, "And Hollis?"

The laugh that came out of his wife froze his blood. "You ask too much. Now leave me before I reconsider the gift I just gave you."

CHAPTER 13

W EEKS BLED INTO MONTHS, and she still hadn't pressured him to come to her. She was giving him time as she'd promised. They were locked in a stalemate, full of flirting and innuendos. She'd been working hard to seduce him with her clothing and mannerisms. The way she spoke, walked, ate even. Everything she did seemed designed to make him want her. To lower his guard, draw him in. Or maybe that's just how she was.

No. He should not underestimate his wife, or she'd have him in her thrall again, ready to drop the hammer like she did with Felix.

He would ignore his urges. She'd made him too terrified to take a lover, so he dealt with his aching manhood himself, letting the images of her that flashed through his mind be enough.

And if he were being honest with himself, the flirting was fun. When Caroline's guard was down, she was playful and vivacious, like she'd been when he'd first met her. Dangerously so.

They'd formed a comfortable rhythm, going back and forth between Roskide and Kierengaard, dealing with petitions and the daily business of running two kingdoms. Despite himself, he enjoyed it—being king—and they complimented each other in their ruling styles.

"What did you say that was?" Breicher asked, pushing his empty plate away.

"Mmm." Caroline swallowed. "A spring harvest quiche. Do you like it?"

He eyed the portion she would not finish in answer. She ate more since she'd become whatever she was, but he still always got a part of her portion. She pushed her plate to him as had become their morning routine.

"Quite the appetite." The innuendo was not lost on him. Caroline picked up a ripe berry, and sucked the juice from the end, before plopping it into her mouth. She'd done that once before, an old trick of hers. An unbidden chuckle rose in his chest.

"What?" she asked, glaring at him.

"You're incredibly transparent."

Caroline made a show of assessing herself. "I have no idea what you're speaking of." Dusting her hands off, she stood and headed for the war room.

Breicher stuffed the rest of the quiche in his mouth, then followed after her. He put his hand on the small of her back and gave her a little domineering nudge into the room, leaning down to whisper, "You know exactly what I'm talking about."

Angus was already there when they arrived, sorting through papers. He tossed a missive in front of the queen and the amused expression slipped from her face.

"No," Angus said, "it's not that. Just a report from the vintner. Looks like the cool season rains didn't affect the vines. Should be another good yield this fall."

He knew what Caroline had been thinking when Angus had given her the paper. Since the massacre at Avondale, things had been quiet along the border. Breicher hardly believed it. The lingering threat of another skirmish was always looming, especially now that they were attempting to rule the kingdoms as one.

But somehow, against all odds, there hadn't been one. Things were too quiet, going too well and Breicher didn't trust it.

The feeling traveled with him throughout the day. Even as he sparred with his nephew, the feeling a shift was about to occur was unshakable. Somehow, he had to know Caroline wouldn't allow this to go on forever.

"What has you so distracted? Doesn't happen to be that wife of yours running around the castle oozing *fuck me* like an official court announcement," Jaden asked, bending over to catch his breath.

Breicher fetched a cloth and wiped the sweat pouring down the back of his neck. It was so much warmer in the south. He'd been here for five years, but it seemed like he'd acclimated so fast being back in Veetula for the few short months he was. And now it was like going through the training all over again. "How long do you think she's going to let things go on like this?" he asked his nephew.

Jaden shrugged, dropping on a nearby bench at the edge of the training yard. "You're sure you won't let it go and give her what everyone can see you both want? I told you what I found, Breicher. Short of desecrating potentially fake graves, what more proof do you need? I think she was telling the truth. It's like you want to hate her."

"Nothing can convince me she isn't cruel and calculating. Even if some of what Hollis showed me was falsified, there are too many other things." Breicher swung, releasing a pinch of his frustration out on the straw dummy.

"Like what?" Jaden asked.

"I don't know," Breicher said. They'd had this conversation a dozen times and he never had a better answer. Still, he said, "The thing with Felix."

Jaden gave an exaggerated groan, getting to his feet. "You can't keep using that one incident as your excuse. You're not Felix. I don't think she's playing you."

Breicher scoffed, taking another swing. "She's most certainly playing me. And you too, apparently."

"You're being impossible." Jaden threw his arms into the air. "What are you going to do when she decides she's had enough of this cat-and-mouse game you two are playing at?"

Jaden stepped back into the ring and readied himself to take the brunt of his uncle's wrath. Fucking and sparring were about the only things that eased their tension when they got like this, and since Breicher was abstaining from the first, the second got double attention. It was the only reason Caroline had begrudgingly allowed him to join them for the few days they'd be at Roskide.

It was his first trip to the sunny kingdom, and instantly he'd seen the appeal. Everything was green. Bright colors were everywhere, a contrast to the washed-out icy world he grew up in. Each night as the sun set over the farmland and rolling vineyards, he wished to ride through the fields enjoying the feel of sun warming his skin.

Breicher hadn't answered his question. He lunged at Jaden, lowered his sword tip a little too far. A mistake which Jaden took advantage of, knocking it aside, darting forward underneath his uncle's defenses. A second later, he was twisting Breicher's wrist, his sword clanked to the ground, and Jaden had him up and over his shoulder. The larger man coughed beneath him, trying to refill his lungs with air as Jaden straddled him. "Like I said, you're distracted. And you didn't answer my question."

Jaden helped his uncle up, watching him as he dusted himself off and placed the practice weapon back on the rack.

"I won't give into her and let her make me look like a fool, so we will just have to be ready to do what we must when the time comes." Defeated, Breicher left the training yard, leaving Jaden with the warning.

Jaden sat there, thinking until the sun had almost dipped completely below the horizon, mirroring the sinking feeling in his gut. If fear was contagious, Jaden would suspect he'd just caught it.

Caroline stifled a gasp. Breicher must not have heard her when she came through the door of his apartments. The bedroom door had been cracked, so she'd nudged it a little further and popped her head in to see if the king was in residence. Breicher leaned against the fireplace with one arm and the other was working himself vigorously. Part of her bristled at the image before her because she felt she should be the one wringing her husband's pleasure from him. The other part of her, the part that was winning, which resided quite a bit lower than her brain, was responding favorably.

"I see you're being a good boy," she said, from the wall where she was leaning. Watching. *Drooling.*

Breicher started, eyes flaring open.

"You were thinking of me?" she asked, allowing a silken texture to overtake her voice. The way his face flamed answered her question.

"Get out," he said, between pants.

"Why think of me, when you could have me?" Caroline walked over to him. He'd been aggressive to her before, handling her like a bag of grain, and she was stronger now. Turnabout was fair play.

She grabbed his arm and spun him around, pressing him against the hearth. Sweat beaded and dripped down his front, making a trail to his lowered pants. Her mouth practically dripped at the sight before her. The way his hard length jutted out toward her as if beckoning her closer.

"You know I don't need ropes to tie you up, husband." She grinned when the compulsion took over, pressing him back against the warm stones. Grabbing the V of his shirt, she yanked, ripping it in two, exposing his chiseled abs, clenching and releasing with each unsteady breath. His eyes tracked her every movement through heavy lids as she dragged her palms across the sweat slick surface, savoring the feel of him. "I like these," she said, when she got to the divots at his hips leading to what was making her mouth water. Gods, she wanted to taste him.

She dropped to her knees on the plush fur rug beneath them, and he groaned, tilting his head to the heavens. A pained grimace sprouted across his features. The real reason for his anguish was seized up beneath his impressive length. Licking her lips, she peered up at him. "Tell me no, and I'll stop."

"We shouldn't," he breathed.

"Was that a, no?" she said, holding his hips, pressing the tips of her nails into his flesh, so it would sting ever so slightly. She wouldn't move an inch until he let her know it was okay.

He gave her a slight shake of his head. She kissed his hip, letting her tongue run up the V of muscle. "So, then it's a yes?"

She pinned his shaking hands to his sides. Unfurling her power into him, she eased any nausea he might be feeling. He wanted to use them, and she suspected it was not to push her away.

"Do it," he moaned. That cost him and she planned to reward him for it.

⋘

Nothing existed outside of Breicher's ache and the spread pink lips and greedy tongue flicking against the head of him, teasing as she ran her fingers up his length. Then he was in her fist, lips closing over him. Each time she moved forward on him, she took him a little deeper, until she no longer needed to use her hand, she had him bumping into the back of her throat.

Watching the queen work for him was what dreams were made of, and it was an effort to prolong the pleasure. Right when he'd think he was at the edge, she'd pull back and tease the tip, giving him a breather, before beginning her languid tempo once more.

As if giving him permission for what he so desperately wanted, she released her hold on him and his fingers immediately threaded through her hair, drawing her down on him more insistently than she'd been moving. "Relax for me," he urged. "I need you to take all of me. You can do it." As he felt her muscles ease, surrendering to the moment, he pressed his hips forward, sliding in the last few inches. When her nose bumped his stomach, he let out a guttural cry. *Gods, what a sight.* Nothing compared to this, and it was only her mouth. He took her over and over again, pressing as deep as he could go.

"Caroline!" Her name was a prayer on his lips, between savage grunts and heavy breaths. She wanted to cry out, too, but he wouldn't let her. Her glassy eyes told him how badly she ached for him from the way he was using her mouth. A whimper escaped her, and he swelled in her mouth. "That's it, Your Majesty. Not much longer."

⋘

Caroline's core clenched. There was the cocky man she'd fallen for. Part of her wanted to force him on the bed and take what she wanted, but she desired to give him this. Something else to visualize. And every time her nose brushed against his tight stomach muscles, a wave of pleasure washed over her. "Are you ready for me?" he asked, and she moaned onto him, knowing the deep vibration would drive him over the edge.

And like that, he was holding her head, keeping himself deep in her mouth as he spilled himself into her throat.

After his convulsions subsided, he released her head. Sitting back on her heels, she wiped the back of her hand across her lips and stared up at the warrior god who'd just claimed her mouth, the way she wished he'd claim her body.

He'd used her mouth so thoroughly tears had sprung forward. Gently, his rough thumbs swept underneath her eyes, wiping them away as he cupped her face. The look on his face, the absolute vulnerability in him at that moment, would have brought her to her knees if she weren't already there. "I wish..." he trailed off, releasing her. Her eyes followed him as his face crumpled from ecstasy to defeat. She knew that look. In his mind he'd given in. *But what had he wished?*

Then another thought struck her. That was bullshit.

Breicher paced to the bathroom and was splashing chilly water on his face when she finally approached him. "I didn't peg you for a selfish lover," Caroline said, sneering up at him as she rested her backside against the counter he was leaning over. He was conflicted, but she didn't care. That he resented being with her was unacceptable.

Breicher eyed his wife, feeling a mixture of satisfaction, finally after all this time, and immense guilt. He was amazed by her. She was the most stunning creature he'd ever seen. How she sensed exactly which buttons to push was anyone's guess. *She knows you*, an unwelcome voice nagged. He wasn't a selfish lover. That was one of the things he prided himself on. Even if it was a woman he was paying, he always made sure to get her off, too, if that's what she wanted.

"What do you want, Caroline?" he said in a voice which was as menacing as he could manage.

"For you to reciprocate. Is that so much to ask? I know you want to." Caroline rubbed her palms across the silky material at her hips, and shifted her leg, so the slit of her gown exposed her inner thighs. "Don't you want to feel what you do to me?" she breathed.

Breicher couldn't remove his eyes from his wife's spread thighs. How was he getting hard again after he just spent himself inside her pink, pouty lips? He had been denying himself for too long. Being around the queen did things to his body that if she were any other woman, he would not have to deny. But even the fact that he wanted her made him feel like a traitor. He had no idea how he'd feel if he gave in to his desire to bury himself deep inside her, but he imagined it would be far worse than how he felt now.

Her delicate hand wrapped around his wrist and tugged. He allowed her to pull his hand toward her body. He was transfixed as she placed it on her hip and then guided it lower over her exposed flesh. Swallowing, he looked up at the queen.

She was staring at him. Her breathy need was apparent in her gaze. Her mouth parted in a quick breath escaped as his hand slid lower, cupping her sex. "Oh," he gasped, feeling the moisture through the flimsy fabric. His fingers were moving on their own accord, now sliding the lacy garment aside.

His cock twitched, renewed the moment the pad of his fingers skimmed through her desire. He flipped his fingers a little deeper and an unbidden sigh formed in the back of his throat at the wetness he had discovered. Making him want her like this was one of her punishments for what had happened with Hollis. She had to know that to him, giving in was a betrayal. That was the only reason she would allow him her mouth and her body after he'd scorned her.

He stilled, his train of thoughts making a shock of ice dance across his skin.

"Gods, Breicher. Don't stop."

A surge of heat shattered the ice crystals at the sound of her begging his name—his real name. He'd had plenty of women cry it before, but none jolted through him like when his name was on her tongue. He pressed his fingers deeper, thrusting, finding her center and used his thumb to massage little circles into the bundle of swollen nerves right above until her hips were grinding into his hand.

Her cool fingers crept over his abdomen and ran up his chest, sending tingles across his skin. Urging him to angle his body nearer, her greedy hands crawled all over his body, eventually discovering the erection he was hoping would stay hidden.

"Oh, wow. Again?" She asked, a little giggle followed by a small cry.

She fumbled to undo the laces of his trousers. Eventually she succeeded and had her grip around him, squeezing and moving in a rhythm she'd keenly observed him using.

Breicher threw his head back at the waves of pleasure cascading out from his cock through his body.

"Oh, Breicher," Caroline cried, the sound interrupting her moans. Tight inner walls cinched down on his fingers as her orgasm shook through her. When it finally passed, she commanded, "Do it again," between pants.

Having a laugh at his demanding wife, he redoubled his effort to bring her to release again. When she was close, he wrapped his hand over hers, still pumping his erection, and squeezed.

Her forehead crashed into his shoulder as she cried out again. Another pump of their hands and he was coming right along with her, thrusting his hips in time with his plunging fingers.

When the aftershocks subsided, she was still leaning her head into him. He grabbed her shoulders and leaned her backwards a little to better see her. Her bright silver eyes were glazed over with satisfaction, and her hands trembled as she ran them across his skin, eliciting gooseflesh.

"Say something," she commanded.

If he didn't know better, he could've sworn that was hopefulness in her eyes. His own narrowed and the constant companion of his—tension—slithered back across his muscles.

"We shouldn't have done that." He released her and turned to hand her a towel to clean his cum off her dress. "Sorry about..." He motioned to the stain on her gown.

She took the towel and wiped it off, looking away. The muscles in her delicate jaw flexed.

"You need to get over yourself," she said, but there was no fire in her voice. "I should go."

Don't go. It was the first thing that sprung forward in his mind. Instead, he said, "Okay."

Damn her. She was only trying to lure him in, he reminded himself. He shouldn't fall for the glassiness in her eyes or how vulnerable she looked as she retreated. It was bait which would make the fall so much harder when she delivered the punch. Like him, she was a predator, and he refused to be her prey.

He steeled himself and let her leave, dropping to his knees the moment he heard the door click shut. How long would he have to do this until she finally gave up? How long could he withstand her constant assaults? Gods, what they had done had been a narrow miss, and this was only a few months in.

Anxiety gripped him as realization struck. Caroline wasn't the type to give up. He thought of the words he'd left with his nephew. They'd have to find another way to solve his problem.

CHAPTER 14

A s Breicher stewed all night, he'd come up with a plan. He walked into the breakfast room they shared wearing a fitting black riding suit she liked.

Caroline took notice, giving him a once over. "Going somewhere?"

He placed a kiss to her temple like the dutiful husband he wasn't, then took a seat opposite her. "I was hoping you'll allow Jaden and I to return to Kierengaard. Petitions are in a few days, and I thought we might oversee them ourselves. It would be valuable experience for him, and me, and you seem like you could use a break."

Caroline narrowed her eyes at him. "You sound like you're up to something," she said, not buying it.

"Well, Jaden is driving Angus crazy," he said, which was true, "and last night you said I was being a good boy." He winked at her and she blushed. Everstal's wicked queen blushed. Gods, he might have to stick his cock down her throat once more before he left, to ensure she was out of his system, of course.

As if reading his mind, her eyes flashed toward the door. No, he needed to get away. Do some work for the kingdoms—anything to get sex off his brain. They were acting like teenagers.

"I'll get Jaden. Be back in ten." Breicher spun on his heel and fled from the room.

Finding Jaden had taken ten minutes. Convincing him five. And another fifteen to get his things together and find wherever the queen had wandered off to. They found her in a garden terrace reclining on a wooden bench, surrounded by rose bushes covered in fat white blossoms. The vines ran up trellises on each side of her and overhead creating quite the picture. As a petal dropped and floated down toward her, she snatched it out of the air, and studied it as if she'd never seen a rose before.

"I've been wondering why they turned white."

Her matching white hair spread across the bench and fell in straight strands to the ground beneath. "I found Jaden," he said.

Caroline sat up, dropping the petal. "I was hoping you'd changed your mind."

She sauntered over to him without fanfare as if she weren't expecting a response when Angus approached. Taking note of him and his nephew, the commander frowned. "Your Majesty, Emmy wishes to see you."

Caroline's features liquified into a sneer. "Tell her she can rot."

"*Caroline*," Angus impressed, lips smashing into a thin line.

She rolled her eyes. "Fine, tell her I'll visit once I've dropped these two off. My king wishes to try his hand at ruling and our lovely Prince Jaden here wants to watch." Caroline winked at Jaden.

Before Angus commented, she'd grabbed their wrists and a cold gust was biting into the exposed skin on his neck and forearms. They were in Veetula.

Breicher blurted, "Your sister's alive?" at her as soon as they landed.

She tilted her head to the side. "You seem shocked."

Her husband coughed. "I am shocked. Your sister's been alive this whole time, and you didn't think to tell anyone? Wait—you have her imprisoned? Emmaline Dallimore has been in that filthy disease riddled prison for ten years."

He hadn't asked her. He'd assumed, *accused*, and it stung. She reached for him, but he stepped back as if he might catch something if she were to touch him. Frowning, she said, "First, I keep a pristine prison as you yourself are aware from experience. Second, you always think so little of me."

Before he had the chance to respond, she disappeared.

"What do you want?" Caroline hissed as she entered Emmaline's apartments in the East Tower to find her half-sister peeling an orange and feeding it to a lover who was wrapped in a sheet beneath her. The man's well-muscled stomach flexed as he sat up. Emmy shrugged as he got up to leave them, but not before giving her a long, languid kiss.

"How much of the crown's money are we spending on him?" Caroline asked. Because the man was too good looking, too perfectly manicured, not to have a price.

Giggling, Emmy grabbed her crumpled shift off the floor, and slipped it on, having to tug it to get it over her full peach breasts. "Not much."

"I expected you to be decent since you'd requested to see me." Caroline plucked another orange off the table, dug her nail into it breaking the skin, and began to peel.

"I've been thinking," Emmy said. "Since you've become," she gestured up and down at Caroline, "whatever you are, that you could free me. Let go of the past."

Caroline raised two incredulous eyebrows as she marinated on the thought. "And what will you do?"

Emmy shrugged, eating another piece of orange. "I don't know." Wistfully, she stared out the window. "Maybe I'll go visit that vineyard you're always talking about. Or I'll go sailing. I've always wanted to take a trip out to the islands."

"Let me get this straight. You want to travel the world, while I stay here and run this kingdom?"

"Kingdoms," Emmy corrected. "You like it, and even if it were to come out that I was alive, I don't think it would matter. You are clearly in charge."

Caroline snorted. "And when you aren't gallivanting around with gorgeous paid bedfellows, spending my coin, where do you imagine you'd live?"

Spreading out her hands, gesturing to her lush surroundings, Emmy said, "Well, here, of course. Technically, it was all supposed to go to me, so this request is only a small thing." Her voice was hesitant, testing.

"I see." Caroline got up, picking up one of the many oversized pillows her sister collected and buried her fingers in it, squeezing. Was this her fate, to have these pleas and demands put upon her by these people on a nearly daily basis?

"What?" Emmy asked, blinking up at her.

"My patience is being tested and I don't like it. Everyone thinks I will just give and give. It's getting terribly tiresome."

Emmy sagged back into her day bed. "So that's a no, then?"

She'd asked Caroline before. It seemed like she came up with some new excuse every year. This was the first time she'd had a valid argument, however.

"I'll think about it, okay?"

Before she stepped away, Emmy bounced up and was bounding toward Caroline, her shift barely covering her thick backside which jiggled with each step. Then she was in her sister's arms, and though she hadn't done anything yet, Emmy said, "Oh, thank you, Caroline. Thank you!"

CHAPTER 15

H ER HUSBAND HADN'T BEEN back but a week before Caroline summoned him to her chamber.

"You wanted to see me?" he asked, leaning up against the doorframe to her room. He was wearing one of the fitted black suits she'd had the tailor sew for him. The collar was unbuttoned so the top of his muscled chest poked out. He stood with his arms folded over his chest and his ankles crossed casually.

Just looking at him aroused her, and it was the same for him. The month he'd been gone had been too long, the memory of what they'd done not nearly enough to sate her. And she was growing tired of him resisting her. They hadn't fooled around since he'd come back from his visit to Veetula, and it almost seemed like he was avoiding her. She understood being busy. She had weeks of work to do and twice as many petitioners as usual to see since she'd been back in residence at Roskide. At least they'd been able to share the burden between the kingdoms.

Caroline yawned and stretched out across the bed, letting her satin nightgown slide up her thighs. She arched her back and wiggled her ass a little, knowing that was sure to draw him in.

Breicher shoved off the doorframe and narrowed his eyes at her, widening his stance. He cleared his throat, waiting. "Not tonight, Caroline. I have some things I need to take care of."

She narrowed her eyes at him. The bulge in his pants was begging to be taken out and played with. "You sure about that, Your Highness?" Rolling over, she traced her fingertips down her neck and across her chest, flicking her nipples as she went. She felt them harden and draw his gaze.

"Come play with me, Breicher. I know you want to," she said, practically purring as she stroked the silky black bedding.

His jaw clamped. He was going to leave. That's what usually happened when the Veetula loyal side of his mind worked.

"Sorry, wife. Another time."

When the door closed, Caroline chucked a pillow at it. "Stupid man," she yelled, which was followed by a low chuckle from the other side of the door.

That perked her up. The outside door of the sitting room clicked shut as the idea struck her. Caroline sprung from bed, threw open her armoire and flung on her onyx traveling cape. She darted through her sitting room, then snuck out the door, closing it quietly so no one would hear.

He wanted her. He just needed a little extra motivation. She could help with whatever he was doing, and he'd get distracted along the way and finally take her. Flipping the hood up over her head, she caught up with him. The soft footfalls of her bare feet didn't make a sound, and the faint swishing of her cape was eclipsed by the sound of his boots stomping down the hallway.

As they neared his room, her trailing silently behind him, her pulse began vibrating rapidly in anticipation. She was determined it was going to be tonight. His desire was a palpable thing humming through the air.

Instead of opening the door to his suite of rooms, he breezed past them and continued hastily down the hallway. Where was he going? In the evenings, he usually preferred to work at the stately desk she'd gifted him after their wedding ceremony.

Her breath caught as she followed him down several winding staircases to the lower levels of the castle where the attendants and guards' dormitories were. Perhaps he was going to visit an old friend from his time in the service. Even though he'd been a traitor, he'd still actually done the service. Probably formed bonds with the men.

Breicher eventually stopped at a door, not in the men's wing. He tapped three times, and she heard a female voice beckon him in from the other side. An icy chill swept through her veins, and she cinched the cloak more tightly around her. When Breicher had slipped inside and secured the door behind him, she hurried down the hallway and pressed an ear to the door. Caroline struggled to keep her breathing even as she listened.

He shouldn't be visiting her again. Breicher feared she'd think they were in a relationship, but Kelsey was discreet. She didn't mind if he was quick and never asked any questions afterward. It was just sex, straightforward, easy.

"How do you want it, handsome?" she purred. Kelsey wasn't the beauty Caroline was—she was... pretty. Her honey locks tumbled down across her slim shoulders, meeting the tips of her small breasts. She was over a foot shorter, with a plump ass. Her cheeks were rosy on the apples which sat below her bulbus blue doll-like eyes.

Breicher made a spin around gesture with his finger in the air and unbuttoned his pants, pulling his swollen cock from them.

"You always want it like that," she whined. "Can't we try something different?"

"Next time, Kelsey." Technically, this was only his fifth visit, and only the second since they'd been formally attached. The first since they'd been married and pleasured each other.

Each time, though, he swore he wouldn't see the girl again, but Caroline had gotten him so escalated tonight, it was either Kelsey, or he'd cave and sleep with his wife. His hand, or hers, wasn't cutting it tonight. He needed to be inside the hot depth of a woman. And he had the feeling if he consummated his marriage, he'd fall for her. Hard. Then she would win, and he'd never live down the shame of it.

He'd probably be admonished if his family knew he'd fooled around with her a few times. His brother's words flashed through his mind, and he grimaced. *It will be a betrayal of your family and your Kingdom.* He would be an Ivanslohe in name, but his family would deny his existence, loathing him on the same level they loathed her. He wouldn't allow that to happen, so here he was with the pretty blonde again.

"You're distracted," Kelsey said. "Let me help." She slipped out of her sheer nightgown and draped herself over the little table in the room that was shared by four women, none of which were expected back anytime soon.

Not that it mattered. He'd be quick, do what he needed, and be gone.

The woman gave her ass a little wiggle, reminding him of Caroline earlier sprawled across her gargantuan bed and his cock twitched. It would be better if Kelsey did it for him, but it was always thoughts of the queen that set his blood afire.

He angled his cock and entered the woman without fanfare, getting to work. Kelsey moaned an approval. "Harder."

Obliging, he picked up the intensity, but even as aroused as he was, there was something missing. Determined, he ground in deeper. He looked up to place his hand on her nape and froze.

A single white rose in full bloom was poking out of a delicate glass vase on the nightstand between the two beds in front of him.

"What are you doing?" Kelsey breathed. "Baby, don't stop."

He grabbed a handful of her hair, wrapping the other around her waist, yanking her up so her back was against his. "Is that some type of joke?" he snarled, directing her head in the flower's direction. Her inner walls clenched tight, and he groaned at the movement.

"Is this some type of game you'd like to play, Your Highness?" she purred. "If so, I like it."

"The rose. Just answer the question." Hot dread sluiced through him, but his pivoting hips seemed to have a mind of their own.

"All the castle workers are clipping them and keeping them in their rooms. It's kind of a superstitious thing."

"Explain," he hissed, the fear mixing with the pleasure in an oddly seductive way.

"Well, see the roses are thought to show if the queen is nearby. It's like a warning system. You know, since she turns them all..." Kelsey trailed off and whipped her gaze to him, her big eyes widening further. "It was red before you got here."

Her whole body tensed, and he couldn't hold back any longer. As the pleasure ripped through him, so did the dread. It was the most haunting moment of his life. "Shit."

Caroline put a shaking hand to her mouth as tears beaded on her eyelids. She'd known he'd hated her once. *Pull yourself together.*

She wanted to slam the door open and rage. She let Felix off easy. Breicher had been there to see it. Did he think she was a simpering fool for him? Perhaps she had become one. What type of idiot marries the man who tried to assassinate them?

A million thoughts flashed through her mind, and she had to put a hand to the wall to steady herself. She had to get out of here so she could think. She'd learned it was never a wise idea to deliver a punishment in a state of rage. Caroline spun and started sprinting down the hallway toward her wing. In the distance, a door creaked open, and she thought footsteps sounded, but she wasn't sure. Focus on your breathing. Put one foot in front of the other. She flew up the stairs, not even getting winded, and flung the door to her sitting room open. Grunting, she slammed it behind her, but a veiny hand caught the door before it smacked into its owner's face.

"Get out!" she screamed.

"Caroline, wait, please. I can explain." Seeing the queen so rattled was doing something to Breicher. It's like all his protective instincts were flaring all the sudden, alerting him to a predator she needed saving from. Except he was that predator.

"How?" she demanded, picking up an ornately carved vase from the middle table with both hands and hurled it at Breicher's head.

He narrowly dodged before a candle stick was flying toward him.

"How could you?" she wailed. "I would have given you everything, Breicher." Caroline paraded around the room, destroying everything she touched.

The sitting room was littered with broken tables, busted pictures from the walls, shattered glass and ceramic objects, and overturned furniture.

When there wasn't anything else to ruin, she stopped, dropping her hands to her sides.

"I would have given you everything." Her voice was a low, broken sound. She looked up at him. "Why?"

He blinked, holding out his hands in supplication. "I just couldn't with you tonight. Not after what I found out about your sister."

"But you still wanted to, with whoever the woman was inside that room." Caroline thrust a finger in the direction beyond the door, toward the woman she'd heard him with.

"I didn't want her. I wanted you."

"I offered myself to you." Caroline rolled her eyes at him and paced into her bedroom.

Breicher followed her. "Being with you feels like a betrayal. Especially after I found out that innocent girl is alive and still being kept in your dungeons after ten years." There, he'd said it, the looming thing that had been bothering him. Another reason in the long line of reasons they shouldn't be together.

Caroline threw her head back and gave a deep belly laugh. Tears were still streaming down her face, and he couldn't make sense of the reaction.

She snapped her cold gaze to him. "Did you ever think to ask for any details about where she was being held and why? Or did you assume the worst about me like you always do?"

She marched over to the little window and stuck her hand out. "Look," she demanded.

Breicher followed and stuck his head out the window to follow where Caroline's finger pointed.

"The east tower. I don't understand." His face relaxed as he finally gathered where this was going.

"Princess Emmaline spent a total of three days in the dungeon before I came to my senses and gave her the entire east fucking tower. She has been sequestered there since that night and for good reason. First, she tried to kill me for all intents and purposes the night of the assassinations, and second, if everyone knew she was alive, it would call into question my reign. I got the power, but she was still the heir. While I was doing whatever I had to do to rebuild this kingdom *your* family had destroyed," she jabbed him in the chest with a pointed nail, "I couldn't afford any disloyalty among the people. Something you might understand if you ever did any actual ruling."

"Caroline, I didn't know." He stared down at her, eyes pleading.

Gods, the pain in her chest felt like her entire body might be cleaved in two by it. The Gods wouldn't have had anything on this husband of hers.

And there was so much he didn't know. So much she'd never shared with anyone. She didn't know why, but she sensed the words bubbling up from the deep crevice inside her where she kept them locked away. Sealed behind the obsidian wall where she hid the memories of her father, the stories of her mother, and the few other happy times she'd had as a girl.

"Do you know what they did to me, your family? He was one of your sapphire eyed cousins, wasn't he? Servius, the sicko with the same muddy hazel eyes you had when you betrayed me." Breicher flinched, but she continued, "Do you know why I'm the monster you think I am?" She looked up at him with steel in her gaze and told him everything.

Breicher's instinct screamed, *Hold her*, as tears streaked down his wife's smooth cheeks while she relived the night she lost her father, her sister betrayed her, and his men had tortured her. And they'd not abused Caroline the Cruel, the woman she was now, but a fourteen-year-old girl. Then she told the story of the time she met the Gods and received her first punishment.

His chest pinched as she finished her tale, and he took a step toward her. She waved him off, not turning to look at him. He'd never seen her look so... *defeated*. But she was right to push him away. He'd just been with another woman, and his skin crawled with his own self-disgust.

"Not even Angus knows all the details of that story," she sniffed, then wiped her eyes on the back of her hands. "Honestly, I'm not even sure why I told you. This marriage is over. You should leave."

"Caroline," he pleaded, voice guttural as she turned from the window she'd been staring out as she spoke. An oily sensation rooted itself in his stomach as he understood his betrayal and how much loving him had cost her. Because she must *love him*. That was the only explanation for her reaction. He thought of Felix. She'd been livid about what he'd done, but not gutted like she was now.

"Your family murdered the only person on this earth who's ever loved me—truly and unconditionally loved me." She paused, the glimmer of a smile traced across her perfect lips. "I take that back. I guess I have Angus. But he knew me then, before my heart had shriveled away into nothing. I should have known I didn't have a chance for love the second I realized even the Gods enjoyed my suffering."

Breicher didn't understand one thing. "You could have had me killed when you returned. Why didn't you?"

"I knew marrying me would be the greater pain for you. Because when we'd kissed, I sensed you felt what I did. Or I thought so, anyway. I felt the battle you'd rage inside your mind. The wanting and despising at once was a fitting punishment. And I wanted the ally, and the marriage made sense politically. I thought I could have it all. Obviously, I was wrong." Caroline pressed her lips into a firm line, her shoulders sagging.

She was confessing everything he'd thought was true. "And eventually, you were going to deliver the final blow. Let me fall for you and then take it all away. Like Felix." Breicher almost wanted to look away as he waited for her to confirm what he already knew.

"You're not Felix, and we got to know each other. I thought you'd see I wasn't a monster or cruel. Not really. And our chemistry is undeniable. I thought... I don't know what I thought." Caroline buried her face in her hands.

"Tell me," Breicher whispered. His heart was thundering so loud in his chest that he could hardly hear her as he spoke.

"I thought we could love each other." Caroline's voice was barely audible, but he heard every syllable. The sensations inside his chest were resonating in a frequency he'd never felt before. It was almost painful and euphoric simultaneously, and he couldn't quite connect a word with it. All he knew was he needed to wrap his arms around his wife and beg for her forgiveness. She wasn't lying. The truth of it was scrawled across her divine features. He'd been wrong. So very wrong.

"What about the massacre at Avondale? All those dead—I counted thirty graves. You said there were only five or six. How was I supposed to reconcile with that?" He was grasping, trying to find some explanation for what he'd done. For why he'd hurt her.

"You should go ask your brother if you want to know the truth. I'm done with this conversation." She took off her cloak, and calmly hung it in her wardrobe. He was unable to look away.

Jaden had cautioned him against taking his brother's *evidence* as the real story. But he'd believed him. Hollis always wanted what was best for him. It didn't add up. And even if she had done terrible things, was he any better? As he stared at Caroline's tear-stained face, his gut told him he'd messed up. Possibly even irreparably, and the ache in his chest demanded that he fix it.

Breicher didn't think before the words tumbled from his lips. "Caroline, I don't think I'll ever be able to adequately express the regret I feel—how much I wish I could take my actions back. I've made a huge mistake." He walked over to her, careful not to move so quickly, it would scare her away. She stood eerily still, taking him in. "I'll pay any price. Take any punishment. Please, can we start again?" Breicher lifted his arms, which were gravitating toward her on their own accord.

She understood his intention and held up a hand halting him. "Don't bother."

Breicher, the King of Veetula and Everstal—the Joined Kingdoms, fell to his knees before his Queen. "I didn't know."

Caroline looked down at her husband, at the tears cascading down his perfectly chiseled features. Even in his agony, he was so beautiful, and she loved him. She had for a while, but had been unwilling to admit it to herself. Maybe since that first kiss before he drove the rosenwood dagger between her ribs. She probably always would. Nothing hurt like the dagger in her heart when she'd heard him giving it to that sex worker.

His brother had sent him girls, but she'd unwisely believed he'd rejected them because she'd seen him do it the first time. She shouldn't have followed him last night after he'd left her room, but she was glad she did. They hadn't been making the progress she'd thought they had. She was naïve enough to think he'd been taking it slow with her—no, who was she kidding? He was still at war with himself. But this, going to another woman for his needs, was unacceptable. It was like the final gust of wind that blew the shards of her black heart away. There was nothing left. He had to go. Queens made tough decisions, and Caroline was used to pain.

"Get. Out." She gritted her teeth and pointed toward the door. Breicher didn't budge. She nudged his chest with the toe of her shoe. "What is wrong with you? Can't you see I don't want you anymore? I'll have the marriage annulled. It was never consummated anyway, thanks to you. Clearly you prefer the company of anyone but me." He still didn't move. Just sat there staring up at her with those achingly perfect sapphire eyes. She didn't even hate him. That's how pathetic she was. "Please don't make me compel you, Breicher."

Even she heard the weariness in her voice as she looked away. "Fine, I'll leave," she said. "But I expect you to gather your things and be gone by the morning."

He'd won. Caroline had no more to give. She focused on the door. She just needed to make it there before she fell apart. After a blur of steps, she stepped under its arch.

Okay, she told herself. Now, down the hallway. She left Breicher on his knees as she made the next few steps away from him, on her way to Angus to have him work up the documents. No sense in delaying it. And Angus had seen her breakdown once before after a particularly brutal punishment from the Gods early on when she thought she might not be able to withstand them and needed to give up the power. She couldn't have it and not use it. He hadn't judged her then.

A shudder convulsed through her body. *Stop*, she chided herself. Queens do not fall apart over wayward men. *Even if they are the one*, a little voice whispered as she made it another few steps.

"I watched my father drive a sword through his own stomach." Breicher's heart was beating fast as he shared his truth with his wife in a last attempt to make her see him. See that he understood how wrong he'd been.

Her footsteps quieted in the hallway as she paused. Good, she was listening. "Your father used so much power that night the final conflict ended. He spread the armies and marched right through, meeting my father behind his own lines. Hollis was eighteen and father made him come along, wishing to instruct him on how to be a proper ruler. I practically thought my older brother was a God. I had just turned ten, and father wouldn't let me come, but I was constantly under Hollis's heels."

"I learned if I were persistent enough, I could persuade anyone. So eventually, the king caved and let me ride a small pony alongside him and Hollis, believing me safe."

"By the time your father's power hit us, Thom had him under control. And he didn't kill him cleanly, Caroline. He tortured him, degraded him in front of his men, making him roll in the dirt and bow before him. Imagine seeing your own father being made to lick his enemies' boots. Eventually, when the amusement wore off, or his power was weakening, Thom compelled my father to rise and impale himself."

"How did you get away?" Caroline asked from the hallway.

She was giving him a chance. This was good. "As soon as Hollis understood what was happening, he swept me off my pony and onto his horse. He rode so fast up that hill behind the armies, I'll never forget it. Thom was so occupied torturing our father he didn't notice. We hid behind a section of wagons and watched our father die by peeking around a corner."

"Days later, we received his head from a messenger with a note that we'd be allowed to be *free* if we'd submit to his reign. Your kingdom knew it as the Peace Treaty, but ours thought of it as an occupation. Veetula wasn't truly free until King Dallimore died. But I'm sorry that meant you had to lose your father. It sounds like you loved him very much."

He must have said the wrong thing because her heel strikes began anew, becoming more distant with each sound. "Caroline?" he called from his position on the floor, surrounded by her shattered things, of which he was one.

CHAPTER 16

Hollis was reclining on his cot, leafing through a pamphlet, when Caroline stormed into the prison. Arriving at cell fifteen, she wrapped her hand around the iron grate and, using her otherworldly stolen strength, gave it a vicious yank. The lock groaned, the snapping metal clacked across the space and the door burst open.

The former king had enough wherewithal to scoot back into the corner at her approach. Caroline hadn't attempted to disguise her state, her puffy eyes, her tear-stained cheeks. Let him see. She didn't care. Rearing back, she hurled a rolled-up piece of parchment at him.

Hollis plucked it from the air before it smacked him in the nose. "My execution order, I presume."

A dead chuckle tumbled from Caroline's mouth. "My annulment decree. Don't look too pleased."

Hollis's face brightened considerably. "Where is my brother? Alive?"

"I don't know, but he's a dead man if he ever crosses paths with me again."

"I see," he said, slipping the ribbon off and unrolling the paper.

The way Hollis's jaw ticked like he didn't like what he saw as he scanned it grated on her. But she was a ghost of her former self, unable to muster the energy to torment him. "You're free." When Hollis didn't budge, she gave a long, exhausted sigh and said, "Go, you're free."

Dark eyebrows furrowed as Hollis's incredulous sapphire eyes studied her, reminding her of the feel of Breicher's gaze. Except instead of a flood of heat, a chill sprung to life dancing across her skin, and she had to hold back a shiver.

"So, I can just leave here, go back to my apartments to continue living my life? No exile?" Hollis still tucked himself back in the corner, wary and very aware of Caroline's ways. That was the smartest thing the man had done since she'd stolen his kingdom.

That brought a brief smile to her face. "I'd think it was lovely if you jumped from one of the castle towers, but suit yourself. It matters not to me. But if you are going to stay here, I expect you to contribute. One wrong step, and you're dead. I'm done fooling around with you Ivanslohe's."

"Why?" he asked.

Caroline threw her arms into the air. "You win. He hates me. The pig's blood and false graves were a nice touch." Hollis hadn't told her about that. It had been her and Angus who'd discovered them. She suspected Hollis had even hired actors to play the roles of the grieving families, though she couldn't be sure.

Slowly, Hollis edged forward, and got to his feet. He took a tentative step toward the open door, and Caroline caught a flinch out of the corner of her eye when she turned.

"You blame me. I wouldn't have hesitated to kill you if the positions were reversed. I don't understand." Hollis fell into step beside her as they left the prison.

"You're a snake, but I blame him. And considering what a conniving, but effective louse you are, I have a feeling one day I'm going to have a use for you. You're in my debt. And I need someone to toy with when I get bored. You'll do quite nicely for that." She shot him the most devious smile she could summon, then vanished.

Angus padded across the queen's chamber. The usually resilient woman had been ruling from bed for a week now. He'd finally got her to bathe, dress and stay on foot long enough to transport them to Veetula to deliver the news of the annulment. Of course, Breicher had refused to sign it, but Caroline's word was law.

Since she'd thrown the scroll of the document in Hollis's face, she retreated to her room in Kierengaard and not left.

"Caroline, petitions are this afternoon," Angus said.

"Execute them all," she hissed from beneath the covers.

"Caroline," Angus said a little more firmly. "We can't start executing people for not paying their taxes."

The covers rustled, then a pair of red eyes popped out, her pale skin and white hair blending with the blankets. "Then have Hollis deal with them. Or Agnes. She's always eager to give her opinion."

"You're acting like an adolescent," Angus said, storming out of the room. He had a great deal of empathy for his friend, but this was getting ridiculous.

Angus breezed by Jaden as he left the queen's chambers. "Where are you going?" he asked the prince.

A sly smile danced across Jaden's lips. "Wouldn't you like to know."

Angus let out a loud groan. "You're going to get yourself killed." Why was he warning the man? If Caroline rid him of the prince that would be one less annoyance he'd have to deal with.

The ache in Caroline's chest was unbearable. It wasn't the acute gut-punching sorrow that hit when she'd heard Breicher with the woman. That had lessened into a gnawing, empty feeling and made her limbs feel heavy, like gravity had doubled its force. Like right then, she swore the bed sunk.

No, the bed did sag like a body dropped onto it beside her. If it was Breicher, he was dead. Caroline's own body rolled toward the figure, but she pushed herself to her knees, throwing off the covers.

Jaden Ivanslohe casually reclined next to her with his ankles crossed and muddy boots on her bed. Even his uncharacteristically wild chestnut hair was littered with dirt and—was that—hay? Caroline gave him a scrutinizing look from head to toe. "You're filthy."

Why it was the only thing she could think to say, she didn't know. It barely took two hands to count the number of conversations she'd had with Prince Jaden outside of the Petitions. And none of them had been remotely entertaining. Well, perhaps a few, but they certainly weren't familiar enough for him to be in her bedchamber, much less her bed.

But here he was, always lurking, observing, and sneaking about, Jaden Ivanslohe. Confrontation didn't seem like his style, but he had been spending more time with his uncle Angus had said. Gods, it dawned on her—if he was here as a messenger... Caroline groaned, reaching out a hand to give him a shove. "Get out."

A sly look that might have been followed by a grin, but wasn't, lit the prince's eye. "You're a disaster," he said, and reached into his breast pocket and pulled out a knife and began cleaning the muck from his nails with it. He wiped the grime on her pillow, then moved on to the next nail.

"Is that rosenwood?" Caroline shrieked. Were these people mad, trying to test her like this?

Jaded chuckled. "What? Did you think you got rid of it all?" He paused, raising an eyebrow at her. "Besides, Breicher said it won't hurt you anymore. And the stuff makes fine knives." He handed the blade to her for inspection.

Her brow wrinkled as she took it from him and turned it a few times in her hand before giving it back. She'd will it into his own throat before it got near hers. "What are you doing here?"

"I noticed my uncle's signature was glaringly absent from the annulment decree. I take it he didn't leave willingly?"

"You're here on behalf of your family to find out—"

"About the fate of the king? No. Because to Veetula, if you're queen, then he's still the king." Jaden let out an exaggerated sigh. "He loves you, Caroline."

"Well, sticking your dick in other women is a funny way of showing it."

At first, Caroline thought Jaden was coughing. From under his breath, a full bellied laugh sprung forth. That set her blood racing. She grabbed the nearest pillow and clubbed him over the head with it. "How dare you, you little shit? This is all your stupid father's fault. I hate the lot of you."

Jaden didn't stop laughing, no matter how many times Caroline assaulted him with the pillows. When he had enough, he grabbed a hold of her wrists and gave them a firm shake, bringing them eye to eye. "Why didn't you tell him you love him? He thought you were playing him the whole time—for one of your punishments."

Caroline thought her head was going to explode. "How is this my fault? Everything I've done—he should have known. If Hollis hadn't been sending him women and filling his head with nonsense about mistaken loyalty—that staged massacre at Avondale. I shared what I learned about our family's history and the deity's maniacal scheming. I kept your family alive and even let you continue to live in Kierengaard for the sake of the dead gods, despite how you people disrespected me. I'd drain the gods a second time just to see the looks on their withering faces if I could." Why had she said that last part? She supposed she wanted to see someone suffer like she was suffering.

Sitting back on her heels, she only then became aware of what she must look like, in her sleeping gown, hair mussed from wallowing in bed. She flipped her eyes toward the mirror. Her face and eyes were redder than she'd imagined.

Jaden's gaze danced across her pitiful form, giving her a moment to take herself in before he started beating his muddy boots on the bed. Crusty clods of dirt broke off, soiling her linens. Apparently, he had enough. "Whelp, looks like you can't stay here until you get the servants to change the bedding." His expression was almost sympathetic as he dragged her out of the bed and over to the wardrobe.

"Why are you doing this?" she asked as he threw the doors open.

"My parents aren't overseeing the petitions. Don't tell them I said this, but they're far worse than you. Everyone in Veetula plays like they're not because of our collective hatred for the Dallimore's and everything they touch." He pulled out a sky-colored gown. "You never wear blue. Time for a change. And it will endear you to the people. That wouldn't hurt." Jaden gave her a pointed look.

Caroline took the dress that was proffered to her. "What a lofty compliment," she said. "You don't hate me too?" Her voice sounded a little shaky, but she didn't care. She'd been through enough.

"I've been watching you, trying to understand you. And no, I don't think I hate you. I think I might actually like you," he said, raising his brows like he was surprising even himself. "Trust me, I'm shocked as well. And more importantly, I believe your story about the Gods."

Caroline blinked at him a few times as he rustled through her drawer of undergarments.

"In my experience, these will work under a dress like this." He tossed her a wink, along with what he'd selected, then gave a forceful point to the bathroom.

Caroline seemed glued to the spot. Jaden raised a challenging brow. "Do not make me bathe you. Unless you'd like to pay my uncle back? One thing would lead to another... Oh, that would be quite devious." Jaden loosened the ties at his throat for effect. He was as handsome as his father and uncle. And he was known to be quite the rake, among both men and women. They hadn't the slightest chemistry though, and no matter how badly she longed for the ache in her chest to stitch back together, taking him up on his offer wasn't going to happen. Not that he was serious. Right? Her eyes darted to the space between his hips to be safe. No bulge. Good.

Jaden caught the movement and gave a little low chuckle. "Trust me, all I'd need is a few peeks of that creamy skin and I'd make things happen."

Caroline groaned as she plodded into the bathroom, piling her hair on top of her head, and dropped her sleeping gown. Chills sparked across her skin as she submerged into the bathwater which had gone cold hours ago. *What was with these insatiable men?* The icy plunge stole her breath. For a moment, the only thing that existed was her body and the thrilling chill numbing her limbs.

As she soaked, Jaden spoke from the doorway. "There are a couple of things you need to know." He paused and waited for her to object. When she didn't, he continued. "I believe Breicher is still your king. I think sending him away was a mistake. He is a good man, the type of man you deserve and who deserves you if you both would let go of your bullshit." He paused again.

"I find your audacity to speak to me so frankly..." she hesitated. She wasn't sure what she thought of it. But if she let go of tradition... Angus spoke to her without fear of repercussion. Moments ago, he'd called her, the queen, an adolescent. She'd always felt the best advice had come from that aspect of their relationship. That is what Jaden might be for her here in Veetula.

"How do you find it, Caroline?" he pushed, testing the boundary.

Caroline looked inward for a moment. How did she find it? She settled on, "Refreshing." The word gave her a sudden exhalation of tension, like a cork being blown from a bottle. It was a pain to admit, but she could use a friend. Still, her anger at Breicher and the decisions she'd made were only those a queen would make. Expecting Jaden to understand wasn't fair.

"What else do you think, oh wise one?" Caroline asked, half annoyed, yet half curious what else the man who was her mirror in so many ways had to say.

"I think my mother was wrong about not accepting the friendship you extended to her. I never understood why our people hated each other. I mean, I get the countless wrongs over the years, but it's like a game of revenge that never ends. But I don't think we are so different. I'm not even sure there are that substantial philosophical differences between our people below the surface level ones. I guess what I'm trying to say is I think we can do this."

Jaded let out a deep exhale after he finished his monologue.

"So, you want a job?" she called out.

His laugh danced through the door frame, and her spirits were lifted on the draft. "Yes, Your Majesty. I suppose that is what I am saying. Though we are going to have to come up with a more palatable moniker for you than *Caroline the Cruel*. What about Caroline the Capricious? Slightly less edgy, and perhaps more accurate?"

"Stop talking," she begged, though her amusement bubbled through. When she finally emerged from the bathroom clad in the undergarments Jaden had tossed her, her skin was bright pink.

Jaden looked her up and down. "First my uncle, now the ice bath. Are you some type of sadist?" He held the dress open as she stepped inside. Having the nephew of your former husband dress you was probably inappropriate on so many levels, but she'd threatened the lives of all her attendants. They'd elected to stop coming to work until she, as Angus repeated, *calmed down.*

They chatted openly while she'd finished getting ready. There was only so much eye makeup she could slather on to cover up her sorry state. Eventually, Jaden told her, "You're making it worse," so she stopped. "You still look beautiful," he said, as if that mattered.

When they entered the hall outside her room, Jaden offered Caroline his arm. She reached out to take it and when her fingers wrapped around his bicep, his other hand clamped on hers, pinning it there. He looked down to her, brow furrowed in as much seriousness a twenty-five-year-old playboy could muster, and said, "If we walk in there like this, you know what it means, don't you Caroline?"

She swallowed down a lump in her throat and nodded. "We're on each other's team."

"That's right." Jaden grinned, then they marched down the hallway arm-in-arm to make good on their unspoken agreement with the world.

CHAPTER 17

"**D**IDN'T I COMPEL YOU to jump off a building?" Caroline asked, watching the former king pour himself another glass of winter's sin. The petitions had lasted until well after her normally scheduled dinner time and she had been hoping the cozy study in Kierengaard had been vacant so she could have a moment of quiet, but it seemed Hollis enjoyed the space as much as she did. And his presence held as much entertainment value as the book she'd been planning on reading.

"Surprisingly, you have not. And I think it's because you fancy me," Hollis said, letting his eyes rove over her fitted knit dress.

"Must have slipped my mind. It's very morose to drink alone."

"Well, lucky me, because here you are." Sauntering toward her, Hollis pulled another glass from the bar cart and poured it to the rim, handing it to her. "Go ahead, since you can apparently handle your liquor."

The tumbler was crystal and still had an "I" in filigree etched into its surface. Caroline ran her finger over the silver letter, her mind skipping to images of her husband—former husband. The thoughts were enough to make her take half the glass in a swallow.

Hollis eyed her with a look that suggested he wished he were the alcohol she was swallowing. The dumb smile spreading across his face sparked an idea. For the last month since she'd released him and exiled his brother, she'd been debating how to punish him for the wedge he'd helped drive between her and Breicher.

"I find you have a certain appeal." Fluttering her lashes, she shot him a mockingly sweet smile. Hollis's eyes brightened, as if he hadn't assessed her expression as she'd intended. His arrogance was staggering even after everything that had transpired in the last few months.

The tufted navy leather creaked as Caroline draped herself across the couch in the center of the room in front of the roaring hearth, setting her half empty glass on the side table. Mistaking it as an invitation, Hollis took the other end, still gripping the bottle in one hand as he sat. "I figured as much," he said, and Caroline choked at the gall of it.

"I see narcissism is a family trait, though yours seems to outdo Jaden and Breicher by a load. There, I guess you've found something you can be king of. *Hollis the Ego King*."

"Oh, Caroline, I thought we were getting along much better. I've been helping with the petitions, contributing as you suggested." Hollis paused as Caroline held her glass out to him, giving it a little shake. He refilled it, giving her a wary look. "I told you it's incredibly strong, remember?"

Shrugging, she tossed the contents back, then held it out again, hiccupping.

"That bad, huh?" Hollis asked. When she didn't respond, he refilled it, then his own. "Might as well join you."

An hour later, the bottle was almost empty, and Hollis's speech was relaxing. *Perfect*.

"You know what I fear, Hollis," she swished a hand in the air, allowing her voice to show the effects of the excessive amount of winter's sin she consumed. "Well, besides death of course."

Hollis leaned forward, resting an elbow on the back of the couch. With his other hand, he absently toyed with the hem of her dress. "Tell me, Caroline."

Cocking her head, Caroline said, "Wait," then giggled. "S'not fair for me to tell you a secret and you not have to share, too."

Hollis chuckled. "Well, that's easy, beautiful. What scares me the most is you. Your turn."

"Well, she said, twirling her hair. I hate spiders, but what I fear the most..." Hollis edged forward even closer. "Definitely snakes."

Caroline crawled across the couch toward Hollis, like a friend might move in a treehouse when they were about to share a juicy secret. "We're friends, right?"

He nodded, eyes insistent. "We've shared an entire bottle of winter's sin, so I'd say it was official." The expression on Hollis's face was of a cat who'd given a mouse nowhere to run. He'd cornered her. Or he thought he had.

"I learned something else when I killed the Gods. It wasn't just the rosenwood that could kill a Dallimore."

Hollis sat engrossed. "Go on," he urged.

"The leaves," Caroline whispered. "They said if the dried leaves were ground up into a powder, it would be the same as poison."

"It's unbelievable no one tried that after all these years," Hollis said.

"I know. And lucky for me, there aren't any rosenwood trees left, so no more leaves." Caroline hiccupped again for effect as she set the trap. Pushing to her feet, she stumbled, knocking her shin on the center table. Shit. She should have healed more of the alcohol from her system before she tried to walk. Flee really. Hollis looked like he was moments from kissing her and that sent a series of cramps to her stomach, or it was the winter's sin.

As Caroline tottered from the room, she wondered how long it would take Hollis to strike.

"She told him what?" Breicher released an exasperated sigh.

"Something that's got him combing the castle grounds for rosenwood leaves. He's determined to use them to make a poison, because she said the Gods told her it would kill her."

"And he believed her?"

"Apparently, she sold it quite well. They consumed a full liter of winter's sin between them, and father said she was an equal participant," Jaden said as he rode beside his uncle. They were off to Avondale. It had taken a full month to convince Breicher, who had been too busy wallowing in his misery to leave his room in the little inn where he was staying. Of which Jaden was footing the bill now that his uncle had no claims to anything, really, of his own.

"Oh Caroline, what are you up to?" Breicher called to the clear blue sky. "If he gets himself killed, it's his own fault. There must be a reason she's keeping him alive. As far as we're concerned, it's best we stay out of it."

When they arrived at the town square, Breicher rose from his saddle, but settled as Jaden passed through the center and kept going. Nudging his horse, he caught up, grumbling. "I told you we're not disturbing the gravesites, Jaden."

Jaden shot him a scowl. "Why is it I'm the only one in this family who will do what needs to be done?"

"I'll go, but I'm not taking part in the desecration you intend."

As they rounded the corner, the cemetery came into view and the thirty fresh graves scattered across the frozen ground like open gashes gave his conflicted thoughts about his wife's new life. No vegetation yet covered the rich brown soil. Winter lasted longer here than in Everstal, and the mounds of dirt looked fresh as the day those who had died were buried.

Jaden galloped ahead. "Looks like your lucky day, uncle."

Breicher rode up to the edge of the surrounding stone wall, quickly dismounting and lashing his reins to a post. They let themselves inside the gate and made their way up the rows. Darkness flooded his vision as his world tilted. A strong hand wrapped around his shoulder for support, but he still stumbled, crashing to his knees like he had the morning Hollis had brought him here.

He couldn't believe it. Jaden wasn't going to have to dig up any bodies to confirm his suspicion. Someone had already done the work for him. A sinking feeling rooted in his gut and instinct told him who it had been.

Long moments passed and Jaden let him sit there, running his hand over the dead grass left where the piles of dirt had been cleared away. Processing what lengths his brother had gone to in order to keep him and Caroline apart was almost too much. His voice caught as he said, "How many are there? The false ones?"

Jaden had finished walking the rows, making his own assessment. "It appears all of the ones on this side are just piles of dirt made to look like fresh graves." Jaden slid his sword into the nearest pile of earth, hitting the hard, undisturbed ground beneath about a foot down. "That leaves seven total on the other side. Someone must have died from their injuries after she fled. Or other causes unrelated to the ambush."

Bile gurgled in his stomach as saliva flooded his mouth from the surge of nausea washing over him. Breicher was going to be sick. Jaden came to kneel beside him, placing a hand on his back as the tears fell. "She knew, but she didn't tell me. Her and Angus must have figured it out. I don't understand."

Jaden grimaced. "Well, you know our queen. She had her reasons, I'm certain." After a while, Jaden stood, reaching a hand down to him. "Come on, let's get back to the city before nightfall."

In the time he'd been sent away, he'd been trying to reason out how he might excuse his actions. He'd almost convinced himself that what he'd done didn't count because he'd been forced to wed her under one of her punishments. But that was a lie... he'd felt what transpired between them on their wedding day and he'd been ready to be with her of his own volition and any excuse he might come up with didn't taste right to him. The simple truth was, he'd been wrong. He'd hurt her, and she was the one still standing again like she always was and would be.

What did he have to do to get her back? This new revelation swirled around in his head as he and Jaden rode in silence back to Kierengaard.

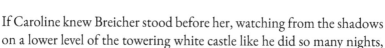

If Caroline knew Breicher stood before her, watching from the shadows on a lower level of the towering white castle like he did so many nights, she didn't let on. It was risky, that she might kill him like she'd threatened if she caught sight of him, but he had to see her. His wife stood on a snow dusted balcony in a loose sky colored gown, staring toward her southern kingdom.

She'd been spending more time in Roskide, now that the petitions were a few months underway, and she'd established a rhythm. The subjects in the surrounding city had even come to appreciate having a weekly audience with their sovereign if the rumors were to be believed. She was still feared, resented, but despite everything things were changing. Caroline was uniting the kingdoms.

And she was doing it all without him. Guilt and sorrow mixed in his mind as she raised a glass of wine to her lips, taking a sip. She set it on the ledge, then gripped the stones, closing her eyes. She took a deep inhale, then exhaled the breath slowly before opening her eyes again. Breicher hated that he wasn't there with her. That he wasn't the one she was leaning on, the one easing her burden.

Instead, he'd become her burden.

No more. In the last month when he'd been licking his wounds, Jaden had suggested he find a way to help her from afar. He'd dismissed the idea, but now he reconsidered. She may not want to see him, or acknowledge he was still bound to her, but he could act as her king by action. Maybe, after her rage had softened, and she saw his efforts to prove himself, she'd welcome him home.

As if sensing his thoughts, Caroline picked up her glass, and turned to go back inside, taking his heart with her.

CHAPTER 18

I T DIDN'T TAKE BUT a week before Hollis was knocking at the door to her suite with two bottles of wine. One was red, presumably for her and poisoned, and the white for him. "Your Majesty, may I come in?"

He wasn't calling her by her given name, which meant it was definitely *poisoned*. She better put on quite the show then. But she should enjoy a full glass or two before the crushed leaves should be taking effect. This was going to be the first bit of fun since... no, she wouldn't go there. Just enjoy this, she told herself. "Hollis," she called. "Come in."

Gesturing to the bottles, she said, "What a pleasant surprise!"

"I figured we should celebrate our new friendship. It's been an entire week since you've threatened to kill me, so I felt we were making progress. May I?" he asked, holding out the red for her inspection.

Caroline made a show of looking over the label. "If you please."

Hollis pulled a wine key from his pocket and got to uncorking the bottles, pouring them each a glass.

What an elaborate effort. He'd re-bottled the wine after he'd tainted it. His thoroughness almost impressed her. Without hesitation, she took the one offered to her, sniffed it, and took a long drink. "Delicious," she said.

Hollis looked overly pleased with himself. "I'm glad you like it."

Caroline studied the man across from her as he sipped his own glass, knee bouncing as if he weren't aware he wasn't nearly as subtle as he believed. She'd told him she could heal the intoxication from her system and what was alcohol but a tastier poison. Fortunately, he hadn't made the connection. His eagerness to end her seemed to outweigh his critical thinking skills, which, based on how elaborate Avondale was, he didn't lack them.

"Another glass?" he asked, springing to his feet.

She chuckled, covering her mouth. Obvious indeed. "Please. What has you in such a good mood, Prince?"

Hollis finished topping her off, then relaxed back in his chair, appearing determined to calm himself. Perhaps he was aware. "I'm having wine with a stunning woman who no longer hates me. I'm eager to see how our relationship evolves. I'm right, aren't I? You don't hate me?" His forehead wrinkled as his eyebrows shot up eagerly.

"Something like that, though I'm still unhappy with the stunt you pulled in Avondale." She frowned as she ran her finger around the rim of the wine glass, causing it to sing.

"Listen, Caroline," he said, and his legs spread even wider than they'd been before. She was sure it was an unconscious movement but telling all the same. "It's one thing for one of us to sleep with you, but love or a marriage wasn't in the cards. Honestly, I think Breicher was looking for an excuse to end it, anyway."

Violet starbursts flashed across her vision, but she seized them before they manifested on her face. It was best to ignore the stinging comment, because there was truth to what Hollis said, and she was still trying to figure out how she felt about that. "Yes, it seems you were right." It was time. Caroline had better start acting poisoned before she murdered him.

Furrowing her brow, she brought her hand to her stomach, and Hollis leaned forward at the gesture. "Are you okay?" he asked.

"I need a second." Getting to her feet, she took a few steps toward the bathroom, then staggered, catching herself on the back of the couch. "Hollis, get help. Something's wrong," she cried as she tumbled to the ground.

❧

"How long is it gonna take her to die?" a rough voice Caroline didn't recognize asked.

"I don't know. She didn't tell me that," Hollis said.

Footsteps shuffled through gravel as the man Hollis had handed her off to carried her across a yard. The cool night air ruffled her hair, and the smell of horses came into her awareness. The man placed her, none too gently, in a carriage and she had to bite her cheeks to keep from wincing aloud. "Go drive. I'll stay here with her in case she stirs," Hollis commanded. The carriage bobbled as he climbed inside, quietly clicking the door closed behind him. Then they were moving.

Caroline estimated they rode two hours through the night to the outskirts of the city, when the carriage came to a halt. She didn't dare open her eyes, but gave a convincing agonized groan at the abrupt stop.

More shuffling, the door creaking open, then the man Hollis was working with seized her wrist with a meaty hand, then she was being pulled through the door, and cradled as they followed along behind Hollis. *What fun.*

Muffled sounds of a lively gathering were taking place somewhere in another room of the building they were entering. They must be going in through a back entrance. "Take her to the room. I'll be up in a bit," Hollis said.

"I don't see why we couldn't have buried her in a deep hole and left her to die there," the unidentified man said, and a whiff of his foul breath hit her face drifting up her nostrils and she almost gagged. His head must be angled toward hers, studying her blank face.

"Until I see her dead body, I won't be convinced," Hollis said.

"We could cut off her head?" The man's voice lifted at the end of the question a little too hopefully. He was nervous Hollis was leaving him alone with the dying queen.

Smart, she chuckled internally. He should be worried.

Hollis huffed, like he'd considered it. "No. I plan to put her bleached corpse on display for all the kingdoms so it will be known she is well and truly dead. Then I will take my rightful throne... *and hers.* We are so close, I can taste victory."

A gruff hand stroked her head, and one of them lifted a lock of her hair, twirling it between fingers, which must belong to Hollis since the other man's were occupied holding her. "She's such a pretty young thing, it's too bad." Hollis's voice trailed off as he left them.

"Very well," the man answered, and started climbing the stairs. Soon after they entered the room, he unceremoniously dumped her on a bed, and the scraping of a chair being moved sounded.

She'd give Hollis a minute to get comfortable at whatever bar he'd nestled up to, probably the one in the inn. Because she knew the former king now and his penchant for winter's sin, she suspected he'd be looking to celebrate the victory he believed firmly within his grasp.

It would be divine. Her punishments always were... especially the dramatic ones where she had to play a long game, draw out her anticipation, then watch the thing snap shut when her victim—no, that wasn't the right word—the wrongdoer was lulled into complacency. She'd let them think they'd won, then strike. She felt the lesson sank in deeper that way.

Ten more minutes. Caroline's heart began giddily thumping but halted as hands once more were laid upon her.

"You *are* a pretty thing, aren't you," the man said, turning her so she was face up. Then he was stroking her cheeks with his sticky fingers and heat from his noxious breath brushed against her lips like he was leaning down to—

No. She reached out to seize the man's voice before he could shout. Then she snapped her eyes open and relished in the terror she caught as he stared at her very alive silver, awake and alert, staring back at him. "Get off me."

The man, an Ivanslohe by the deep shade of blue of his eyes, blinked as he scrambled back like she was the collapsing ledge of a cliff, and he was moments from tumbling into the ravine below.

"I'm going to let you speak if you promise not to yell. Sound good?" she asked, sitting up on the edge of the bed.

He nodded vigorously.

"What were you doing a second ago?" Caroline leaned forward, placing her hands on the bed on either side of her and the man, a cousin of Hollis's.

"Checking to see if you were still breathing."

Caroline gave him a surprised face. "Quick thinking, but try again." A thought and she had ahold of him, and had him trembling before he admitted, "I wanted to see what all the fuss was about. I wanted..." The man gagged even as sweat formed on his brow. "I wanted to know what was so great that Prince Breicher would betray his own family for it."

"I see. So, you were going to have a little sample?" she asked, wondering how much of a taste the man would have taken had she not stopped him.

Across the room, he plastered himself to the wall, seeming to use its solidity to hold himself up. "Maybe," he said, voice cracking with effort.

"Do you have a knife..." She paused, inclining her head so he'd supply his name.

"Chauvin, Your Majesty."

Caroline let out a wicked giggle. "Why so formal all of the sudden, Chauvin?" When he didn't answer, she continued. "It's the blade for you. So go ahead and get it out of whatever pocket it's stashed away in and slit your throat, so I don't have to. Your participation in an assassination attempt against a queen is unforgivable. Your death will be a mercy compared to what I have in store for your cousin, so be grateful."

Chauvin tried to scream, but she caught his voice before a sound burst from his mouth. His hands, under her compulsion, dug a knife from a pocket inside his coat, which he'd taken off and laid across the small table in the room.

Struggling to speak, Chauvin half spit and half mouthed the words, "I'll take Hollis's punishment. Whatever you planned to do to him, you can do to me."

Caroline kicked her feet, which dangled over the side of the bed, back and forth how school children do. "But you don't have enough life to pay for the two of you. Now be a good boy, say *Thank you for your mercy, Queen Caroline*, and slit your throat."

Chauvin murmured, "Thank you for your mercy, Queen Car—" catching short as the deadly red line drew across his neck. Horror flashed once across his wide, glassy eyes before they went lifeless. Chauvin thudded to the floor.

As she stood, Caroline straightened her clothes, then stepped around the blood pooling, staining the porous grey stones. An excited chitter fluttered about in her stomach as she left in search of Hollis.

Caroline's prey sat in the middle spot at a navy felt-covered game table in the center of the room and had an unlit cigar loosely clenched in his back teeth. Tossing a few gold coins on the table, Hollis asked the man dealing cards, "Can't we raise the stakes?" The other players, eyeing the coins, shifted in their seats anxiously, like they wanted out, but were afraid to offend the royal.

Stepping behind him, keeping her footsteps soft, she traced her fingertips across his shoulder, then up his neck. Caroline threaded her fingers in his hair, knowing he would assume it was one of his many lovers or a sex worker who had found him. His overconfidence made things easy for her. Hollis didn't flinch until she gripped a handful of hair tightly and yanked his head backward, so they were eye to eye as she stood over him. The cigar fell from his lips as his mouth dropped open.

"Gods," he swore. A confused grimace turned into realization, and he said, "You lied."

Caroline bopped him on the nose. "Exactly. You're quite clever. Unfortunately for you, I am far cleverer. Oh, and thanks for warming my seat for me."

Hollis, becoming wan, pushed back from the table, and held out the chair for Caroline, moving it forward as she sat.

"Go fetch me a glass of wine." Caroline turned to the dumb struck players at the table, then reached out and scooped up the gold Hollis had deposited. "Don't worry, we won't be playing for this. I like to get my thrills in other ways." Caroline acknowledged the dealer, patting the stack of silver which had been in front of Hollis and said, "Deal me in."

When Hollis set the wine on the table, Caroline snatched it up and sniffed it. She gave it a swirl, inspecting it in the light, then shot a wink to Hollis before taking a taste. "Heel," she said, and pointed to a spot on the ground beside her where a chair had been before he'd gone for the wine. Hollis stood where she pointed, then slowly lowered to his knees as rivulets of sweat dripped down his temples from his battle against the compulsion.

Leaning over to him, she said, "Don't worry. I will not kill you like my father did yours. *Yet.* You and I are becoming quite good friends, don't you think? We have so much fun left to have before I end you. Right now, I need you to learn your place."

Hollis looked like he was clamping his jaw so hard his teeth would be crushed under the pressure, and everyone was watching them. "Oh, my guard dog is upset because someone tried to kill me tonight, which I believe is impossible. His distress is pointless." Shrugging, Caroline picked up her cards, throwing out a few coins.

Caroline was terrible at cards, but she was having a delightful time. On her third glass of wine, and at least that much for the others at her table, she'd convinced them to tell her stories of Hollis. None of what they were sharing painted him in a positive light, but they had her doubled over laughing. "He didn't?" Her voice was gleeful as she covered her eyes in a mocking gesture.

"That's what Carla said. When he didn't show up in her bed that night, she thought he'd found someone else, but when he stumbled through the kitchen on his way out the next morning, she realized how right she'd been. Her mother, Old Mean Marge, whose tits hang to here—" The woman gestured to her stomach, below her belly button. "—came out after him wrapped in a sheet, beaming."

The woman, giggling behind her palm, shot a wary glance to Hollis who was still heeling at Caroline's side and went on. "Marge gave him a swat on the tail and asked when she would see him next. She said he didn't say a word and his face was as red as an apple."

The server brought several plates of small bites to the table and passed them around. Caroline looked at Hollis. "Is that true?" she asked. He managed a glare at her, but she held out a piece of sausage wrapped in flakey bread, wiggling it in front of his face.

"Yes," he hissed, which only made the giggles turn into outright laughter.

When Caroline could hold it together long enough to speak, she said, "Good boy." Then, "Open," in a voice that she might use for a real dog. Hollis had no choice but to open his mouth so Caroline could plop the food into it. Tussling his hair, she turned back to the game she was sorely losing.

When she'd finally spent all the coins Hollis had bought in with, she tossed the gold on the table. "Looks like I've found something I'm beyond terrible at. But you all have been lovely. Tonight is on me."

Before anyone could protest, she placed a hand on Hollis's shoulder, and they vanished.

Before anyone could protest, she placed a hand on Hollis's shoulder, and they vanished.

"I don't know about you, but I had a fantastic time." Caroline couldn't help but beam at the former king.

"I hate you," Hollis grumbled as they appeared back in the study in Kierengaard. Getting to his feet, Hollis stretched his limbs out. He'd spent hours in the supplicant position, and she imagined he must be terribly stiff.

"Me?" she said, in a mockingly demure tone. "But I thought you fancied me?"

Hollis flinched as she threw what he'd said the day he'd given her the idea. "Back to cell fifteen, I assume?"

"Only if you wish." Caroline headed for the door.

"Is that where you took Chauvin?" Hollis dared.

Turning, she caught his eyes with her own flatly serious expression. "He's dead."

Hollis blanched, stumbling back a step. "You killed him?"

Caroline shook her head. "What did you expect, Hollis? For me to forgive and forget? Roll over like the weak and flippant woman you believe I am? I've been merciful to your family because of your brother, and I was attempting to start things without bloodshed between our families for once."

"I haven't killed you because you are a former king who *some people* still respect, and I still have use for you. I'll send someone to take care of your cousin's body. Next time, you might weigh the potential consequences before you fuck with me. Understand?"

Three different veins were bulging in Hollis's beet colored forehead, but he forced himself to say, "Understood, Your Majesty."

"Good boy. Don't wander off too far. I wouldn't want my asset to step in front of a carriage by accident." Caroline winked before she turned and sauntered from the room, pleased with her first step toward breaking her former rival.

CHAPTER 19

"SO, WHAT DO YOU do for fun, Caroline?" Jaden asked, scratching meaningless symbols into the margins of the parchment before him.

She raised an eyebrow at him from across the table. "Rule?"

"Dead Gods, you're such a bore. What does my uncle even see in you except a nice pair of tits?"

Angus cleared his throat at his own spot at the furthest end of the table, but kept reviewing the treasury ledgers that had arrived from Veetula's royal bookkeepers that morning when the queen and Jaden arrived in the war room in a whirl of her power.

Caroline looked down at her chest. "I've always thought they were rather small?"

"If I didn't think Breicher would somehow find out, I'd offer to give you a free evaluation." A wolfish grin spread across his face as he overtly stared at her chest.

She shot him a warning glance. "I dare you to mention his name again."

Jaden shook his head vigorously and stuck his tongue out at the queen. He would not fall for that trick again. The last time he'd flaunted their *blossoming friendship* before her, she'd reminded him she was still queen and watched him, with the groomsman who was supposed to be doing the job, from a balcony sipping pink wine while he'd mucked the horse stables.

"Can we please focus?" Angus hissed under his breath.

"I amend my former statement: you two are quite the pair of bores," Jaden said, leaning back in his chair so it balanced on the two rear legs.

"If you're not going to contribute anything, I'd suggest you'd go find some castle girl to amuse yourself with," Angus said.

"Don't exclude the men, Angus. They deserve my attention, too. That new stable hand sure looked in need of some *entertainment*, didn't you think?" He gave Angus a lazy smile. "And I've already told you what I think of your idea, and so has the queen, but you can't seem to drop it."

"It's an absurd idea, Angus." Caroline brushed the crumbs of a crisp bread she'd been munching on off the paper Angus handed her.

"Here me out. With the king..." he cleared his throat. "*Former* king in exile, the people in Everstal are getting antsy. Your subjects in Veetula still fail to acknowledge the annulment, especially considering that you are allowing the prince to collaborate with Jaden implementing your policies in the outlying villages—a decision I cautioned against. There's even a rumor that another assassination attempt might be in the works. So, the paper you are holding is a list of the most eligible men in the two kingdoms, with stars next to the ones from the north—which I think would make a better alliance. But you're going to have to bed the man, so your pick."

Caroline whined as she looked over the list. It had been almost a year since she'd banished her husband and had the marriage annulled. Wasn't that long enough to get over a broken heart? Each morning when she looked in the mirror, she swore the darkening circles under her eyes smudged a deeper shade of violet. That meant more makeup, which she wasn't accustomed to.

Maybe Angus was right, and it was time for a change. Something had to get her out of this rut. "Are you sure it's a good idea?" she asked, narrowing her eyes at her commander.

Angus noticed the dark circles long before the queen had admitted she hadn't been sleeping. The woman was suffering and suffering badly. He needed to do something to distract her and do it quickly. Jaden seemed to think she needed to end the exile. The prince Caroline had taken into the fold voiced his opinion a little too liberally and too often if anyone asked him.

And it's not that he was jealous of the man. That was absurd. At first, he'd even thought Caroline had planned to take the man as a lover, but she claimed there was no spark between them, even though Jaden teased at it enough. Besides, a new king would be the perfect chance to solve the queen's apathy and the several political problems arising too.

He just didn't think he could handle seeing her so broken again, the way she'd been the night she'd sent Breicher away. She hadn't told him what had transpired, but it had devastated her. Caroline hadn't been herself afterward. But Jaden had come along and somehow gotten the woman he respected most in the world out of bed and somewhat back to her testy self.

Angus eyed his sovereign, wondering if he'd misjudged whether she was ready for this. He was about to retract the suggestion when she looked up. It was that spark in her eye he missed most. "You need to do something, Your Majesty."

꿍

Her commander only used the formal address when he was saying something she didn't want to hear. She supposed he was right. Pressing her fingers into her shut eyelids, she tried to ease the strain. "I'll do it. But I want to meet them, to get a feel."

"You mean you want to see which one strikes your fancy—"

"No, Angus. I don't really care about that anymore. I just want to get a sense of which one might be the least traitorous out of the bunch. Make them all wear costumes, or better yet masks. What they look like matters not to me." Caroline clicked her fingers on the table as she stared off into the distance, thinking.

"A masked ball at Roskide?" Angus asked, surprised at his queen's unusual suggestion. "We've never had a party here before."

Not before they'd lost their parents the night of the Peace Ball, and they eventually cordoned off the Great Hall. He wasn't even sure how to go about putting one together. "Umm, so that is a, yes?" Caroline's gaze had wandered off again. She'd been doing this a lot lately, which worried him. Fortunately, she remained completely focused during the Petitions at both Everstal and Veetula.

"Mmmhmmm."

Angus tracked her gaze, which was focused longingly out the north window. "Perfect," he said, snapping the ledger sitting before him closed, drawing her attention back to the present. "Any other requests?"

"No, I don't care." Caroline got up from the table, then stopped short, turning. "The decor should all be black, the candles, linens, even the roses. Dye them if you must. I want to make sure my suitors know what they are getting themselves into."

✦

As the queen stormed past, Jaden, who'd been trying hard to keep quiet, looked up from his stack of correspondence. "Are you sure this is a good idea?"

The queen ignored him and kept walking, so he shoved his chair out and stomped across the room after her. A firm hand wrapped around his bicep and a shiver went down his spine. Jaden turned to Caroline's commander.

"I've known her much longer than you. Trust that I know what she needs."

Affronted, Jaden sneered down at the delightfully calloused hand cutting off his circulation and peeled each of Angus's fingers off one at a time. He looked the intimidating man square in the eye. "Considering I'm the one who got her kicking and screaming again, I wouldn't be so sure of that, *commander*."

Jaden could tell the man was holding his emotions in check by the way his jaw clenched when he'd said commander. He wasn't intentionally mocking him. He was such a stalwart at times. No fun. Always the stoic commander. And the dam was near cracking. Jaden didn't want to be the man on the other end of the sturdy man's fists, so he spun to chase the queen down the hall, shaking his shoulders out as he jogged to catch up.

"Your commander needs to get laid," Jaden said, when he finally caught up to Caroline.

"Good luck with that," she huffed. "Trust me, I've tried to set him up with plenty of women. He's just not interested."

Jaden raised an eyebrow.

Caroline shook her head. "Have at it, prince. I'm guessing you won't have any better luck than me." The queen paused, walking for a moment, then skipped through an open door and to a balcony overlooking the training yard. She grabbed his forearm before he made his presence known. They stood in the shadow of a column and watched Commander Angus Straihan begin his assault on a straw target with a wooden long sword.

Jaden's hands went to his collar, clutching it closed. "Gods," he said.

"He's been like this ever since I've known him. Like *that*, ever since his body began to fill out."

Jaden's pulse thrummed. He couldn't tear his eyes away from the man and the relentless exercise taking place.

His face flushed, and Caroline, witnessing his rose stained cheeks asked, "Think you could beat him?"

He swallowed. "I supposed it wouldn't hurt to try? I may not be the towering warrior my father and uncle are, but I still have the Ivanslohe Gift from the Gods." Jaden figured he ought to be able to hold his own, considering his unnatural strength and vitality, even against the formidable man below. *Surely.* He winced as Angus struck and the burlap holding the target split down the middle, straw exploding outward into the commander's agitated face.

Caroline twirled her white locks as she patted him on the back. "Consider it a dare from your queen." Tilting her head up at him, she winked, then charged off in whatever direction she'd been going, leaving him in the shade unsure of what he'd been after her for.

It took a month to plan the masked ball. Jaden enlisted a few ex-girlfriends who were still friendly, as the queen had no interest in party planning. The women, thrilled to use their skills and be this close to all the gossip, had willingly grasped Caroline's hands as she transported them from Veetula to Everstal. They'd spent the first two days walking around, struck stupid by the beauty of the place. It's lushness, the crystalline water in the bay visible from Roskide a wonder that never failed to amaze him either.

But they were doing so well at their task, he hardly needed to lift a finger which was a sign you were doing your job properly. When the experts you brought in managed it and you didn't need to do anything at all. That's how he'd found himself fingering the leather wraps on the handle of two short swords, staring down Angus in the training yard. It was a fine line to walk with Caroline and her dares.

"You sure you want to do this?" Angus asked, not even trying to hide the arrogant edge to his voice.

"I'm fully confident you'll be no match for me." He was terrified.

Angus huffed, like he sensed the thoughts swirling inside his mind. "Caroline put you up to this, didn't she?" It was a growl and Jaden swallowed the lump of tension knotting itself in his throat.

Breicher and Hollis could beat him, even on a bad day. Some of his cousins too, but he'd yet to come across someone outside the family who he thought might challenge him. He leaned his sword against his thigh as he wiped the sweat from his palms on the back of his pants. Gods, it was sweltering here.

As soon as he'd picked up his short swords, Angus charged.

Jaden brought the weapons up in a block, arms straining as Angus's blow landed. His eyes widened as a thought struck him. "You're trying to scare me off." Angus grimaced. Oh, that pissed him off. To think this man thought so little of him that a few hard swings of a sword would intimidate him. Did Angus not realize he grew up fighting men much more skilled than him?

Jaden ducked another blow, using his lighter form to nimbly spin under Angus's outstretched arm and deliver an elbow so hard to his side, the other man stumbled a few steps. He'd thrown him enough off balance that when he darted past, then twisted, jutting the shorter sword forward, Angus was barely able to get up a defense in time.

But he did, and the forearm to his chest sent him tumbling into the dirt. A second later, Angus's knee was in his gut and a knife he'd pulled from some hidden pocket at his throat. "Yield," Angus demanded.

Oh Gods. Angus was like some type of amber skinned angel hero. He blinked a few times, taking in the halo the sun had formed around his head, blocking anything beyond from his vision. That strong jaw, those supple lips, the hulking body pinning him to the ground was something else entirely. Jaden's heart lurched as a grin crawled across his face. "Never."

With a quick roll and a swipe of his legs, he had Angus on his ass, disarmed, and nailed to the ground. As Angus thrashed, throwing his weight around underneath him, Jaden employed his grappling techniques. That was one thing he excelled at. The men in his family might have had more physical power, but the wrestling technique common in Veetula took strategy. Within a few moves, he had the large man in an unbreakable hold. Unbreakable, he figured, for someone who knew nothing of the sport.

"I yield," Angus ground out. Jaden, of course, following the sports rules, immediately released the man, backing away so he could get to his feet.

Oh, this was fun. A wide smile lit his face. Angus was pissed, and he was giddy. He eagerly leapt up, waiting for his opponent to retaliate. "Again," he said, getting into position.

Instead, Angus dusted his shirt off and charged away from the practice ring, never once looking back at Jaden. Even as he rounded the corner, the commander's shoulders stiffened.

Jaden tried to shrug it off, but the nagging sensation that had punched into his gut when Angus had turned his back wouldn't quit. Not even as he waged his own war against the re-stuffed opponent.

"What happened to you?" Agnes asked, as Breicher stormed into her parlor.

Breicher looked rough. He hadn't shaved in days, and when he and Jamison had sparred that morning, he'd been so distracted from the news he'd received, he'd slipped up and let a few of his cousin's punches through his defenses. Chuckling to himself, he thought of the few that had made it through his cousins in return. Partially because he needed somewhere to funnel his aggression and partially for the role Jamison had played in the scene in Avondale he'd been a part of.

But they were family, and after a few sessions in the ring, he forgave him. He'd do the same with Hollis, eventually, assuming Caroline took him back and didn't kill Hollis along the way.

Breicher flung the envelope on the table his sister-in-law was sitting at, sipping tea. She picked it up and turned it in her hands, not needing to open it. "I see you found out," she said. "What are you going to do?"

Slumping down into a chair across from her, he put his head in his hands.

"It's been a year and Jaden said she won't budge when it comes to me. She takes no notice of anything that I've done. I've written her dozens of letters—she hasn't responded to one. I'm about ready to lay myself at her feet and let the consequences be damned."

"Let's not be dramatic," Jaden said, slipping into the parlor right as the attendants came in with breakfast. Seating himself, he took out his napkin and placed it in his lap. "It's so nice we can do this. Too bad a certain unraveling former king can't spare any time to join us."

"I fear your father is getting worse, Jaden. It would be best for you and your sister to prepare for the inevitable." Agnes reached across and patted her son's hand.

When the attendants had set breakfast and left the room, Breicher said, "And what would be *the inevitable*?"

Agnes finished chewing the bite of sausage she'd plopped in her mouth. "She's going to kill him, eventually. If she doesn't do it because of his most recent scheme, I'll be shocked."

Jaden lurched back in his chair, drawing both their attention. "I guess we're just going to let that happen?" When neither Agnes nor Breicher refuted, Jaden continued. "Mother, you no longer care if your husband lives or dies? Your children's father?"

"Of course, I care, darling. But, I mean, I've hardly spent a moment with the man since..." she patted her pursed lips with the pad of her finger. "Oh, yes. The night I tried to spare our youngest child from living under the thumb of a tyrant."

Both Breicher and Jaden stiffened.

"Seems I forgot I'm dining with two of her biggest fans. Lucky me." Agnes flicked a winter berry across the table at Breicher.

Catching it in mid-air, he popped it into his mouth, then said, "-Agnes," his tone lowering in warning.

Agnes huffed. "Oh, don't scold me. I used to be your queen and I would still be your queen if Hollis wasn't too lost in his alcohol induced stupor to get us out of this, so a little respect from someone in this family would be appreciated." Right as she spoke, the door to her bedroom cracked, and a tousled looking man poked his head out.

"Excuse me, Your Majesty," the man said, then made his way toward the door. "I must be getting to work."

"Evan, my dear," Agnes called after him. "I'll see you again tonight, yes?" There was a hopeful lift to her voice as she waited for the man to reply.

A blush crawled across his broad cheeks, and he gave her an eager nod before slipping out the door.

Both Breicher and his nephew were staring at her, slack jawed. "What?" she said, raising a hand to the flush at her neck. "Evan has been keeping me company. You know how your father and I are—don't look so shocked."

"He's younger than me," Jaden blurted, running a hand across his face. "The things you wish you could un-know."

"He's completely legal and *very effective*." When Jaden gave an exaggerated whine, Agnes said, "I thought we were talking about our little queen."

A relieved expression melted the horror off Jaden's face. "Caroline isn't that bad. She's actually quite pleasant, though a little stubborn, which brings us back to your problem." Jaden eyed Breicher as he reached across the table to where Agnes had discarded the invitation to the ball. "We need to find you a mask, uncle. I have a plan."

CHAPTER 20

T HE KNOWLEDGE THAT THE finest and most eligible men in the
kingdom were about to vie for a shot at his wife made the muscles
around Breicher's head feel like they were going to seize up and crush
his skull. She may think their marriage annulled, but that wasn't how it
worked in Veetula. Especially with the royals.

He couldn't fathom what Angus had been thinking, trying to remarry
her. He made a mental note to throttle the burly man the next time he
saw him. Everstal might accept the imposter, but Veetula never would,
and an uprising would surely ensue. Even though she'd cast him away
from Roskide, he was still her king.

And like he'd once overheard her say, he'd choose when to discard
something that was his. In this case, that was her. And he'd never discard
something so priceless. He knew that now and he was determined not to
go down without a fight.

Breicher glared at himself in the mirror as he tied the grey wolf mask on
his face which matched his steel-colored suit. He laughed at the irony. He
knew his wife. She was making them wear the masks to send a signal that
she didn't care who was behind it. She and Angus believed the king to
be a figurehead at this point. Jaden had confirmed as much. After it had
failed with Felix, the merchant she'd built, then with him, she was done.
His amusement was hidden behind the mask that would allow him to
sneak into the Great Hall where he would take back his queen. He used
a rosenwood needle to pin a closed white rose to his lapel. That was the
only hint he'd give of the man beneath the mask.

Breicher took the stairs two at a time as he departed the little inn that sat midway up the mountain on the single road which wound its way up to Roskide. The carriage he'd ordered was waiting on him when he stepped outside. He had full access to the purse of Veetula still via Jaden, so he used it, making sure his attire and his arrival would blend in with the other suitors.

After a long and nausea-inducing ride full of twists and turns up the mountain, Breicher arrived at the ornate iron gates which were flung open in welcome. He looked up at the imposing pink castle and memories of everything they'd been through flooded through his mind.

She would never forgive him. To her, she'd been trying to connect with him. Make their marriage into something more than the sham it had been. *Her punishment.* He'd given her nothing but a few orgasms with his hands and mouth.

If she would have told him sooner what had happened that night of the Peace Ball, to her, maybe he would have understood. If she'd told him she loved him, maybe he wouldn't have let Hollis have such an influence over him. It might have changed things. But they'd had that conversation a day too late.

Not a day when by that Caroline didn't think of him. It's like her mind had blocked off the bad parts and only remembered the man on his knees with tears rolling down his face.

"Caroline, you look so... forlorn." Jaden leaned down and kissed her cheek.

"Why are you going along with this tonight? I know you don't agree," she said.

"Can a man be a libertine and a hopeless romantic at the same time?" he asked, adding kohl to his own eyelids. Jaden slipped his mask on, showing her the effect of the makeup and handing her the stick. "You need more."

Caroline's shoulders sagged as she added a thicker swipe of the black product on her upper lids.

"You know it's okay to still be in love with him, right? He's still hopeless for you."

Caroline spun. "No, it isn't. I'm supposed to pick out the new King of the Joined Kingdoms tonight, Jaden. I wish you'd stop bringing him up. Isn't it enough that I'm letting you work with him?"

Jaden gave her a deep frown, then pulled a box from his pocket. "I got you a present, darling." He gave her a knowing look, pulling the box out of reach as she grabbed for it.

Angus cleared his throat. "Don't tease the queen."

"You're already in dangerous territory, Jaden Ivanslohe," Caroline admonished. Poor Angus. Jaden was becoming a little too intrigued by her commander. She'd thoroughly explained that relationships weren't really Angus's thing, but that only seemed to draw the prince more.

Jaden turned to Angus. "It's my present. I'll give it to her whenever I like. Unless you plan to do something about it?"

A glare shot from Angus to Jaden, who was still blinking innocently, as if he didn't know he was blatantly flirting. "Then how about you put the box back in your pocket," Angus said.

"I'll give it to her later. It will be more appropriate then, anyway." He shot Angus a smug look in return, then dragged Caroline up from her stool. "You're ready. We need to quit stalling and get down there and get you a king."

<hr>

Red wasn't typical for Caroline, and she stood out in the color that had been Jaden's suggestion. The man had a mind as keen as hers for the politics of running a kingdom, including a much-appreciated gusto that enlivened the monotony of ruling. He'd imparted that gift into her attire for tonight.

Beaded fabric wrapped the column of her neck, sweeping closely over her figure down to her hips, where sheets of gossamer scarlet draped to the floor like overlapping rose petals. The look was what Queen Cerise had tried to create for Emmy for the peace ball, but overblown. While her front was completely and demurely covered, her arms and back were exposed. The dress's opening dipped so low on her back it was almost indecent. But that wasn't the most shocking aspect of what they'd designed.

She'd piled coils of white hair atop her head and wove ten in-bloom scarlet roses through like a crown. Caroline eagerly anticipated the effect the red flowers would have—the rumors. Since she'd drained the Gods and subsequently the roses, stories about what had happened to the queen and the roses that were a symbol of the kingdom had swirled. Had the color drained like the light in the queen's own soul? Was the hue the cost she paid for even greater power? Had the last Dallimore perished? Some had claimed the day the roses bleached, they'd shriveled first, then rebloomed white, signifying Caroline's rebirth.

Tonight, she and Jaden had them dyed red. For a few hours, they'd stay that way before the dye would turn them black, the dye killing the cut flowers.

The rumble of voices inside the Great Hall hushed as her footsteps echoed from the corridor behind the main banquet table which was piled high with decadent treats and black flower crusted sculptures. Like she ordered, swaths of black glimmering fabric draped the tables and hung from the ceiling in undulating bunches giving the space an ominous feel. Even the music, if it had a color, would be black. It matched her mood perfectly.

Her heartbeat clapped loudly in her ears as it jumped erratically higher and higher. It struck her then. She didn't want to do this. The sinking sensation that pulled her down each stair like quicksand and into the awaiting crowd, seemed to say, *This is wrong.*

Caroline gritted her teeth, tamping down on her traitorous heart. Angus had been right. She owed it to her people to make this impartial decision. Ruling the Joined Kingdoms took quite a bit more out of her than it had when she'd just had her own to deal with. Of course, Jaden and Angus made the burden easier, but in these early years, she liked to oversee everything as closely as possible. Having a partner, like she'd had those short months with Breicher, had felt so effortless. Surely there was a man here who could fulfill that role.

A rough hand grazed the small of her back. "Your Majesty," a deep voice uttered. Caroline turned, heart momentarily skipping. The man standing before her with a head bowed and a glass of sparkling wine extended wasn't Breicher. None of them were, she reminded herself. Forcing a smile, she took the glass and greeted the man behind the mask.

"Tell me of yourself, Lord Elmshorn. Why would you make a fine king?" Caroline said, racking her brain, trying to extract what she remembered about the Master of Bridgewater and the sprawling Elmshorn estate. There wasn't much.

Only a few petitions had warranted enough elevation to come through to her from his region over the years. The local magistrates adeptly handled conflicts in Bridgewater, where Lord Elmshorn held the jurisdiction. It was a point in his favor. The rough hands which indicated he used them were another plus. But judging by the narrow red pout and flaring nostrils that poked out from his feathered fox mask, he might be a little tiresome to look at, not to mention should she need to bed him at some point.

"I'm a businessman, Your Majesty. I'll let these other men tell you of your beauty, as I imagine you already know. If you are looking for an equal, a man who can rule beside you, all you need to do is consider at Bridgewater. My father served yours faithfully..."

She shouldn't be tuning him out. On paper, she already understood everything he was saying. Her eyes darted through the crowd. "Yes, yes. I see your merit, Elmshorn," she said, patting his forearm. "I will definitely consider it."

Elmshorn took the glass, a little speechless after Caroline downed it and held it out for him. "More?" he asked, a little too hopefully. Shaking her head, Caroline turned slipping into the crowd to find something, or someone more interesting.

Another set of hands, *too forward hands*, gripped her shoulders and there was warm breath at her ear. "I'd be lying if I didn't say I was insulted when I received the invitation, Your Majesty. Why put on this charade when you know my offer still stands?" a smooth voice whispered into her ear.

Her anxious heart guttered. For a second, she thought the possessive touch might have been him. But what would be the point of that? She'd only send him away. The last thing she needed to do was be confronted with those blue eyes which seemed to pierce her like a dagger. "Not now,

Hastings. We've been through this." Caroline shrugged away from Lord Hastings' clammy touch meaning to walk away. She didn't remember seeing the man's name on the guest list, but Roskide's guard knew Hastings. He probably smooth-talked them into letting him in. Once upon a time, he had been a regular fixture here.

Hastings gripped her elbow squeezing insistently and tugged her back toward him. She spun, jerking out of his grip. "Are you mad?" she asked, eyebrows pinching as she glared up at him. "Get your hands off me." Just the feeling of another man's hands on her made her feel the need to scrub at her skin. She steeled herself. No, she had to get used to the idea because she would be giving one of these men permission to touch her... eventually.

Wide eyes stared back at her from under the mask that covered the upper half of Hastings' face. He gave her an uneasy laugh. "Caroline, when I heard you'd married that prince and that he'd been your guard, I didn't know what to think. It made sense when I thought about how possessive he'd been that day and it made me sick to think of how he manipulated you—"

Caroline's open palm was flying before she could stop it. A loud crack silenced the room and all heads turned toward her. Hastings stepped back, stunned. Damn it. She was too volatile for this. Angus and Jaden were swiftly approaching her from either side of the room.

"But Caroline," Hastings said, rubbing at his cheek as Angus latched onto his bicep.

"Don't worry, Your Majesty. I'll take care of him," Angus said, leading the man away. Caroline's head cocked quizzically as a pained expression crossed Hastings' features when she didn't intervene. With a dejected slump of his shoulders, he let Angus guide him out of the room.

Jaden didn't speak and she could almost hear his admonishment as he put his hand around her waist and led her to the outskirts of the room in the opposite direction. "I know what you're thinking," she said when they got out of earshot from the crowd.

A smirk flitted across Jaden's face, but he didn't say anything. Didn't rebuke her, or judge her. All he said was, "You know you don't have to do this, right?"

Caroline shook her head as he rubbed her shoulders reassuringly. "But I do have to do this, Jaden. Queens must do difficult things." It was the mantra she repeated so often to herself these days.

Jaden gave her a sorrowful nod. "Very well. Then let's get back after it." He led her back into the mele, releasing her once he seemed to determine she'd collected herself.

After listening to a few more pitches, and refusing a few more glasses of wine, she found what she was looking for. Jaden had warned her only men from Everstal would dare attend, but Hollis had promised her a selection of Veetula's finest. The first favor she required of him. Initially, it appeared Jaden was right in his assessment, but standing next to Prince Hollis were six rather robust looking Veetula men. That would send a message. She sauntered over to them, letting the fabric swish with every movement of her hips.

"Prince Hollis, won't you introduce me to your friends?" Caroline surveyed each of them. Of the six, three pairs of sapphire gazed back at her through different animal face masks. She held up her hand before Hollis answered. "Wait. You three are cousins?"

The man in the middle gave a nervous glance in Hollis's direction. "There could be no better match for you than an Ivanslohe."

Angry bursts popped across Caroline's forehead, and she had to hold her hands at her sides to prevent them from squeezing her temples. "I had an Ivanslohe, Hollis. But if I recall, you were adamantly opposed to our union. Now you are offering me another one?" It was taking all her concentration not to scream. "This seems rather distasteful, even for you, don't you think?" she asked, tilting her head to the side. She addressed the blue-eyed cousins. "Thank you for coming, but I'm afraid there are some lines I can't cross."

Caroline didn't fail to note the relief relaxing the faces of the three men as they bowed and took their leave, returning to the party.

Right as the color drained from Hollis's face, a prickle tickled up Caroline's spine. She knew who Hollis had spotted without needing to look. Kicking herself for electing not to wear a mask, a brilliant smile would be her only outward defense to shield the warring emotions wrecking her insides. He hadn't dared to show his face, obeying his banishment until now. The punishment was death, she'd told him, if she ever saw it again. And though Breicher had worked with Jaden, she never *saw* him, so she permitted it. Besides, he was effective in getting things done.

Sometimes, though, she'd scent him in a room, or on a piece of furniture and the memory of him would wash over her in a wave and she'd have to steady herself. Then the sounds of what had transpired in that room echoed in her mind, threatening to double her over. The only reason she resisted the urge to spin on her heel and strike him down was because of the strength of the elation welling in her. Out of the corner of her eye, she caught Hollis nudge the man next to her.

"Hollis, why don't you go find a window to jump out of?" Caroline blinked in mock sweetness at the former king who grimaced but left them.

"Don't worry," she winked at the men. "I didn't compel him. Tell me your names. I'm eager to know them." Gods, she wasn't being subtle. But she would flirt and hoped Breicher would see every single second of it, down to the moment she chose which man would be her new husband. It hadn't been the plan, but she would choose tonight for him to see. Take the lucky man to bed with her, and force Breicher to stand outside the door while she moaned in pleasure. The three tall men before her seemed up for the task.

"Jamison Flaxfeet," the one who Hollis had nudged spoke up. Shiny auburn hair fell in soft curls down the sides of Jamison's face. The rest was tied neatly at the nape of his neck. "I've been dying to meet the woman who was responsible for the death and torment of so many Ivanslohe men." A wicked smile lit his face as he extended his open palm for her, lowering his muddy hazel eyes.

The man was good looking in a rugged way and almost as tall as Hollis, who, based on the three standing before her, had come through on his favor she'd called in. Caroline placed her fingers in his, and Jamison brought them to his lips. "Oh," she said. "You must be referring to the team of assassins my commander and I dispatched. There were quite a few sapphire-eyed murderers among them."

"Precisely. And what a magnificent creature you are, just as Hollis promised, if I may say, Your Majesty."

Placing her finger under his chin, she raised his head from where it was still bowed, so his eyes met hers. "I was only fourteen then, Jamison. Imagine what I'm capable of now."

Jamison let his eyes roll over her figure as he stood to full height. "Quite intriguing."

Turning, Caroline assessed the next man. Dex Winningham, another hazel eyed suitor, introduced himself, then Geoff Strongman stepped forward and did the same. *What strange family names.* All tall, muscular, handsome. They all had family land, ran successful businesses, and had no attachments. She could do worse.

Caroline was quite enjoying herself when Angus stepped to her side. "Making progress?" he asked. She'd spent more time with these suitors than all the others in the room combined and Angus was here to move her along.

Caroline tapped the tip of a painted nail to her lips. "I think we can safely narrow the field to these three." Three grins broke out across from her, but she flicked a wrist at them, addressing Angus. "I think a Veetula husband is a good strategic move. The union would show the people we intend to have balance, camaraderie, and prosperity in my Joined Kingdom."

Breicher still hadn't shown his face, but she had a feeling he was watching her intently. Time to draw him out of hiding. It wouldn't do to allow her people to see him defy her exile. Embarrass her like this. A memory arose. She'd once threatened to have him follow her around crawling on all fours. That would be a fitting punishment.

"What's going on in that pretty little head of yours?" Jamison asked, a flirtatious smirk tugging up the side of his mouth.

Caroline wanted to roll her eyes. She was leaning more towards Dex or Geoff. But Jamison would do perfectly for bait. "Let's see. I was thinking of your dossiers, weighing which of you had the most to bring to the table." She bit her lower lip for effect and stared up at them. She shot a quick, doe-eyed glance at Angus. "I can sample the offering?"

Dex made an amusing choking sound, but Angus kept his face neutral, even though she suspected he wanted to throttle her. He had come to stand next to her because of the looming threat stalking somewhere on the outskirts of the party. "You are queen, Your Majesty. You may do whatever you wish."

Splaying her fingers across her eyes, she began to chant a nursery rhyme in her head, changing which man she pointed to with her finger. By now, a small crowd gathered around her, and the spectacle of choosing a husband based on a riddle was sure to delight them. She stopped it a beat short, though no one knew, and landed on Jamison. "Looks like you're first. Perhaps we can go to the terrace *alone,*" she said a little loudly, "and you can show me what you're all about."

Jamison's teeth flashed, and a self-satisfied expression took residence on his face, officially striking him off her list. She was done with self-important men. Still, he was incredibly attractive, and a little kiss wouldn't hurt. Besides, when she sent him packing after their whole audience knew what had taken place on the balcony—she chuckled inwardly—*that* would be an ego damaging blow.

Bouncing on the balls of his feet, Jamison stepped forward, offering his arm to Caroline. She tucked her fingers into the crook of his elbow, allowing him to lead her across the room, all the while butterflies swirled relentlessly in her stomach. Before they'd made it halfway, heavy boot steps sounded behind them, approaching more quickly than they were moving. Beneath her hand, Jamison tensed, and she knew she'd drawn out her prey.

The helpless man beside her suddenly wasn't there anymore. She spun. Breicher had grabbed Jamison by the collar, towed him backward a few steps, and was now in his face, seething righteous venom. A thrill zapped her heart making it double its beat. Then a surge of warmth spilled through her as her exiled love attempted to fight for her. *No,* she chided herself. *He is nothing to you.*

Breicher took a deep breath, and growled, "You've come to court my wife, cousin?"

Caroline huffed, then shot a furious glare Jamison's way. "He's your cousin?" She buried her fingers in the fabric of her skirt, squeezing the fine material so hard she was sure the points of her nails were piercing the garment. Searching the hall for Hollis, she narrowed in on him stomping back through the parting crowd.

"Eye drops, remember," Breicher said in a hushed voice to which she responded to with a frown. Obvious, if it weren't for her rapidly fraying nerves.

"It seems to me that your wife doesn't want you anymore," Jamison hissed.

A low grumble emanated from Breicher's chest, causing the butterflies in Caroline's stomach to turn into soaring eagles. "You're mistaken," he growled.

Caroline gasped. She might have passed out if it weren't for the iron rod she was willing her spine to become. Plastering on her own self-important smirk, she said, "You always were cocky."

CHAPTER 21

M AGENTA AND VIOLET BLOTCHES partially obscured Breicher's vision. It was how they described it when a person had a blackout rage episode. But killing his cousin wasn't on the agenda for tonight. He had a wife to win back. Releasing his hold on his cousin, he stepped forward to his subtly trembling wife.

"Why are you getting these men's hopes up when you know it is me you want?" he asked her in earnest.

Or what he thought was earnest, because Caroline folded her arms across her chest and said, "Not good enough, Breicher. Your swagger isn't going to get you out of it this time."

"I know," he said, lowering his eyes, letting her see the shame he felt for the pain he'd caused her.

By now, everyone in the room had their eyes on the two royals and the challenging suitor. It was how Breicher had intended it to go. Make enough of a scene that he had everyone's attention so he could do this for all the world to see.

Breicher fell to his knees before his wife, pulling the mask off so she could see his face. He looked up to see her hand across her chest as if she could cradle her heart. She still loved him. Jaden had told him how she'd suffered, but he'd thought she only needed time. When Jaden tossed him that wedding invitation, he'd known he'd been wrong about that too.

What he'd found, he'd needed to fight for. Lay down his life for if that was what was required. What they'd found wouldn't just fade in a year or two. He'd given her space to get her anger out, but what they had was enduring. He knew it. They'd truly seen each other that day. And that was real.

"Caroline, I am so terribly sorry that I hurt you." Tears fell freely down his cheeks. To be so close to her made a cascade of emotion crash over him and he would let the world see.

"Breicher, what are you doing?" she said under her breath. "I told you I'd kill you if I ever saw you again."

"Then kill me if that is what you wish." Breicher pulled the ornamental blade from his belt and pressed it to his chest. "I'll do it if you wish. Anything for you."

A firm hand grabbed his shoulder, then wrenched the knife from his hand. Hollis's angry voice stole his attention. "Breicher, get up. You're embarrassing our family. I had this handled. You shouldn't lower yourself before her."

Hollis was trying to pull him to his feet and the entire crowd, including Caroline, had taken a step back. Breicher jerked his shoulder, trying to get out of Hollis's grip. "Get your hands off me. You've done more than enough damage."

Hollis stumbled back like the words had struck him. "I'm trying to help you. Someone needs to save you from yourself."

"I don't belong to you!" Breicher bellowed. The onlookers stumbled backward another step bumping into each other. But like they couldn't resist, collectively they leaned in.

"Then who do you belong to, Breicher, if not your king?" Hollis's voice had the edge of a parent who'd scolded their wayward child for the same mistake one-to-many times.

Neither of them said anything, but both their eyes darted to the queen.

"Traitor!" Hollis hissed. "I thought it was a passing fancy. She's a nice conquest, but not enough to betray your family."

"Don't speak of my wife that way." Breicher gritted his teeth so tightly his jaw was beginning to hurt.

Hollis huffed. "Jamison's right. Your *wife* doesn't even want you. She is gleefully looking for your replacement as we speak." He gestured to his ruddy, red-headed cousin still lingering at the ready. "Your cousins were prepared to..." Hollis flipped his hand through the air like he was searching for the right word. "He's prepared to *deal* with the queen in your place until whatever ridiculous infatuation you have has dissipated. You should be commending him for his loyalty to our family. For his sacrifice. Not admonishing—"

"Come on, Hollis. We should go." Agnes approached and tugged on Hollis's sleeve. She gave a wary glance toward Caroline, tugging again a little more insistently.

Hollis wrenched his arm away from Agnes. "I'm not leaving until my brother comes to his senses. Maybe I went about this all wrong and you should have bedded her. Fucked her enough to get her out of your system."

Breicher shook his head. He could almost laugh. "You don't get a woman like Caroline out of your system."

"If you choose her over your family, a woman who doesn't even want you, you will be disowned. An Ivanslohe no longer." There it was. The ultimatum that Breicher had known was on the edge of every conversation he'd had with his brother.

"Hollis, please," Agna urged. "Don't you see you can't break them apart?"

Hollis's eyes widened in horror as he gaped at his wife. Before Breicher could stop him, the back of Hollis's hand was soaring toward Agna's cheek. Right before it struck, it froze. Agna put a trembling hand to her cheek where she would have been hit had Caroline's power not halted her husband. Jaden came forward, putting his arm around his shaken mother, pulling her into his side. With his free arm, he fished out a little box from his pocket, and tossed it to the queen.

Caroline, still silently observing like the crowd, caught the package. She tore her eyes from the two men and regarded the navy box. What an odd time to present a gift. Gingerly she tugged the white satin, then opened the lid. The box slid out of her frozen fingers, and the clink of metal chimed across the silent space. Her wedding ring rolled in a foot wide circle then stilled between her and Breicher.

She couldn't think even as her body knelt, reaching out to graze the white gold. A phantom weight encircled her ring finger like the piece of binding jewelry was making itself known. Like it agreed with Jaden and Breicher.

They will see me as weak.

Caroline's legs shook as she stood. She needed to get out of this room. Everything was becoming tight, like that cramped crevice her and Emmy had hidden in as children. She should have held her breath then. Her breath caught now. Voice trembling, she begged, "Why are you doing this?"

His wife hadn't picked up the ring. She'd looked at it, but only stood. Were he and Jaden wrong? He held it out to her again to take before putting it back in his pocket as she only looked at him with distant eyes and a half vacant expression. "I'll keep in until you're ready to take it back." A hot tear traced a path down and dripped off the plane of his cheek. He got to his feet, defeated. "I'll wait as long as you need me to. But when you're ready, please let it be me."

Behind him, laughter lanced a new hole in his heart. Hollis bellowed triumphantly. Was he insane? Did he think the queen was going to let him disrespect her like this? But Caroline was paler than usual and though her back was ramrod straight, her eyes glazed. This was just another thing he put her through.

"Shut up, Hollis," he growled.

"I tried to warn you. But you trusted her over your own family, and now you look like a fool. Everstal's Cruel Queen strikes again." Hollis raked his fingers through his perfectly tousled hair, indignation dripping from a huff. "She'd played you, Breicher. She's still playing you even though she's tossed you aside. Why can't you see that?"

It was like Breicher's body had a mind of its own. His hands wrapped around the fine material of Hollis's jacket, and he was in his brother's face. "I said do not speak of my wife like that."

Hollis thrust his head forward and a crack split the atmosphere. Breicher touched the blood trickling from his nose, then his fist was flying. Outside of sparring, he'd never struck his brother. For Hollis's part, the man looked just as surprised, when knuckles cracked across his jaw, despite the fact he'd instigated the fight.

"How dare you?" Hollis demanded, then swung.

Caroline stood, a little perplexed, as the two Ivanslohe brothers traded blows, then tumbled to the ground, grappling. Hollis's elbow struck Breicher across the temple and blood from his already broken nose sprayed across the room. Then he was on his feet again.

"Caroline, do something. They'll kill each other," Jaden said.

Jaden shook her gently. Did he think Hollis would kill Breicher? *That he could?*

Breicher angled down like he was going to drive his shoulder into the other man's chest, driving him to the ground as he charged. The glint of metal brought her back to reality. Right as Hollis pulled the blade he'd taken from Breicher and stashed somewhere on his person, Caroline released a thought. Both men froze.

Murmurs erupted in the crowd as she circled the men. Hollis's hand still tightly gripped the gilded weapon, but she pried it from his white knuckles. Then she spun it, addressing him. "How dare *you*?"

The moment she'd seen the weapon, she made her choice. And the former king's audacity... Caroline edged up to Hollis so close she tasted the wine on his breath. Perspiration formed across his brow as he fought her control. "How dare you come into my kingdom and threaten something that is mine?"

"You have too much power. The Gods failed us when they gave it to your family. And now, with what you've become, there's no stopping you. You claim you want balance, but we all know as soon as we let our guard down, a tyrant will emerge."

Caroline didn't flinch as Hollis spit the words at her. "You've been watching me rule for a year and you think so little of me? So deeply entrenched in the old ways... it's a pity. You could have been a part of something truly monumental." Caroline stepped away from the man and faced Breicher. But not before she said over her shoulder like it was an afterthought, "Go climb into that window." A lazy hand waved toward one of the few tall openings in the Great Hall. "Somebody help him. And Hollis, stay there until I decide your fate." She didn't turn as a flurry of heel strikes rumbled through the space, doing her bidding. Agnes cried out unintelligibly as she clung to Jaden, but she ignored her.

Caroline didn't dismiss the party goers. She pressed her shoulders back and got control of herself. She wanted them to see her conduct this punishment. See her rule. There were representatives from every territory in the Joined Kingdoms. She'd been spreading the message, but now she had a captive audience.

Walking in a circle, tapping the blade on her palm, Caroline scanned the crowd. "By now you've heard the story of the divide which led to the old ways?" Some heads nodded, but some looked at their companions, faces lit with confusion. "What you've heard is true. I'm the monster capable of overthrowing, not just one, but five gods. I took Love first. It was easy to destroy, naively opening itself to me until it was too late. Then Life and Death, then Justice. I saved pain for last. You see, we'd become friends of a sort."

Slowly, Caroline spun to make sure everyone in the room saw her face. "Few know what I am about to tell you. Many looked at what the gods had given my ancestors, our Gift to bend others to our will, as an abomination. What you didn't know is what we paid for that power."

Caroline let out a low chuckle, lacking humor. "Imagine, sitting, eating breakfast with your loved ones, then a cool breeze whisks you away to a world of emptiness. A void where five demons wring a pain from you so vicious your vision went white, and fire felt like it would consume your soul. Minutes or hours later, after they exacted their pound of flesh, they dump you back in your home. Sometimes you'd be unable to see you were wrought with blinding pain, other times you'd arrive with the flesh flayed from your bones. If you'd been a little greedy with your use of the Gift, every other bone in your body might be shattered, only to slowly heal over the course of a day."

She scanned the voyeur's green and sallow faces. Many with hands covering their open mouths. "And still, for our power, my ancestors and I used it over and over again, accepting the consequences gratefully. Every time I'd come back, I'd think it was worth it—anything to keep my people safe from our adversaries in Veetula. But over time, I grew to hate the Gods and resent them for what they'd done to my family. When I had the chance, I stole their power and ended the gods without a second thought. That's the type of monster who rules you."

"I planned to exact vengeance on the Ivanslohe's and all the frozen northern kingdom, but as Pain died, it let a little secret slip. A thousand years ago, when they bestowed our gifts upon us, they also pitted our people against each other, all for some sick desire for amusement. So many people died because of the Gods' boredom—it made me ill. But I'd learned a lot from Justice over the years and brought mine down upon them. Now we are free, and I plan to rule the Joined Kingdoms differently in light of their treachery."

Caroline took a few long breaths, and no one spoke. Walking over to Breicher, still hunched over from where she'd frozen him, she ran her fingers through his hair. Heart aching for what she had to do, she released her hold on him. "You may kneel." He was fairing far better than his brother, since Breicher was beyond fighting her compulsion.

"Many of you here are from Veetula. The truth is, I grew up hating you as much as you did me. But then, you see, I met Prince Breicher. He drove a rosenwood dagger into my heart, but instead of dying making him a hero, I became this—" She gestured to herself, letting a hand linger where the blade had slipped underneath her ribs. "And we formed an attachment." Caroline gently ran a thumb over the swelling sapphire eye that was already erupting with an angry purple.

"Unfortunately, there are some royal traditions common in Veetula that I find unpalatable," she said, shooting an angry glance in Hollis's direction. As she spoke, she continued to heal Breicher. "And our arrangement could not last. It was to my benefit that Everstal doesn't hold the same marital laws as Veetula, which we'll be changing as you would expect."

"Prince Breicher has worked tirelessly with Prince Jaden this last year to enact many of the new laws, so I will forgive him for our little interruption tonight, but—"

Jaden cleared his throat loud enough to interrupt the queen. Was she going to talk forever? He was going to be in nine kinds of trouble when this was over, but someone had to do something. His nimble fingers fished inside his jacket, pulling the tightly coiled parchment. He slid the ribbon off, letting it fall to the floor, then unrolled it. The queen's stare beating into him was hard to interpret. Surely, she wouldn't punish him.

But he knew her well enough now. Caroline prided herself on never going back on her word. She'd ended it with Breicher. In her mind, they were irreparably over, regardless of what she actually wanted. Fortunately, he held the loophole. Or at least he prayed—or hoped, he supposed, since the gods were no more—that she'd see it that way.

Jaden's voice trembled as he said, "His Majesty didn't sign the document." He bowed as he extended it to her for effect. When she didn't take it, he held it out so other ball attendees already crowding behind him could get a closer look and see for themselves that King Breicher's signature was nowhere on the annulment. He'd inadvertently boxed her in. His vengeful queen. He hadn't known she'd give the speech. But this piece of paper was the one chance, should she choose to use it.

Only incoherent utterings came from the now raucous onlookers. Jaden wrestled his hand to stop shaking. It wouldn't look good that one of her closest advisors was terrified of her. Not that he was... exactly, but this was cutting it close. A gentle hand slipped around his waist and Jaden turned to see his mother reading the document. "This doesn't seem to be binding, Your Majesty," she said, bowing her head in deference.

Angus approached, his teeth notably gritted. Jaden gave him a look that said, *You better not fuck this up or I'll find ways to terrorize you endlessly.*

Angus snatched the piece of paper from Jaden and gave it a once over. He eyed Jaden, frowning before saying, "They're right. The document hasn't been properly executed."

Caroline's heart thundered in her ears. She had caught the subtle flick of Agnes's eye up to her husband as she bowed. Knew what agreeing with her son would cost her. It was only because of her interference that Jaden hadn't been disowned. If she let Hollis live, what would it mean for his wife?

Time seemed to crawl, though she suspected it was moving much faster outside her mind. Breicher still knelt before her, head raised, like the day she'd left him in her room in tears, surrounded by the evidence of her fury. He resembled a fallen angel as he'd sat there and begged, those beautiful blue eyes pleading. In her black heart, she'd known why he'd done it. The war which had raged inside him: his family and his loyalty to his kingdom or her. Being with her was a betrayal on so many levels to him. But she'd forgiven him long ago and redirected her anger to the dead Gods and his brother for egging his conflicted mental state along.

Still, her pride would keep her from the man she so clearly loved. Who was on his knees before her and all the Joined Kingdoms. Caroline flicked her eyes to Jaden. He knew. So did Agnes beside him, and Hollis, considering how hard he'd worked to keep them apart.

A wayward thought struck her. If she sent Breicher away, Hollis won. Everyone who didn't believe she could make peace had won. Sure, she could take a Veetula husband, but it wouldn't be the same. She wouldn't let them win, Hollis or the Gods, or the many people from her kingdoms who still opposed this symbolic union. Even Angus, who'd been quite ready to act at her side this whole time, appeared to have accepted the inevitable. She, it seemed, was the last tower to fall.

A cruel slash lit his wife's face. After a nausea inducing pause, Caroline said, "Well…" Her voice had a velvet edge which slid across Breicher's skin like a silent invitation. This was the woman he knew. The woman who saw him like he now saw her. That he'd so longed to touch and taste. *No, worship.*

Caroline continued, "I suppose this changes things. What do you think, Breicher?"

YES, his mind screamed, but he didn't allow his face to show his eagerness. Now was the time to act like the king she needed him to be, *wanted* him to be. Breicher looked up at his queen—his wife and let the smoldering need he felt for her body and soul radiate from his eyes. Her nostrils flared ever so slightly as she took him in, as if she needed a little extra air. He let the corner of his mouth tick upward, knowing she'd read his thoughts precisely.

A collective silence spread across the room, and everyone drew forward in anticipation. This was not how they'd expected the night to go at all.

Breicher stood, wiping the blood under his healed nose on his sleeve, and took the parchment from Angus, tearing it in half. The ruined document fell to the floor like a relic of another time—lost to the present moment—to the future. He would adapt to the new ways, forgive the suitors who'd shown up from Everstal to win his wife. What he'd done this last year had proven that. But it wasn't their law in Veetula yet and the men, including his own cousins, no doubt prodded here by his brother, wouldn't be so lucky.

He eyed the nearest three, then sought the other cousins who were lingering at the edge of the room, still attentively watching. "You dare try to woo *MY WIFE*?" Breicher let his anger bubble up as their faces blanched. "According to the still intact Veetula law, the queen and I are still married, which means you've blatantly flaunted the law and disrespected your king." Breicher took a cue from his wife and emitted a dark rumble. "You're in over your head, boys." Snapping his fingers, he commanded, "Guards! Take them away and find a dark hole to store them in until I have time to get to it."

He shot a simmering glance at his wife. "I have a feeling I'm going to be busy for a while." Caroline gasped as he swept her into his arms.

As he carried her from the Great Hall, he turned to the man precariously poised on the window ledge. "Be careful, brother. It's a long drop, and the wind rises at night."

CHAPTER 22

"**B**REICHER, SLOW DOWN, MY king." His wife's voice was breathy with need as Breicher kicked her door open.

"I'm sorry," he said, in between the kisses he was planting on her lips, her jaw, her neck. "It's like finally being able to breathe again—I want to inhale you." Like an animal mawing its prey, he couldn't keep his hands from pawing her.

Grabbing her ass, he pulled her into him, showing her how much he needed her. When she groaned, his teeth clenched in pleasure, but he'd bit down a little too roughly on her nape and she cried out. He jerked back, and brought his hands to her neck, to inspect the red mark he'd caused.

Caroline gave him a coy smile. "You don't have to stop. I like it."

Oh, he knew that, but he'd save that for another time. This time, it needed to be about her. About the forgiveness she was extending him. Though it went against everything in him, he said, "I think we should talk."

Caroline's face pinched into the purest distress he'd ever seen on a person. "Is talking really necessary?" Her greedy hands roamed down his chest, un-tucking his shirt. She deftly unbuttoned it, then ran her hands across his chest as she pushed it off his shoulders.

※

Talk? Her husband wanted to talk? She had something far different in mind. Reaching up on her toes, she kissed the base of his neck, then his collar bone. She moved her focus across the tensed muscles, kissing and licking until she came to his nipple, all the while she was undoing his buckle and pulling his pants down over his hips trying to get at the glorious prize he stored there.

Right as she was about to get him in her hand, his fingers wrapped around her shoulders, and he pulled her away enough so she could look at him.

"I need to apologize to you."

She snaked her hand in between them, taking what she wanted. "Can't you play and apologize at the same time?" His grunting only encouraged her, until his hand wrapped around her wrist.

The other tipped her chin up toward him. "If that is what you want, then that is what I will do."

Ugh, he was serious. His slacks had fallen to the floor, but she tugged his undershorts back over his hips. "I suppose we better hide this then."

"I wouldn't want you getting distracted." Breicher reached up and unthreaded one of the red roses from her hair, showing it to her in question, before untangling another.

"We dyed them. For effect. I wanted to make a statement."

The gentle way he was releasing her hair from its arrangement made her heart squeeze. He turned her, so she was facing the full-length mirror in her room and moved her hair around to her front and began unlacing the neck of her gown. "You deserve so much better than how I've treated you. What I did was dishonorable, and I deserve whatever punishment you could have given me. I understand that now. You once asked me if you were a fool. I see now that I was the fool."

"I need you to know that Jaden told me what you and Angus discovered about what Hollis had done and he took me there, and I saw it with my own eyes. At first, I was angry that you didn't come to me with it, but over time I understood you didn't tell me because you wanted me to trust you—to believe in you. And I failed you in that. When I realized it, I didn't think I deserved you. Staying away was my way of punishing myself."

Caroline shuddered as his hot breath met her skin as he pressed a kiss below her ear. "I don't know what the future holds, but I want to promise you I will spend it making it up to you, making you proud that

I'm your husband. Being the king you need to stand beside you and making sure not a day goes by that you don't know what you mean to me."

The night breeze drifting in through the window trailed across Caroline's skin, like a whispered kiss, as Breicher lowered the front of her gown, exposing her breasts to their reflections. Rough fingers trailed from her neck, down her spine. A moment later, his palms slid into the material and were guiding the dress off her hips, leaving only a barely there piece of lace held together with a few ribbons.

Breicher ran his hands over her in featherlight touches, across her stomach, her breasts, before squeezing with a little more firmness. The warring sensations clashed in the most luscious way. The way they merged with the pretty words he was saying made her heart sing. And her core ache. "And though I know I have no right, I will do everything in my power to make sure you understand that you are mine and mine alone," he said. The grin he gave was feral, and he caught her as her knees buckled. Perhaps she wasn't done with cocky men after all.

Breicher set his wife on the bed, then crawled on it after her. Why couldn't he just let an apology be an apology without having to stake his claim? He swore whatever the Gods had done to his family line had made them all half animal. He looked away, a little ashamed, as he reached down to pull the last shred of clothing from his wife. Soft hands gently guided his face back toward hers. His eyes fluttered open, and the luminescent silver that stared back at him could have struck him dead.

He was in love with her. Gods, what a fool he was. His traitorous heart wouldn't stop singing her song. His betraying eyes wouldn't stop following her. His lecherous mind had thought of nothing but her since she'd exiled him. Hollis had thought it was his wounded pride or a momentary infatuation. His anger toward his brother simmered anew. Was the remorse drowning him ever going to stop?

He gave her a pleading look. *Just end his misery now.* He cupped her cheek as if she were glass he might shatter. "I feel like I'm going to spend the rest of my life apologizing to you."

The way she grinned made him a little nervous. She knelt between his spread knees so they were face to face and clasped his jaw in her cool hands. "I see you, Breicher. And despite everything, I love you."

As she kissed him, her benevolence lapped over him like a warm wave. Any hesitation flowed away in the ebbing tide. He'd dreamed of finding a wife that he loved, an equal. Instead, he'd gotten a queen and a goddess. He shuddered as he deepened the kiss, the feel of his wife eclipsing every thought in his mind.

He pulled away for a moment to give the words room to burst out. "I love you too, Caroline." He'd think of another, more eloquent way to say it one day, but the simplicity of the words rang true to him as he repeated the feelings of his heart. "*I love you.*"

Caroline's silver irises pulsed, his own glowing blue a reflection in hers. Had the Gods ever imagined such a pairing?

"Then show me," she answered, laying back on a pile of silken pillows. Her alabaster skin shone like moonlight against the black bedding, her white hair absorbing each flicker of candlelight.

When she spread her knees, baring herself to him, it was as if the heavens had parted and were calling him home. He wanted to grip his chest as his pride swelled. She was his—really and truly his. No games, no punishments. Just their two souls intertwining, the way she'd know they would, if he'd let his guarded and hate filled heart open to hers. The urge to cover her with himself was almost unbearable, like some primal mating ritual.

Slow down. He had to take this slowly. Savor the woman who was gracious enough to let him back into her heart. Show her she hadn't made a mistake trusting him with it. He positioned himself between her legs, lifting her ankle to his mouth, knowing as he ran his hot tongue against her cool skin, the heat would dance in gooseflesh across her body.

Caroline clenched and jerked beneath him as Breicher kissed and sucked his way up her thighs. He kissed right at the edge of her center, teasing. He nudged her clit with his nose, then extended his tongue right through the pool of her desire. She was dripping for him and he shuddered at the taste of her. At the knowledge of what he did to her.

With every lick and thrust, he made sure she knew just how thoroughly he intended to show her how he felt. She was writhing beneath him, and he was enjoying every second, his cock throbbing with every twitch. Right as he brought her to the precipice, as the early tremors in her legs and her inner walls flexed, he eased his tongue out, giving her a few teasing flicks.

"Don't stop, don't stop." Caroline sobbed when he pulled his mouth away from her sex. "Damn you. And they say I'm cruel," she said, trying to shove his head back down where she wanted it, but he swatted her hands away. Her eyebrows lowered as she sat up and glared at him making him suspect she wanted to tease him about how he owed her. She didn't joke, though. It was too soon, and they needed this. She gave this to him—*her*—without any room for question. Caroline flopped back onto the pillows to allow him to continue his ministrations at his own pace, slow and languid. Leisurely, to show her now that he had her, he'd take all the time in the world to make her feel good, because they had that now and he wouldn't waste it.

His wife was pouting for sex—practically growling. He crawled up her body and sucked her lower lip into his mouth. Gods, he loved this woman. But this first time, he wanted to make an impression, take her to the edge repeatedly until, when she finally came, he'd show her all the beauty of the universe in a single moment. The first of many gifts he planned to give his wife.

"I want all of that pent up sexual need seizing up around my cock, Your Majesty," he said, his voice lust drunk against her ear. Her head tilted back into the pillow as he nudged at her entrance, while nipping her neck. "Breicher, please," she demanded.

She swore to the dead Gods. This man had her so tightly coiled she might explode. He quaked above her as he pressed himself inside. A helpless whimper escaped her throat, and she dug her heels into the bed, pushing herself further up on him, wanting—no—*needing* more. Meeting her desperation, he forced himself the rest of the way inside her and she gasped, feeling her inner walls cinch down around him. It almost hurt, taking all of him in.

She'd known. Somehow, she'd known it was him the moment she'd seen him. Despite everything, they'd persevered. If it hadn't been for Jaden's quick thinking with that document, she might be missing out on the shuddering man above her.

"Gods, Caroline," he moaned, retracting a little. "If you don't relax, this is going to be over very quickly."

"Kiss me," she said. Breicher obeyed and when his tongue swept against hers, the taste of herself on him made her eyes roll back in her head and her body ease into the rhythm of him. He was right—this was going to be quick.

Giving her swift, shallow strokes, it didn't take him long to bring her to the edge again. When he stilled, not letting her climax, taking his own breather she suspected, Caroline let out a desperate wail and beat at his chest. "I hate you," she cried.

He grabbed her hands, tugging them above her head. "Be a good girl, Caroline."

She tried to jerk away, but he held her firm, reaching his free hand beneath her ass, angling her toward him so he could press in deeper. Her face teetered between anguish and sublime pleasure. "I think I'm going to die," she moaned as he nudged over and over the deepest part of her core in slow, agonizing strokes before taking her to the edge once again. He did it twice more, seeming to only keep a thread of control himself.

She was Caroline Dallimore, Queen of the Joined Kingdoms, panting, begging, practically crying beneath this man as he worked her. Never before had she been so thoroughly splayed open, emotionally and physically and the man above her appeared as if he never experienced anything more satisfying than witnessing the lines of ecstasy etching her face. The Gods had wrung every ounce of pain from her body over the years. Breicher seemed determined to do the same with pleasure. She deserved no less.

"Release me," she demanded. "I swear to everything holy if you do that again, I'll make you cut out your own heart."

Her husband's taunting laughter reverberated through her. Sexy, cocky bastard. Of course, Breicher would laugh at her threats. Look at the puddle of pleasure he'd melted her into. The way he worked his hips—she couldn't even make herself feel like this. She was utterly his—her king.

When he finally released her hands, she dug her claws into the back of his arms and clung to him. She squeezed tighter, digging the tips of her nails in deeper, and Breicher's head kicked back, and he moaned at the ceiling thrusting forward. A sharp sensation jolted down her spine which seemed to mirror his experience. His full body shudders and that sublime pleasure-soaked expression that almost looked like pain told her his release lapped at the edge of a crumbling damn. The intensity in his luminescent sapphire eyes, that stare penetrated her, blasting past the obsidian wall she protected her black heart behind. Breicher's gaze dove into her depths finding *her* somewhere in the chasm of her tarnished soul. And dead Gods it felt good.

Everything about him was perfect. Caroline savored the weight of his muscular body pressing down on hers, into hers, like the entire summer night sky coming down to visit, cloaking her in its warmth. Finally caving to her demands, he moved relentlessly, driving her pleasure higher and higher. Stars burst through her vision as her body tensed, the first wave of violent pleasure rocketing through her. "Breicher," she cried, hanging on his shoulders as each crash hit, only to be superseded by the next. She wasn't aware of time. She felt infinite. Her only sensation was of acute bliss pulsing outward from her core.

Caroline was breathless when the aftershocks, which seemed to be timeless, finally subsided. She peeled her eyes open to see Breicher above her, watching. "You're incredible," he said, his voice guttural, as he brushed her sweaty strands out of her face. "Otherworldly."

"Did you?" she asked in a voice that rang uncharacteristically sweet for her. *Ugh, what was he turning her into?*

Breicher sighed as he peeled himself off and she hated him sliding out of her, away from her.

"Yeah," he said, climbing out of bed to retrieve a cloth to clean up the mess they'd made. "Shall I have a bath drawn, my queen?"

The muscles of his ass flexed with each step as he walked away, and her lips parted to draw in a quick breath. How long would it be until she could have him again? "Just come back to bed and tell me about the wonders of this famous Ivanslohe blood you have."

A chuckle sounded from the bathing chamber at what she implied. Caroline propped herself on the pillows and brought a knee up, casually resting her wrist on it, knowing exactly the display she'd be giving him when he reentered the room.

"Haven't had enough, have you? I had a feeling you'd be insatiable," he said and murmured something about thanking the Gods and his luck. Breicher sucked in a quick breath when he stepped back into the room. The expression on his face was dead serious as he stalked over to the foot of the bed, eyes zeroing in on her glistening sex. Before she blinked, he shot a hand forward, wrapping his fist around her ankle then tugged her to him. His hands latched on her hips, and he flipped her over, so she was face down on the blankets.

She could feel his eyes burning into her center, how he'd positioned her giving him the perfect view. The aftermath of them was still warm as it slid down her thighs. "I've made quite the mess of you," he said, taking the cloth and wiping before it dripped on the bedding. When he seemed satisfied he'd gotten everything he gave her a swift smack on the ass and a cry leapt from her lips, even as her core jolted.

"That was for making me wait so long to take me back." Another smack. She groaned, fisting the blankets as he kneaded her stinging flesh.

"That was for all the times you tried to seduce me, driving me to madness."

Oh, Gods. Caroline pressed herself back into him, hoping he pressed something of himself inside her soon. When his hand landed this time, the fingers of his other slid inside her, granting her wish, and she screamed.

"And that was for making me your helpless fool."

Breicher moved his fingers slowly, but intently, using his thumb to graze against her clit. Each time he entered her nudging that exact spot, a little bolt of lightning danced through her body. Caroline could melt into the mattress, it was so good, but she wanted more. She wanted him. "Please, Breicher."

Hearing her cry his name was all he needed, and Breicher was at attention again. Pulling his fingers from her, he kneed her legs wider and climbed between them. He lined himself up, then reached forward, grabbing her shoulder. Breicher sunk himself inside with one thrust.

When he was fully buried, with her ass against his stomach, he leaned over her wrapping an arm under her belly, pulling her closer. He rested on an elbow, fisting her hair. Her beautiful face, half hidden pressed into the covers, pinched under the onslaught as he gave her steady, determined pulses. Licking up her neck, he said into her ear in a rough low tone, "How do you want it, Caroline?"

She whimpered at his words and was panting again when she breathed, "Harder."

He'd already had her once and was a little worried it would be too much. "Are you sure you can take it?" he asked, sucking on her earlobe.

"Don't hold back," she demanded, between breaths.

"I'm a lucky, lucky man," he said, and unleashed himself to give them both what they were craving.

Leaning back, he tugged on her hips until she was on all fours, and he had easy access to her clit. Then he went to work pounding away relentlessly until she began trembling and cried out with her first orgasm. He paused, letting her breath even out before he started again. This time, he would give her multiple.

He was taking her so hard, pressing himself so forcefully inside her, he'd need to scoot forward every few minutes. Every few orgasms a more apt description. The Queen of the Joined Kingdom's was getting deliciously limp he was so thoroughly fucking her.

Breicher pressed down on her shoulder blades until her arms buckled and only her sweet ass was up in the air for him. He took ahold of her hips, pulling her back on him, meeting each thrust so all she had to do was lay there and accept the pleasure he was giving her. "You are so perfect," he said, right as the tingling started. "It feels like—it feels like—"

Fireworks erupted across Breicher's vision as his body kept pumping into his wife as if under a spell. Somewhere in his awareness, he sensed her clamping down around him, her fingers reaching back digging into his thighs, pulling him deeper. Stars danced as his body was dipped in heaven, as he spilled himself into his goddess.

"Are you okay?" he asked, a little worried he'd hurt her in his rapturous state. Caroline flopped forward on her stomach, and he turned her over to find a silly grin had spread her mouth wide.

"What type of ridiculous question is that?" she asked, twirling a lock of hair.

A lucky man indeed. "I think you're going to be sore tomorrow." A little twinge of guilt niggled at him.

She giggled. "You forget, your *goddess* can heal herself."

His cheeks warmed. "Did I say that out loud?"

"Oh, yes you did, Your Majesty. What a mighty compliment. I'll be sure to let you fuck me senseless, often, as I quite enjoy your euphoric mutterings."

Caroline broke into a fit of laughter he couldn't help but join. Trying to put on a serious face, he picked up the half messy cloth and offered it to her. She took it to prevent any leakage as she waddled to the bathroom. "I feel highly undignified," she said, slipping out of view.

"The last thing you could ever be is undignified, my goddess." Breicher crawled under the covers letting them warm him like the rush of love he felt as he awaited his wife.

CHAPTER 23

T HE MINUTE SHE CRAWLED back in bed, Breicher wrapped his arms around Caroline, placing gentle kisses all over her face. His chest was so full it might burst open. "Did I tell you I'm quite hopeless for you?"

She chuckled. "You did mention that."

Caroline yawned, her eyelids lulling lower with every blink. He moved back to lay his head on her chest, his ear pressed to her heart. If she let him, he might spend the night like that, in the cocoon of his wife's body. Finally, he understood. Submitting to what was between them hadn't made him weak, or a traitor. He never felt more alive or more powerful as he lay there in her arms.

Breicher started as something caught his eye. "I thought you said they'd turn black after a few hours."

"They do," Caroline said, gesturing to the now black roses he'd pulled from her hair littering the floor. Their color, illuminated by the moonlight streaming in through the window, wasn't mistakable.

"But..." Breicher trailed off.

❦

Caroline's eyes tracked her husband's, to the object which had garnered his attention.

As if in its own moonbeam, on the nightstand, lay in full, glorious bloom, a single crimson rose.

ACKNOWLEDGMENTS

Thank you for taking the time to read *CAROLINE THE CRUEL*. I hope you enjoyed Caroline's story—I had a ton of fun writing it. If you want to find out what happens next for Caroline and Breicher, AND the next couple in this series of fantasy romance stories, Angus and Jaden, be sure to sign up for my newsletter so you'll be the first to know when it is published.

If you enjoyed the *Caroline the Cruel*, even a little, I would be honored if you went over on Amazon or Goodreads and left a review. I know leaving a review can be time consuming, but it helps us indie authors more than you know and may help other readers become exposed to our work.

I want to say thank you to a few very special people whose support, insight and feedback was invaluable to me in the writing and publishing process.

My husband, Max, and sister, Kristen, spent countless hours listening to me talk about characters, working through plot holes with me, and just generally supporting my path to becoming a published author, and ultimately bringing this story to life. One couldn't ask for a more supportive and amazing family.

I will be forever grateful to the following beta readers who helped me understand how my work was being received from a reader's perspective with chapter notes, inline feedback, and thorough reader reports and impressions. Thank you to: Virag Viszus (@nerdy.bookdragon), Megan K. Hill (@_megan_kat), Anakha Ashok (@iawkwardturtle), Victoria.K, Hailey B. (@prose.before.woes), Ashley T. (@_chamberofbooks).

Finally, I am grateful to have worked with an outstanding editor, Roxana Coumans of Roth Notions and proofreader, Belle Manuel.

About the Author

Jennifer is an artist, small business owner and author of the new adult adventure fantasy Skyborne series and an upcoming new adult fantasy romance. She holds a Bachelor of Fine Arts with a minor in Art History from the University of Central Oklahoma. Jennifer enjoys creating and paints with that same imaginative stroke throughout her writing.

When she's not writing, you might find her whipping together her favorite dark chocolate mousse, power walking a beach in a tropical destination, or lost in the minutia of one of her excel spreadsheets. Jennifer lives with her husband and two dog children in Oklahoma City.

Find me on Instagram @authorjmwaldrop or TikTok @authorjmwaldrop
and my website www.jennifermwaldrop.com for:
Updates on my current WIP, giveaways and more.

ALSO BY

JENNIFER M. WALDROP

Skyborne Series

Realm of the Banished

Realm of the Skyborne

Read the peek of chapter one of Realm of the Banished next.

REALM OF THE BANISHED

CHAPTER ONE

A S SENSATION CREPT BACK into my overtaxed limbs, the fog clouding my mind began to clear. I gasped, taking in the change in my surroundings. A heavy mist clung to the lush foliage surrounding me. *No... steam,* I thought. My eyes were adjusting to the gloom as I realized whatever power that hit me must have sent me, not just to the edge of the Swath, but well into it. The thick, squat trees created a dense and shallow canopy where I could see moss draping over the branches. Droplets of moisture clung to the moss, making the few tiny rays of sunlight creeping through the canopy strike them and refract and glow with the light. I thought they would have glittered with any movement if the air wasn't so still and stagnant.

The last thing I remembered was fleeing with all my remaining speed toward the border of Eastdow. If I could have made it across, the Covenant would, *or should* have protected me from Darius and his gang from Drakestone. I fled, all the while wondering if retrieving the ember was worth the cost. For almost ten years, every moment of my existence was devoted to my training, all designed to sneak through Drakestone and retrieve this relic I now carried. I'd spent years learning the regional dialects and perfecting my shifts so they would come so effortlessly I'd slide unnoticed through the maze of the mysterious northern territory.

I tried to determine where exactly in the Swath I landed. Time was not on my side, I knew, but I couldn't help but wonder where it had all gone wrong.

My advisors and instructors had almost convinced me I was the one who would bring the ember home. They dubbed me their very own *Chosen One*. It was ridiculous. I bristled at the thought. They began training me when they detected the extra inklings of power I developed during my adolescence, which, in the past, would have bloomed at adulthood—unheard of in my lifetime. The seers claimed I was the one from the prophecies who would end the banishment and bring us home to Idia. It was a pleasant idea at first, the idea of being a fated hero, but when my power never grew into anything more, distrust blossomed. Now that I was kneeling in a steaming marsh deep in the Swath, I knew they had been wrong about me and the alleged prophecy. Yet, I had done it. I could hardly believe it.

I surveyed my body. Though I'd traveled what had to be miles, I did not have a scratch on me. Only what felt like would bloom into some fine purple and black bruises on my thighs and rear from where I had landed and tumbled. I had no explanation for what had happened to me. One minute earlier, while running, I glanced back to see Darius—my former lover—'s loaded crossbow perfectly aimed at my back, then blackness. Thinking of him now made me wince.

The forest was warm and moist, and the air clung to me, making it hard to breathe. The fall knocked the wind out of me, but I was recovering quickly. I knew they would keep searching for me. If my internal compass held true, it was unlikely they'd be eager to join me on this side of the Swath's barrier. The pools in this forest ranged in temperature from scalding to bathwater warm. Fortunately, my fall hadn't landed me in one of the deeper, hotter pools.

Scanning, I noticed the angle of one of the few streaks of sunlight permeating the canopy had moved past forty five degrees, suggesting daylight was running out. After everything I'd been through, the last thing I wanted to do was die in this Makers forsaken forest, knowing full well the bloody treat I'd make for the creatures who lived here.

With that thought, I identified east and began making my way. I chose a path that would put me in the Swath longer than I preferred but would not land me at the feet of Darius and his gang. It was a risk, and according to my knowledge, no one had ever escaped the barrier, so the odds were good I'd die here. Still, it was useless to be idle. As I walked, keeping so quiet as to not attract the attention of one of the many horrors that lived in this forest, I couldn't shake the feeling that the pervading quiet that hung in the air was wrong.

Wrong. Even for this place.

It made no sense. I knew that Skyborne, who crossed the invisible boundary of the forest's edge, never escaped it, which meant some silent, hungry creatures were lurking alongside me under the canopy. There were stories and legends of death sentences carried out by executioners who pushed the condemned at spear point across the invisible boundary. I thought of the chilling illustrations I'd seen in books of the hooded men with lengthy poles prodding the ill fated past the Swath's barrier, depicted as a shimmering wall. The condemned would spend hours frantically running hands along the interior, searching for a way to escape, becoming increasingly desperate as the hours drag on and the forest sounds near. Sometimes, they would last days. Lingering at the edge of the forest must have been terrifying, knowing what awaited them inside. While a clever deterrent, it was still a cruel punishment. I shuddered, imagining being eaten alive.

The strip of forested area called the Swath lay in the center of the large continent. The Swath did not belong to any of the six territories surrounding it. On the other three sides, each territory had two neighbors and a sea border.

I admired the fore mothers' architecture and the seemingly equitable system the matriarchs birthed for their new realm and the Skyborne who crossed over with them. Since then, however, half of the territories shifted to a patriarchal system. The foremothers intended that each of the six territories would alternate the ember's guardianship, so no one territory would ever hold power over the others. They considered using a single central location, but considering the central location of the Swath, they decided on an alternating watch. The agreement continued effortlessly until it was time for Drakestone, who was fifth in the rotation, to pass it on to Eastdow. Some dead Dsiban Regent refused to relinquish it.

There was a rustling near but not within my range of vision. I heightened my senses and pinpointed the direction of the sounds. They were coming from the direction I was heading. Next to me, the moss stirred as if in the wind created from something passing.

A foot squelched in the mud. Something was right there. I flicked my gaze toward the sound and met a pair of eyes glowing with intensity. Green, the color of sour fruit.

Shit, shit, shit.

I'd sensed my death was imminent before, though maybe that had been my pessimism and not a premonition. But now? Was this it? When I was so close to delivering the ember and this assignment's end. With my freedom in sight, I could either run now like I had never run in my life— on already drained legs and a stomach that hadn't seen food for days—or fight. Whoever or whatever those eyes belonged to would likely enjoy one of my bruised thighs before long.

Regret flooded in. I wouldn't be in this situation if the full powers of the so-called prophecy had befallen me. I still accomplished the task, regardless, which gave me more than a little pride.

Fight.

I stood, gathering my reserves as the creature approached.

"Give me the ember," an otherworldly voice echoed in the forest.

The voice came not from the creature directly but from all around me. My arm hairs stood on end from the eeriness of it.

"Not going to happen," I said defiantly, reaching for my breast pocket. The ember hummed under my touch as if in agreement.

"Then you will die, and I will have it anyway," its slippery voice echoed.

I knew my life was forfeit, but I stared toward the eyes, seeing it sensed I carried the ember and that lying was futile. I refused to let it sense my fear. "I find it hard to believe you'll let me live either way." I drew the long knives I had managed not to lose in my fall, motioning to it invitingly, "Shall we?"

As the creature came nearer, I could see long, narrow black pupils in the center of its iridescent eyes glaring down at me from a bulbous head that towered over me. The yellow green skin on its gangly limbs was molting and limply wrapped around a plump, vaguely humanoid body like an aged, sagging canvas. Recognizing my surprise at its girth, it cackled. "Yeesssss, girl, our diet improved when your kind showed up in this realm, our realm of the banished." It rubbed its fleshy belly, taunting and sloughing skin off as it did. A slimy grey tongue flicked over its cracked lips as it watched me. I could tell it was enjoying making its live prey squirm.

"What—*who* are you?" I asked, eyes wide.

It sneered and gave a light laugh, its flesh jiggling.

"Answer me," I demanded, becoming increasingly nervous. I pushed the hairs that had slipped from my braid out of my face.

Continue Reading...

Ingram Content Group UK Ltd.
Milton Keynes UK
UKHW012109220323
419017UK00014B/173/J